Dawood Ali McCallum: international playboy, gambler, sportsman and—rumour has it in Swindon—Nobel laureate.

Well... actually, he lives in the UK with his wife and two children and drives a terminally uncool green car with a dent in it that he is too mean, or apathetic, to get repaired. But he does tell a good story.*

His writing career includes speeches for a West African President, Ethiopian government ministers and several British High Commissioners. His articles and short stories have been published in India and the UK. His first novel, *The Lords of Alijah*, was published by Viking-Penguin India in 1997.

According to his Mum.

Taz

Dawood Ali McCallum

Muriel + David
With thanks for
all the walks, warmth
and happiness over the
years

Dawood Ali McCallum
May 2007

PENGUIN BOOKS

PENGUIN BOOKS
Published by the Penguin Group
Penguin Books India Pvt. Ltd, 11 Community Centre, Panchsheel Park,
New Delhi 110 017, India
Penguin Group (USA) Inc., 375 Hudson Street, New York,
New York 10014, USA
Penguin Group (Canada), 90 Eglinton Avenue East, Suite 700, Toronto,
Ontario, M4P 2Y3, Canada (a division of Pearson Penguin Canada Inc.)
Penguin Books Ltd, 80 Strand, London WC2R 0RL, England
Penguin Ireland, 25 St Stephen's Green, Dublin 2, Ireland
(a division of Penguin Books Ltd)
Penguin Group (Australia), 250 Camberwell Road, Camberwell,
Victoria 3124, Australia (a division of Pearson Australia Group Pty Ltd)
Penguin Group (NZ), 67 Apollo Drive, Rosedale, North Shore 0632,
New Zealand (a division of Pearson New Zealand Ltd)
Penguin Group (South Africa) (Pty) Ltd, 24 Sturdee Avenue, Rosebank,
Johannesburg 2196, South Africa

Penguin Books Ltd, Registered Offices: 80 Strand, London WC2R 0RL, England

First published by Penguin Books India 2007

Copyright © Dawood Ali McCallum 2007
The moral right of the author has been asserted

All rights reserved

10 9 8 7 6 5 4 3 2 1

ISBN-13: 978-0-143100-522   ISBN-10: 0-14310-0521

This is a work of fiction. Names, characters, places and incidents are either the product of
an author's imagination or are used fictitiously, and any resemblance to any actual person,
living or dead, events or locales is entirely coincidental.

Typeset in *Weiss* by SÜRYA, New Delhi
Printed at Gopsons Papers Ltd, Noida

Contents

PART I

BURNING BRIDGES

1

The name is Armitage Shanks. A bad joke at the best of times, which this surely isn't.

The name is Armitage Shanks, and tomorrow I'm going to die.

Do you have any idea what it means to know you're going to die? Can you imagine it? Can you? I can't. Even now. At one level, I know the fact. Tomorrow, some essential, some literally vital, part of me will be destroyed. As a machine, a functioning entity, I will simply cease to work. Be switched off. Closed down. Cease to be. My body will remain, but what happens to all that explosive, passionate, confused essence? How can it just end?

Two things trouble me above all others; firstly, that I will die indoors. Secondly, that I will die hot, sweating.

The fact that I know the time precisely, or that I'm in a country not my own troubles me less. Strange.

When I first arrived, I was taken with the others on the back of an open lorry to a run-down army barrack. There we were made to sit on a concrete floor. More and more people were herded in; the heat, the day, and of all these bodies together, were insufferable. We weren't allowed to speak, or look up, or around at one another. We had to sit with our knees up, and our hands linked around our legs. First I was scared. Then, the sheer bloody discomfort of the situation became the dominant thought. My buttocks ached, and my muscles stiffened. The heat grew stronger; a couple of the younger men began sobbing. One of them was hit with a rifle butt. After a while, somebody vomited. Someone else could not control their bowels any more.

I don't know how long we were held there. After a while, the pain and discomfort all became one. It absorbed me, and I lost track of time. I never passed out, or fainted or slept. I just ceased to differentiate between sensation, thought and emotion. All became one.

When they split us up and moved us to various prisons, I was held first in a cell with fourteen others. There was one hard, vicious bastard who was the cell lord. He was, I think, a Somali, although none of us ever told one another much about where we were from or who we were. Informants, you see. Grasses were everywhere. So I never knew what he was picked up for, but he made a bee-line for me; thought it would be fun to take a whack at the white guy. He'd killed men in that cell; everyone knew it, but he was never charged because no one cared. It cut down the numbers they had to feed. They never even reported the deaths; just dragged the body out and went on indenting for the allowances for funding the full complement, pocketing the spare. Someone once said that according to the paperwork, there were fifty-three men in that cell, even though it could barely hold fifteen.

Neat scheme.

Besides, the Somali kept the peace, ensured there was no trouble.

So what did I do? What any determined survivor would— made myself indispensable to him. I think in the end he really came to like me—he was certainly very angry when they took me out of the cell.

There's a familiar smell here—familiar from way back. It took me a long time to place it. I thought for ages it was simply the reek of fear. Then, suddenly, I awoke one morning and knew exactly what it was—as clear and certain as if I'd first smelt it only the day before.

The Slaughter House on Pound Street.

Then, after weeks, I was moved from the big cell to a smaller room, with only one other prisoner. He was a Shi'ite; a Koja. He had been jailed for killing his six-year-old daughter, because he said when he heard her voice, he heard the voice of the man who plays with dogs.

He was completely mad; barking, if you'll forgive a pun in very poor taste. Hardly ever slept. His eyes were bright, like a man with malaria. Ridiculous though it may sound, he was good company. An ideal cell-mate. He was obsessively clean, careful, and private. In places like this, other people's bodily functions take on dramatic significance; he never even broke wind. Not once. He was determined that, before they executed him, he would convert me to Islam. In his insanity, he kept me sane. Exercising my mind by teaching me prayers, and lecturing me. The real torture in prison is the grinding, relentless monotony. Except for two meals a day, served (ha!) at the whim of the warden, there is no pattern. Nothing to structure and dissect the day. The lassitude, the torpor-induced surrender to their erratic timetable, their unexplained agenda. Meal times, bowel movements, sleep. That's all there is. Other than hour after hour of sitting, staring at nothing. This is when moral fibre comes to the fore.

Well, call me shallow but I'd exhausted my inner resources within days. After a month, I couldn't even be bothered to dream.

That's why Islam was such a gift from God. Suddenly, so much to learn, practise and do: language, process, movement and a glorious, disciplined regimen the guards could interrupt and frustrate but could not impose on. Requirements, restraints, deadlines. All the dos and don'ts you think you would love to be free of but for which you (or at least I) physically ache for once they are taken away.

In return I taught my cell-mate a Gene Pitney song I'd liked as a kid: Not much of a trade really. Eternal salvation for 24 *hours from Tulsa.* When, without really thinking about it, I told him I'd become a Muslim, he laughed, and capered and kissed me. Told me I already was. From that moment on, he treated me like a younger brother, or maybe a son. He sat awake, watching over me, when I slept. He sat awake, talking incessantly to me when I was awake. He would guard me from everything he could protect me from: insects, and insults. He would snatch the food we were given, pool it, then give me the best. I suppose he loved me. I certainly came to love him and found sense in his crazy, obsessive ways.

There was some problem about his sentence; it was postponed indefinitely. In the end, the date of my execution was set before his day came, and I was moved to a single cell. As my life expectancy progressively shortened, so the quality of my accommodation has, in step, improved.

When they decided to kill me, they gave me my first medical check. The doctor complimented me; apart from worms, he said, I was remarkably fit. Good one.

I can't remember how long ago now I was sentenced to die; a few weeks. Maybe three months. I lodged an appeal; not that it mattered. An appeal was lodged for me, automatically. When it was turned down, automatically, three days ago, they told me I would die today, at 9.15 in the morning. Friday morning.

I'd had my last weekend, and I hadn't even realized. And in all that time, no one had asked me a single question. Weird, eh? Still, I guess that's what happens when you are Armitage Shanks.

Once your appeal is turned down, various things follow at specific points in time. Forty-eight hours before you are to die, you get a haircut, your nails are trimmed and in theory, at least, the clothes you were arrested in are returned to you.

They couldn't find mine, but someone very thoughtfully rang around, and found for me the clothes an Indian businessman had died in. They are somewhat too large for me, but they're clean—apart from one rather troubling stain upon which I would rather not dwell—and of high quality. I'm wearing a pair of vintage Levi jeans, and a t-shirt which assures me Mumbai is a twenty-four-hour, non-stop adrenalin rush. Is it?

Maybe it's the tradition of respect for the dead that I guess exists in all cultures. In the last few days, I've been treated with such profound courtesy...

Thirty-six hours before your time, they give you writing paper. As much as you want. I'd heard this, but never really believed it, not really. You're not allowed to write to anyone; merely to write. Or rather, you can write to whoever you want. It just won't get posted. It goes on to your file. Christ knows why.

Christ.

Why did I write Christ? A last-minute relapse? Old habit, idiom, or simply exhaustion? I'm very tired, and my hand aches. I'm afraid to stop, however. Because if I stop, I will sleep. Then, when I awake, it will be simply to die. I'm not scared, or maybe it's just that I've been scared for so long I don't notice it any more. At the very least, I'm not more scared than normal. Tired, though, that's for sure, and a bit of me just wants to get it over.

I've got a photo of you. It's in front of me now. I'm afraid I've never heard of you, but the guy whose clothes I'm wearing must, I suppose, have been a fan of yours. I found your picture—it looks like it's been torn out of a television guide in a magazine—in his pocket. Underneath is your name, and the words 'Good Morning Mumbai, 07.00.'

They gave me the choice of his other belongings, too, this dead guy, your fan. He had a paperback book of poetry. Classics. Coleridge. Keats. I thought about trying to learn 'Kubla Khan' by heart but I don't have enough time, so then I tried to make up extra verses, complete it. I tried doing it straight, then in a kind of pastiche. I think that's the word— what a time to want to extend my vocabulary! I wonder, if I asked for a dictionary, whether they would give me one. Shall I try?

I've written a will. It's the jeans, you see. Much sought after. I've left them to one of the guards—the one I'm absolutely sure they won't fit. Cruel, eh?

Why am I writing this? Who even cares what I do? This letter will never be sent. They know it. I know it. They know I know it. So why am I writing to a total stranger who'll never receive this and why are they letting me do it?

They're indulging me, I suppose. And I'm indulging myself. I used to carry on writing to Father Christmas long after I accepted he didn't exist. I found it comforting to kid myself. You're my Father Christmas, except that I've got no more Christmases left, no more wishes and, from the way the sky is lightening, not very much more time, either.

∾

The man with the prison haircut and the overlarge Levi 501s sat at the table bolted to the floor and wrote. He wrote with a ballpoint pen, a freebie from an airline. His face was set in a permanent frown of concentration. As he tired, the child in him came out, and the tip of his tongue protruded from the corner of his mouth. It was well through the night, he didn't want to know what time. His cell was lit by a single forty-watt light bulb. Beyond the cell door, with its peephole and clumsily welded metal plating, the sounds of sad men sleeping could just be heard. Ill at ease, throat-clutching snores. Groans, coughs and muttered blasphemies.

The man with the prison haircut and the Levi 501s paused, sat back from the table, and scratched the bridge of his nose.

He felt the air change; the pre-dawn chill. There was no glass in the high, narrow window of the death cell. Only thick, rusted, wire meshing. He had been plagued by insects, and dust. He had been caught, and chilled, by driving rain. Torrential rain. Now, a breeze, carrying a hint of the desert, and wild herbs, under heavy grey clouds, made him homesick, though he had no idea how or why.

He felt a pitching, sinking sensation in the pit of his stomach as he heard the door bolts sliding back. He fought down gasping panic, and forced himself to turn and face the door. Die with dignity, he reminded himself. As yourself. Then they don't win. The guard whom he had befriended, whose home was up in the hills, stood at the threshold of the cell, hesitating to enter, unable to meet his eye. Two others lurked behind him, like sneak thieves.

'Is it time?' he asked, surprised and pleased at the steadiness of a voice he hadn't used for many hours.

'It's time,' murmured the guard.

There was a noise, a flurry outside. The guards turned, and stood aside. A young priest, red-haired and pink-faced, pushed past them.

'The Lord be praised!' he cried, his harsh Ulster accent, so out of place, tugging a last smile from the condemned man. 'They called me, my son, asked me to be with you. What can I say? Thank the Lord I got here in time.'

The priest turned to the guards: 'You'll give me ten minutes with him, to hear his last confession, will you not?'

The guards, all devout men with too much on their

consciences to be disrespectful to priests of any cloth, shuffled uneasily, and looked uncertainly at one another. There was a strict timetable to be followed; they did not have the authority to amend it. Nor were they particularly keen to return to the governor and seek his permission.

The condemned man saw their discomfort and, illogically, felt for them.

'It's kind of you to come, Father,' he said, 'but you should know I am a Muslim'.

The red flush returned. The priest ran a hand through his hair. 'Oh, they told me... It doesn't matter. No, of course it matters. Is there nothing I can do? Shall I walk with you to...'

The prisoner shook his head, then felt ludicrously sorry for the crestfallen priest. This... *boy* who called him Son.

'Just hearing your voice has been comfort. I've planned out, precisely, every step of this journey. Where my thoughts are going to be and what prayers, and poems, and names and places and silly things I'm going to think about. I'm not sure I can get through it unless I keep to that plan.' He held out his hand. 'Sorry.'

The priest stared at the extended hand for a moment, confused. Then, gripping it in both of his, he shook it vigorously. 'I wish there was something I could do,' he murmured sadly. 'I'll pray for you.'

A resigned smile, and a shake of his head. Then, silent still, the prisoner turned, and left with the guards.

Alone in the cell, the young priest tried to gather his waltzing senses. His pulse pounded in his temple, and he feared for a moment he would faint. He slumped into the chair, still warm from the last heat of the condemned man's body. He looked at the pages of tight, neat text. He reached out and picked up the picture of the woman torn from a magazine. Furtively, he glanced back towards the cell door, still ajar. A moment's further thought, then all indecision left him. Briskly, he folded the sheets of paper over once, then once again, and thrust them inside his cassock. He sat a moment longer, trying to get his thoughts, his breath, and pulse under control. Then he rose, and walked to the cell door. 'Can anyone tell me how to get out of here?' he called out.

His question was greeted by guffaws of hollow, bitter laughter, curses and a particularly offensive, wincing, blasphemy.

༃

'... So from me, Ash Kumar...'

'... and me, Taz Dhar...'

'... and all of us here at *Good Morning Mumbai*, have a good one.'

Ash Kumar eyed the camera, a lop-sided grin in place as the studio lights dimmed. The floor manager winked and held up three fingers. They were three seconds out on the close. Not bad; anything less than five seconds, either way, was as near to seamless as made no difference. The recording light blinked out, and Taz Dhar sniffed loudly.

'Fuck, I was sure I was going to sneeze during that last feature,' she murmured.

The tension left Ash Kumar's shoulders and back. His posture eased forward, his shoulders rounded and his ludicrously boyish face sagged.

'I saw you digging your nails into your palms; guessed some part of you was itching, twitching or aching.'

Taz looked at him sharply. 'What are you getting at?' Her eyes narrowed, she sniffed again, and rubbed her nose. Ash Kumar began patting his jacket pockets; breast, then hips, three times each. It was the same every morning. Taz looked away. He's like a machine; programmed, she thought.

He found the single cigarette he carried, in his left breast pocket, where it always was, and brought it to his mouth.

'Anybody got a match here?' he called out, his perfectly modulated voice muffled like a poor ventriloquist's by the cigarette held between his lips.

'Prat!' Taz groaned. This was a routine that pre-dated the channel's smoking ban, and was, through indulgence and an appeal to constitutional rights, the sole exemption tolerated. Around them the technicians looked up, smiling at each other and at Ash Kumar. A few shook their heads, the same every day; what a guy! Just one of the boys, with just brains enough to realize he'd got the crap the market was buying that week. A sound man disengaged himself from his equipment, and leaned over the wide, reconstituted wood desk that looked, on screen, like teak. He held a lit match forward, cupped in both hands, like an offering towards Ash Kumar. Kumar leaned forward no more than three inches, drew the flame into the cigarette, his heavily made-up cheeks drawn in, then stretched back, nodded gratefully, and immediately blew the smoke out in a thin jet.

'Doesn't even inhale. Wanker,' Taz mumbled.

Kumar turned to her, his right arm draped over the back of his chair. Smoke from the cigarette ran up over the back of his hand, and curled up from his cuff.

'Got something to say, Taz?' he asked.

'No, no,' she smiled, shaking her head, 'nothing at all'.

Kumar shrugged, and carefully removed the microspeaker from his ear, wary, as always, of his hair. As Taz reached for hers, the voice of the floor manager breathed, 'Taz honey, Mr Mehta wants to see you as soon as you're through here.'

She glanced up questioningly to the control box. The floor manager, his face sallow and haunted, illuminated from below by the light of a dozen flickering monitors, spread his arms, and shrugged. He was tired, she could see that. He had to be, or he would never have called her honey. A clear breach of the channel's avid pursuit of gender-neutral language.

Ash Kumar caught the look, and frowned. 'What is it?'

'SK wants to see me, PDQ.'

'PDQ?' repeated Kumar, puzzled.

Taz's eyes flicked skyward: 'Pretty damned quick,' she explained. 'Oh, shit, do you think they caught my nose twitching?'

'Not a chance,' Kumar reassured her. 'They'd never have picked it up; not with me on screen as well.'

'God! You're a narcissistic son-of-a-bitch!' said Taz, rising.

'Thanks,' said Ash, uncertainly.

'Maybe they're going to offer me a raise,' said Taz with a confidence she didn't really feel.

Kumar had an instinct for uncertainty in others. 'Or maybe they're gonna give your job to that pushy little lesbian on arts and culture.'

'You're a real charmer, Ash, know that? Anyway, just 'cause she's pushy doesn't mean she's gay.'

'Ha!' he cried, triumphantly. 'Gotya! You're not meant to say that; you're meant to say, "Her sexual orientation is not an issue here."'

'Well, she isn't, and it isn't.'

'No? But she's certainly pushy, isn't she? And she's got her beady little lesbo eyes on your job too, hasn't she?'

❧

Taz paused to catch her breath outside S.K. Mehta's office. It had been two weeks since she had last been up to the fourteenth floor; then it had been to receive a few words of warning as a result of a series of complaints received about the tone of voice she'd used in an item about back office support centres she'd titled 'Cyber-Coolies'. Pretty standard kind of complaint—the sort SK was normally pleased to receive—except that the channel sucked in serious money from the specific company she had chosen as an exemplar, and which proved to have a fat wallet but an extremely thin skin.

Then, the title on the door had been 'News Team Leader'; now it was 'Current Affairs Coordinator'.

She knocked, and went in.

S.K. Mehta was tall and balding, in his early fifties. As the years passed, and his career stagnated, he had adopted a range of affectations; a bow tie, bifocals suspended around his neck on a red cord, and snuff. Taz suspected he really saw himself as a gloriously old-fashioned literary figure. On the wall of his office, amid the inevitable framed awards and pictures of a younger him with a previous generation of Bollywood heart-throbs and political big hitters, hung a half dozen Spy caricatures of long-dead British press barons and judges; pot-bellied, gloomy men, in top hats or tweeds, identified by a single initial in inverted commas beneath their distorted images.

S.K. Mehta was devoted to all things English. Taz had always suspected that's why, against all the odds, she'd gotten her job.

The room smelt faintly of eucalyptus and menthol; the prime constituents of his favourite inhalation, which he bought on his regular trips to London, and carried home. His A/C was set, as always, two degrees below ambient. He leapt up from his chair as she entered, his face crumpled with concern.

'Taz!' he cried, moving quickly round the side of his desk to take her hands in his. 'Good session today; what were you, two, three seconds off? I liked the way you handled the piece on mafia dons. And that call from the guy in Vile Parle! It was really good.'

They stood awkwardly for a moment, SK still holding both her hands in his. He seemed unsure quite how to go on.

Eventually, he led her toward the low sofa bracketed between the coffee percolator and a massive potted palm—the Comfort Corner.

'Oh, shit,' thought Taz. 'What is it, SK?' she asked.

SK looked away. 'I don't know how to say this, Taz. We've had a letter...'

Taz groaned. 'Not cyber-coolies again?'

SK shook his head. 'No, nothing like that. At first we thought it was fan mail, or another crazy wanting to kill you: that's why it was opened for you. You know the policy: Privacy with Protection. But it isn't. It's personal. We've only read the covering letter, but it's, er... obviously pretty serious.' He crossed back to his desk, and picked up a bulky envelope. 'I'm really sorry. Really, I am. If you want to be alone when you read it, just say. Or if you want me to call anyone, then that's OK too. We're all here for you. You know that.'

Taz thought immediately of her mother in the UK, and her heart rate increased and her stomach churned. As she reached out for the envelope, her hand shook. The stamps were British, but she didn't recognize the handwriting. She took out the inner envelope, and the single sheet of paper. She scanned it quickly; it made no sense. She read it over, aloud.

'By the time you receive this, you will, I am sure, have been told through official channels of Armitage's death. I grieve for your loss, and pray that the Lord will give you strength to meet this tragedy with the same fortitude and resolve he displayed.

'I had the privilege to be with Armitage in his last few moments in this life. I am sure it will be a comfort for you to know that he died with courage and dignity. His last hours were devoted to writing you the letter I enclose. I have not read it; I do not think he would have wanted it read by anyone other than you. I am sorry to say I did not know Armitage well, but in the short time I spent with him, I recognized in him the strength and dignity that can only come from knowing that he would be meeting his God reconciled to his fate and at peace within himself.

'I pray that he will find peace and that the Lord will comfort you in your loss at this time.'

Taz looked up, her eyes bright and hard. 'Is this meant to be a joke?' she asked, quietly. 'Did Ash put you up to this?'

'You don't *know* this guy... this Armitage?'

Taz shook her head. S.K. Mehta blew out his cheeks, and massaged the back of his neck.

'Phew! You think this is some lunatic playing a joke?'

Taz shrugged. 'Who knows? He just signs it 'Father Thomas'. Not very funny, though, is it?'

'You want me to trash this?' S.K. Mehta asked, reaching for the letter.

'No.' said Taz. 'I'll glance through the stuff in the envelope later. Is that it?'

'Well, it was going to be; but while you're here and while I'm geared up to it, we may as well get all the bad things out of the way. You want some snuff? No? You mind if I do?'

He took a tiny mother-of-pearl pill box from his trouser pocket, and tapped out a small mound, the size of the head of a drawing-pin, onto the back of his hand. He raised his hand gently to his face, holding the mound first to one nostril, and inhaling briskly, and then the other. He brushed the last remaining traces of dark, pepper-like snuff from his hand, holding his breath.

'Wow!' he gasped, with an apologetic smile. 'Powerful stuff! Crumbs of Comfort. The Thinking Man's Coke. We're letting you go, Taz.'

'What?'

'We're letting you go. Sorry.'

Taz frowned and rubbed her nose. 'Well, thanks for the forewarning; it's pretty early to be making a decision like this, isn't it? My contract's still got fifteen months to run.'

SK closed his eyes and screwed up his face. He pulled out a large red and white handkerchief and buried his face in it as a massive sneeze exploded, muffled.

He blew his nose, inhaled deeply and leaned back. 'We're going for severance. Sorry, but it's not my decision. I was going to tell you at the end of the month. You get a pretty hefty pay-out; you've got a good contract. Solid. Sorry.'

'Severance? Blimey, you must be keen to get rid of me! I've got a right to know why, surely?'

'What can I tell you? You know the suits are worried about the ORG-Marg Intam ratings; they hired in some hot-shot media consultant who's done hours and hours of attitude modelling, and they say you're too... Asian Fusion.'

'What?'

'Asian Fusion. That's what they said. Your mix of Agony Aunt and Shock Jock. East meets West. A woman who speaks her mind, in tune with the wider world. That was the thing to be pre-9/11, apparently. But now—and excuse me, but these are their words, not mine—being sneered at and scolded over our foibles and failings—they have a weakness for alliteration, you will notice—smacks too much of hankering after some kind of foreign approval, and that's just not *Aaj Mumbaikar*, which is, so we are informed, what we need to be. We no longer seek the approval of the big, wide world: we are the big, wide world. You were intriguing, and you were cool, but now you're passé. Sorry.'

'*Passé?*' Taz repeated, chewing her bottom lip. 'I just can't believe this. I've changed the way I dress, the way I wear my hair, the way I talk. Shit, I've even changed the way I spell my name. I am simply incapable of being passé.'

'So you've changed the way you spell your name; big deal. Everybody changes their name in this business. You know what Ash Kumar was before?'

'Yeah. Joseph Jacob Fernandes. Everybody knows that. That's not the point.'

'Well, that's the word we paid big bucks for; passé'.

'So what about Ash? Are you severing him too?'

SK shook his head.

'Well, why not? He sure as hell isn't *Aaj Mumbaikar* either.'

'No,' SK conceded, 'he isn't. He's Evergreen.'

'Evergreen? And that's OK, is it?'

'Apparently. Old is Gold still holds good, so they say. Oh, and you're an NRI.'

'I know I'm an NRI; that's why you gave me the job!'

SK nodded. 'In 2001. Then, it was good to be an NRI. Then, if you were an NRI, you were worldly, sophisticated, and successful. One of us, yet not so. Something more. Then, our upper quartile viewers were NRIs tuning in across Canada, the States and Europe. Now, it's not so... now. The NRI demographic has changed, and its purchasing power apparently shrunk away to nothing. Then, it was doctors, lawyers, accountants. Formers, movers and shakers. Now, it's the ill, the unemployed and the aged that tune in from the diaspora. Now, they're the bad end of the business. The end we'd be happy to let slip away.'

'That's it?'

'No. Not all of it. The War On Terror; Iraq; Human Rights. Uncle Sam throwing his weight around. Here and now, to be an NRI from the West is to be tainted with questionable ethics. In bed with the bad guys. And to be a British NRI is to be... compromised. Uncertainly imperialist, arrogantly confused and, well, definitely not *Aaj Mumbaikar*. Sorry.'

'So I'm a passé NRI.'

'With a substance-abuse problem.'

Taz sat dead still. She felt the room closing in around her, then suddenly expanding out. She thought for a moment she was going to pass out, or throw up. Control. This conversation was way out of control. She thought desperately about how to respond. Insulted? Furious? Conciliatory? Amazed? Time. She needed time.

'Am I?' she asked, quietly. Shit, she could see how SK got his job and kept it. Wrapped up in the affable, increasingly eccentric packaging was a real killer.

'Aren't you?' SK asked gently. 'There's a specialist who runs a discreet clinic in Andheri who says so. He plays squash with someone on the board. Says you display several of the symptoms on-screen. Told us what to look out for, and suggested if we keep a camera on you when you're off-screen, he'd look over the tapes to be sure. For free; seems he's quite a fan of yours. Keen to help. You're rubbing your nose again; he says that's a classic symptom.'

'That's not a symptom,' Taz sneered. 'That's a fucking cliché.'

S.K. Mehta held up both hands. 'We're not out to crucify you, or pry into your private life, or even justify a decision to get rid of you. We don't need to; there's provision in your contract. You've been good for this channel, but you just aren't any more. That's all. We still care for you as a person. The channel's even prepared to come in on a three-way deal with this guy's clinic, if you think it would help.'

'So who replaces me?' she asked bitterly.

'Kavita, from arts and culture.'

Taz shook her head. So Ash had been right, after all. Had he known, or had it just been a lucky shot? The instincts of a true survivor? 'I might have guessed.'

'She's young, fresh, street-real and home-grown. The consultant guys said she's *desi* and totally *Aaj Mumbaikar*, and thus just what we need right now.'

'Ash says she's a lesbian,' said Taz vindictively.

SK smiled, 'Even better! Not, of course, that her sexual orientation is an issue here.'

'So, when do you want me out of here?'

'As soon as you like. Kavita's all lined up to take over; you can stay with it for another week, or go now. Up to you. If you want my advice, I wouldn't hang around. Take off for a couple of weeks with what's-his-name, and think about the offer about the clinic.'

'I'm not seeing what's-his-name any more. We split three weeks ago. My life's a mess right now, SK.'

Her voice was almost pleading. Hard man though he was, SK knew she'd hate herself if she thought she'd grovelled.

He looked at his watch.

'Could be worse, Taz,' he said, brusquely. 'You could be your buddy; what's his name? Armitage?'

Taz snatched up the envelope, her eyes blazing. She held it to her, while she extended her right arm, first clenched, index finger extended upward.

'Spin on it, SK!' she spat. 'You fucking, shit-bag toss-pot.'

She stormed out, slamming the door behind her. SK stood in the middle of the room, smiling. 'That's my girl,' he murmured proudly, as he jotted down the expletives on a velvet-covered pocket pad he kept for just such gems. 'So gloriously foul-mouthed. And oh, so predictable.'

2

The sky was a bright, translucent grey, like old porcelain. The ground was wet. The grass sparkled with overnight rain. The flaking limestone slabs of the old graves nearest the church were darkened, so the pale lichen blemished them in starker contrast, eczema on an old face. The church clock struck the half-hour. The minister re-checked his notes.

The name of the deceased was unknown to him; that was nothing new. He was well used to intoning anonymous, impersonal eulogies for a deceased he had never met and about whom he'd merely got the sketchiest confection from the bereaved relatives. The hubbub this memorial service had already caused was, however, something quite out of the ordinary for him. He walked out to the porch, removed three out-of-date announcements, and surreptitiously folded up and thrust into his pocket a hand-written notice about a bring-and-buy sale in the village hall. It was still two weeks to the sale, but he felt that the clumsy poster with a spelling error in its heading lowered the tone.

He looked down the flagstoned path to the arched gate, mossy in the perpetual shadow of the massive yew. There were already half a dozen estate cars cast like beached dinghies at odd angles on the high verges beyond the coned-off area around the church gate. Men in jeans and waterproof jackets smoked cigarettes beside cameras on tripods wrapped in polythene. Sound booms topped with fluffy microphones dipped beyond the wall like a herd of mechanical giraffes.

A reporter spotted him in the shadows of the porch and cheerily shouted out an invitation to come over and chat; the vicar shook his head, smiling politely. The bishop had told him what to do. No media personnel beyond the gate other than the Indians who had arranged the whole thing—and then only as mourners. No reporting or filming in the churchyard; no comments from himself until after the service, and then only the most nondescript platitudes...

There were even spectators. He could pick out almost a dozen, in raincoats, anoraks and plastic rain hats. Locals, come to see what all the fuss was about. He recognized two of his own parishioners, but couldn't immediately recall their names. A shame they didn't display such interest in attending church, he thought uncharitably. He nodded vaguely in their direction, but they didn't see: their attention was totally absorbed with the clutter and drama beyond the gate. He shifted his gaze up to the sky. He rather hoped it would start to rain again. There was to be no burial, of course. There was no open grave waiting: there was no body to put in it, but the sound of rain against the large stained-glass window, and the smell of wet earth and damp clothes seemed to him equally vital ingredients of a true English funeral.

He wondered, momentarily, what the actual interment had been like, indeed if there had been one at all. Hot, hurried and undignified, he assumed. He had never travelled outside of Europe, but had sat through sufficient films about missionary work, hosted plenty of fund-raising lectures and read more than enough articles full of leper colonies and disaster relief to set clear in his mind a pretty unattractive image of what it would have been like. He liked funerals—proper, well-proportioned funerals. Liked the sombre, measured ritual. The sound of his own, solemn voice echoing to the centuries-old beams of his beautiful little church, prompting perhaps a few tears, and a sniffed, manly struggle or two against the emotion his oratory would wring from the desperate mourners.

Back in her apartment, Taz kicked off her shoes, and walked through to the kitchen. In the sink, a half-dozen-odd china mugs and three tumblers lay on their side half-submerged in cold water laced with detergent which had thrown a greasy ring around the sink a fraction above the surface of the water. The bovine maid she had reluctantly taken on with the apartment was out, thank God. Well, at least now she had an excuse for letting her go. She disdainfully lifted a coffee cup from the sink with thumb and forefinger, and rinsed it beneath the tap. She switched on the kettle and whilst waiting for it to boil, tossed a half-teaspoon of granulated coffee into the mug. She watched as the granules dissolved in the residue at the bottom of the mug. She bent towards the cupboard beneath the sink, drew away, and then bent again, and reached inside, among the detergents and spray polish, for the half-bottle of Peter Scott she kept for emergencies. She broke the seal— glorious sound!—and poured a generous measure into the coffee cup, and when the kettle clicked off, topped the cup up with boiling water. The woody aroma of hot alcohol filled her senses, comforting her. She cradled the hot mug in both hands, held it to her face, and inhaled gratefully.

One of Raj's shirts—the heavy-duty cotton check he'd worn on winter evenings and then, when the collar started to fray, for odd jobs, or when he thought she wouldn't notice— was still draped over the towel rail beside the fire exit. It wasn't quite three weeks since he'd moved out. She'd hoped at first that he'd deliberately left the shirt behind to give himself a pretext of coming back. Passing time made that increasingly unlikely. Now, she was almost superstitious about removing it. If she packed it away, threw it out, or sent it on to him, it would be a final, irrevocable acceptance of his departure.

She wondered if she could ring him; losing her job was surely pretext enough. If she was going to, it had to be now. Before she sipped her coffee.

He could tell, even over the phone, if she'd been drinking. She looked at the telephone, then at the steaming mug.

'Fuck him,' she thought, and took her first sip.

A substance-abuse problem! The puritanism of fashion, nothing more, she assured herself. Like the changes of job title on S.K. Mehta's door. Like the obsessive pursuit of gender-neutral language when all the same shitty power structures were in place, and all the same issues were in play. Twenty years ago, her ability to turn in a thoroughly professional performance every morning after nightly boozing it up with the best of them would have been regarded as a plus point, far more likely to have helped a woman compete successfully in a man's world than playing around with the words. The whisky-laced coffee eased her anguish, and boosted her confidence. She was glad too she hadn't rung Raj. Grateful, too, that SK had not let her crawl. Pious git! Who the hell was he to lecture anyone on addictions? SK, with his snuff and... Suddenly, she wanted to cry.

She sniffed, rubbed her nose. Maybe she'd ring her mother. She was surprised how upset she had been when she'd thought the letter was bad news about her. Surprised how relieved she had been when it had turned out not to be. But not just now. Not just yet. It would be early morning in the UK. If she called before breakfast Ma would instantly infer disaster and set about attributing it to her. Whatever she did, she decided she was not going to drink any more, at least not this morning, and she wasn't going to get maudlin.

So what was left?

Tidy up the apartment, fire cow-face when she saw fit to drag her fat ass back in from the shops and make something to eat. Great. She wasn't sure whether she'd go back to the studio, or simply ask them to send her things on to her. Didn't know if she'd enjoy saying aloud to Ash all the things she'd said under her breath over the years, or get more satisfaction out of the thought of how much his ego would be bruised by her showing she could just walk away from nearly five years of working with him without so much as a goodbye. But right now, she needed something to occupy her mind.

When she had arrived back at her flat, she'd still been clutching the letter from the priest, and the sealed envelope it had enclosed.

Well, what the hell? In the land of the visually challenged, the one-eyed gender-neutral person is the gender-neutral monarch. Or president, of course, if it happened to be a republic. In a crazy world, there was considerable comfort in surveying the evidence of someone being more reality-challenged than you. She took the coffee through to her bedroom, retrieved the letter from off the telephone table in the hallway where she had tossed it, and settled down to be reassured.

ॐ

Half an hour later, her coffee cold and untouched, her shoulder aching where she had lain awkwardly, and her eyes bright and dry, she rang the studio and asked for S.K. Mehta. When he answered, she said simply, 'I think it's for real. I need to talk to you. Can I buy you lunch?'

ॐ

She was at the restaurant before SK. It was the best part of an hour in honking, congealed traffic from her apartment; no more than a ten-minute walk from the studio.

She had been determined to be there first. It allowed her to choose the table. She ordered herself a whisky and soda which she downed quickly and handed the glass back to the waiter, and a Bisleri, which she placed piously before her. She took out the first few pages of Armitage Shanks's letter and was reading them again, absorbed, when S.K. Mehta arrived.

'This had better be worth it,' he warned, pulling the chair out, and sitting down with a sigh. 'You want a drink?'

'What is this? A test?' she asked, irritated.

S.K. Mehta shook his head. 'No. Just an offer. Your dependencies are not my problem any more; you're off the payroll. What's that, water? Want something stronger?'

'What are you having?'

'Me? Just nimbu-pani.'

'Then I'll have the same. SK, I think this guy might be for real.'

'So you said on the phone. So you've got a fan who died overseas. That's sad. But so what?'

'He didn't just die, SK. He was executed.'

'Wow! Where?'

'I don't know. Somewhere hot.'

'Well, that certainly narrows things down a lot. There was a bunch of guys executed in Iraq, but that was months ago. I don't recall any other stories...'

'Nor do I. Nor does anyone. I Googled it. Nothing. That's what makes this so bloody weird. Here, read this.'

She handed him the first page of Armitage Shanks's manuscript. He put on his bifocals, screwed up his eyes and glanced over the crumpled pages.

'I don't get this wisecrack about his name.'

'Armitage Shanks? It's the name of a major sanitaryware manufacturer in the UK.'

'Sanitary wear? What, like tampons and towels?' he asked, looking slightly nauseated.

'No. Like basins, baths, sinks and toilets.'

'Oh. So he's Angrez too?'

Taz shrugged. 'I guess.'

SK read on, at first snorting irritably, then becoming increasingly absorbed. When he had read to the end, he folded the papers over and handed them back to her. He took off his glasses, and polished them with his napkin.

'What do you think, SK?'

'I don't know. It's as you said: weird. Are you ready to order?'

'SK, I want you to assign me to find out what happened.'

SK's eyes widened. 'You want me to pay you to go off round the world to look for a dead guy who's named after an English toilet? And he's not even from Mumbai? You must have a bigger substance-abuse problem than I thought.'

'I really think this could be a big story, SK. I believe in it.'

'Good for you: do it freelance; I can get you an advance on your severance if you've got a cash-flow problem.'

'That's not the point. I don't want severance. I want an assignment. This assignment. Think about it: this guy, out there. All alone. Facing a cruel death in a foreign country. And as far as you or I or Google can tell, nobody knows a damned thing about it. Handled right, his story could be big. Really big. Breaking news, not just all-India, but syndicated globally. The channel could be the new *Al Jazeera*.'

'Yeah,' said SK, uncertainly, 'but does it matter?'

'Matter? This poor guy's been topped, and nobody knows? I think it matters. Don't you think it matters?'

'To the channel, I mean. So some guy gets switched off somewhere hot. So what? There are Brits on death row in Texas, and Australians in Indonesia. There's an Indian days from execution right now in Pakistan, and nobody gives a damn about that. Every year, two or three Indians are executed in Saudi Arabia, and we invite Saudi princes to the Independence Day Parade. What's the big deal? Like I said, if you believe in it, and I'm really glad that you do, do it freelance.'

'I don't think I can, SK. I'll be honest with you: I don't think I can handle this, not on my own. It's my story, but I need the channel behind me, and its contacts. Even if this doesn't make sense in terms of its simple newsworthiness, it makes business sense, you must see that? Look at it this way: you save the severance pay. Keep me on salary to do this story, and I'll waive any claim to severance if you don't use it, or me, when I come back. Fair?'

'I don't know. The only foreign stories anyone's interested in are about Pakistan, NRIs and China, preferably all negative. This isn't about any of them. Supposing, just supposing for a moment, that this guy is for real: how do you know he's not someone you knew in the UK; where's the angle for us?'

'Look, he doesn't even know I'm from England. See here, he says 'your country' when he's talking about this dead Indian businessman. He thinks I'm Indian; it isn't me he's writing to as a person. It's to the channel. It's to us.'

SK sat back and stared at Taz. She knew he was making up his mind. Yes! It was still in the balance. She sat dead still, and waited.

'No, Taz,' he said eventually. 'I can't do it. It may be your story, but it isn't ours. It isn't right for us, and we both know you've got no experience as an investigative reporter. Sorry.'

He'd expected her to be angry, disappointed. For her to argue, yell and curse. Instead, she seemed almost resigned.

'OK, SK. You win. Let's have that drink, and let's eat. What'll you have?' They ordered, and sat in awkward silence. The wine arrived before the meal, a South African red. Taz took a glass gratefully, drank it quickly and accepted a refill. She needed the extra confidence it would give her. SK sipped at his, uncomfortable, keen to get the meal over quickly.

'Would you say this was a pretty high-profile place, SK?' Taz asked suddenly.

'I guess so. Why?'

'Oh, nothing. How's the family?'

'They're fine. Asha is driving Gauri up to Pune to get her settled into college; she starts her first year. She's really scared.'

'What's she studying?'

'Physics. Can you believe it? My little girl is going to be a physicist. Makes me feel so old.' He paused, and reached for the wine. 'You're planning something, aren't you?'

Taz nodded. SK smiled, and shook his head.

'OK, let's have it.'

'Well it's this, SK. Somewhere around dessert, I'm going to get up, and walk out. I may throw a glass of water in your face, or I may knock something over. Something to get everyone's attention. Then I'm going to claim you demanded sexual favours of me in return for trying to persuade the board to keep me on. That is, unless you agree to send me on assignment. Ah! Here comes your salad.'

It was Taz's turn to wait, unsure what would happen next; whatever she anticipated, it certainly wasn't SK's guffaw of laughter. 'Oh, Taz! You're great! You really are! Do you think anyone would believe you?'

'Does it matter? To the channel, I mean? I think I could make things pretty unpleasant.'

'Believe me, the channel could make things much more unpleasant for you. I'm not threatening you, just warning you. They'd go public about your drinking. Make sure you'd never work again. You're burning your bridges behind you, Taz, and that's always a high-risk strategy.'

'So it's risky. Big deal. I took the precaution of looking at the blurb we send prospective advertisers: 91 per cent of our breakfast-time viewers who stay through to 9 P.M. are women. Of those 64 per cent are in the thirty-five-to-fifty, upper-quartile, greater-disposable income bracket. If I don't screw the channel on gender, I'll fuck you on age: do you really think these well-heeled ladies of a certain maturity will still tune in to a channel that says you're past it at thirty-nine? So the channel will say I've got a booze problem? Ditto. Big deal. Maybe I'll claim it's cocaine, procured for me, by you, at work. Who knows? It might even make me *Aaj Mumbaikar*.'

'OK. Let me think about it.'

'Fine,' Taz smiled sweetly. 'Go ahead. Eat your salad. Enjoy. Just be sure to make up your mind before we get to dessert, or ring Asha to prepare herself for some extra dry-cleaning bills.'

❧

SK had it played just the way she asked. Next morning, with the lesbian sitting in her old chair—looking cowed and gauche, Taz noted with satisfaction—Ash Kumar eyeballed No. 3 camera, one eyebrow raised, and like a character from a third-rate war movie, announced: 'Good morning, Mumbai. This is Ash Kumar, with the 7 o'clock news. With me, Kavita Durga. Taz Dhar, my co-presenter for the past five years, and my friend, is on special assignment. We'll be bringing you her story exclusively here on *Good Morning Mumbai*. In the mean time, as the UK adopts new laws on screening for terrorists, Kavita will be taking your calls, texts and e-mails on what you think this means for the Indian travelling overseas.'

An hour later, Raj called round on his way to the office, on the pretext of finally collecting his shirt. She made him coffee, and offered him breakfast. He shook his head.

'No time,' he told her, as he sipped quickly. 'Associate directors meeting at a quarter to nine. Is it real, you know, about this special assignment? Is it true?'

'Of course it's true,' she snapped. 'It was on *Good Morning Mumbai*, wasn't it?'

'I thought maybe you were taking a break to, you know, to...'

'Dry out?'

'If you're comfortable with that. I was going to say, get help.'

'Well, I'm not. You want some more coffee?'

'Where is your "special assignment?"' The way he said it made it sound like a euphemism for something sham, and hollow.

'Abroad.'

'Really? When are you leaving?'

'Soon.'

'Maybe we could get together before you go. For dinner. Or something?'

would cope manfully with the disappointment of their mother's annual visit being cancelled, but was determined not to give him the opportunity. 'I won't hear of it. It would be crazy, and it would be unfair. You go. I'll probably still be here when you come back. In any case, I'm going to be out and about most days: London, chasing up leads, that sort of thing. It would be crazy for you to cancel your trip. You know that. It would be unfair to Asghar and Saena.'

They were sitting in the front room of the house that Taz had bought her mother three years earlier. It was a relatively new house, in a relatively new estate, in a relatively old village, six miles east of Swindon. Taz had arrived, announced only by a phone call from Santa Cruz, the previous day.

Asghar and Saena, in Toronto, had two children. Boys: Amar, aged six, and Saif, three. Taz didn't really like either of her nephews, felt terribly guilty about the fact, and compensated with extravagant gifts and exaggerated responses to key landmarks in their progression. She knew her mother had no intention of missing out on two months with her only grandchildren. Certainly not to spend time with her.

Other people's descriptions of her mother tended to range across a narrow bandwidth from 'marvellous' to 'magnificent'. She was one of those semi-nomadic dowagers who criss-crossed the world between family homes with the same assurance they used to board the bus from Kampala to Nairobi. Small, frail and tough as old boots, Najmabehn Dharwalla (she had never forgiven Taz for truncating her name) was a woman so slight you could image a gust of wind blowing her away, yet a glimpse at her set expression and that lathe-straight back told you she would face down a couple of armoured divisions. A woman to be admired, respected: to be spoken of with pride and affection, but not, unfortunately, an easy mother to love.

They'd never really been close: Najmabehn always seemed to Taz to regard her with a slight frown that Taz had of late started to recognize in unexpected reflections of her own features. There was always that whiff of disapproval and disappointment. That sense of failed attempts and frustrated hopes. It had never even occurred to Taz to tell her mother the truth about her current position at the channel: it would become just another strand to weave into the mesh of regret that shrouded their sterile relationship. So they did what decent people in such circumstances do: they did their duty. Taz was the ideal distant daughter. Far away, independent. Earning respectably, contributing generously. The house, a down payment on a little car, and the yearly ticket to Toronto. (Asghar could not be expected to contribute similarly. After all, he had a family to think of, didn't he?) Najmabehn reciprocated with loyal expressions of pride in Taz's achievements.

Taz looked round the living room. Home? This was no home to her. There were things she recognized from her childhood; the last and least fragile of the few possessions her mother and father had bought with them in a suitcase from Kampala. The African carving and the little ivory elephants. There were old school and graduation photos of her and Asghar. There was even the badly painted model of the *Millennium Falcon* Asghar and their father had made when Asghar was eight, and Papa was first ill. There were several large studio shots of the grandchildren in Toronto as babies and as toddlers. There was clutter, and familiar trivia, and stuff she'd asked her mother to look after whilst she was working abroad, but nothing which made this place home for Taz. It felt more like an under-funded and half-hearted museum of her past. Idiosyncratically gathered, illogically displayed, unenthusiastically curated.

Except, of course, that there was Pudding. The stray that had somehow adopted her when a fluffball kitten, a year or two before her divorce, and which had stayed with her until she had moved to Mumbai. That kitten was now an arthritic and lugubrious brute which cost her a small fortune in vet's bills, and continued to treat her with the disdain verging on contempt with which he had won her heart from day one.

He was on her lap, now. Asleep, as he seemed to spend twenty-three hours out of every twenty-four, purring contentedly. She scratched him under the chin, and the rhythm of his purring changed, but otherwise, he remained, as always, indifferent to her advances.

'I feel terrible, just leaving you here,' her mother grumbled.

'I'll be fine,' Taz insisted. 'Really. Pudding will look after me, won't you, boy? Anyway, I've got a thousand and one things to do. I'm going to be out most days. You go ahead and have a good time.'

Her mother watched Taz play with the cat with a mixture of distaste and jealousy. She could not bring herself to touch the creature, and only took it in because Taz had begged her to, and she was very aware Taz was paying the mortgage on the house, but she and Pudding both loathing excessive displays of affection, had become comfortable in each other's distant company over the years and she resented Taz assuming she could just walk in and reclaim him. 'I rang Mark to tell him you were here,' she said with studied nonchalance.

The tremble of irritation that ran through Taz was sufficient even to disturb Pudding, who raised his head sleepily, and looked up at her with narrowed eyes. 'You did what?' said Taz quietly.

'You know he likes news of you, always asks after you. Likes to know how you're getting on. He's proud of you, like we all are. Besides, I thought he'd be company for you. You don't have to see him, although I think you ought to, not if you don't want to. Don't sulk.'

'I'm not sulking. I'm thirty-nine. I don't sulk. I show my disapproval. I haven't sulked since I was fourteen.'

She and Mark Letcombe had been married for six years. Hard now to believe, listening to her mother championing the interests of her ex son-in-law, what a god-awful drama there had been about her marrying outside the community. But in spite of, or perhaps because of, the tempest their engagement had unleashed in both families, their short marriage had been spectacularly undramatic. As time passed, passionate opposition cooled, angry in-laws grudgingly acquiesced and finally everyone ended up surprisingly fond of one another. And remained so. Mark's parents still had Taz's mother over to stay at Christmas and never failed to remember Taz's birthday. Taz sent them a card every year for their anniversary and had flown home the previous year for Nanny Letcombe's funeral. At which, much to her embarrassment, she had wept buckets. She and Mark had been easy and comfortable together; been good friends for what seemed like forever before they married. They could have remained easy and comfortable with each other, had it not been for their increasingly irreconcilable desires for children (him) and recognition (her). A job in India provided a convenient excuse for an amicable termination. Done with respect, affection and a genuine concern for the other's dignity, that too had been easy, and comfortable. The right thing to do in the circumstances, like switching off the life-support of a vegetating beloved.

With hindsight, Taz thought it was probably that casual cosiness which had ultimately smothered their marriage; she couldn't even remember them ever having a real, honest-to-God, voices-raised row. These days, they too exchanged birthday cards—Mark always sent her one with a cat on it—and a newsy e-mail at Christmas. She knew her mother still hoped they would get back together again; she suspected Mark cherished similar ambitions in that direction too.

'I'll call him,' she said, with a resigned sigh.

'Promise?'

'I said I will, didn't I? *Bas.*'

'Very *Raichand*,' said her mother, obscurely.

∾

Taz drove her mother to Heathrow in a hire car, and parked in the short-term car park at Terminal 3. After a stilted series of farewells, concluding with them brushing their cheeks against each other in some distant semblance of a kiss, she left the car clocking up parking fees at an astronomical rate and travelled on into central London on the tube. What the fuck? She thought. The channel will be picking up the tab. She bought SK his snuff at Smith's on Charing Cross Road, and trudged, with no great urgency, along wet pavements toward Trafalgar Square.

As she walked, a sense of desolation and loss seemed to seep into her like damp through a holed shoe. From the moment she had been greeted on arrival at Heathrow by the studiously polite immigration officer, who had taken such great pains to pronounce her name correctly, she had become increasingly aware of a different feel to England post-7/7. In the past she had been regularly reminded of her perceived identity as at her best an Asian, at worst a Paki: an obvious, convenient, ubiquitous classification. This trip, for the first time, she was conscious of people no longer reacting to the colour of her skin, but to the sound of her name: the shutters, if not actually coming down as soon as someone realized she was a Muslim, were at least slid into place, ready and at hand, if needed. This was an interesting new twist in the responses of the traditionally suspicious and the naturally bigoted who, not so very long ago, would have been offended if anyone thought they could tell a Muslim from a Sikh. But it was even more noticeable in the careful way the polite and politically correct spoke enthusiastically about 'ordinary, decent British Muslims' and deliberately included her, drew her in, as though to say, 'It's alright, we understand. We know you are really one of us: British, just like us.'

Except, she suspected, she wasn't. Not really. Not any more. It was, as with her marriage, not about who was right and who was wrong but about how much, and how quickly, empty ground opened up between two parties growing inexorably apart as both changed in different ways, reacting to different stimuli and embracing different priorities. And, again like her marriage, she found that much she had once loved, always assumed permanent and had thus taken for granted had withered away to be replaced by new things, foreign, vaguely threatening and infinitely strange.

She had last been in the UK a year earlier, just for a few days, for Nanny Letcombe's funeral. It must have been three years since she had been in the centre of London. It had been a beautiful, bright autumn day, she recalled. That city now seemed Atlantis-like, and she was sure she was idealizing it. Since that day, it seemed to her, the population had significantly bulked up and dumbed down. For example, she had never been conscious then of the casual use of the word 'fuck' which now echoed around so, a constant in many different accents and intonations. She decided that as its currency was now so devalued, she should stop using it. Where was the shock value if every clutch of workers huddled, smoking on the steps of their office routinely used the word as padding simply to modulate the pace of their verbal exchanges? When lumpen mothers cursing sulky toddlers felt it an entirely appropriate addition to their lexicon of rage? What was the point when you heard it, high-pitched, tossed indifferently between giggling schoolgirls waiting for the bus home? Why bother when a High Street fashion chain realizes it can retail its merchandise far more successfully by changing its name from French

Connection to FCUK? And then put slogans on their tops like 'FCUK me!', just in case anyone had missed the reference.

I've become old. She thought, glumly. Middle-aged, middle-class and pompous.

But it wasn't just that. When did there start to be so many uniforms on the street? When did the sight of a policemen in body armour on a busy corner, his folded arms resting on a machine gun slung from his neck, fail to turn heads and raise eyebrows? And who the hell were all these Community Support Officers, dressed in blue and draped in pseudo-police paraphernalia, proclaiming an authority and a competence they did not have? And what about all these cameras? They seemed to be everywhere. Watching. Recording.

Absentmindedly she made a dash across the Strand, out into slow moving traffic, as she would have in Mumbai, but here the anticipated blast of a car horn was accompanied by a furious voice that called her a stupid cunt. She turned, shocked, to see a young Asian, his face twisted in fury, glare out of the window of a silver BMW and throw her a vicious finger gesture. Why should he be so angry? How could he possibly care so much? And when did boys like him start to call women like her cunts? God! She glanced down at the pavement and recognized, like an old friend, a red splash of discharged betel. She suddenly felt very far from anything she really cared for and fought back the urge to cry. What kind of society had this become when everyone watched what they and everyone else said so carefully, imprisoned by propriety, desperate to avoid the risk of being labelled racist or sexist, yet felt so at liberty to spew out a barrage of obscenity at the least provocation?

Being pre-menstrual, she reminded herself, realizing suddenly that if she was, it didn't mean having to be pathetic. But that was how she felt: utterly pathetic. She thought of half a dozen stinging retorts she should have made to the now far distant BMW and gave herself a firm talking-to for being too slow, and so weak.

She strode more briskly up the Strand for Somerset House, in search of the Registrar of Births, Marriages and Deaths.

Her heels echoed as she walked on cobble through the imposing vestibule of the neo-classical palace, and emerged into the vast, draughty courtyard beyond. She stopped, shoulders hunched against the cold rain that blew across the deserted space, and studied a map which proudly proclaimed 'What to see and what to do at Somerset House' in a purple, friendly typeface. What the hell was this? Galleries, Collections, Exhibitions, Restaurants. A uniformed security warden, an elderly West Indian in an orange reflective jacket and a peaked cap wrapped in plastic, asked her if she needed help, and shook his head when she mentioned the Registrar's Office.

'Hasn't been here for years, love,' he said. 'Most people look up that sort of thing on the Internet nowadays. Except the old folk, of course.'

She looked down, feeling her face flush, and he added sympathetically, 'But at least once every day someone turns up looking for it. Especially...'

'The old folk?' she offered.

He shook his head. 'Foreigners.'

She walked across the courtyard to the Seamen's Waiting Hall and sat, alone, beneath vast portraits of Nelson and Hardy, sipping a cappuccino in a paper cup from The Deli and feeling deeply sorry for herself. She looked out through tall, rain-streaked windows across a muddy Thames at low tide to the unlovely blockhouses and towers of the South Bank. The National Theatre, The Royal Festival Hall, The OXO Tower and the Shell Building. Temples to a future of brash functionalism built five decades ago, now a dated and dreary backdrop to the barely revolving London Eye, huge beyond

Waterloo Bridge. What was she doing here? What was the point of this... charade? She felt like one of the damp sightseers on the Eye, trapped in a capsule on a faked flight, rising in the air yet firmly anchored to the ground, trying to spot familiar landmarks and find some recognizable pattern in the sprawling confusion before them. She had no more idea of how to find this Armitage Shanks than a five-year-old child. Did she even really care who this poor fuck, sorry, fool, she corrected herself, had been and what had happened to him?

She got out the copy of the papers and covering letter she had received and lay them out on the table in front of her. She folded them and was about to tear them up, then stopped herself. Another pointless gesture. They were photocopies. She decided instead to make some calls. As she searched for her mobile—she had forgotten how many pockets you end up with when you have to wear several layers of clothes—she failed to notice a figure, similarly well wrapped up against the weather, quietly enter the waiting room and sit at the furthest table.

She called Mark's number. He was out, as she had expected, hoped and planned. She listened to his desperately cheery voicemail OGM, then just said 'Hi, it's me' and promised to try and call back.

Duty done.

Next she autodialled S.K. Mehta.

'Taz?' he asked, groggily.

'Hi, Boss,' she chirped, with a cheeriness she didn't feel. 'How's tricks?'

'It's night here, Taz,' said SK, yawning. 'We get up at four, remember? Try to bear that in mind when you call next.'

'Whatever. I got you your Crumbs of Comfort.'

'What? Oh, good. Thanks. Well...'

'No, listen. Don't hang up. Look, you know you said that, well, if I felt, you know... I wanted to...'

'Give it up? Taz, you've only been there, what? Three days?'

'Four. But that's not the point. You were right when you said I have no experience as an investigative reporter.'

'And you were right when you said you were the one who should do this story. Perhaps the only one who can. I realize that now. Think about it a bit more and call me tomorrow.'

What was there to think about? Here she was, all alone... and then something Pappa used to say came back to her: 'A member of our Community is never alone. Sometimes in your life that will make you feel good. Most times, it will probably make you feel bad, but whatever you do, never forget it.'

She smiled at the memory and found the mobile her mother had left with her. She clicked down through the contacts list. Abbas, dentist. Amir, an accountant, as were Hamzabhai, Hasan, Saif and Qu'aid. Not likely to be of much use, as far as she could see. Husain and Bashira, pharmacists. Ditto Fatima and Imtiyaz. Similarly irrelevant. Mansur and Murtazar had a wholesale business in Sheffield. Munira was a secondary school teacher in Bristol. All good marriageable careers but not much help to a lost wannabe private eye. And then she saw it, smiled, surprised that her mother would have kept this number, and wondered how she could ever have taken so long to think of it. Yusuf Kaka!

Quite what Yusuf Kaka did these days was a mystery. He had property, flats and terraced houses that he rented out. He owned a printing business and held shares in a restaurant, but always managed to make these undoubtedly lucrative sources of income seem irrelevant to whatever it was he was really into. Something disreputable, clearly, because Ma and her brothers never spoke of him, did their best to ignore him at family gatherings and acknowledged him only icily at the mosque, solely to avoid gossip and uncomfortable questions. He had always been an enigma. Trained, much to his family's disgust, as a butcher, he had been the only one with a readily transferable skill when they were kicked out of Uganda. For the arrival of a flood of East African immigrants gave rise to a surge in demand for familiar food. Someone who could cut meat the way they did at home, halal, too, mind you, was not likely to be short of work for long. Yusuf Kaka was almost immediately out of the camp and in serious demand. Travelling from one butchery to another, from abattoir to farmyard to slaughter and joint meat for the Asian market. He seemed able to go on forever with virtually no sleep. Cutting as clean and sure at the end of an eighteen-hour day as at the start. Indefatigable, indiscriminate and, as anyone who had seen him at work would confirm, so much more than a skilled journeyman. There was a grace in the sight of him skinning a chicken or jointing a leg of mutton that transcended the reek of stale fat and dried blood, the damp terrace house cellars and chilly backyards in which he worked. Soon he had his own *goshtwallah*'s. Then a second. Then four more. Then rumours began that more than meat was passing though his chillers. A lot of it hot and none of it halal. That's what they said at the masjid, anyway. Inevitably, this gave Yusuf Kaka a powerful romantic appeal to his nieces and nephews. He was a tall man, bald and pot-bellied now, but still a charismatic presence. Always better dressed than his siblings, if rather more flashily than most of the community's men thought fitting, he was the first of the refugees from Uganda in the 1970s to own the now ubiquitous BMW. He was a regular and generous contributor to various charitable and community initiatives, Islamic Aid, the Mosque Building Trust, the Khubbrastan Fund, and forked out unstintingly for numerous jamans. Meat supplied free for all occasions. He had always seemed to be someone people turned to in order to solve difficulties that otherwise defied resolution, be they difficulties with landlords, or more latterly, tenants, planning authorities or jamat members. A man, valued, whom some partly admired, and others mostly respected, whom many feared but few liked.

Except Taz. He had never seemed that terrifying to her. As the only other rebel in a family remarkably light on freaks and ferals, she had won his approval and affection at an early age, and through misadventures, crises and narrowly avoided disasters kept his high regard. And as a regular visitor to Mumbai, for ziarats and other less specific engagements in Bhindi Bazaar, Yusuf Kaka was actually the relative Taz had seen most over recent years, for he never failed to call her and invite her out to dinner whenever he was in town.

So she rang her father's youngest brother, with a genuine feeling of anticipation and affection, but Yusuf Kaka was, predictably, not picking up calls. She told his voicemail she was in the UK, left a summary of what she was doing, and said she wanted to see him. He lived out toward Saffron Waldron somewhere. She wondered about heading out there now, but glanced at her watch; and decided to leave it till the next day. She left the Seaman's Waiting Room feeling much more positive. The only other occupant waited a furtive minute, then rose and followed her out.

By twenty to ten the first mourners began to arrive, neat and sombre, with expensive, muddy shoes. Parking had been arranged for invited guests in the field across the lane, but several days of rain had swelled the clay and pooled on its surface so that even the two dozen bales of exorbitantly priced straw the farmer had forked around the entrance did little to keep the mourners' feet dry.

The vicar had little sympathy; the deceased had, as far he was aware, no real connection with his parish, or even the

Christian faith if rumour was to be believed, and he was pretty sure his church had been selected for the service solely because of the picturesque background it would provide. A further example, if one were needed, of just how obsessively inclusive and commercially avaricious the Church of England had become. Still, he mused, sourly, what could you expect of a church which ordained women and embraced homosexuals?

He frowned; he really must snap himself out this cynical frame of mind. In little over half an hour, the service would begin, and no matter what their motives for choosing Coombe Wootton, he had a duty to perform. A vocation still to fulfil. So what if he found it difficult to sympathize with someone going out to the back of beyond and getting himself killed? Who cared if what would now follow was little more than a theatre more appropriate for a Bollywood blockbuster than a serious act of remembrance? Did any of them really care for the deceased? No. But then, if he were to be honest, nor did he, and it was hardly his place to sit in judgement. He had a job to do; no, a calling to fulfil, and he also had his instructions.

His instructions. He knew, in his heart, that it was those very instructions that were at the root of his uncharitable frame of mind. The bishop had made clear that the media were not to encroach beyond the gate—but his church, his lovely little church, was so beautiful, so picturesque. He wanted it seen, and photographed, and televised, and resented his bishop's ruling. He was to prostitute his calling, but could not glory in his wonderful church. Pride, of course, is a sin, but fortunately for him the Church of England was less harsh on sin than in former days for he was guilty of a sinfully massive pride in his pretty, pretty little church.

He hadn't told anyone to do it, it had just happened. As soon as word got out that the memorial service would take place at Coombe Wootton a determined army of helpers had descended upon the church to polish every inch of old wood, and furiously Duroglit the brass, and bedeck the Norman walls with some of the most beautiful flower arrangements he had ever seen. The graveyard had been tidied. Edges trimmed and long grass trimmed. He could have wished that the avenue of flowering cherries that stretched from the gate to the porch had not been quite so ruthlessly pollarded: their boles stood bare and gnarled in arthritic fists. But even that only served to add to the stark beauty that framed the glorious little chapel. The place, quite simply, was a picture, and he was inordinately proud of it.

And no matter what the bishop said, once the service was over, he would, he decided, make sure those nice people hunched up in thick parkas got their chance to capture it all on film. For the glory of God. And Coombe Wootton.

∾

It was gone nine by the time Taz got back to Heathrow, picked up the car and drove back to her mother's house. She hadn't eaten, but she wasn't particularly hungry. She had thought about stopping somewhere for food, but couldn't work up the enthusiasm. She was sure she would find something around the house that would do. She was less and less troubled these days about what she ate, and when. She was more conscious of her desire for something to drink.

There would, of course, not be a drop of alcohol in her mother's home. Pappa had taken a drink on rare occasions, and had kept a bottle of something or other in his long-disposed-of garden shed, to which he and Yusuf Kaka would retreat to sip discreetly from coffee mugs. Of course, everyone knew what was going on, but as long as it wasn't blatant, wives and mothers could politely overlook it and pretend not to notice the fumes, and fuddled, guilty smiles.

When refuelling the car, she bought a bottle of Bells. When had petrol stations in the UK started selling booze?

When she opened the front door, and flicked on the hallway light, Taz automatically called for Pudding. It was something she always used to do; even when she was married to Mark. 'You care more about Pudding than you do about me,' he used to grumble amiably. 'If the house burnt down you'd only ask the fire brigade to look for me once you were sure that bloody cat was safe!'

There was a pink envelope on the mat inside the door, with her name—well, Esme—on it. She recognized Mark's handwriting.

She knelt, and picked it up. He'd always called her Esme, though now neither of them could recall why. Inside was a card with the picture of a cat in a Victorian garden on it. He had written 'Welcome Home' inside. She wondered if he thought that in her memory their garden had looked like that: it hadn't. Not to her. She shook her head, and lay the card on the telephone table in the hallway.

She walked through to the sitting room, switching on lights as she went. It would take some time for her to get her bearings properly. She turned on the TV then knelt and opened the sideboard, where her mother kept a range of glassware. She poured some whisky into a cut glass tumbler which, she realized bitterly, was one of a set her mother had given to her and Mark as an anniversary present, and which had somehow found their way back.

She wondered where Pudding was; a late burst of wanderlust, maybe. These days he had to be forced out to 'do his business', her mother had assured her with glum satisfaction.

The whisky eased the tension in her. She ran her hand through her hair and felt suddenly grubby and tired. Luxuriating in the spirit warming her, and in the solitude, she stripped off her clothes and left them in a pile on the floor.

She realized that the house was centrally heated, and that the radiators were full on; she was surprised. She'd associated her mother too strongly with cold, draughty places. Prudence and parsimony. For someone who had been born and bred in Africa, Najmabehn had a remarkable tolerance for the cold. She had a theory that the human body's thermostat could be reset to function across a completely new temperature range once in life, but only once. And there was no turning back. One of the reasons she gave for not coming out to Mumbai to visit: she was sure she wouldn't now be able to cope with the heat.

Taz remembered her mother ringing a couple of years back to say that Asghar had suggested radiators would be a good investment, and then a few months later sending her an article torn from a woman's magazine about hyperthermia among elderly Asians and the breakdown of traditional family structures. Taz had taken the hint the second time and sent her the money to have central heating installed, never really expecting her mother would bring herself to get it done. Still less would she have expected that she would actually turn it on if it were installed. Childhood memories of getting undressed beneath the bedclothes, and of being scared to stretch out because the bottom of the bed was so cold it immediately made her want to wee, and that would involve re-crossing the arctic landing to the icy bathroom, were still too strong. When she finished her drink, she would take a shower, she decided, as she stretched, naked, in the warmth. Then she'd worry about some food.

The house, closed up all day, smelt fusty; there was a tang of old people's homes—Taz realized guiltily her mother was aging, it was there in the smell. There too, evident in the fact that things weren't quite so carefully dusted as they would once have been. This was an old lady's house. A lonely old lady's house. Taz paused in front of the full-length mirror in the hallway. She looked at herself, naked. Her mother was not the only one who was aging, she told herself, frowning at her reflection.

She had always been brought up to believe herself plain. Pappa used to call her his beautiful girl, but her mother had had no time for vanity in a child, nor for offering reassurance to a skinny teenager. It still came as a shock to Taz that anyone could find her attractive, yet people did. She had the fan mail to prove it. She looked at herself, critically. Her face was unlined still, as long as she put effort into fighting back that inherited frown. A haircut wouldn't go amiss, and her legs could do with a waxing. Otherwise, she thought, she was, all things considered, in pretty good shape. Her skin, clear, and unblemished. Breasts good, belly flat-ish. She turned suddenly, and looked down at her left calf muscle, then at its reflection. She'd been conscious of a blue vein there for the past couple of months; she screwed her eyes up, and looked down, then at her reflection, then down again. Had it got worse? Was it the start of a varicose vein?

Taz realized her glass was empty. She was about to go and refill it, then decided first to put on the silk kimono she'd brought with her. It was upstairs: still unpacked in her case.

Leaving the empty glass on the hallway table, next to the telephone, she ran lightly up the stairs—as much to demonstrate to herself something about youth and energy as anything, and felt for the light switch in her bedroom.

The sour odour she'd been conscious of since she'd returned struck her with renewed force; maybe there was something wrong with the toilet in the bathroom next door.

She opened her suitcase, and the reek hit her like vicious fingers thrust up into her nostrils. There was Pudding. Burst like an over-ripe fruit. Split so that his entrails and viscera spilt out of him, drenching the still neatly packed clothes in blood and excrement.

His eyes were half open, and his lips were drawn back over his tiny, yellowing teeth.

The stench, and the sight, sent her reeling against the wall. Nausea rose up sour, with the whisky, in her throat. She gagged, and turned. Bitter tears stung her eyes, and she had to feel her way to the door, and out of the room. On the landing, her pulse convulsing, she lurched forward, clung to the banister rail and let out a wail of anger and horror. Her breath came in short, shallow gasps. She pushed herself away from the banister, and staggered down towards the telephone in the hallway. She needed help; she needed someone here. Now. To make sense of this, and to calm and comfort her. As she reached for the phone, it rang. She snatched it up.

'Curiosity,' a man's voice said.

'What?' she gasped.

'Curiosity,' the voice repeated.

Anger now flooded into her where before there had only been confusion and revulsion.

'Who is this?' she screamed.

'I can see you, Miss Dharwalla,' the voice said, sounding amused. 'Nice tits.'

She looked at the door. It was locked, but the frosted glass was uncurtained. She threw herself back against the wall, sending the tumbler flying and dropped down, to squat curled, tight and tiny, amid the shards and splinters and the voice on the telephone breathed its satisfaction. 'Curiosity,' it said again, and the line went dead.

4

'He said he could see me,' Taz said again. The policeman nodded, sympathetically.

'He must have been watching you—waiting for you to

find the cat. Probably sitting out in the road, in a car. Did you hear a car engine?'

Taz shook her head. She sat at the kitchen table, wrapped in her mother's heavy dressing gown, hunched over a mug of fortified coffee the policewoman standing silently by the sink had made for her. The policeman, a Deputy Chief Inspector with a south London accent by the name of Bignall, was heavy-set, balding and running to fat. She imagined he must have been a hard man in his day. One of those big, swaggering tough bobbies so beloved of TV dramas, but one for whom the last few years looked like they had been spent sacrificing eyesight, posture and pride to a desktop and a keyboard. He sipped noisily at the tea with two sugars he had asked for, and tried not to look at the portion of her right breast the dressing gown left exposed. Between them lay five pages of witness statement that the Woman Police Constable had laboriously transcribed from words Bignall had half dictated and half prompted from Taz. A booklet emblazoned 'Victims of Crime' which, he had explained, talking as though reading an autocue, contained answers to lots of questions that often occurred to people later, another, entitled 'Islamic Hate Crimes', and the address and phone numbers of the nearest counselling service and the local Victims Support group. Poor Pudding had been photographed, and he and her luggage had been carefully removed for further tests. The area around the house had been searched. Locks on doors and windows had been checked. More crime scene investigation would follow, but it could wait for daylight. So far, it seemed whoever had done this terrible thing to Pudding had left no other evidence of their visit.

'Can you describe his voice?' Bignall asked.

'Nice. Well-spoken, not too deep. Middle-class, cultured. Not young, but not really middle-aged. A slight accent, but I couldn't place it. Oh, and a slight lisp on the "s" in "curiosity".'

'Very good,' said the policeman, adding to the statement. 'Not many people would notice so much.'

'My job. Or it was. I mean, voices. Voices were important in my job; the job that I had. That's why. Professional skills.' She suspected she was rambling, stopped and took another sip of coffee.

'I thought I knew you,' said the young policewoman, pushing herself away from the sink. 'You used to be on the radio, didn't you? *Late Late*, wasn't it?'

'No,' sighed Taz, 'that was Sophie Johnson. I was on its forerunner, *Talk the Night Away.*'

'Yeah, that was it,' agreed the policewoman, nodding. 'You were good.'

'Thanks,' said Taz, glancing round at the slender, earnest young WPC. She looked south Indian: dark, with short, cropped hair. Her eyes were wide, and unblinking. Taz found something vaguely unnerving about her. 'We used to call it the Graveyard Shift,' Taz continued. 'You know where the studios are? Well, you can imagine what a night was like there. Lost on a deserted industrial estate, surrounded by locked-down business units selling cut-price tiles and used computer parts. Desolation Island. And the calls: the drunks, the lonelies and the nutters. Exactly the kind of people you'd expect to be listening to a radio talk show at 3 A.M. My apprenticeship.'

'Well, we all thought you were great. We used to tune in whenever we were on nights. Do you remember that caller…'

'The voice, Miss Dhar,' said Bignall, pointedly, with a sidelong glare at his colleague. 'You're sure it was no one you know?'

Taz shook her head. 'No one I know would do something like that.'

DCI Bignall looked doubtful, but did not pursue the matter. 'Did he sound drunk? High? Was he excited? Threatening?'

'Yes, threatening.'

'Tell me again what he said.'

Taz sighed. 'He said that he could see me, that he was

watching me. He kept saying "Curiosity". Over and over. "Curiosity".'

'... killed the cat?' suggested the policewoman, and both Taz and the DCI turned to her.

Taz groaned. 'Oh, I get it. Really smart. Really fuck... bloody clever.'

'What do you think it means?'

Taz shrugged. 'Warning me off. Off the thing I'm working on.'

'And that would be?' asked Bignall.

'A story. For the TV channel I'm with now in India.'

'Tell me about it?'

'Why not? Now?'

'If you like. Or tomorrow will do. We'll be back to finish off...' He glanced at the WPC.

'The victim impact statement?' she prompted.

'Oh yeah. Would you care to make a statement about the impact this has had on you as a victim?' he asked, studiously neutral.

'No,' said Taz.

'Can I ask why not?'

'Because I'm not a victim. I may be someone's target, but I refuse to be anyone's victim.'

Bignall smiled. 'Good for you, love. Have you got anyone who could stay with you tonight?'

'No. Yes. A friend, I think.'

'Would you like us to call them? Might be wise to have someone here, don't you think? Just for company.'

'It makes sense,' she agreed. 'I'll call him.'

'You do that,' said Bignall, stretching. 'And while you do, your fan here, WPC Sitaram, will make us another cup of tea. And while she does that you can start to tell me what this warning is all about. Just to pass the time, while we wait for this friend, you think, to appear.'

∽

Mark was there within an hour; the image of concern. Good old solid, dependable Mark.

'You've put on weight,' she said, as the police left.

He looked down, and patted his waistline, ruefully. 'Missing your cooking,' he said.

Was that meant to be funny, she wondered? She had never been any sort of cook.

'Too much convenience food,' he added, realizing he'd got off on the wrong foot. He picked up the leaflet the police had left. 'I'm glad you called me. In trouble again, eh, Esme?'

She frowned. 'Is that how you see me? A victim?'

He shook his head and she noticed how carefully his thinning hair was combed. 'Not at all! No one could think of you as a victim. It's just that...'

'Just hold me, Mark. Stay with me tonight. Please. I'm very, very scared.'

Without realizing she had moved, she was in his arms. He smelt wholesome, and comforting. Of good soap, and warm, woollen clothing. He held her close. Tight. She recalled how safe she used to feel, with him. How long it was since she had felt safe. How, even when making love with Raj, she could still feel alone.

'I assumed...' he began.

She pulled back slightly, and kissed him gently. 'Don't assume anything. Not beyond tomorrow morning. Just tonight, OK?'

They made love. In her mother's bed. It was exciting, because it was different, but it was somehow reassuring and comforting too, and safe, because it was the same, as it had been, when they were married. Physically, it was good. It had been a good twelve years earlier, when they had first made love. It had still been good, eight years later, when they had separated. But it hadn't been enough then, and it wasn't enough, now.

His gratitude, evident in the confidence of his movements and the generosity of his smile as he looked down at her, was both touching and infuriating. It distracted her. She came, comfortably, reassuringly, unexceptionally. Afterward, she poured them both a drink. The telephone rang. They looked at each other; Mark picked up the receiver. It was SK.

'Who was that?' SK asked, as soon as Mark had passed the phone to Taz.

'My ex. Mark. He's staying for a while.' She looked across at Mark, and he winked at her. She smiled, and looked away. 'I got your snuff.'

'You told me. I thought your ex was called, er, what's-his-name?'

Taz turned from Mark's trying, supportive smile. 'Different ex. Listen, SK, Mark's here because I got threatened. About my curiosity. Some weirdo broke in and killed my cat.'

'Wow! Pudding?'

'Yes, Pudding! How on earth could you remember that when you can't remember what's-his-name was called Raj?'

'Because you talked more about Pudding than you did about what's-his-name. You think this is about Armitage Shanks?'

'What else could it be?'

'I don't know. What are you going to do, Taz?'

'Do? Do? What I came here to do, of course. Some bastard cut up Pudding. How can I stop now? I'll call you tomorrow.'

'Be careful, Taz.'

'Who's Raj?' asked Mark, with poorly feigned nonchalance as she ended the call.

'No one,' said Taz, surprised she could say that without a pang of conscience.

They were saved more difficult conversations by the return of Bignall, the DCI, and WPC Sitaram, the former, chipper and smelling vaguely of fried bacon, the latter, eyes red-rimmed with exhaustion. Of course, it was a Saturday morning. She guessed the previous evening's binge-drinking, street thuggery and domestic viciousness would have kept at least the more junior of them both pretty busy throughout the night.

'You know,' said Bignall, resuming the chair he had occupied hours earlier at the kitchen table, 'I was thinking about what happened. It's what someone who really wanted to get you where it would hurt most would do. Vicious, mean and personal. A jilted boyfriend, perhaps? Do you have an ex who could have done this?'

'I'm her ex,' said Mark. 'Well. One of them, apparently.'

The policeman eyed him warily. 'And would you happen to have a key to this house, Sir?'

Taz, smiling, listened to Mark's horrified protests, made them all tea, and told them all she knew about Armitage Shanks.

'Who else knows about this?' Bignall asked two cups later, folding over and returning the copy of the papers Taz had shown him.

'No one,' said Taz, frowning. 'Well, obviously my boss...'

'And his name would be?'

'S.K. Mehta. I can give you his contact details. Obviously, he's in Mumbai.'

'Well, I think that probably rules him out then. Here?'

'Only my mother and...' She paused, noticing how Mark was shifting uncomfortably. She sighed. 'Well?'

He shrugged. 'It was your mother's suggestion, Esme,' he almost pleaded. 'We, she, thought that if we, well, I, put the word round about what you were looking for, it might help.'

Taz glanced at the policeman, who, eloquently expressionless, avoided her eye.

'And you spoke to...?'

'Hardly anyone, really. A couple of people at the Home Office, and a chap I went to school with who's now something important in the FCO. They all said the same thing. That it must be a practical joke. Impossible. Just couldn't have happened.'

'And you were going to tell me this... when?' asked Taz.

'Straight after breakfast,' Mark assured her.

Taz turned to the policeman. 'What do you think?' To her surprise, Bignall turned to WPC Sitaram and raised an eyebrow.

The policewoman shrugged. 'A quarter of a million people are reported missing every year in the UK. Of course, most of them turn up after a few hours; almost all are accounted for within a few days. But that still leaves thousands who aren't. It doesn't sound impossible to me that one of those thousands may have ended up in a situation which led to them being executed abroad. But that no one would know? Depends where, I suppose. Implausible maybe, but not impossible.'

Bignall glanced at his watch. 'Sorry. I'll need the names and details of the people you've both spoken to about this matter. We can pick them up when we do the full forensics.'

The doorbell rang. Yusuf Kaka, in whom a first-generation immigrant's innate distrust of the police had matured to near paranoia, nodded coolly toward Taz and studiously engaged Mark in a conversation about football. Bignall took the hint, rose and left, with a nod toward WPC Sitaram.

The policewoman switched off her radio, and paused on her way to the door. Checking they were out of earshot of Mark and Yusuf Kaka, she turned to Taz. 'We've met before,' she said, quietly. 'You came to an Open Day at the Asian Girl's Club I was in as a kid.'

'Strangely, that doesn't make me feel good,' said Taz. 'I suppose you're going to tell me you were only twelve then?'

WPC Sitaram laughed. 'Fourteen, actually. We all thought you were so cool.' She paused, as though considering her next words carefully. 'Mr Bignall is far too senior to be able to spend much more time on this. I'll probably be your point of contact. Can I give you a bit of informal advice?'

Taz nodded.

'If I were you I'd think I'd be a little bit more careful who I confide in from now on, and what I chose to tell them. In particular, I would strongly recommend you don't tell anyone what you intend to do next.'

'OK. Thanks. Absolutely,' said Taz. 'Er, if you were me what *would* you do next?'

'It's obvious, isn't it? Find the priest. He's the only real lead you've got.'

❧

The people from the television channel in India were late. The vicar seethed with impatience; he knew the organist was reaching the end of her sparse repertoire of sombre music. The bishop had made it clear; the Indians were to be there. Waited for, welcomed, and treated with respect. But for how long? These people were notorious for their cavalier attitude to timekeeping: should he begin without them? It really was too bad! Heads turned among the gawpers beyond the wicket gate and the low wall. With a heartfelt sigh of relief he saw three cars crash through the cones, bump up onto the verge, and halt, carving, he was sure, thick scars on the neatly trimmed grass around the gate.

The vicar shook his head; car doors flew open and the Indians burst from their vehicles like they were detectives in an expensive television series. The dozen or so men, five of them lugging equipment, he noted disapprovingly, half ran, half walked, ludicrously stiff-legged, tugging at their unfamiliar jackets, and straightening foreign ties. The single woman with them was the one he had spoken to, he assumed. She and the man called Mehta had arranged the whole thing; all her idea, apparently. Each hissed an apology from the corner of their mouth as they scurried past him to find somewhere to settle within. He nodded to the churchwarden, who hurried off to the organist. Extending his chin to correct the lay of his collar, the vicar walked into the body of the church.

He could hear the organist's gratitude in the first few familiar bars.

'I am the resurrection, and the life, sayeth the Lord,' he intoned, solemnly, as the congregation rose. 'He that believeth in me, though he die, yet shall he live; and whoever liveth and believeth in me shall never die.' The old, old words, and the resonance of his tidily modulated and solemn tones complemented the organ and restored his confidence. The church was beautiful; if pride was a sin, false modesty was a greater one. His little church was a triumph. A fine place for any life to receive its final celebration.

They had asked for the full burial service, rather than a simple memorial. Shocked as he had been when he'd first heard it mooted, he had now to admit he could see their point. There should really have been a casket, borne with fortitude on strong shoulders, progressing pace for pace behind him. The Indians, according to the bishop, had actually proposed that. Talked in all seriousness about filling a coffin with bricks, or bags of sand. Really! Not even the bishop, with his beady little eye on the main chance and an almost indecent appetite for anything that smacked of diversity, could quite stomach that one. So there was no body, nor any pretence at such; nothing tangible. But they were still determined to have the full service. So be it. After all, the vicar thought, bitterly, they were the ones who were paying.

'We brought nothing into this world, and it is certain that we can carry nothing out. The Lord giveth, and the Lord taketh away. Blessed be the name of the Lord.'

5

'Are you sure this is the place?'

'According to your policewoman friend, Google Earth and the Ordnance Survey.'

'Well, I suppose…'

'… we'd better go in'.

Taz had forgotten Mark's habit of finishing her sentences for her and how bloody irritating she used to find it.

'No, I'll go in. You can sod off and find us somewhere to have lunch.'

'It's a long walk, Esme.'

'It will do me good.'

'It's pretty cold…'

'Then I'll wrap up warm! Shit, Mark, when did you become such an old woman?'

It was Monday, mid-morning. They had spent a large part of the weekend at Mark's flat huddled over his laptop. Or at least Mark had. Taz couldn't understand why what they had been doing was called surfing: it seemed far more to her like something a wading bird would do. About as interesting to watch, too. Staring, glassy-eyed. Hunched over, barely moving, silent and intent. Searching, and then stabbing down, hopefully and usually pointlessly, in pursuit of some elusive flash. She had been amazed at the range and breadth of resources devoted to Catholicism, and had to discipline herself from asking Mark to wander off down interesting but irrelevant byways of obscurity. She was surprised at how adept Mark was at this sort of thing: How fast his fingers moved over the keyboard and with what confidence he checked and dismissed potential sources. She was grateful to him, for her own IT skills were rudimentary to say the least. That's what researchers and staffers had been for at the channel. The laptop that had been perched beside her on screen had been little more than a prop: viewers' e-mails had appeared on her autocue.

She was grateful, yes, but a touch resentful too. She hadn't expected Mark to be yet another of the growing army of people who made her feel old and clumsy. She had always thought of herself as more technically adept and socially in tune than him. Bored, she found her thoughts drifting and her eyes wandering. She couldn't help but notice how attractive, tidy and comfortably furnished his flat was, on the top floor of an imposing Edwardian town house. High-ceilinged, airy and uncluttered. And how not one thing of their life together, other than a single photograph, did he now display. He had clearly adjusted to a single life better than she had, she thought, sourly, and she resented that too.

They had clicked through dozens of Catholic directories, websites, resource centres and networks, to no avail. Hardly surprising, really, Mark assured her airily. After all, the Internet, umpteenth wonder of the world though it may be, was incapable of the intuitive leaps that would enable their priest to be located on the scanty data they had. Father Thomas: surname unknown; parish unknown; nationality unknown; age unknown. Had fairly recently worked abroad. Somewhere hot. Even the most powerful and sophisticated search engine needed something a little bit more capable of manipulation than that to work with.

So it was thanks to WPC Sitaram that they were here. She'd told them what a couple of unofficial calls first to the Immigration and Nationality Department, then to the British Embassy in Ethiopia had suggested might be the name and present location of the elusive Father Thomas. But even then they could find no reference to the place on the Internet. He seemed to have been sucked deep inside some kind of Roman Catholic black hole. Unlisted in any directory, unacknowledged in any source they could access and, apparently even unknown to the local priest, to whom, in desperation, Taz had turned. They had located it only from the post code Sitaram had provided, which Mark checked out on the AA Route Planner. Even then, with addresses and satellite images on screen, quite what 'Our Lady of the Sorrows' was had been impossible to tell. Now, as they sat in a warm car at its unmarked gates after a good mile and a half of precarious driving along single-track lanes, and stared at it through steamed-up windows, all they could see was a distant, anonymous country house almost entirely masked from the road by high hedges of rhododendron and laurel, located far down a long private driveway. In a small, populous county in southern England, it was as close to remote as it was possible to get.

It was still. Quiet. But what was it? What purpose did it serve? It lacked the outward symbols of a place of worship, the buzz and clutter of an educational institution, or the self-important trappings of a centre of administration.

Taz was about to leave the car when her mobile rang. It was Yusuf Kaka.

She was not particularly surprised. He had called her at almost hourly intervals throughout Sunday. Having only learnt on his arrival on Saturday morning of the break-in, he grumbled at her not calling him again that night. He seemed to regard the matter as a personal slight. His proposals for dealing with whoever had broken in and killed Pudding were characteristic: robust, of undoubted practicality but questionable legality. Having paced around the garden, out along the road and into the park, following the route the police had checked out, just in case they might have missed something, he had urged Taz to have a couple of his 'friends' around to keep an eye on her, and promised swift and terrible retribution to whoever had done this thing to his favourite niece.

He had also taken away a copy of the Armitage Shanks papers. Taz felt a slight qualm handing a set over, bearing in mind WPC Sitaram's warning. But after all, she consoled herself, she had already confided in Yusuf Kaka. It was too late, and anyway, he was family.

'*Kem cho, Beti*, are you alone?'

'Yes, well no. But it's only Mark. We're in his car in...'

'Don't tell me where you are. Can you get out and talk?'

'I was just getting out.'

She glanced across at Mark, and pulled a face. He groaned and shook his head. He had always thought Yusuf Kaka at best an over-dramatic charlatan, and at worst a third-rate gangster. Why on earth did Taz have to call him, of all people?

Taz walked a few paces away from the car. 'Go on.'

'That thing we were talking about...'

Taz sighed. 'Yes?'

'Forget about it. There's nothing to find out about. Absolutely nothing. Do you understand me? Nothing.'

Taz frowned. Yusuf Kaka sounded almost frightened. Something she had never heard of and would have found difficult to imagine. But there could be few other explanations for the urgency and near desperation in his voice.

'What's going on?'

'Nothing. I'm just telling you. Go back to Bombay.'

'I can't. I don't have a job there any more.'

'That I can help with. I'll be in touch. I'll see what I can do.'

Taz returned to the car, told a huffy Mark briefly what Yusuf Kaka had said, made arrangements to meet him later, and set off down the drive to Our Lady of the Sorrows.

The weather had cleared, as they had travelled across country. Now, though it was bitingly cold, the sky was bright, and as the sound of Mark's Renault faded, she could hear birds singing. Somewhere, far away, there was a repetitive throbbing of an agricultural machine doing she had absolutely no idea what. If London had seemed foreign to her, rural England was a different planet. She looked around, ashamed that she could not name a tree, or recognize a birdsong. Would it have been any different in India? Well, yes, actually, it would. She could name at least four Indian trees, and knew the calls of a few birds too. Why?

Back in Kampala, Ma had fed the birds. Cast out a sprinkling of grain each morning. She had continued to do so when, as refugees reliant on benefit payments and rank bundles of second-hand clothing, they had first shifted from the mothballed RAF base to the comparative luxury of a council flat in Swindon. But every morning, she would grumble about the lack of colour and drama in the drab little creatures that pecked at her offerings. A metaphor for their new life, Najmabehn clearly felt.

Taz spotted a gaunt figure unenthusiastically raking up a few leaves, and walked over to him, surprised to glimpse beneath his loosely tied scarf, a clerical collar.

'Cold morning,' she said brightly, rubbing her gloved hands together. 'I'm looking for Father Thomas Quinlan.'

The priest, a woollen hat pulled down over his ears and a dewdrop hanging from his nose, straightened up stiffly and studied her for a long moment. 'He would be expecting you?'

'Oh, yes,' she lied, without hesitation. After all, she reassured herself, smothering a murmur of conscience, she wasn't a Christian. To lie to a member of the clergy of a faith not your own can't be any worse than lying to an ordinary member of the public, can it? And she did that all the time.

'Go on up to the house, and you will find someone there to help you.'

She walked on up the gravel drive and climbed the half dozen steps up to the big double doors. She paused, and looked back, to see the priest she had spoken to still leaning on his rake, watching her. She raised a hand in acknowledgement, but he neither returned the wave, nor looked away. Shaking her head, she pushed one of the doors open, and entered. Inside, there was again, the silence. And a smell of something: beeswax polish, disinfectant and incense. In a corridor of closed doors, she spotted one slightly ajar, and as she approached it, heard from beyond, a low murmur of male voices.

She eased the door further open, and a group of priests, sitting around in a circle, paused, and looked up. The youngest turned, with a sigh, irritation giving way to polite concern as her looked at her.

He seemed ludicrously young: more like a teenager kitted out as a priest for a fancy dress party. But then again, as she looked at him longer, maybe not so young. She noticed the swelling veins on the back of his pale freckled hands and his hair, ginger, was cut short, but not so short as to disguise the fact that it was thinning. His small features were certainly boyish: a tiny turned-up nose that must have made him look cheeky and mischievous and utterly adorable as a child. His eyes were bright beneath brows that were little more than a faint orange smudge. He was slightly built and looked like he needed someone to look after him. Yet the other priests, all older, some by several decades, seemed to be looking toward him as a figure of authority in their midst.

He frowned as he looked at her, and reached for a pair of glasses. He polished the lenses, put them on, and stared, blinking, at her.

'Can I help you?' he began, still frowning quizzically, his Ulster accent heavy and angular. 'Do I know you?' he asked.

'I don't know. My name's Taz Dhar.'

His eyes widened. Quickly, he made his excuses, rose, and walked with her out into the lobby. She reached into her bag for the letter.

'Not here,' he said. 'My, you look half frozen. Come. We'll take a cup of something in the refectory.'

They walked through to a surprisingly modern kitchen with a dozen tables, and rows of stainless steel chairs. Taz could have screamed with impatience as the priest boiled a kettle, poured steaming water onto teabags in bright blue mugs, and searched through tins of biscuits for something to offer her. When they were finally seated, Taz held up his letter. 'Did you write this?'

The priest nodded. 'You look different from the photograph.'

'Older, probably,' said Taz. 'And shorter. That's what most people say.'

'No. It's your hair. Cut differently. Was he family...?'

Taz shook her head. 'I'd never met him. Didn't you read what he wrote?'

Father Thomas studiously broke his piece of shortbread into three pieces. 'Just the first few lines. I wanted to do something for him. Perhaps for my benefit as much as his. Said he was a Muslim, although I am not sure if that was just .... something to say. But I was there and wanted to do something for him. He had a picture of you, and your name, and the name of the place you work. That was all I needed to send you his letter. But you never knew him? Now that's a very strange thing, don't you think?'

'The whole thing is a very strange thing,' she said, trying to order the various questions she needed answered in her mind. 'Where did it happen?'

'In a prison, just on the Ethiopian side of the border, such as it is, with what used to be Somalia.'

'What were you doing there?'

'I was part of a CAFOD project. You know CAFOD? The Catholic Agency For Overseas Development. I was working with a team of Ethiopians to help build awareness of legal rights and entitlements.' His face twisted and he added, 'I wanted to do something important.'

He paused. 'So Armitage Shanks didn't know you? But he wrote to you. That's a very strange thing. And you didn't know him, but you're here trying to find out what happened. That's a very strange thing too.' He folded his arms, and leaned back, angling his head to one side, like a dog catching a distant whisper. 'But then, you're a reporter, aren't you? So maybe it's not so strange after all. Is that why you are here?' he asked, suddenly wary. 'For a story?'

'Yes,' she admitted, 'I'm here for a story. But it's not just any story, is it? Not for me, or for you. It's personal.'

'Because he wrote to you?'

Taz shook her head. 'No. Well, maybe at first. But not for long. It's personal because this story is my only chance of keeping a job that I love and can't be without. It's personal because someone broke into my house and killed my cat and threatened me because of it. It's personal too because though I never knew him when he was alive, I feel I want to, need to, know him now.' She reached into her bag, and took out photocopies of the pages Armitage Shanks had written. 'Wow! I guess you being a priest prompted that confession. Although…'

'You're a Muslim. Just like he said he was.'

She frowned. 'Yes. I hadn't thought of that. Do you think that's significant? Anyway, I keep the original safe,' she said, although she wasn't quite sure why, as she offered the sheaf of papers to him. 'Do you want to read what he wrote?'

Father Thomas glanced at the papers for a moment, clearly tempted, then handed them back. 'No. I don't think I do.'

'Can you tell me about him, about what happened?' The priest took a deep breath, then filled his cheeks and exhaled noisily. Again he tilted his head. His mouth hung open and his eyes seemed to focus on something far away as he organized his thoughts. 'They came for me in an old pickup. Told me there was a man to be executed, and that I had to go, to be there with him. Said it was in the rules. They weren't local police or prison officers. I don't think they were *federali*— federal police—either. I wasn't quite sure who they were. They were hard men, that was for sure, but like many Ethiopians, devout, serious and very focused on due process in individual cases. They wanted me to go with them right then. One of them even started waving his AK-47 around and shouting at me. But the others stopped him.' He smiled, distantly. 'That whole area is primarily Islamic, but these guys were Christians. They hated me as a *ferunghi*, a foreigner, but their fear and respect for the cross I wore was stronger.'

'I told them that I couldn't go with them, not right then. I had a woman lying on the kitchen table, dying. They could hear her screams. She'd been raped, and stabbed. Several times. Some inter-clan thing, I guess. Or a marriage by abduction that went wrong. Rights and entitlements! She'd been brought to us because her people assumed the nuns were nurses. They weren't, not that it mattered. There was nothing anyone could have done for her. I told the policemen I'd follow them to the prison, as soon as I could. After all, she was already on her final journey. No turning back. Only the time of her departure was still in the hands of the Lord. The man in the cell, as I said to them, well, his time was at the whim of man, not the dictate of the Lord. She had to take priority.'

'They left me a map. Told me where to go. Left a couple of foot soldiers too, to make sure I went. I stayed with the woman till the end. I didn't even stop to wash the blood off my hands. Then I let them drive me to the prison. I only just got there in time... That's not quite true. Not quite fair. I think they would have given him more time if he'd wanted it, but he said he didn't. Said he knew what he was going to do and how he was going to do it, and had thought it all through. What was it he said? Something about knowing about what thoughts he was going to think and what songs he was going to sing or poems he was going to say. Said he was a Muslim, did I tell you that? Yes, I did, didn't I? Anyway, he was very clear that an Ulster Papist praying in his ear was not part of his scheme of things.'

'How was he? How did he sound?' prompted Taz, quietly.

'He was scared, for sure. But he walked out and met it, didn't wait for them to come to him and drag him away. He was prepared. But not like a religious man, you know? More like a businessman. A professional. Going to a meeting where he knew the agenda, had read the papers and got the figures straight by heart: prepared.'

Taz looked around, feeling tears pricking in her eyes. 'Tell me what he looked like.'

The priest shook his head. 'Not sure I can.'

'But you saw him!' Taz cried, suddenly leaning forward. 'You must be able to tell me what he looked like. What he sounded like. How old he was. You must.'

The priest leaned forward too, so that their faces were no more than a few inches apart. 'Remember, it was a badly-lit cell, and I only saw him for a few seconds. I'd been awake all night. Most of the night before that too, come to that. It was shortly after dawn; I was tired. You wouldn't believe how tired. He was scared, pale and I'd never seen him before, and I only saw him, literally for a few seconds. I'm sorry, but right now, I couldn't even tell you if he had a beard, or how tall, or what build he was. I'll try. Try to remember more, I promise, but right now, I'm sorry.'

Taz slumped forward. She thought her head would explode. Like some massive change of pressure; like an aeroplane dropping through turbulence, or a diver coming up too fast. Since WPC Sitaram had told her to look for the priest, she had convinced herself that if only she could find him, she'd finally make real progress. But all this seemed thin stuff. 'Isn't there anything?' she asked, her voice little more than a gasp.

'There was his voice.' He paused, and then continued. 'Very English. Oh, and his clothes. I remember he was wearing a pair of jeans.'

Taz leapt up. 'For Christ's sake! I knew he was wearing jeans! I knew he was English! What is wrong with you? What kind of a person are you anyway? You turn up and you watch this guy marched out to be turned off, and you feel you've done your bit once you've bothered to post his last letter for him. God Almighty! You ask me about if this is personal? Well, it certainly doesn't seem to be to you. Don't you feel any personal responsibility? Wasn't it your God-given, basic, human duty to tell someone? How come not one word of this is in any newspaper or on any television channel? Don't you think you should have reported this?'

'I did,' the priest said, quietly.

Taz ran both hands through her hair: it really felt like her head would explode. 'I'm not talking about what you told some project coordinator to justify your petrol allowance, or what you shared with your confessor to salve your conscience for not taking his last confession. I'm talking about proper authorities: government agencies. Why didn't you tell them?'

'I did. Really, I promise you. I did: But they'd already heard about it. You need to understand what that area is like. Not much law impinges on people there. The hand of the authorities lies light, and true power is distant. The execution was entirely illegal. Unauthorized. They said they'd already heard rumours about it, and had begun to investigate. They thanked me and asked me to fill out a statement, which I did. I assure you, I reported it.'

Taz slumped back. 'You mean the British government knows all about it?'

'The British government? What business is it of theirs?'

'But he was English! You said it.'

The priest shook his head. 'I said that was how he spoke.

How he sounded. I checked his papers. He was an Ethiopian citizen. That's how he was born. That's how he died. That's about the only thing no one denies.'

'Did it ever occur to you that he might have had false papers? He might have been oh, I don't know, a secret agent or something? Don't look at me like that. Don't you dare laugh! I know it sounds crazy, but there must be such people, mustn't there?'

'I'm not smiling because I think you're crazy, but because I thought of that too. I went to the British Embassy. And when nobody would talk to me, I wrote to them. I even got an acknowledgement. Would you like to see it? Oh, I told the British authorities alright. And they told the Ethiopian authorities that I had told them, too. And then, somebody told my bishop. And then I was sent here.'

'What is... here?'

'Here? Oh, a very interesting place. The last chance saloon. The final retreat for the misunderstood. Hospice for the lost. Last grasp at redemption for the terminally tormented. Those good gentlemen you saw me with when you arrived. Shall I tell you about them? Well, let's call the first one Father John. When you interrupted us, Father John was extolling the wonders of a single malt called Dalwhinnie. Mother's milk and angel's breath. Nectar and ambrosia all yours at around thirty pounds a bottle. Then there's Father Charles, a good, a loving man, but with what some of his parishioners thought was an excessive interest in the physical and spiritual development of one of his altar boys. Father Michael, now with him, it's a matter of some maladministered funds and a bit of injudicious borrowing to try and cover the losses. We have yet to learn where the money went. And then there's me.'

'They sent you here for telling the truth?'

'In a manner of speaking. You see, unlike the other members of the circle you broke into, I was not sent here as a result of any acknowledged or even whispered misfeasance. I am here to minister to the temporal and spiritual needs of my troubled brothers. This is not correction that you see, this is my vocation. Not purgatory, but a privilege, however it may seem to you. Indeed, out there, in a more prosaic world, one would say I have had a promotion. Now I must return to my neglected friends. I have a responsibility to them, and I have left them alone for too long.'

Taz stood up, and held out her hand.

'Father, I said some awful things. Unjust things, and I'm sorry. I hope it works out for you.'

The young priest smiled, took her hand in a firm grip, and shook it. 'And for you too. I hope you find what you are looking for. But remember, only from within can you tell a sanctuary from a cell.'

❧

The vicar turned from the altar, and surveyed the rows of fashionably clothed mourners, like a teacher looking at a class he suspected was about to disappoint him. He half smiled, sad and professional. His gaze fell on the Indians, nodding encouragingly at him and urging him on. Of course. Deadlines. How predictable that they should swan in late, then demand he keep to their timetable. He tried to calculate the time in India, but almost immediately gave up. He treated them to a slightly patronizing smile, and deliberately held the silence for a few moments more. He needed no advice, and would brook no instruction on timing in his own church from them or anyone else, thank you very much!

'We come together today, not to mourn a death, but to celebrate a life. A life, cut short, far away.' He lifted his gaze from the Indians, and looked around. The wry smile playing on his lips hinted that he alone was privy to great secrets that could offer comfort, and a solace of sorts. 'A life, cut short, far away.' He repeated, savouring the sound of it. 'A young life, snuffed out, in its prime.' He paused, and shook his head. 'A life full of promise, never now to be realized.' He heard a sad little sniff, and someone cleared their throat. That was more like it!

'It is hard for those of us who mourn to say farewell, and to make our final parting, especially when nothing physical remains of the one we have loved, here among us. People talk dismissively today of ritual, yet ritual has its place, in all societies. Ours is no different in that. Some may argue that those of us gathered here today to mourn this parting are denied a fundamental of that ritual with nothing of substance left behind. Yet I say that is not so. What any of us leave behind, of lasting value, of true substance, are those that we have touched, and warmed, and cared for, and perhaps, in our own small way, influenced for the better. Christ says to us, in the Gospel according to St John, in my Father's house there are many mansions; if it were not so I would have told you; for I go to prepare a place for you. And if I go and prepare a place for you, I will come again, and will receive you unto myself; that where I am, there Ye may be also. Peace I leave with you; my peace I give unto you; not as the world giveth, give I unto you. Let not your heart be troubled, neither let it be afraid.'

The vicar raised his eyes to the roof beams, and a single venal thought about the restoration fund flashed unbidden across his mind like a kingfisher across flat water, and was gone. He sighed, and allowed his double chin to tremble with emotion.

'Let us take comfort in the words of the Lord; let us pray.'

On the journey back to her mother's home, Taz spoke little about the meeting. She could sense Mark's desire to hear how it went, but there was just too much to think about. What now? Where could she go next?

When they got in, she checked her e-mails. Amid the spam and trivia, she found a message from Yusuf Kaka. Strangely innocuous: expressions of goodwill and a promise he'd talk to someone in Mumbai. Hardly worth sending. She sent back a terse thank you, and hit delete. The next message was from a Hotmail account she didn't recognize, headed Armitage Shanks. She opened it. Untitled and unsigned, it gave a name and an address in Germany. She sent off a reply, but it bounced back. The account no longer existed. Of course! Yusuf Kaka. How typical of his Byzantine mind. She noted down the detail, mentally thanked her mysterious uncle, and Googled flights to Frankfurt.

6

Taz Dhar strode through the cavernous arrival halls of Frankfurt-en-Main, her brand new Samsonite wheelie clattering in her wake.

Few of the disembarking passengers had baggage to reclaim; the morning city-hop from Heathrow was populated with WiFi Warriors. Laptop nomads, travelling light. In front of her, three silver-haired German businessmen in jeans and light jackets, their upper lips lost under luxurious moustaches, whispered and laughed, like guilty school boys.

She'd bought the cheapest ticket she could find on the Internet and had even taken the coach, well before dawn, down to the airport. It was the first time in more than twenty years that she'd travelled by National Express. As a kid she'd headed off with Ma and Pappa on shopping expeditions to

Brent Cross, returning, loaded down with purchases, on a coach full of similarly burdened Asians. Now, she was the only Indian among a busload of dozing central Europeans: Poles, Bulgarians, Czechs. Wan, young and scruffy, heading into the airport to do the shit jobs that two decades earlier had been the exclusive preserve of Punjabis and Gujaratis. Well, her motivation was the same as theirs. Now that this was for real, she had to be very careful about the expenses she was running up.

She even wondered if there would be time to look for a cheaper hotel in Frankfurt.

Mark had offered to drive her to Heathrow, as they stretched, sprawled side by side on her mother's sofa with a family-size packet of Kettle Chips between them, watching a DVD. But it had been a sulky, grudging kind of offer, interspersed with half-gasps of exasperation. Why did she have to go? What was so bloody important about it? Had she forgotten what happened to Pudding? Didn't she realize it could be dangerous?

She'd got up, and poured herself a drink.

'It's my job,' she had said simply.

'No it isn't. Anyway, I thought...' he had begun, but she'd turned on him, surprising them both with her anger. She felt him using his vulnerability as a weapon, wrapping her round with it. Ensnaring her with a dependency from which she had escaped once, and within which she had no intention of being entrapped again.

'I told you. Didn't I? I fucking told you. No assumptions. Whatever you thought is your responsibility. Your problem. Not mine. Right?'

He had turned away, but not before she had seen how much he was hurting.

'I'm sorry,' she had sighed, running her hand through her hair. 'Maybe when I come back...'

'Maybe I won't be waiting,' he'd said, peevishly.

They had slept, a DMZ of chilled sheets between them that neither attempted to cross. She'd taken a taxi to the bus station. She'd known he was awake, but pretending to still be asleep, as she prepared to leave.

∾

She took the train into the Hauptbahnhof, at the heart of the city, and walked down the Kaiserstrasse to the imposing splendour of the Frankfurter Hof. To assuage her newly discovered public transport and pedestrian conscience even further. She swapped her reservation for the cheapest room available, showered quickly, slipped a couple of new friends from the minibar into her handbag, and asked the hotel to get her a car to take her to the address she had received. Spoilt by too many years of being driven everywhere by someone else in Mumbai, she dismissed any thought of driving herself in a hire car. The driver was a slender, swarthy man with a mass of overlong, thick black hair. He wore dark trousers and an imitation leather windcheater, buttoned to the neck. An identify card dangled, stark against the dark plastic, from his up-turned jacket collar.

He smiled, even white teeth appearing beneath a pencil moustache. She watched him as he pulled his stomach in, and straightened, glancing down at her legs. 'Fräulein Dhar?' he asked, his voice rich as strong coffee. His accent, double-guttural: the staccato rhythm of German, catching on and chopping at a cross tide of something much more familiar. 'Welcome to Frankfurt, business trip?'

She nodded, and took from her handbag the addresses in Rastatt the semi-anonymous e-mail had given.

The driver glanced at it, then looked up at her, as though seeing her for the first time. He smiled, 'From India?'

'England,' she said.

His eyes widened. 'I know who you are!' he cried, beaming. 'Big star! I watch you every day on StarPlus.'

Taz recalled SK's uncharitable profile of their NRI viewers. It figured.

'You want to go to Rastatt.' He led her to a gleaming black BMW, got in and switched on the radio cassette. Tinny and distorted, Nusrat Ali Khan gave it his all, indifferently interrupted, by traffic updates in breathy German. They headed out of the city on to a busy four-lane highway, and the black BMW cruised easily into the fast lane.

'You know, all the big stars stay at the Frankfurten Hof. Shah Rukh, Hrithik, Preity. I've seen them all. Now you. And you are first in my car. Big day for me!'

Taz laughed, and the driver glanced across at her, and beamed.

'What's your name?'

'My name, is right here,' he said, touching the hotel ID badge. 'Sidiq.'

He told her it was a privilege to drive her. Asked if she would like AC, or heating. She shook her head. 'Neither,' she said. 'And don't patronize me. OK?'

'Patronize? What's that? I am showing you respect. Simple. I treat you like I would treat my mother.'

'I don't want to be treated like your mother. I just want you to drive me to Rastatt. How long will it take?'

'I love you modern Indian ladies! So direct. So sensible! Just like in the movies. Maybe a couple of hours. Good, fast, German roads, all the way. We can be there maybe by three. You tired, or hungry? You want pee-pee? You just tell me whenever you want to stop. OK?'

They drove out of Frankfurt in easy silence, and held a steady speed down the A5, past exits for Darmstadt and Mannheim. Taz dozed, waking only when her head jolted back, or lolled forward.

'You German?' she asked, to try and keep herself awake.

Sidiq grimaced. 'I came here to work in a garage. My father sent me to work here because he said I would learn how to really care for cars. You know the nearest I got to an apprenticeship? I swept floors, cleaned toilets and learnt German from evening classes for guest workers. I came to Frankfurt because there was a Hindi movie festival and it turned out lucky for me. I got work as a driver. I married here, a girl from a good family from Hyderabad, but we couldn't go for wedding there 'cos her passport has a problem'—Taz could surmise the sort of problem, and suspected Sidiq may share it—'I've got a son and two daughters here. We have a school to teach them prayers, and the Quran, but they speak German, and a little Arabic, but not their father's language, or their mother's. Life is shit here, for people like us.'

He spoke as though he had confided nothing more significant than the weather forecast. Taz looked away, discomfited by his indifferent bitterness, and could think of nothing to say.

'Kids smash the windows at the mosque. Call us names; paint swastikas on the door. These Germans, they're shit bastard people, you know? Not like people back home. There's no freedom here: you got to be exactly like they tell you to be. Especially now. Got to keep your head down and your mouth shut. This is a shit bastard country. You need to be careful. Really, I mean it. I'm telling you this because I feel like you're my ...'

'Mother? Yes, you said.'

Sidiq laughed. 'OK. But you just be careful. They all hate us. All shit bastards. I wish we were back in India.'

'When were you last there?'

Sidiq shook his head. 'Never been back. My mother died. Then my father, three years ago next month. One day, when I can afford to... maybe I'll go, visit their graves. Visit you. Become your driver. Then maybe become a big film star too.'

'I'm not in the movies. I'm not even on television any more.'

They lapsed into a renewed silence, until they passed Karlsruhe, a harsh industrial landscape of factory chimneys, steam and prefabricated sheeted roofs, and Sidiq asked her to read out the address they needed to find in Rastatt.

'Drei Mohren Strasse,' he repeated, with a hollow laugh. 'You know what that means? Three Moors Street. They have a custom here, after Christmas time. Three men make their faces black, and come and give out presents to children. Shit bastard people.'

They had to stop twice to ask directions. Eventually, they found Drei Mohren Strasse, a neat and careful street on an estate of grey concrete houses with red tiled roofs. Each identical building, a two-storey block comprising four flats, with neat and anonymous gardens in front, separated by driveways leading to blocks of garages at the rear. They pulled up beside No. 83. Taz checked the name above the doorbells; Ruhl was the third. The upper flat, on the right of the shared front door. She rang the bell. There was no answer. She rang twice more, and returned to the car.

'No problem,' Sidiq assured her. 'You hungry? Let's eat, then come back, and do what you do in films, what is it? A stake-up?'

Taz glanced at her watch. 'A stake-out,' she said, absently staring back at the closed door. 'Must be at work, I guess. What time do people come home here?'

Sidiq started the car. 'Depends what he does. What kind of food do you like? German food is...'

'Shit bastard food?' she suggested.

Sidiq laughed. 'All cream and pig meat. That's why they're all so fat, and ugly. And Indian food here is not much better. You like Turkish food? You eaten Imam Beyldi, no? Let's eat Turkish.'

They were back outside 83 Drei Mohren Strasse an hour-and-a-half later. Sidiq had watched with satisfaction as she had first picked at, then eaten with greater enthusiasm, the aubergines swimming in oil that he had ordered for her. His pleasure turned to frowning disapproval when she had ordered beer, and he had pointedly ordered a diet coke for himself. They'd finished their meal with small cups of strong coffee, which, with the beer, left Taz thinking longingly about a bathroom, as they sat in the car across the road from 83, eating their way through a box of sweet, flaky pastries, and sticky slabs of pistachios cemented together with honey.

After the best part of an hour, a blue Volkswagen with a noisy exhaust drove up, swung into the drive that separated 83 from 85 and pulled up outside a garage at the rear. The driver, a short, stocky, silver-haired man, leapt out with surprising agility and swung the garage door up.

Taz licked her fingers, and wiped them surreptitiously on the car seat as they watched him walk round to the front of the building, and unlock the door.

'Him?' asked Sidiq, his voice muffled with a cheekful of adhesive confectionery.

Taz shrugged. 'I guess.'

'You want I should go and ask?' asked Sidiq, brushing crumbs from his shirt front and lap. Taz nodded.

Halfway across the road, Sidiq called out to the man at the door. Even from where she sat, Taz could see the fear and suspicion evident on the face, and echoed in the slightly crouching poise of the man, as he turned, seemingly uncertain whether to stop, or to throw himself through the doorway, and slam the door behind him.

She couldn't hear the words, but she could see Sidiq pointing over his shoulder at her, the man at the door squinting, and shaking his head. She could see he was edging further in, and suspected that if she didn't move in now, they would lose him.

'Herr Ruhl? Hugo Ruhl?' she called, as she ran towards them.

'I have nothing to say...' he began, in German, then stopped, and looked at her as though he had seen her before.

'You speak English?' Taz asked, taking advantage of the pause.

He nodded. 'Of course.'

'Can I speak to you?'

'About...?'

She took a deep breath. 'About Armitage Shanks.'

He stared at her, a blank, neutral half-smile on his face. He was giving nothing away.

'You are?'

'Taz Dhar. I...'

Ruhl shook his head. 'Your name means nothing to me. You will have to do better than that. Who sent you?'

'He did. In a way. You knew him, didn't you?'

'Knew him?' Hugo Ruhl seemed confused, as though what she said made no sense, then his eyes saddened at her use of the past tense. She noticed for the first time that he had a sticking plaster over the bridge of his nose. 'Perhaps. What has happened?'

'Can we talk inside?' asked Taz. Ruhl glanced at Sidiq.

'Wait in the car, Sidiq,' Taz said, without taking her eyes from Hugo Ruhl's. 'Please.'

Ruhl led her up a flight of concrete stairs to his own front door.

'How did you find me?' he asked, as he simultaneously turned two keys in two different locks.

'My... sources,' she gasped, still short of breath from her run; she hadn't realized how out of condition she was. 'I was told you could help me.'

She followed him into the flat. It was beautifully furnished, modern, tasteful, yet in its own way, as anonymous and impersonal as everything else about Drei Mohren Strasse. It was more like being in the showroom of an exclusive furniture store than in someone's home, she realized. Like he'd bought the whole ensemble, en bloc, out of a particularly expensive catalogue.

He left her standing in the narrow hallway while he walked through to the kitchen. He rummaged noisily in the refrigerator and dug out two bottles of beer. He held them up to her, and she nodded, gratefully.

'May I, er...' she asked, holding up her hands.

He pointed to the bathroom. When she emerged, he was sitting in an armchair, in a lounge of chrome and black leather, dominated by a bookcase filled with pristine paperbacks of uniform size which spread the entire length of one wall, their spines forming oblong orange and blue tiles. They too seemed arranged purely for aesthetic effect.

He pointed to another chair, beside which he'd placed her beer, condensation already forming on the bottle.

'I appreciate this,' she said. 'You seeing me. I realize it's an intrusion but need to know...'

'First,' he interrupted. 'Let us talk of what *I* need to know; I need to know who you are, and why you are here.'

Taz quickly told him about the letter, her assignment, and the anonymous e-mail giving her his address.

When she'd finished, he nodded. 'So he's dead?'

'I'm afraid so. Can you tell me about him?'

Ruhl glanced up at a collage framed in a stark black mount which dominated the wall opposite the bookcase. A clutter of images, mementos and memories, intensely personal. Totally out of kilter with the rest of the anonymous apartment. Places, faces and objects. Mostly tropical. Many old. Images of buildings. European. Tropical. Lists. An image of the dust jacket of a book, H.G. Wells's *Time Machine*. Postcards: a fat woman in a straw hat next to a basket of dried fish. Sunrise over a temple dome somewhere in Asia. Two men smiling in a garden. A railway ticket. A lapel pin of a flag, green, red and black. A prayer, entitled 'Sanctuary', translated, on browning newsprint. An invitation to an Embassy function. And faces. Grinning out of fuzzy, colourful snaps. Glowering in monochrome passport photos. Reserved and erect in formal group portraits. She started to recognize the same four or five people, time and again. All men, various ages, mostly white. Usually in short-sleeved, open-necked shirts. Often wearing sunglasses. And at the very centre of the collage, at the heart of a boozy night-gathering outdoors somewhere hot, sat Hugo Ruhl, smiling, surrounded by these men. Their faces were red, red with the sun, and flushed with pleasure. Wide-eyed, caught, almost as though—despite the way they had crowded together for the photograph—they'd been snapped unawares.

'Is Armitage Shanks in that photograph?' Taz asked, too quickly.

Ruhl's pale eyes gleamed suddenly. 'You don't know...' he paused, as though to catch his breath '... what he looks like?'

'No. Just the letter, that's all I've got. Do you want to see it?'

She handed the photocopy over and Ruhl took a pair of half-moon glasses from his breast pocket. He put them on carefully as though whatever the sticking plaster across his nose covered was still tender. He read, fast.

'Yes,' he murmured. 'This is a hand I know. The writing of an old friend. You are sure he's dead?'

'On the word of a priest. There are no announcements, or press reports, or apparently any official knowledge, but the priest says he died; why would he lie?'

'Why indeed? Why would a priest tell a lie?' murmured Hugo Ruhl, like he was toying with a riddle.

A new excitement seemed to pulse through him and he looked suddenly much younger. His chin trembled, and when he spoke, his mouth was twisted, as though he wanted to cry and laugh, at the same time. 'Look how determined his hand is; barely a tremble,' he said, in a way that she assumed was for his own benefit, except that he said it in English.

He shook his head. 'Hell of a man.' He flicked on to the last page. 'See? Even here, right at the end. Such confidence! Such courage!'

He handed the letter back to her, and took off his glasses. 'So he's dead? And as a result, you have found me. You know, he told me not to come back here; told me an old Jew in Germany was no safer than an Armitage Shanks in Africa. Where did he die?'

'In Ethiopia,' Taz said, quietly.

Ruhl shook his head vigorously. 'No, not in Ethiopia. Impossible.'

'That's where the priest saw him. On his way to the execution shed,' Taz said.

'So it may be, but that's not where it happened.'

'Well, that's what the priest said. Ethiopia.'

'And why would a priest lie? Drink your beer.'

Taz took a quick sip of the heavy, yeasty liquor and licked froth from her upper lip. 'Tell me about him. Please.'

Hugo Ruhl glanced up at the collage and shook his head, sadly. 'The man that wrote this letter was a good man—a kind and generous man who was a good friend to me when I most needed a friend. He's right in his description: good food, bad company, terrible jokes. But he was also a man who wanted to leave his mark. To make a difference. Someone who perhaps tried too hard to do good. Lost sight of what was right and what was wrong. Tried too hard to make that difference. And finally, he ended up the wrong person in the wrong place, at the wrong time.' A corner of his mouth turned down, and he seemed to be lost in some memory. 'And I played Judas to his Christ.'

'How long did you know him?' Taz prompted.

'Me? Oh, seven years. Eight, maybe.' He sniffed. 'We worked together, on all sorts of things. You don't know who told you about me?'

Taz looked away and shook her head. 'Sorry, just an e-mail, mentioning your name.'

'And where I lived?'

'Yes.'

'And on that you came to find me?' he said, doubtfully. 'Who is that man in the car outside?'

'Just a driver I hired.'

'That's not a licensed taxi.'

'It's a private deal. Forget him. He's no one.'

'He would have smiled at you saying that,' said Ruhl, holding up the letter. 'No one. Non-People. Those who don't matter. Why did he write to you?'

Taz reached out for the letter, and pointed out the parts which explained about the Indian businessman, and her photograph. Hugo Ruhl smiled, an affectionate, sad smile, that sparkled, tear-bright. 'That sounds like him—yes, just like him. A romantic. He could have written to me, or to the others. Or to the Pope, or his Prime Minister, or God Almighty. All sorts of people. Instead, he writes to a pretty woman he's never met. You feel... involved with him? Because of this letter?'

Taz shrugged 'In a way, yes, I guess so. I feel I owe him; God knows what or why.'

Hugo Ruhl laughed, like a proud mourner. 'He had that effect on people, always.' He glanced up at the collage, and Taz's eyes followed his, but which picture was he focussing on? 'But Ethiopia? No. Not in Ethiopia... '

He spread his hands, in a gesture of resignation, and conclusion.

'There's a lot I want to know...' she said, and was surprised to hear her own voice plead.

'Not now. Not today. I will tell you everything. But at another time and somewhere else.'

'Tomorrow?'

'Yes. Maybe tomorrow. But not here. You must never come here again. You being here changes everything. You know the bar at the end of the road, the Drei Mohren? There. It's better that I meet you there.' As though persuading himself, he added, 'Yes, that would be best. Eight o'clock. Tomorrow. Now...'

She rose and reached out to shake his hand. For the first time, she noticed the patches of deathly white skin that marked the back of his right hand.

'Until tomorrow,' he said, quietly, as though she was already so distant she would be unable to hear, no matter how loud he spoke.

❧

Sitting, arms folded, in the black BMW parked across the road from Hugo Ruhl's apartment block, Sidiq was a handsome image of sulky truculence. The tight line of his lips, and the artificially erect poise echoed for her, ludicrously enough, her mother, in maximum disappointment mode.

'Right!' she said, briskly, as she flopped into the passenger seat, determined not to accommodate his petulance one iota. 'We need to be back here at eight tomorrow night.'

On the journey back to Frankfurt he brightened considerably. He even began to flirt with her. At first, she thought she must be reading the signs wrong, some kind of cultural difference, perhaps, she told herself. When not even the most generous interpretation could explain away the implicit overtones, she interrupted his enthusiastic description of her charms to ask him, simply, how old he was.

'Twenty-five,' he said. Undeterred, he turned to her, swinging a smile in her direction like a searchlight beam.

'I'm just,' she said, 'just, I say, biologically, old enough to be your mother, God help me. You say you're married, and you've got a family. So let's just move on from holiday resort Romeo stuff, huh?'

To her surprise, he laughed eagerly. To her growing irritation, she recognized relief. 'I thought it was expected; sorry. I thought, you know, lonely famous lady, handsome young guy. You know. From now, I treat you with respect. Like my...'

'Employer?' she asked, hopefully.

'No! Like my mother's youngest sister.'

Back in her hotel room, she showered, and ate from room service, and drank, and rang SK, and got no response, and rang Mark, and got no answer there either, and drank some more. She tried to watch television, but fell asleep in the armchair, wrapped in a thick towelling hotel bath robe, with her hair tied up in a hand towel. When she awoke, her neck was stiff, and when she unwrapped the towel from around her head, her hair stood out in spikes and broken waves.

She thought about washing it again, but couldn't be bothered. She began to make herself a cup of coffee, but had the last, minute scotch from the mini-bar instead. She slept, and lost the next morning in a morass of frustrated telephone calls and some uncomfortable, headachy, introspection.

Sidiq called for her at four. She was at the Drei Mohren in Rastatt by seven.

❧

The Drei Mohren was the most antiseptic bar she had ever been in. Scrupulously clean; new. Scrubbed, lacquered and brightly lit, laid out like a Swedish pine kitchen on special offer, reeking of spray polish and carefully designed simplicity. You could perform open heart surgery on the bar, she thought, with less risk of infection than in most UK hospitals. She sat at a table by the window overlooking the empty white concrete car park, waiting and watching. Barely any traffic drove past on the estate road. Only one other person sat in the bar; a plump old man with a trilby hat on the back of his head, and a face tanned and lined like a farmer's. He perched on a bar stool, sipping beer from a tall thin glass.

Whenever she finished her small beer, the empty glass was immediately whipped away, the table wiped, and a full glass carefully placed before her on a brand new beer mat, with a neatly folded paper napkin beside it.

The imitation beech floor, and the highly varnished pine tables and chairs were unscratched. It was like drinking in the front window of a furniture shop. She thought of Hugo Ruhl's flat, and wondered if the entire estate was like that. She glanced at her watch; time passed slowly.

Sidiq had dropped her off, and promised to be back for her by nine. He intended to return to the Turkish cafe and pass the evening drinking coffee and watching football on TV. She looked across at the bar; the fat man with the trilby on the back of his head looked round and nodded to her. She nodded back. Silence. She wished she had something to read.

When Sidiq returned at ten past nine she was still there; alone. Fuddled, nauseous and bloated on gassy beer. He shook his head sadly as he watched her pay her bill, and they left. They drove round to Ruhl's apartment in 83. It was in darkness. She rang the doorbell, leaning on it for thirty, forty seconds. No answer. She felt sick, and old, and heavy and stupid. She should have seen it coming; should have recognized his concern over being found. Realized that all he wanted was a chance to get out. To hide from whatever it was that had brought him back to Germany, and his pathetic attempt to lose himself.

Pathetic? That was rich, coming from her. She cursed herself, for her naivety and stupidity. The channel was right; she wasn't up to it. She was just another amateur. A no-hoper. SK was right. Mark was right. Everybody was right, except her. She wasn't fit to be out on her own. Didn't stand a snowball's chance in hell. One lead, that was all she'd had. And that an uncle's gift-wrapped little treat for an indulged niece. Which she'd duly followed up and promptly fucked up.

Well, he wasn't there. Standing in the street outside and cursing herself wasn't going to change that. She walked back to the car, and saw in Sidiq's eyes a kind of patronizing sympathy that really pissed her off.

He was as good as his word; he was treating her like his mother's youngest sister. Assuming Auntiji was a congenital idiot too.

'What do you want to do now?' he asked.

'What do I want? I'll tell you. I want the picture on his wall. In the main room.'

'How you going to get it if he's not there any more?'

'I'm not going to. You are.'

Sidiq blew out his cheeks. 'You kidding, right?'

'No, I am most definitely not kidding. Remember the famous-lady-handsome-young-guy routine? Well, this is how it really works. I say and pay; you go and do. Whatever it takes. And I say I want that picture.'

Sidiq shook his head, while his low rumbling laugh shook his shoulders. 'You movie stars, you think everything is that easy? You just pay, and you get what you want, yes?'

'Yes,' she said. 'That's about it. There should now be only two thoughts in your mind: how much, and in what currency?'

'It's dangerous. Very dangerous,' Sidiq observed.

'All commercial transactions carry with them an element of risk. That can be factored into the negotiation. How much?' she repeated.

'OK.' said Sidiq. 'A ticket to India and a job.'

He looked at her hopefully. She frowned.

'Shit, Sidiq,' she said. 'Can't you just take money?'

'No,' he insisted, sensing victory. 'A ticket and a job.'

'It's not what you think, believe me.'

'You went, yes?'

'So?'

'So, who are you to stop my having the chance you had? So it isn't what I think; let me have the chance to find that out. Let me have the chance you had, and my wife and my children too. Get me a job back home, I get you your picture.'

'I don't know. If I get you there, sort out the passport problems, how about that? But that's it. No strings after that. No coming running to me afterwards, for a place to live, or a handout, or anything.'

He beamed, ingratiatingly. 'Done deal. No strings, no nothing. I'll be OK, if I can just get to Bombay.'

'You and fifty million others.' She sighed. 'OK. I just may be able to do it. I don't know, but I think I can. Will you trust me to try?'

'You're my aunty; of course I trust you. Get in the car.'

She frowned, confused. He looked up, raising his eyes to the roof as though amazed at her simplicity. 'You seen the locks on those doors? You think an amateur is going to get in there? You think these shit bastard people don't ring the police as soon as they see even Ein Mohren in their streets after dark anytime other than Christmas? How many you think have been watching us, behind their net curtains? How many already called the police? Number one, we get out from here, or were you thinking of standing and watching? Number two, we get a professional.'

'A professional?'

'Sure! You want a car stolen, I'll do that for you myself. But breaking into a house? You gotta know what you're doing. I can find you somebody, but that will cost extra. Maybe we could let him keep whatever else he can take? That will reduce the cost.'

'No!' she cried, horrified. 'Absolutely not! Christ, what do you think I am? You tell me what it will cost, and I'll pay him. But only the big picture in the black frame; nothing else is to be touched. And minimal damage getting in and out. With a statement of what he's damaged so I can send money for the repairs. Got that?'

'Got that. It will be like you say. Done deal.'

The final notes of *Crimmond* not so much faded, as seemed to leach away, deep into the stonework of the little church; a spiritual seasoning, adding a faint remnant of its own to the echoes of many decades, of centuries of such sounds of celebration and commemoration.

There was a wave of rustling, of paper and clothes, as people folded hymn books and bent forward, to lay them down. The vicar waited until the congregation had, at his invitation, seated themselves. Now was his time; he'd prepared a few words, as they had asked. Carefully chosen, words rounded and fitting.

The vicar glanced at the Indians, and felt again the pang of regret that the bishop had forbidden filming during the ceremony. He had practised the brief sermon several times before a mirror; something he hadn't done since the first eighteen months after his ordination. He only had very second-hand information to go on; only what had appeared in the reports, on television, and in the newspapers. Heavy on hyperbole; thin on fact. Well, he had told himself, men of his calling had been making stories with meaning out of what, to others, might seem no more than a series of disjointed events long before there were reporters, and newspapers, and television channels.

He took a deep breath.

'When I was a boy, growing up not too far from this parish,' he began, then paused, frowning thoughtfully as though the words were coming to him fresh, for the first time. 'When I was young it was still common to talk about Africa as the "Dark Continent" and India as "The Jewel in the Crown". People talked about the white man's grave yard, and the white man's burden, with no hint of embarrassment.'

He paused, and looked around, shaking his head, with what he hoped was a sardonic smile. 'How clumsy. How offensive and archaic those expressions sound to us today. Naff, I believe, is the expression today's young people would use. How naff they sound. Yet in their day, they were sufficient to lead less selfish generations to find unmarked graves in the far, mysterious corners of a long passed Empire.'

SK scratched the side of his nose, to hide a smile. He had wanted Father Thomas, the priest that had been there at the end in Ethiopia. They had tried to get him to conduct this memorial service. Had offered serious money to get him before the cameras here, or back home in the Cathedral of the Holy Name. Or better still, one of the churches in Bandra: St Theresa's or maybe St Joseph the Worker. That had the right tone about it. But no, the authorities had explained, politely but firmly, that a Catholic priest couldn't actually carry such a service for one who had so clearly specified he was not of the faith. Left no room for doubt, really. None at all.

Pompous, SK had thought it. Narrow-minded, pig-headed and short-sighted too. So not *Aaj Mumbaikar*. So he'd settled for the picturesque, instead. There was after all, a link to the deceased here, even if it was somewhat tenuous. So the deceased died a Muslim? He must at one time at least have been happy to be called a Christian and his passing could thus be commemorated here at Coombe Wootton. God bless the ever accommodating Church of England.

Father Thomas would have heightened the poignancy, though. But no, he'd have to settle for what this sad old fossil could offer by way of the dramatic and the symbolic. Still, you couldn't fault his delivery. He glanced across at Ash Kumar, and found, not at all to his surprise, that Ash was rapt, absorbed by the vicar's oration. A pair of ripe hams, SK thought. One sizing the other up. He could just picture old Ash up there in the pulpit: he had the same kind of innate sense of timing. Instinctive. And the same shameless exploitation of a situation, and an audience.

'Unselfish, did I say? Today, it is fashionable to question the motives of those who long ago met untimely deaths in distant places. To suggest that they were driven by personal greed, or arrogance, or an over-weening belief in their own racial or moral superiority. Perhaps there were such, undoubtedly there were. Undoubtedly too in the large hearts of many good men—and women,' he added, with an unctuous smile and a nod to the Asian woman sitting, head bowed, between SK and Ash Kumar, 'such unworthy motives occasionally found fertile ground and took root. Maybe it was so with the man for whom many here searched. A man who reached out to them, quite literally, from the lip of the abyss. Called out to them. For simple comfort and a fleeting companionship caught in a final, scrawled letter. A man who signed himself Armitage Shanks.'

Not at all bad, acknowledged SK, grudgingly. Set up a juxtaposition, build up the tension. But, he realized, shifting uncomfortably on the hard wooden pew, when the preacher starting that far back, we're here for a long time. A very long time.

And in this business, time could be critical.

To stop himself looking at his watch, SK glanced around the little church, and was moved by its overwhelming Englishness. Tears pricked his eyes, and he couldn't decide whether it was the weighty dignity of the service, or the sense of eternal continuity buildings this old always engendered within him. It was perfect; right down to the smell of chrysanthemums and lilies.

He tried to spot Mark; he was sure he should be able to, from Taz's description. He guessed Mark was the slightly round-shouldered guy up ahead in the second row who was obviously wearing a suit purchased for weddings and funerals a good ten years ago. It was expensive material, sure. But even the darts in the back of the jacket looked dated. SK smiled to himself. He could guess what the lapels would look like!

Yet for all his sneering, he envied this Mark, if Mark it was, the smug indifference, the confidence verging on arrogance which would allow anyone to wear a suit like that within a half-mile radius of a television camera.

He glanced surreptitiously at his watch, raising his cuff above it on the pretext of scratching his wrist. The service had started late, because they'd taken a wrong turning. Not that it really mattered. Still, he was annoyed that they had been the cause of the delay. Knew it played to all the worst stereotypes. He was getting bored, he knew. He was no longer listening to the vicar's words, and merely following the movements of everyone else in the congregation.

Like everyone else in the world, his attention span was shrinking. Day by day.

He thought about how much Taz had managed to find out about Armitage Shanks, and how much it had cost.

They'd got photographs, and notes of her interviews, and

even this memorial service was part of the story; maybe its culmination. But he knew that there was still something, if not missing, not yet in the right place. Like a kaleidoscope which needed a final shake for the true pattern to emerge. Or thread which, when plucked at, and tugged, would not cause the loose tissue to unravel, but would pull the whole slack weave together, tight, neat and deadly as a silken straitjacket.

❧

'SK? Hi! It's Taz. You're a hard guy to get hold of.'

'The time difference, Taz. Try and remember that when you call next time. Please. What is it?'

'You notice there's an echo on this line? And a kind of a time lapse kinda thing? There wasn't, when I spoke to you in England. Strange, huh?'

She could hear SK sigh. Time lapse or not, she knew from old he was about to patronize her.

'Listen, Boss,' she said quickly. 'I've had to pay out some big money, and unless you want to enter the murky world of illegal immigration, I'm going to have to fork out a lot more.'

She listened, with satisfaction, to SK make sounds like a small water heater in the final stages of terminal collapse.

'What are you talking about, Taz?'

'I've got a photograph of Armitage Shanks.'

SK paused. 'Is it something we can use?'

'Not yet,' she admitted. 'I'm sure it's a photograph of him, but he's with some other guys, and I'm not quite sure which one he is. And there may be some… copyright and ownership issues too. But we're getting nearer.'

'The photo's from this Ruhl guy in Germany?'

'Yes. He seemed like he wanted to talk. But then he just disappeared. Ran out on me. Story of my life, I guess. Men letting me down.'

'You're getting maudlin, Taz,' said SK, unsympathetically. 'Have another drink.'

'You can be a real shit to me, sometimes, SK. You know that?'

'I'm paying dearly enough for the privilege. So what are you going to do next?'

'Go back to England, and see if the priest can tell me which one of these guys is our man. Maybe go to Ethiopia. Find out what really happened there. But I've got a photograph now, and I've spoken to someone who knew Armitage Shanks, and to the priest who sent me the letter. SK, it's like, well it's like he's really, well, real.'

'You've got a wonderful way with words, Taz. Whom do you have to pay for this photo?'

'One of our viewers. He says he thinks the Lesbian is a sorry replacement for me by the way. A young man called Sidiq who's going to be one pissed-off ex-fan tomorrow morning when he turns up here expecting to pick me up, together with a ticket to the dream factory only to find an abject apology and a great deal of your money. It's a shame it's going to end like this. He's been like a, well, a nephew to me. Still, life goes on.'

'You never fail to amaze me, Taz. E-mail your notes. And a scan of the picture. I want to be able to see him for myself.'

She replaced the receiver, and lay back on the bed, holding the stolen collage at arm's length above her.

It was still in its frame; black lacquered wood, the surface so perfect it could have been plastic. A collection of apparently unlinked things. Together, did they tell a story? And the picture in the middle. Armitage Shanks and his friends.

But who was Armitage Shanks, and who were the friends?

She rolled on to her side, and curled her legs up, still holding the picture in both hands, her arms stiff. It looked like a farewell party for Ruhl; he was the centre of attraction. He looked drunk, and happy. More erect, confident and, well, just simply more alive than the man she had seen. She guessed he was a man who liked warmth; the hot sun of Africa, and the comradeship of good friends.

But which one was Armitage Shanks?

The four men around Ruhl ranged in ages from, she guessed, mid-twenties, to mid-fifties. The two men sat on either side of Ruhl, leaned in towards him, their hands abnormally large around the glasses that they held. They seemed much of an age; hair cut very short, almost shaven-headed. They were smiling, but they looked as though they were holding their breath, too.

To the right, there was another man, standing. He had his left hand on Hugo Ruhl's right shoulder. He leaned forward, so that his head was only a few inches above those of the seated men. He was older, heavier. His hair was greying at the temples, and whilst the younger men wore tee-shirts, he wore a bush shirt. With the exception of Hugo Ruhl, they were clean-shaven.

Beside the standing man, another figure, older too, and blurred slightly, as though he alone had been moving. He had a darker complexion, a receding hairline and dark eyes, and wore a loud patterned shirt, and spectacles.

The composition of the photograph was unusual, from low, angled up so that the flash threw shadows behind onto a trellis bedecked with a creeping, brightly flowering plant, and fat chinese lanterns.

Taz swung herself from the bed, and picked up her glass from on top of the mini-bar; it was empty. She thought about another drink, but there was only vodka and fruit juice left.

She took out the miniature bottle of vodka, looked at it, turned down the corners of her mouth, and put it back on the fridge shelf. She took out a tomato juice, pulled the ring opener, and poured the glutinous contents into her glass. She reached back in, and took out the vodka.

She picked up the photograph; she thought she could work out what had happened. The camera was set on automatic, the man on the extreme right having pressed the delay firing button, and then raced round to be in the photograph. Yes, the slightly frozen, forced grins of the others then made more sense.

There were six bottles of beer on the table; plates too; cards and an ash tray. She glanced at their hands, the hands that were visible. None seemed to be smoking, yet the ashtray was cluttered with butts.

She wondered what else she should try and deduce from the photograph; wondered what a professional would look for, then reminded herself, sternly, that she was a professional. She put the photograph aside, and drank the fortified tomato juice.

Suddenly, she felt depressed. The thrill of getting the photo, taking risks and breaking laws in a foreign land, and getting away with it, leaked from her, leaving her feeling uncharacteristically guilty about what she was about to do to Sidiq. Well, she told herself, there are bigger issues at play here. If this turned out to be the story she was beginning to suspect it could be, she'd make it up to him. Make good her promise. Redeem herself.

She crossed to her suitcase, and took out a photocopy of Armitage Shanks's letter that she had shown Hugo Ruhl; she didn't trust even herself with the original.

I've got a photo of you. It's in front of me now. I'm afraid I've never heard of you, but the guy whose clothes I'm wearing must, I suppose, have been a fan of yours. I found your picture—it looks like it's been torn out of a television guide in a magazine—in his pocket. Underneath is your name, and the words 'Good Morning Mumbai, 07.00.'

They gave me the choice of his other belongings, too; this Asian guy, your fan. He had a paperback book of poetry. Classics. Coleridge. Keats. I thought about trying to learn

'Kubla Khan' by heart but I don't have enough time, so then I tried to make up extra verses; complete it. I tried doing it straight, then in a kind of pastiche. I think that's the word— what a time to want to extend my vocabulary!

Without quite knowing why, she wanted to cry. She picked up the photograph again. Well, she thought I've got a photo of you too, and it's in front of me now. But which one of you is Armitage Shanks? Which hand wrote that last letter to me? Which one of you died, alone, abroad, determined and scared, focusing your final thoughts on me, a sad, semi-drunk, demi-celebrity, total fuck-up?

She determined that, whatever else she did, or didn't do, as soon as she got back to her mother's house, she'd read 'Kubla Khan'.

And arrange a proper memorial service for Armitage Shanks. And look up the word 'pastiche'.

∽

The vicar was approaching his high point, SK suspected. He was in full swing now. The little church rang with his voice, and even SK had to admit he was good.

'A lonely death in Africa,' the vicar boomed, a tremble in his voice seeming to resonate with sincerity. 'A death, alone. Yet there are here people from more than one community. More than one country. More even than one continent. Come to reflect. To celebrate, commemorate and, yes, to mourn this tragic death. This sad and tragic death. Of one who had achieved so much, and yet had so much more still to give. This loss has a sense and a purpose, which transcends our simple understanding of it. It is a cliché that the Lord moves in mysterious ways, yet move he does through these events. He has called us to come together, today. Many of us brought to this place for the first time, just as he called a man who called himself Armitage Shanks to go to Africa.' The vicar threw his shoulders back and moved slightly from side to side, and suddenly let his voice drop low, so the congregation had to crane forward to catch his words. 'In his final moments, that lonely man reached out, to a young woman far away, and the Lord called her to go in search of the truth about that tragic, lonely man. What happened, on that journey to find an elusive truth, we will probably never know. But somewhere, a dear one was taken from us, and this we mourn. But we mourn for our own loss, as we gather today to celebrate the life as well as to mark the passing of the person who just a few short years ago took her wedding vows in this very church. Someone who on that day became Mrs Mark Letcombe. Someone whom many around the world knew so much better simply as Taz Dhar.'

PART II

FIGHTING FIRES

7

The meeting was scheduled for four in the afternoon. The first sunny afternoon for several days. The venue, a face-lifted and refurbed Seventies office building on Kennington Lane. South of the river, and not at the fashionable end, up toward the bridge, where the Secret Intelligence Service had its HQ and where ex-Prime Ministers maintained pieds-á-terre in St George's Wharf. Human traffic through the glass doors, on which was etched 'Honiton House', was pretty much all one-way: out. After all, it was POETS day—Piss Off Early, Tomorrow's Saturday—and the sun was shining. Home, a lawn in need of a quick trim, a clutch of kids at a childminder or a body pump class at the local gym, all whispered more eloquently through the open-plan offices and wide corridors, where smart screens flashed a surreal mix of housekeeping trivia and BBC World news headlines, than did the dull grumble of prosaic duty.

A few of the departing staffers paused on the wheelchair access ramp to light up. Others headed off fast for the Oval Tube, next to the cricket ground, or strode up past the shabby tenements of local authority housing and the twenty-four-hour Tesco toward Vauxhall. DCI Bignall and WPC Sitaram sat on the only two chairs in the reception area and waited. Looked like it would be a long time before she got home tonight,

Anuradha Sitaram reflected grimly. Another function missed. Further promises broken and more good intentions frustrated. Another weekend of murmured disappointments and repeated regrets loomed ahead.

The departing workers, in a chorus of good wishes for the weekend, thrust the security passes which clearly differentiated the warranted officers from the civilian staff into pockets and bags as they approached the door. Although anyone who had spent much time around the police could easily distinguish one from another without the need for badges. Fellow officers could tell Sitaram and Bignall were cops just as easily, even though neither wore uniform, and more than one cast them a sympathetic smile as they passed.

'You're here, just in case,' said Bignall for the umpteenth time. 'Chances are you'll be sitting around here for an hour or two, then we'll head home. Sorry if this is screwing up your weekend, but, as they used to tell us during the miners' strike, just think about the overtime.'

Anu Sitaram said nothing. She still didn't know what to make of Dave Bignall. He was three decades older and three ranks higher than her, and whilst she was a simple beat officer, he was head of the county special branch, charged with protecting the state in general and the people of Wiltshire in particular from the threats of international espionage, global terrorism and internal subversion. He treated her with a mix of paternal indifference, professional courtesy and sexist condescension which she found unsettling and impossible to work out how to respond to, and she still didn't understand why he'd been dealing with the Taz Dhar case in the first place, or, come to that, why he seemed so keen to keep her involved. He was far too senior and specialized to be handling what seemed most likely to be an act of domestic viciousness, and she was far too junior and inexperienced to be 'point of contact' for a case as potentially significant as this.

She glanced up. Meeting rooms, with walls of sheer glass, surrounded the atrium in which they sat, stretching up for four floors. Almost all were empty. The few still occupied were clearly gatherings coming to an end. Casual body language, easy smiles, papers and laptops being packed away. The meeting rooms, she noticed, were named after cities, a different continent for each floor.

Dave Bignall sighed once more, and wished he still smoked. He was pretty sure the next hour or two would be a patronizing exhibition of how far out of the mainstream Wiltshire Special Branch was. Ironic really, because that was precisely why he'd applied for a move from the Met to a provincial backwater like Wiltshire. Lush, green rolling hills, picturesque villages with thatched cottages and cricket on the green, neat farms and undulating downlands. That's what he'd wanted to see out the last few years of his service wandering amidst, after twenty-five years of frontline territorial policing in some of London's most deprived and divided boroughs. But that was before 9/11, Her Majesty's Inspectorate of Constabulary's Thematic on Special Branches and the creation of Muslim Contact Units. And Dave Bignall, who'd virtually invented community policing in Tower Hamlets, the borough with the highest Muslim population in Britain, back in the Eighties when it was new, edgy and a real risk, knew far more about Muslims in Britain than anyone else on the force.

'We were originally called the Special Irish Branch. You know that? Only concerned with Fenians and mad Paddies and violent Republicans. If only it still was, I'd have been OK.' He reflected, glumly. 'Anarchic Plebs.'

'I'm sorry?'

'It's an anagram of Special Branch.'

'Did you just make that up?'

'Mmm. Give us a bit of paper. How do you spell your name? Anuradha Sitaram? OK.' He frowned, scribbled for a moment or two, then held the paper at arm's length. 'A Radiant Asharum. A drama Sharia nut. Shame you're not a Muslim. That would be a good one. A harridan Ma at us.'

'That's amazing!'

'Yeah.'

At five past four, Dave Bignall's name was called from reception. He handed Anu the paper. 'See what you can do with David John Bignall. I expect three good ones by the time I get back,' he said , as a birdlike woman with the cough and poor skin of a heavy smoker led him, chatting, husky-voiced, about her imminent weekend, up to the second floor and pointed him in the direction of Oslo.

'Welcome. Good of you to join us,' said a large man in his early fifties, with the ruddy complexion of an outdoorsman, cropped hair so fair it looked almost white and a soft transatlantic accent, as he strode forward to shake Dave Bignall's hand and usher him in. 'Now we're all here, let's get on. I'm sure we've all got places to go and people to do. DCI Bignall. Can we call you...'

He glanced down at the file in front of him, and frowned. 'Dave,' Bignall offered. 'Dave will be fine.'

'Right. Great. Well, welcome Dave. Tea and coffee is on the trolley behind you. Help yourself. The chocolate digestives are particularly good. We saved you one. No? OK. First of all a big thumbs-up and thank you to our friends in the Met for providing the facilities and hosting this little gathering, and thanks to Dave here for coming all the way up from Swindon.'

He made it sound like he'd trekked through jungles, forded rivers and crossed three mountain ranges rather than simply boarded a near-empty high-speed train a couple of hours earlier.

'Introductions are probably best kept to a minimum. I'm Gord. Accredited across the river. Rohit there is with us, via Interpol, from India.'

A well-built man with soft, dark eyes, a thick moustache and pock-marked cheeks smiled and nodded.

'And Tim? Well, Tim is from another part of the security sector with offices in Euston.'

Tim, who sat abnormally straight, was trim, fit, expressionless. He was short, stocky, with a slight paunch. He looked like he used to work out but was not at his peak. As though he was on an injury break. He had short, spiky hair, and heavy eyebrows on pale skin. He said 'Hello' in a broad northern accent Bignall struggled to place. Yorkshire, perhaps? Bradford? Strong, but studied, like he was determined it should stay patently provincial.

Gord picked up on Dave Bignall's failure to register the euphemism 'With offices in Euston,' he offered, again. 'And Tim is here because, well, it's a case of "Euston, we have a problem".'

'Is this about Armitage Shanks?' Dave Bignall asked.

All smiles faded. Gord looked pained.

'No,' said Tim. 'It's about a Tasneem Saifuddin Dharwalla. You know her.'

Dave frowned. 'Taz Dhar? WPC Sitaram and I attended a crime scene at her mother's house in Chiseldon last Friday. She was there then.'

'Bit beneath your dignity, I'd have thought,' Gord observed. 'Don't get me wrong, we're all for hands-on and managing by wandering around. Jeez, we invented it. But I'm intrigued that the local head of Special Branch would go out on a Friday night to this one in particular.'

Dave shrugged. 'My call. My patch. My choice, for which I'm accountable to my chief, not to you.'

Gord put up his hands in surrender. 'Whoa! Easy! No criticism. No problem. Of course we're not challenging your actions or your judgement...'

'Well, we might be,' said Tim from Euston.

Gord treated him to a 'profoundly unhelpful' glare and continued. 'Bear with us, Dave. Just talk us through this please. Off the record, just to help us out.'

'She's well known locally, and a Muslim. There was no one around in the Muslim Contact Unit, and I didn't want whatever was happening to get out of hand. A mosque was fire-bombed in Swindon a week back. Things are tense.'

'Missing the action, perhaps, Mr Bignall?' asked Rohit Shastri, amiably. 'I find the same now I'm deskbound at headquarters. Gets to all of us.'

'Thanks, Superintendent Shastri,' said Gord, seemingly in danger of losing control of the meeting. 'And you asked Sitaram to accompany you?'

'I asked for a WPC. As you know perfectly well it's standard police response when the caller is female to have a WPC along.' Standard police response to a feeling of intimidation, pending backup, being to confront the threat face-on, he instinctively went on to the offensive: 'Why are we even talking about this? If someone doesn't offer me a good reason in the next five minutes, I'm out of here. The detail of this matter is confidential and I have as yet no idea what your interest is. I have told you WPC Sitaram was just there because…'

'She's female?' offered Gord, smiling. 'Yes. You said. Standard procedure.'

'And when did you find out she was already acquainted with the subject Dharwalla?' asked Tim from Euston.

'Why?' asked Dave, eyes narrowed. He had taken a profound dislike to this Tim. 'I ask again: What does this have to do with any of you?'

'Oh, various reasons,' said Tim, airily. 'Among them the fact that she got the security liaison officer at the British Embassy in Ethiopia out of bed on a Saturday morning to ask about a certain priest. Presumably that was with your call.

Your patch. Your choice, for which you're accountable to your chief?'

Silence. Dave Bignall refused to surrender eye contact and stared back at Tim. Now he was sure he hated him. Almost as much as he hated Anu Sitaram at that moment. 'I need a comfort break,' he said, rising from his chair and stretching. 'Help yourselves to another cup of Met coffee while I take a walk.'

∿

Anu Sitaram glanced up as Dave Bignall strode toward her. 'Handling valid job.' She said. 'An anagram of David John Bignall. It's the only one I've got so far.'

'Not for very much longer, thanks to you. Come with me on a comfort call.'

She followed in the wake of the fuming Dave past the toilets and down to the canteen in the basement.

'I thought you needed the loo,' Anu said, suspicious.

'I'll manage. You know, I used to have irritable bowel syndrome. Then, a couple of years ago, it seemed to disappear. I said to my doctor, does this mean I'm better, and he said "No. It just means the rest of you has caught up in the pissed-off stakes. You now have total irritability syndrome." And days like this bring on my symptoms big time.'

They purchased a drink from a glowering West African woman who had been wiping down the laminate surfaces of the tables, and who tried, unsuccessfully, to persuade them the canteen was closed. Dave simply smiled, shook his head and invited Anu to make her selection.

She took a bottle of mineral water. He took a plastic cup, stuck it beneath a coffee machine, and handed over a five-pound note whilst he waited for the cup to be filled.

'I've cashed up,' said the woman, the corners of her mouth turned down in disgust. 'No change.'

'Then I'll have to owe you, won't I?' retorted Dave, snatching the fiver back and thrusting it into his pocket.

They sat at a long refectory table. Anu wondered if every police station in Britain had a canteen layout like this. Certainly, it had been a constant in all the ones she had visited.

Dave took a noisy sip. They sat for a moment in companionable silence. Canteen cool.

'Right,' said Dave, after the appropriate interval. 'Let's get a few things clear. What's going on upstairs is called an LCS; a Liaison and Collaboration Session. Joined-up government. No silos; no Chinese walls. The security services, intelligence agencies and law enforcement all working together in harmony as one seamless whole. Full disclosure. Complete candour. Total bollocks. As it ever was, you and I are on the same side and those guys upstairs, well, they aren't. And what you and I say to one another stays between us. Now pin your ears back and listen hard. There's a guy up there who says he's from across the river. That's Security Service. Box to the likes of me. MI5 to you. There's a tosser called Tim from Euston, and I have no idea who he is, but if the boys from Box are happy to sit in the same room with the unlovely Tim, and look to his lot for help when they're in a flap, then he's clearly not 6, and I think I'd prefer to remain in ignorance. And there's one of your kith and kin from the subcontinent who says he's a cop, but I don't believe him. He's accredited by Interpol though, so as far as you and I are concerned, we have to assume he's kosher. For now, at least. Or should that be halal?'

'I've no idea. I'm Uniform, remember?'

'Good one. Anyway, they are all acting very cagey, and they've got a serious case of the screaming habdabs about your friend Ms Dharwalla.'

'Look, Mr Bignall, I really don't know why I'm here. I'm...

'...a midge's dick away from being done for abuse of office. Did you get the whereabouts of that priest from our Embassy in Ethiopia for Taz Dhar?'

Anu sat dead still and counted her heartbeat. Surely that couldn't be what this was all about? Of course not, she told herself. OK, so a couple of phone calls to find the whereabouts of Father Thomas was unauthorized: she had said she was a police officer and given her details and thus, strictly speaking, had committed an offence, but a matter of national security? Come on! 'Should I be speaking to my federation rep?' she asked.

'Young lady, if you have done what they say you have, we are way beyond disciplinary. No trade union brief can talk you back from where you are now. You've had the misfortune, or plain crap judgement, to stray deep into where the meat-eaters roam. Worst of all, you've dragged me in there with you. How could you have been so dumb?'

'But you said I should do all I can to help her.'

'Don't you dare try to lay this on me! You know perfectly well what I meant. Visits, assistance with counselling and insurance claims; the usual stuff of a family liaison officer. Not breaching standing orders, professional etiquette and national security to help your pal. Right now, I'd happily to see you crucified for what you've done.'

'I thought you wanted me to do it,' Anu said in a small voice. 'I thought you were encouraging me to demonstrate my initiative.'

'I dare say that's so, Constable,' Dave Bignall sighed sadly. 'You wouldn't be the first good cop, and sadly you won't be the last either, to go down for trying too hard to show your initiative. But you're an adult, and a fully trained officer. You are wholly and solely responsible for this.'

She looked down, her face burning, her eyes pricking and her stomach churning. Don't let me cry, she silently prayed. Don't let him see me this scared.

Dave crossed his beefy forearms on the table, and leaned forward. 'Listen, I've got two daughters older than you. Both of them in the force. One's a sergeant in the Met, the other in her first year at Hendon. And I love them both dearly. But even if they screwed up like this, I'd let them sink or swim on their own. There is only one reason why I might help you out of this, and even then only if, from now and forever, you do exactly as I say. And that is that much as I loathe you for dragging me into this mess, I hate those cowboys and Indians upstairs even more. Now, are we working together on this?'

'Yes, Mr Bignall,' she murmured, like a chastened infant.

He glanced around, and met the malevolent stare of the glum waitress, waiting, damp cloth and spray disinfectant in hand, to wipe down their table and switch off the lights.

'If that was a yes, you'd better call me Guv'nor from now on. Now, come with me upstairs and let's get this sorted. And when we head back for Swindon tonight, think of an anagram for 'I am a silly but remarkably lucky cow'. Better still, write it out 100 times.'

'Yes, Guv'nor.'

∾

Two floors above, in Oslo, three men waited, trying to look unconcerned.

'You think this will work?' asked Rohit Shastri.

'Setting a thief to catch a thief?' suggested Tim.

'Sending what you call a 'Paki' to find a 'Paki'?'

'Your words, Superintendent Shastri,' said Gord, primly. 'Not ours. Not mine.'

'But your problem, gentlemen,' Rohit Shastri assured them. 'And it seems to me to be your approach. I'm only here because we have an ongoing investigation which may cross over what ever you are considering and we want to avoid a Blue on Blue. But while we're waiting, let's just look at the logic of what you're doing. Taz Dhar is thirty-nine, a first-generation East African immigrant. Anuradha Sitaram is a twenty-four-year-old police officer from a Hindu family who've been in Britain for fifty years. Taz Dhar is a barely functioning alcoholic bent on self-destruction. Sitaram is a vegetarian teetotaller who works out three times a week. Dhar has made her living out of attacking the respected and the powerful, only very occasionally with any justification, and then usually by accident. Sitaram is a model police officer. Two Chief Constables' commendations already, and an award for gallantry under active consideration. A Hindu rule-follower and a Muslim mould-breaker. One plays squash for the county, the other drinks for England. It would be hard to find two more different people.'

'They both come from Swindon. That's about the only link between them.'

'Yes, we'd picked up on Ms Dharwalla being a Muslim,' said Tim. 'If things become difficult that may be relevant. This sect she belongs to, Gord. Islamic extremist links? Could she have been radicalized?'

'Not so far as we know. The only one we're currently taking an interest in is, interestingly enough, her paternal uncle, Yusuf Abbas.'

'Money-laundering and possible links to terrorist cells in Mumbai,' Rohit completed impatiently. 'We have an interest in him too. And we wouldn't want him disrupted at present for operational reasons. As for the rest of them, you couldn't find a more conservative, introverted, financially motivated and profoundly worldly bunch. Anyway, she's not even a practising Muslim. She converted for her wedding and our records show she never reverted when she divorced. The only community we have her down as belonging to is an irresponsible bunch of female writers and broadcasters known collectively as the Mumbai Clitoratti.'

Gord couldn't resist a furtive chuckle. Tim smirked.

'If this Dhar woman is such a pain in the rear end, why are your lot so concerned about her?' asked Tim. 'She's not even one of your citizens.'

Rohit smiled. 'Maybe because we have an affection for the rebel. Especially when they are entertaining and somewhat larger than life. And that's one count Taz Dhar never falls short on.'

'You sound like a fan.'

'Oh, I am.'

'As, of course, was the late owner of the clothes our man was wearing when he embarked on the big step to his next life.'

'The dead Indian businessman?' said Gord. 'Yes, I'd forgotten about him. You know who he was, Superintendent Shastri?'

'Oh yes,' said Rohit, smugly. 'It's not our policy to let one of our citizens disappear overseas without us knowing what happened.'

'Nor ours, Superintendent Shastri,' said Tim, 'believe me'.

The door opened. Dave re-entered. 'Let's talk,' said Dave. 'I've asked WPC Sitaram to join us. I think you'll want to hear what she has to say.'

∾

'Tasneem Dharwalla, better known as Taz Dhar, used to be on Wiltshire Radio, back in the mid-Nineties. She was a talk show host,' began Anu. The four men sat in silence: concentration, polite smiles, watching her carefully. Rohit Shastri looked her up and down, checking her out unashamedly, as only an Indian man can. She could guess what he was clocking. Thin.

Hair shorn, as though it were an irrelevancy, no make-up. Breasts small. Good complexion, at least a hell of a lot better than his. She returned his scrutiny with a simple stare in the hope of putting his vulnerable masculinity under threat. It usually worked for her, and it did again now. He looked away.

Mid-thirties, she guessed. Not bad looking but a bit too soft around the edges. Full, pursed lips gave him a permanently petulant look. His hair was parted in the middle and swept back. Carefully. So maybe we're thinning on top and a bit sensitive to the fact? He wore a rakhi thread, she noticed, faded and thin, and like the others, an open-necked shirt and casual jacket.

'Ms Sitaram?' prompted Gord.

'She was controversial, right from day one,' Anu resumed. 'Clever. Funny. Rude. A very different sort of role model for girls of my generation. Until I was sixteen I went to a club for Asian girls. It was well established by the time I went there. It had been started much earlier: around 1985, following a rape at the local college. A Goan girl, Asian parents, you know the sort of thing. Wouldn't let their daughters out to evening classes, let alone youth clubs, Guides or anything like that. My folks aren't like that. I went for the sports. Anyway, Taz Dhar came to the club. Local celebrity, you see. Handed out the prizes for various things. Bollywood dancing. Gymnastics. I won a cup for trampoline. That's the only time I actually met her before last week, although I'd listened to her talk show plenty of times. And as she got more famous, and then went to India, well, there was local press coverage. The *Evening Advertiser* would do the occasional feature. She was guest of honour the year before last at the Swindon Mela. I was on duty there but didn't see her. I could hear her speech over the PA system. Caused a bit of a stir. People said she was pissed, but I don't think so. Just being herself. I admire her. I always have. So when we went to her mother's house, and saw what some sicko had done to her cat, and how scared she was, well, I wanted to help her.' She paused and looked at Dave, who nodded, almost imperceptibly.

'WPC Sitaram suggested it might be worth finding out a little more about this Armitage Shanks business and I agreed that we should assist Ms Dhar to trace the priest that sent her the letter. As you said earlier, my call, my patch, my decision. Questions?'

Anu sat back, suddenly exhausted, and slowly inhaled. Again she glanced at Dave, who looked bored and indifferent, with profound gratitude. No one seemed inclined to say anything. Then Tim from Euston cleared his throat, paused and looked at Dave. 'May I?'

'Be my guest,' said Dave, airily. 'After all, we're all on the same side.'

Tim turned to Anu. 'Have you seen her or spoken to her since you gave her the priest's address?'

Anu shook her head.

'Do you know where she is now?' Again, negative.

'Has she tried to see the priest again?' asked Denis

'Yes,' smiled Tim. 'Unsuccessfully. He's a busy young man. Called away to a Vatican event of indeterminate duration.'

'So where is she now?'

'Sigint says Addis,' said Tim.

'And again in English?' asked Dave, prompting a smile from Rohit. 'For the benefit of our guests.'

'Signal Intelligence currently places her in Ethiopia. She made a series of calls on her mobile phone from Addis Ababa yesterday. Ms Sitaram?'

'That would make sense.'

'Why?'

'That's where the alleged execution took place.'

'How do you know?' asked Tim.

Anu shrugged. 'Taz Dhar must have told me.'

'That's interesting. You see, she didn't know that before she spoke to the priest. Yet you say you haven't spoken to her since then. So I ask you again: how do you know?'

Dave frowned. Not good. Not smart. 'Her ex-husband,' said Anu. 'He told me. Said she asked him to say thanks and to let me know where it happened.'

'That accords with the intercept record,' confirmed Gord. He looked to Tim. 'And we know what she was doing in Germany?'

Tim nodded.

Gord was clearly not satisfied. With a sniff of irritation, he continued, 'Where she went, who she spoke to, what about?'

Tim gave him a long stare. 'It's done.'

'Well, we haven't seen it.'

'No need. It's contained. Dealt with.'

Stand-off. Silence. Then Gord turned to Anu Sitaram. 'You know, Anu, Ms Dhar is not only causing us a great deal of worry, and the British taxpayer considerable expense, she may also be placing herself in considerable danger. And as this situation progresses, she may have to struggle to distinguish between friends and foes. None of us want to see any harm come to her. Least of all you, I imagine. So, in the words of the late, lamented Vladimir Illyich Lenin, What Is To Be Done?'

8

Taz Dhar stood on the balcony of the Ras Amba Hotel, wrapped in two shawls, chilled still, but luxuriating in the night scents of the city—coffee, incense, wood smoke and charcoal—and feeling every inch a traveller. How could she ever have doubted this was what she should be doing? God! If she'd realized investigative reporting was like this, she'd have deep-sixed studio work years earlier.

She had been turned away from the Hilton down in the heart of the city, which was full of aid workers and World Bank review teams, and from the obscenely opulent Sheraton, a floodlit oasis of indulgence besieged by dismal shanties, which was not taking bookings either. But this frustration had turned out to be a blessing as neither hotel had anything approaching the charm of the tiny, cheap little Ras Amba, clinging to the side of a steep hill and offering a glimmering panorama of Addis Ababa, ice-bright through thin air by night. Thin indeed: on her arrival in this, one of the highest capital cities in the world, Taz had found herself gasping and dizzied by the exertion of simply picking up a bag that had seemed a very great deal lighter when she had checked it in nine hours earlier. Frightening, until she realized that this was nothing more than the effect of functioning 8,000 feet up on a pair of lungs that hit peak performance on the humid fug at sea level in central Mumbai.

High though the city itself might be, the skyline of Addis was surprising low. Scarcely any buildings rose up more than two floors. Most were single-storey, squatting low beneath red-rusted or newly galvanized tin roofs, scattered haphazardly, like a deck of cards tossed across a lumpy bedspread of browns and greens. The absence of tall structures made the night sky seem abnormally vast, and the resulting lack of polluting illumination meant that the sky was chock-full of stars, save where distant hills rose up beyond the airport three or four miles out at Bole on the other side of the city. Yet the night was so clear, and the uninterrupted view so wide, she could watch, as though it were all happening in miniature, silent aircraft approach, land and taxi to a halt before the new glass and metal lightbox of a terminal.

She sipped at a Harar Beer, and thought the image (which for no good reason she felt should be captured in monochrome) would be completed if only a cigarette was held elegantly to the side of her face as she contemplated her next step. That would fit with her new persona: the investigator, alone, on a balcony overlooking a city in Africa. The night hawk on its high perch, watching for the movement that would simultaneously reveal and condemn her prey. Unfortunately, she couldn't abide the smoke, which made her sneeze, and the smell and the sheer bloody grubbiness of the whole business. The legacy of too many mornings-after, retching as she had bundled the previous night's reeking party clothes into laundry bags. And if she had any doubt about that, she had been forcibly reminded of the fact since her arrival. Shame, really. Still...

The Ras Amba sat in pretty gardens of narrow, sharply stepped terraces, carefully watered, regularly clipped, interminably swept. For the Ras Amba, though cheap and basic, was not short of labour. Her room, one of a mere dozen or so identical dark cells on three short floors, was sparsely furnished and poorly lit, dominated by a low, heavy ceiling. The sheets on the bed were musty and cold. The threadbare carpet damp. The towels in the bathroom, where loose taps finally emitted, after a guilty ten minutes of watching water gurgle slowly down constricted drains, a weak stream of lukewarm water, were worn thin and edged in tattered threads. Food was basic and the choice limited, but oh, that view, and the simple sense of homeliness that no amount of detailed planning, franchised staff development packages and expensive design can give a hotel, more than compensated for these shortcomings.

It was a contact of SK's who had recommended the Ras to her. There were other, better hotels, more central, better appointed, even with the Hilton and Sheraton out of the equation, but this one was a favourite of his, and she was grateful to him, if for little else, for his choice.

His name was Vijaya Rama Rao, a professor of

psychometrics in the department of psychology at Addis Ababa University. A chain-smoking, edgy, serious man. Polite, distant, and pathologically uninterested in her reasons for being there. He made it very clear when she rang him, tired and turned away from the lobby of the Sheraton, that he was helping her only because SK was an old friend. On meeting him at the Ras Amba, to which he had directed her taxi driver in crisp Amharic over her mobile phone, she found that very easy to believe: of an age, and with similar exaggerated eccentricities, Rama Rao and her (should she say ex-?) boss may inhabit very different worlds on separate continents but still had a great deal in common. Both hid their intelligence behind a façade of other-worldliness, yet each clung ruthlessly to the cutting edge of their chosen professions. For Addis Ababa University, although an under-funded institution in a desperately poor country, punched well above its weight academically, and, as Rama Rao ensured she was aware, his personal publishing record and citation rate stacked up respectably against anyone in the second-tier institutions in India and more than a few of those tenured to the leading universities worldwide. He would answer her questions, find her accommodation, a driver and car, but had no wish to know anything about what she was doing, thank you, and wanted that made abundantly clear to anyone and everyone she might meet. A long tradition of Indians lecturing and teaching in Ethiopia there may be, but these were not good times to come to the attention of the authorities in Addis University, which could boast an even longer tradition of student dissent and political unrest and was thus the subject of relentless scrutiny from the security services.

Not a good time to be asking unfortunate questions either: eighteen months on from a bitterly disputed election, bombs going off daily in buses and markets, hundreds of people rounded up and held on charges of treason, deaths at the hands of the police in demonstrations and in custody. No, not a good time at all. That's what he said, but it was a description Taz found hard to reconcile with the reserved dignity and quiet kindness with which she had been met since her arrival. Addis felt to her, she told Rama Rao, far safer than the centre of London, which prompted the first smile she had witnessed cross his thin face, but it was not a pleasant thing to see.

'Ethiopia,' he had assured her more than once, 'is different. Different from anywhere else you have ever been, different from what it may seem to you to be, different from what anyone will tell you it is. Here, everyone has a secret. No one answers a question without thinking through the implications of the answer they give. Anyone could be an informer. There's stern authority here, and there's raw power, but only very rarely will you find they reside in the same place, or are exercised by the same people. That's the way it's always been here. The faces may change, and the names of the parties, but nothing shifts, down in the political permafrost that envelops this country.'

'And you have your position to consider,' Taz added.

'Yes, I do. And the disapproving tone of your voice is not lost on me. I also have an Oromo wife, and two children whom I want to see survive to be something more than Ferangi-fathered members of an unempowered and alienated people.'

The morning after her arrival, she visited the British Embassy, a vast estate with its own pub, clinic, stables and extensive rides in glorious gardens. Yes, they recalled the strange priest and his story. No, they couldn't comment other than to remind her that the alleged execution, even supposing it took place, and that was a fact about which there appeared to be significant doubt, was a) an extra-judicial killing, b) of an Ethiopian citizen with no links to the UK and c) already under investigation by the appropriate authorities. No, they couldn't tell her who those authorities were.

They could however, and did, hand her a printout of the UK Foreign and Commonwealth Office Travel Advice for Ethiopia, which sternly reminded her of the need for extreme caution at all times and, when she mentioned where the priest had said the execution had taken place, pointed out the recommendation not to travel anywhere near the Somali border, adding that, should she choose to ignore that advice, she would find that her travel insurance would automatically be invalidated. It was only then it occurred to her that she didn't actually have travel insurance.

Making a mental note to ring SK to check she was covered on the channel's corporate scheme, she thanked them and asked for the address of the local chapter of Amnesty International. She was not terribly surprised to learn that there wasn't one. Instead she was given a directory of local human rights NGOs. She asked instead for directions to the CAFOD office and was told its main partner in Ethiopia was the rather ambitiously named World Organization for Freedom, Democracy and Justice. She decided that would do for a start, and left.

As instructed, the officials she had met promptly cleared their diaries for the next hour the moment the heavy metal gates slammed closed behind her departing car, drafted and e-mailed individual reports of their discussions with her to London, and then returned to more routine matters, safe behind the high stone walls of their compound, and within the comfortable assurance of their quietly professional patriotism.

∾

'She's just checked in at the Embassy,' said Gord, studying the screen of his mobile. 'Headed now for some NGO.'

'Still in Addis?' asked Tim from Euston, exchanging a glance with Gord. Gord nodded.

'As long as she stays in Addis this is containable,' said Tim, as though thinking aloud. 'She's safe as long as she stays there.'

Anu Sitaram opened her mouth to speak, but paused and looked toward Dave Bignall, who shook his head ever so slightly. Silence.

'Well, Anu. What is to be done?' repeated Gord. 'You say you like Ms Dharwalla and you have already persuaded Mr Bignall here to go far out on a limb to help her, but she's getting into ever more risky situations. We can't continue to monitor her erratic wanderings around the world like this. It's too costly and it's too dangerous. On the other hand, Muslim or not, she has yet to break any laws, so we can't stop her doing what she's doing. Would you like to help us bring her home and make her safe, and in the process, redeem your little error of judgement?'

'Of course I would,' Anu assured them. 'But I think you're underestimating her determination and her strength. Nothing will make her stop until she finds out who this man Armitage Shanks was.'

'Then she's going to be looking for a very long time,' sighed Gord.

Rohit held up his hand, his eyes not leaving Anu. 'I agree with Ms Sitaram's assessment of the situation. Taz Dhar isn't going to stop, and she needs to be watched. I think we may be able to help one another after all.' He turned to Gord, and seemed to be speaking only to him. 'Would that be of interest?'

'Carry on,' said Gord.

'Why not let us handle Taz Dhar in Addis? Don't forget we already have legitimate interest there over our deceased compatriot. Then, as soon as we get the subject back to the UK, she's all yours again.'

'I think that might be a mistake,' warned Tim.

'Freedom is not worth having if it does not include the freedom to make mistakes,' observed Rohit.

'Lenin?' asked Dave.

'Gandhi,' said Rohit.

❧

Ethiopia is different. That's what Rama Rao had drummed into her. One of the many ways this was evidenced was by the fact that jobs with NGOs, the preserve of the passionate enthusiast and the worthy volunteer elsewhere were, in Ethiopia, among the best paid and most well resourced in the country. Accordingly, the World Organization for Freedom, Democracy and Justice, which had its offices in a converted bungalow in a suburb of Addis, sat behind guarded gates, in a well-tended compound dominated by three gleaming four-by-fours with the organization's name and logo—five hands reaching up for the scales of justice superimposed on a globe—on their doors, above smaller print which declared the vehicles a gift of the people of the European Union. In good works as in any other sector of human activity, success breeds success and achievement stimulates investment. And the World Organization for Freedom, Democracy and Justice, or WOFDAJ, was universally lauded as a success story. Founded four years earlier by a full member of the ruling party, with close links to a number of ministers, WOFDAJ was perfectly placed to lever sizeable development partner funds. And that was because it sat sufficiently distant from government to allow donors to say with conviction that they were not supporting the regime, whilst being close enough to mobilize political power and state resources in support of its aims. What those aims were remained vague in the extreme. Its few critics dismissed WOFDAJ and its charismatic leader, Ato Mesfin, as little more than slick chancers, who would enthusiastically embrace any cause that came with dollars, euros or any other internationally negotiable currency attached to it. Certainly, their portfolio of projects and funders listed in the glossy annual report that Taz studied as she sat in the reception area that would have not seemed out of place in a lawyer's office in London or Delhi, could most generously be described as eclectic. Everything from literacy classes for street children in Bahir Dar to food security strategy consultations in the Afar region, courtesy of money from a dozen bilateral donors, the World Bank, six German Stiftungs and of course, the European Union and CAFOD.

Ato Mesfin, Taz had been told by a slender and stunningly beautiful young woman with tightly braided hair and a gossamer thin shawl, stark white in raw cotton, draped elegantly around her shoulders, was not available. One of the programme officers may be able to see her if she wouldn't mind waiting. Would she care for tea or coffee?

The programme officer was a sharply suited thirty-something with a Canadian accent and a smile of such charm and warmth that Taz found herself beaming down at him, for she was a good head taller than him. He introduced himself as Ato Haile, asked the inevitable questions about whether this was her first visit, how she found things, where she was staying, and oh, and would she like another cup of coffee? His smile faded and he grew progressively more grave and uncomfortable as she began to explain what she was doing in Ethiopia, and he glanced around nervously as she spoke. He suddenly interrupted her, suggesting they go out to get coffee, despite the fact that the place seemed to be awash with the stuff. He led her, in a flurry of earnest small talk, the sole purpose of which seemed to be to ensure that she could not say anything more in the building. They went back through the reception, out of the gate and across the rutted and dusty road to a small hut with battered metal tables and chairs around it. He ordered 'Buna' for both of them and gave a sibilant hiss, with the hint of an 'r' toward the end, signifying acknowledgement, acceptance, agreement or conclusion to confirm the order. The Amharic equivalent of the Indian head roll, the ubiquitous 'OK'. Only after their coffee arrived, treacle-thick and highly aromatic in tiny chipped cups, did he relax and ask Taz what she wanted from him.

'I met a priest who was working out here on a CAFOD project...'

'Father Thomas?' asked Ato Haile. 'Red hair, kind heart, awful accent?'

Taz laughed. 'That's him.'

'How is he?'

'Fine, I think. He's now some kind of counsellor at a retreat for failed priests.'

Ato Haile grinned. 'I should think that would suit him very well. Better than what he came out here to do. We handled the logistics for the project he was on. I met him several times. Before and... Well, things didn't turn out well. Did he tell you what he was doing?'

'Something about legal rights and entitlements?'

'That's right. A gender empowerment initiative. Funded by CAFOD and the Japanese. There're a number of things about the Somali region that are...'

'Different?'

'You bet! The people are semi-nomadic, most of the men are addicted to *khat*, and are stoned stupid after 10 A.M. Many people live on smuggling across the border from Somalia. You want a refrigerator or a new microwave? Go to Jijiga and you'll find the best of white goods stacked up under armed guard next to rows of starving people waiting outside the US Consulate for the daily food handouts. There are all sorts of tribal and ethnic struggles going on, and as in a number of other areas here, a process called marriage by abduction. When a young suitor takes a shine to a maid but can't afford the bride price, he and maybe a friend or two kidnap her, rape her, then return her to her family with a renewed proposal for marriage. Of course, she's now damaged goods: forget the bride price now, Daddy is only too happy to accept any offer. That's how it usually works. Sometimes things go wrong. That's what had happened when Father Thomas was out there. A girl about fourteen. Stabbed because she put up too much of a struggle. Then there was this man they say was hanged in Jijiga Jail...'

'Armitage Shanks?'

'Yes. Odd name. Especially for an Ethiopian, wouldn't you think?'

'Father Thomas said he sounded English.'

Ato Haile smiled. 'Close your eyes and listen to my voice: do I sound like an Ethiopian? When I talk over the phone people assume I'm an American or Canadian. This man could have been one of us, but the name...'

'It's a toilet and bath manufacturer,' said Taz.

'I know. I looked it up on the Internet. It's also the name of a 1980s Punk Band and a pub football team in England, the title of an on-line comic and of a song by a band called Green Day. It's also a pseudonym of choice among bloggers and people who wish to remain anonymous on those sites which enable you to find long-lost friends. There are hundreds of Armitage Shanks out there, but none of them, other than the bath company, are really called that, or I assume, expect anyone else to believe that that is their real name. So he could have been an Ethiopian who studied in the UK, and was up to something illegal under the alias Armitage Shanks. Especially in the Somali region. Who knows, he might even have been smuggling porcelain with the name Armitage Shanks on it. Make sense?'

Taz thought for a while: although Ato Haile's analysis sounded thoroughly rehearsed, especially for someone who supposedly hadn't actually been expecting her, she had to admit it also sounded depressingly reasonable. But it didn't fit with the content of the letter, and what about the picture from Hugo Ruhl's apartment? She didn't actually know which one of the men pictured was the man who had written to her: Ruhl had looked toward the montage, but could he have been looking at another image? There were plenty of dark-skinned men in the other pictures. There were also plenty of Ethiopians who were of such a fair complexion they could easily be mistaken for a tanned European. Could one of the men grouped around Ruhl in the picture have been Ethiopian? Maybe...

'So they hanged him? This smuggler, or whatever he was.'

'That's what the complaint says. Personally, I don't think they did.'

'Why?'

'Have you ever been to Jijiga prison? No, of course you haven't. Well, I have. Several times. It's the only prison in the entire region. A tiny place, designed by the British or the Italians or whoever had decided they were responsible for peacekeeping in that area about a century ago. It's a single-storey building around a central courtyard. Looks more like a small stockade in a cowboy film, with guards walking the walls looking down onto the prisoners. It was designed for around sixty convicts to be held in conditions colonial administrators considered adequate for native criminals at the end of the nineteenth century.'

'Which would have included a place of execution?'

'Probably. But that was a hundred years ago. Now, there are over 200 prisoners in there. Most of them sleep in rows out in the open: convicted killers stretched out side by side with juveniles on remand and violent lunatics—there's no asylum, you see. There's massive overcrowding and no privacy. Nowhere to erect a gallows, and I can promise you, the last time I was there, nowhere high enough to set up a beam and accommodate a drop. Look, this is one of the things we do: human rights and custody care, funded by USAID. We know what to look for. We can tell when and where extra-judicial executions are being carried out, and there are two things I can tell you: one, whoever this man was, he did not die in Jijiga prison. Two, you do not carry out extra-judicial executions by hanging when you have a small armoury of AK 47s, piles of ammunition and an entire desert to dispose of the remains in.'

'So it simply didn't happen?'

'If I had to bet, I'd say there was this man in Jijiga prison but I know it was not under that name, because when Father Thomas told us what had happened we asked a few friends in the Prisons Commission. This man, I suspect, *did* genuinely think he was being taken out to be killed there and then, and that's what he told the good Father. But I think there would be more talk about it if it had really happened. I think the official report was only created because they knew the foreign priest had somehow been dragged into whatever was going on and would raise the issue, and they needed to be able to show it was being dealt with.'

'But what about the soldiers, or policemen, or whoever they were who fetched Father Thomas in the first place? They obviously thought something was happening. That an execution was about to take place.'

Ato Haile shrugged. 'Who knows? Maybe they were trying to scare their prisoner into confessing to something. Maybe they thought the sight of a real live foreign priest would finally convince him he was going to die. Maybe they really did kill him, although if they were going to, I don't think they would have advertised it quite so spectacularly. Whatever the reason, no one has been able to find one of these soldiers to interview, or even identify where they were from.'

'And Jijiga is the only prison in that area?'

'Where did Father Thomas say they took him?'

'To a prison. That's all.'

'Then it had to be Jijiga.'

∾

It was decided. Tim from Euston registered his grave reservations but in the absence of any other suggestions, Gord concluded the tone of the meeting was to agree to Rohit Shastri's proposal. They broke up shortly after, the others to head back to their respective offices or homes, leaving Dave, Anu and Rohit to talk through precisely how the newly-agreed joint operation would proceed.

'I have to tell you, I know bugger-all about Ethiopia,' grumbled Dave as he checked the flasks for the last dregs of coffee. 'Or India, come to that. My good lady wants us to go there when I retire, but with my dicky tummy, I'm not so sure...'

'You'd be very welcome, Sir. Come and visit us anytime,' Rohit assured him with a politeness so excessive Dave suspected he was taking the piss. He treated Rohit to a jaundiced stare through narrowed eyes: he was not going to tolerate being mocked in front of the newest recruit to his team, no matter who this geezer was, but the disarming smile on Rohit's face gave him pause.

'Yes, well...' he muttered uncertainly, giving Rohit the benefit of the doubt that he, like Anu, was simply trying too hard.

'Me neither, Guv,' offered Anu, keen to hear how it sounded, and won herself a paternal grin from her new boss. 'Never been further south than Aya Napa, Guv.'

'Don't overdo it, Sitaram,' said Dave. 'No one likes a lick-arse.'

'Sorry, Guv.'

∽

'This is a massive fucking error of judgement,' fumed Tim as he and Gord strode briskly back up Kennington Lane toward the river.

'I'm not so sure,' said Gord. 'We have Sitaram tied in nicely. One potential problem defused. And I'd welcome some alternative suggestions. I didn't hear many at the meeting.'

'I have several, but you could hardly expect me to explore them in the presence of the Old Bill and his Indian Oppo, could you?'

'I don't see either of them about now, Tim,' said Gord irritably, breaking into a sweat as he struggled to match the pace his furious colleague was setting. 'They are doing their jobs: planning their operation to save Ms Dharwalla, so while they and she are safely engaged elsewhere, why don't you follow their laudable example and do yours? Feel free, speak away.'

'We have an idea.'

Gord sighed. 'No you don't. An idea in an organization is like a virus in a network. Especially in one like yours. You have a policy recommendation. Which we would be willing to hear. But perhaps you and your psychotic chums could try and make it rather less costly and somewhat more risk-neutral than the last few, eh?'

9

Taz found it difficult to sleep in the Ras Amba. It was not the inadequacies of the hotel; she was quickly reconciled to its limitations and idiosyncrasies, and it was in an under-populated district of a quiet city. But even here the still of each night would be regularly ripped apart by the sudden roar of a heavy vehicle, climbing hard through low gears. Then there was the cry of the muezzin, bells tolling at churches without number and the howls and barks of a pack of dogs that would work themselves up to a frenzied crescendo and, as though strictly orchestrated, abruptly halt, leaving the subsequent silence charged and every bit as disturbing as the preceding din had been.

There was a steady churn of Ethiopian guests at the Ras Amba, few of whom stayed more than a night. Local courting couples would drift in too, to sip coffee and soft drinks in tense silence in the bar or on the terrace. There were several Europeans staying in the hotel: foreign aid workers from charities and NGOs which paid bottom-dollar subsistence, and three German couples who'd come to adopt Ethiopian babies. Taz said hello to them at breakfast and again in the bar in the evening, and beamed dutifully at warily held infants, but otherwise had little to do with them.

She had been in Ethiopia for more than a week and, to be frank, wasn't sure quite what to do next. She had travelled out to Jijiga, against all advice, and found it every bit as bleak and intimidating as Ato Haile had warned her it would be. At every dusty street corner, men lay on thin mats and gazed, dull-eyed and vacant, into space, a bunch of *khat* and a cheap plastic flask at their side. Where two or three gathered, no conversation took place. No smiles, or any other form of acknowledgement. Only the same eternal stare. She had walked past the prison, and confirmed for herself the truth of Ato Haile's account: No one could be killed there without a hell of a lot of other people knowing about it.

In the grim hotel in which she had lodged, the only other guests were three Korean contractors and a tall, sombre man in a wide-lapelled blue suit who held court daily in the sparsely furnished restaurant at lunchtime. At midday, every day, he would sit down alone at the centre of a long table covered with a sticky plastic sheet, remove his jacket and heave off the khaki canvas shoulder holster and the heavy pistol it cradled. With great care, he would drape the jacket over the back of his chair, lay the holster and gun on the table in front of him and sit, in silence, and wait. At intervals, other men would arrive, nod, and follow the same ritual. Within an hour, the table was groaning under the weight of steaming mounds of thick pasta, bowls of oily sauces, fat hanks of roast mutton, and a dozen holstered guns, as the diners ate in silence. Then, one after another, they would rise, nod, pick up their weapons, and leave. Not a word spoken. By 1.45, only the host remained, presiding over a deserted table still laden with food. Outside, the queues for free handouts grew.

Taz was surprised how much like a homecoming it was to return to the Ras Amba after Jijiga. Everyone seemed genuinely pleased to see her back, and each of the staff who asked her about her trip laughed when she described her impressions of the Somali region, and assured her the rest of Ethiopia was, well, different.

Ram Rao came to check she had got back safely, studiously asked no questions about what she had seen, done or learnt, told her he would be unavailable for the next week, and left her with a request to ring SK. A call, for some reason she couldn't explain, she was reluctant to make. Mark had phoned every other day, but she hadn't returned his calls either. She was progressively, consciously and willingly giving way to a profound lassitude, a sense of comfortably drifting that she thought should probably be a cause for concern but out of which she had no desire to snap herself. She couldn't even be bothered to eat out, and settled for the hard, steamed vegetables, fried fish and leathery steak that dominated the menu in the deserted restaurant. Addis, she had been told, was home to one of the best Italian restaurants in the world, just a ten-minute taxi journey away, but she stayed where she was, sipped her drink, studied the limited menu and settled, settled. She had eased comfortably back into the Ras Amba, learning, she wasn't quite sure how, through some form of osmosis she assumed, the first names of the reception, restaurant and bar staff, the room cleaners, and the security guards, big men with proud moustaches, in khaki greatcoats and green peaked hats who stamped to attention and saluted her briskly every time they saw her. The manager, a broad-shouldered man in a leather jacket, with a pencil moustache and a gold tooth, greeted her delightedly every morning, shaking her hand enthusiastically and asking her how she was. She had a return flight booked for the next Saturday, four days hence, but as the date of her planned departure grew nearer, she thought maybe she would stay on for another week. Not because she could think of anything else much she should be doing in Addis, but because she could think even less of anything else she should be doing elsewhere, and if she were being honest with herself, which she wasn't inclined to be just then, the Ras Amba was becoming a safe haven from the harsh realities of failed relationships, lost jobs and frustrated assignments that would insist on being confronted whether she returned to the UK or headed straight back to India.

The fifth night after her return from Jijiga, as she sipped at her drink and debated if she could work her way through another congealing plate of Spaghetti Bolognese, or whether she should settle for the soup, the only other customer in the restaurant, an Indian in his early forties, persistently tried to catch her eye, and smiled as though he wanted to pick her up. At first, she was simply amazed. Since returning to the UK, and lapsing into her ponderous post-marital relationship with Mark, she had ceased to think of herself as a single woman, and had become increasingly indifferent to her appearance. In the last few days she had reached levels of slovenliness which would have caused fellow members of the Mumbai Clittorati to shake their heads sadly and look up the number of a good detox and spa. Having studiously avoided his eye, she had glanced up as a shadow fell over her, surprised and momentarily confused, to find him smiling down at her. He wasn't bad looking, she acknowledged. Smartly dressed, and a man who moved easy. He wore a polo shirt, and fawn trousers, above the waistline of which there was the paunch of a man who, as Ma would say, liked his food. He held himself erect, and trod lightly, so that he made little sound as he moved. His hair was still wet at the ends from the shower. He was freshly shaved too and smelt of wholesome things. Sandalwood and peppermint. She tried to imagine how she must look to him; grimy, she suspected. Sweat-stained, crumpled and more than a little rough around the edges. She had meant to wash her hair when she had showered at midday, but had simply let the tepid water run through it and left the shampoo unopened. She wasn't quite sure why. However as a result, her hair hung lank and straight. She had not put on any make-up, and, she couldn't remember when she had last shaved her legs. She wore the same t-shirt she had the day before and the day before that.

She frowned up at him; you must be desperate, mate, she thought.

'May I sit..?' he asked, leaving the question hanging in the air.

She shrugged. 'It's a free country,' she said.

He placed his glass carefully next to hers. 'Is it? Maybe a heavily mortgaged country might be more on the button.'

What was it about this place that seemed to make everyone a philosopher? And of a profoundly gloomy school too. He was talking bollocks, but just listening to the sound of his voice, the accent, the intonation and the confidence made Taz suddenly feel a massive loneliness, and deep nostalgia for Mumbai. A heartfelt longing for Indian company. She was ashamed of herself as soon as she felt it. Surely she was more of a citizen of the world than to be reduced to tears by an Indian voice after only... what?.. a couple of weeks away? Three? But at that very moment just such a feeling threatened to overwhelm her.

The only people she had spoken to in the last few days were Rama Rao, and the hotel staff. And Rama Rao, twenty years a resident in Addis, was Indian in name only. No one, not even Rama Rao, if she were to be honest, had been unpleasant to her, and even his prickliness would be well inside manageable elsewhere, but the foreignness, the effort to catch meaning amid strange intonations, and the otherness of the sights, sounds and smells pierced in and weighed down on her—she had never before, she realized with some surprise, spent time alone anywhere other than the UK or India. God, what was she thinking? Some globe-trotting news hound! Her attempts at being a reporter in Africa were little more than minor excursions out of the hotel into a very sanitized Africa— other than her couple of days in Jijiga. A bland, neutral, packaged Africa. In a capital city laid out for foreigners to access with ease. But still, she had to confess, she found Africa too intimidatingly dark.

'Have you eaten?' she asked, suddenly.

Surprise and pleasure dragged an attractive smile across his face. He shook his head.

'Neither have I. But this is my third whisky and soda. If I

don't have something to eat soon I'm going to lose interest in eating, and then I'll feel dreadful all night. How long have you been staying in this hotel?'

'A week. Just under actually.'

'Do you eat here every night?'

'Not often. Mostly, I eat at Castelli's, or Blue Top. If I eat here, it's room service.'

'I eat in the restaurant every night. I've had everything on the menu except the pasta and cheese thing. I'm still trying to pluck up the courage to attempt that. Pathetic, isn't it? Do you want to eat with me?'

'I would be honoured,' said the Indian, suddenly formal.

Taz sighed. 'Do you think you know who I am?'

He shook his head.

'Good. In that case stop being so fucking prim. What are you drinking?'

'Beer.'

'Why did you come over to talk to me?'

'Because you are on your own. And so am I. I thought...'

'Interesting, isn't it, that two people who look like us automatically communicate in English. I mean, it's OK for me. It's my first language. Well, my only language, really. I don't speak anything else, other than a smattering of poor Gujarati, you see. And schoolgirl French. Do you speak Gujarati?'

The Indian smiled. 'A bit. Not very much.'

'Would you sooner we had this conversation in Gujarati? It would give you a profound advantage over me. Mine is shit. So I couldn't be clever at your expense. That would be good, wouldn't it? What are you drinking? Oh, you told me, didn't you?'

The Indian leaned forward, took his empty glass and turned it upside down on her table. 'I'm not drinking anything, now. I came to your table, because I am bored of eating alone. I'm an Indian; communal dining is hard-wired into our DNA.

I want someone to talk to while I'm eating, but someone who's not going to talk to me about management information systems. That's the business I'm in, you see? Management information systems. They're interesting, very interesting. But not all the time, especially not at mealtime. Tonight, I saw you sitting here, and I thought, why don't I go and see if we could eat together. Here, or outside. On the terrace. We could talk about anything.' He smiled, 'Anything other than management information systems, that is. We could even brave the terrifying pasta and cheese thing.'

Taz nodded. 'What's your name? No, don't tell me. I'm remarkably good with names. Dilip? Krishna?'

The man laughed, lightly. 'Kirk. My mother saw her first episode of *Star Trek* when she was expecting me. Brought on the labour, apparently. So Kirk it had to be. Funny, isn't it?'

Taz shook her head, emphatically. 'No. It's not funny. Why do parents do things like that? Don't you hate explaining to everybody why you're called that?'

The man called Kirk shrugged, and smiled. 'When I was a kid, yes. Everyone laughed at me, teased me. Now, it's interesting. When you're young, all you want to do is fit in. Then, when you are an adolescent, you want to be different. Then, when you reach adulthood, you want to be just like everyone else, but perhaps just a little bit more so. Married, but to the most pretty wife. Cleverer children. Higher salary, larger house, newer car. Then, as you get older, again, you want to be different. I'm in that stage, I want to be an interesting individual again, so, I'm grateful my mother called me Kirk. I like being Kirk. And you?'

Taz frowned and shook her head. 'I don't feel strongly about it one way or the other.'

Kirk tried to hold back a smile, but it tore his face into a laugh which closed his eyes, and creased his brow. 'Not what do you think of my name! What's yours?'

Taz began to laugh too. 'Sorry. Tasneem. That's what I was named. Then I got a job. My name was too long. So I became Taz. Stupid, too, huh?'

'You see, already we have so much in common! Will you have dinner with me?'

'No. Because you're too good looking, and you're too nice and I'm too pissed. If I have dinner with you, I'm gonna want to spend the evening with you. If I spend the evening with you, I'm going to spend the night with you. If I spend the night with you, I've got to wake up with you tomorrow and I find it difficult enough waking up with myself. Do I shock you? No? Oh well. I'll take a drink with you, my oddly named new friend Kirk. But we'll eat at separate tables. We can have coffee together afterwards, and maybe even a brandy or two. But I don't want to get too close to you, because I like you already, and I've already got too much, or too little, in my life right now to be able to deal with any further clutter. Does that make any sense at all?'

Kirk slipped his left hand into his shirt pocket. He leaned forward, and placed a photograph on the table in front of her. 'My wife, to whom I have been married for thirteen years, and whom I love dearly. We have two sons. Who, incidentally, have proper, sensible names. I can feel my hand reaching for my wallet to show you their photograph as I speak. I don't want anything other than something or someone to help me pass a long evening far from home. Nothing more, nothing less. Except that I have told you my name, and why I am here. You have to do the same.'

'I told you, my name is Taz, or Tasneem, or something along those lines.'

'And why you are here?'

'That's simple. To find a grave, lay a ghost, and commemorate another lost wanderer's death.'

'Did he have a stupid name too?'

'Yes he did, as a matter of fact. Armitage Shanks.'

'Then we will raise a glass together after our meal, to the spirit of Armitage Shanks: fallen member of the Stupid Names Club.'

∽

Anu Sitaram and Dave Bignall sat in a two-year-old Skoda Octavia in a car park behind a small row of shops in Saffron Waldron, and watched. Both, for different reasons, found what for most of their colleagues was a mind-numbingly dull part of the job a source of unanticipated excitement. As a result, they had chatted volubly and easily from the moment they had collected the car to half an hour earlier, when they ran out of things to say, and an uncomfortable boredom set in.

Anu was excited simply because it was her first time out of uniform and on any kind of detective work. Dave, because he thought stuff like this was a good decade behind him and being out on the street made him feel, if not young, at least considerably less antique.

He'd told her all the war stories: tales of tackling street gangs, and organized crime in the Eighties and Nineties. The big jobs and the bad boys and the stuff that went down and ones that went wrong. Softening, he told her about setting up the meetings with community leaders that stopped his borough sliding into the rioting that defined the summer of 1980. About being the only cop to be invited to attend Id functions and occasional Friday prayers, and the awareness of Islam that had landed him in Special Branch, against his will, preferences and best judgement. About being in charge of policing half of the Mall during Princess Diana's funeral. What to his younger colleagues were the tedious reminiscences of a fossilized boss on countdown to his golden handshake were new, edgy insights into a different world for Anu. She told him about her first raid on a crack house in Park South, the joys of policing the Oxford United-Swindon Town grudge match at the County Ground and the machete-wielding smackhead she had talked down—a bit of recklessness for which she had been put forward for a gallantry award. He nodded, impressed, and responded with a couple of football match horror stories of his own.

They touched lightly on the challenges of being an Asian woman in the police, and moved on. Dave told her about his daughters, and his only son, recently divorced. Anu told him about her Dad and the sports equipment business he worked in. How they had sponsored her to go to various camps for aspiring athletes when she was young.

They lunched in situ—Dave on a Big Mac and a diet Coke, the packaging of which lay balled up on the back seat of the car, and Anu on dried fruit and sunflower seeds from Holland and Barrett. Now that they had run out of things to talk about, they stared in silence at the back door of the largest of the butcher's shops owned by Taz's uncle Yusuf.

'We should have brought a tape,' said Dave.

'It's a CD player, Guv. Shall I put the radio on?'

'Nah.'

'What do you think is going on here? This Armitage Shanks thing. Those seemed some serious guys you were meeting with. '

'No idea, Sitaram,' yawned Dave. 'And frankly I don't really care. I have spent my whole professional life trying to avoid people like them. I hate all this cloak-and-dagger stuff. Bollocks, most of it. Give me a straightforward villain like Yusuf Abbas anytime. At least he and I know which side we're on. Those blokes, they live in a murky world where everything is suspect and everyone is compromised, and they love every moment of it. My concern, and yours too, is to ensure as far as we can the safety of Ms Dhar. That's it.'

Anu smiled. 'Did you ever listen to Taz Dhar when she was on Wiltshire Radio, Guv? Her phone-in programme was from half-past midnight to around four. Music, news, loads of ads, but mainly her. Some of the things she used to say! She was like, fearless.'

'Nah. She was long gone before I moved out to the sticks. Fearless you call her? You may as well say brainless. I've met... what?.. two, maybe three people in my life I think you could call fearless. Two villains and one cop. There were two things they all had in common: no sense of proportion and a violent, messy end.'

'Do you think that's what's going to happen to her?'

Dave shrugged. 'A flask. Next time we do this, CDs and a flask. Tea. Coffee makes me piss. Who knows what's going to happen to her? Right now, that's more the problem of our friend... Superintendent Shastri, isn't it?'

Anu frowned. 'Can I ask you something, Guv?'

'Sure.'

'If I was white, and a bloke, you'd have called me Gunga Din, wouldn't you?'

Dave turned to her, shaking his head sadly. 'Give me some credit, Sitaram. I'm not a complete fucking dinosaur.'

'Sorry, Guv.'

'Actually, I would have called him Imran Khan.'

'He's from Pakistan.'

Dave let his mouth hang loose, in a parody of vacant imbecility. 'Duh! I know that, Siraram. I just wanted you to know that if I did choose to be boorish, inappropriate and crass, I'm perfectly capable of doing it in a sophisticated and multicultural way.'

❧

Taz and the man called Kirk slipped easily into an easy, amiable acquaintance. After their first night of eating at separate tables—dining out in parallel, he had called it—she and Kirk had shared a table at breakfast and in the evening, and thereafter coordinated their mealtimes.

He had clearly been telling the truth when he said he was looking for someone to talk to. He was a voluble and easy companion. He showed her photographs of his home, and his family, and talked about the places he had been. His work seemed to bore him, even though he was a partner in the business, and he was much more keen to talk about what had brought her to Africa and about her life before Mumbai, and in particular about radio phone-ins, a subject with which she was well out of touch, but one by which, apparently, he was fascinated.

Although she told herself it had nothing to do with these light and easy meals with Kirk, she had waxed her legs, started wearing salwar-kameez instead of knee-length shorts and loose t-shirts, and even booked a half-day session with the beautician at the Sheraton Hotel.

She wondered if they would sleep together. He didn't seem particularly keen, just happy to have someone to talk to. She guessed that if he made a move, then they might. It would all depend on the timing, and the moment. She was not particularly troubled, either way. Whatever happened, more important than whether they went to bed together was, for her, the preservation of the Stupid Names Club of three (one deceased). She was starting to get tetchy about her inability to sustain relationships. For that reason, this right, pleasant, easy, almost trivial dining room acquaintance took on a deeper significance. If it happened, it happened. She wasn't looking for anything special. He was pleasant company, she was lonely, and after all, he would be heading back for Delhi in a couple of days. Just the kind of ships-passing-in-the-night type of relationship she needed right now, with no strings, and no commitment longer than could be counted in hours for her to agonize over.

Although a good story-teller, he seemed equally happy to listen to her talk about her interest in Ethiopia. He was a surprisingly good listener. And when the talking faltered, they sat in companionable silence on the terrace of the Ras Amba and watched the world walk by below.

Then, one evening, he looked toward her and said, 'I'm really a problem-solver; my partners are the techies. Big picture: high-level, that's me. That sort of thing. These days the machinery can look after itself, identify its own glitches, and put right most of them itself without the client ever even knowing. And if it can't, it can send a message automatically to system support which will kick in, 24/7. The clever bit comes in matching the capability of the technology to the needs of the customer. Questions about whether technology can do this or that are so last-century: it can do everything. It's no longer about bolt-ons and bespoke add-ins to meet the client's needs, but what facets of the capability they have purchased as the basic package is surplus to requirements. IT now is like a great sheet of cloth, and our job is to be the tailor who designs, cuts and shapes that cloth into a suit, or a dress, or a shirt. The only question now is, what do you want?'

'I thought you said we weren't going to talk about your work?' said Taz, smiling. 'I don't have a problem with it. Sad git though I must be, I'm actually finding it interesting. Talk away to your heart's content, Kirk, but it's your rule.'

Kirk laughed. 'Sorry, sales pitch. What I am trying to say is my work is about listening, analyzing, and reflecting back. That's what I do, and without false modesty, I'm good at it. And those skills are at your disposal, if you want them. You seem to me, if you'll forgive me saying so, stuck. You've come here to find out something, you think you've found out all you can, but you don't know what to do next. Well, I'm here to help. If you want.'

Taz sat on the terrace with her feet up on the low balustrade. It was a cold day, with low cloud and frequent showers. The walls of the houses below had mud splattered to a couple of feet off the ground up their sides, making them look as though they were progressively returning to the earth from which they were made. The city seemed particularly verdant and strangely silent mid-afternoon. The few people about were huddled in shawls, leather jackets or khaki grey coats and carried umbrellas, or long staves. Their heads were swathed in scarves or in shadow under faded baseball caps. Across the road from the Ras Amba, a child lay next to a telegraph pole, legs crossed, his face covered in sacking. Three old men walked past with a herd of goats, barely sparing a glance for the child. They were draped in long shawls, and wore sandals and had skinny, bare legs. They could have been Old Testament shepherds, from a dozen deserts thousands of years earlier.

'I don't know...' She had been only half listening. She found herself mulling on colours and places: an electric tropicana of Mumbai; the sedate greys and gentle pastels of the UK, and the khaki-drab, beige and stark white of Ethiopia.

And then, as if to prove her wrong, four skeletal young men trotted past in bright yellow and green shell suits jogging uphill backward.

Kirk followed her glance. 'What cinema is to India, marathon running is to Ethiopia,' he said. 'The maker of dreams. The escape route by which the poorest can win untold fame and glory.' He paused, then continued, 'Remember: I'm here if I can help.'

His words made her think, uncomfortably, about Sidiq.

'Until the day after tomorrow,' she said, and was surprised at the note of sadness in her voice. She hoped he didn't hear it.

He stood up and stared over the balustrade. 'That kid's moving now,' he said. She hadn't realized he had been monitoring the still child too. 'Didn't I tell you? I'm staying on a few more days. The possibility of another contract...'

ॐ

Yusuf Abbas left his shop at 4.47, and strode briskly across the car park to his six-month-old BMW M6 coupe. He stopped and stared, expressionless, at the heavy white man and slender Asian woman getting out of a car and walking toward him. Inwardly he groaned. They reeked of the law.

'Mr Abbas?' Dave and Anu took out their warrant cards, Yusuf Abbas nodded, and they put them away. 'It's about your niece, Tasneem Dharwallah,' Dave began.

For the fist time, Yusuf Abbas showed some reaction: his eyes widened slightly, and he shook his head. 'Is she...'

'She's fine, Sir, as far as we know,' Anu reassured him. 'It's just that... '

'She's got herself into something risky,' Yusuf Abbas finished for her. 'I know. I told her so myself. We are on the same side on this, believe me.'

'That's a first,' said Dave dryly, recalling his words to Anu. 'So where can we talk? I assume you'd prefer it not to look like this is about those cigarettes which should be in a bonded warehouse outside Harlow but oddly found their way out of your back door half an hour ago.' He put up his hand to stop Yusuf Abbas's denial. 'We were sitting here. We saw it. Your people are getting sloppy. But it's another of your seemingly endless supply of lucky days. Customs may want their fags back, but right now, we've got other fish to fry—or should that be smoke? I'll give them a ring later.'

'Later?'

'Yes, later. How much later depends on how much you can help us with your niece. Now I imagine some of your less socially skilled tobacconists will soon be getting tense about us talking here, and will be looking for the baseball bats and the nail guns, so shall we pop down the M4 for an hour or two?'

Yusuf Abbas nodded once, muttered something that neither of them caught, and followed them to their car.

∾

'What do I know?' began Taz. 'Well, this letter arrived from...'

'Before you start, can I suggest we try this another way?' asked Kirk. 'Who, what, where, when and how. First, who? Who are we talking about?'

'Armitage Shanks.'

'Are you sure? Let's be absolutely precise: what does he say in the letter?'

Taz re-read the first few lines: *'The name is Armitage Shanks, a bad joke at the best of times, which this most certainly isn't. Armitage Shanks. I like good food, bad company and terrible jokes. The name is Armitage Shanks, and tomorrow I'm going to die.* It seems pretty clear to me.'

'Is it?' Kirk wondered. 'Perhaps, let's carry on: what?'

'He's going to die. That's what he says. And for that we have the corroboration of the statement of the priest, who was with him at the end.'

'Well...'

Taz sat forward, nodding. 'I get it. You're going to say he wasn't actually there at the end: okay. So he *thinks* he's going to die. He believes he's going to die, and the priest can confirm that he met a man who was taken out of a cell thinking he was on his way to his execution. Maybe he was, maybe he wasn't, but clearly that's what he firmly believed.'

Kirk smiled: 'Good! So we have this man, the name

Armitage Shanks which may or may not be his, and the fact that he believes he's going to die.'

'Not just die: be killed. Executed.'

'Okay. Where?'

'Jijiga prison.'

'Sure?'

'That's what the official complaint says. Also, everyone agrees that he was in the Somali region. Jijiga is the only prison in the region. It had to be there.'

'Did it? Probably. But we could check that with the priest, couldn't we?'

'The priest's disappeared.'

'Has he?' said Kirk. 'Well, well! Interesting. Back to our man. Where did he come from?'

'Ato Haile says he could have been smuggling across the border.'

'If we really think broadly here, and include the whole world in our purview, he could have come from anywhere, couldn't he? He could have gone anywhere afterwards. All you know for sure is that this man, who wrote the letter to you, was in prison, somewhere in the Somali region, believing he was under sentence of death. When?'

'That everyone agrees on. On 28 March, 2006.'

'Okay. How? Specifically, how did he get there, and if he was killed, how did he die?'

Taz shook her head. Kirk thought for a moment. He glanced up at the sky and watched as buzzards and vultures circled lazily, rising on an urban thermal, then dropping and swooping on one another: killers in casual play. She followed his stare.

'What else is there?' he asked.

'He talks about others. *I was picked up with the others*... He talks about an appeal process, so there must be some paper work involved in that. The clothes of a dead Indian businessman... converting to Islam. The slaughterhouse on Pound Street.'

'Pound Street? I wonder where that is. Could that help?'

Taz shrugged. 'Maybe.'

Kirk smiled down at her. 'Well, that's not too bad, is it? We've got two things to follow up: confirm with the priest if and when he reappears that it was Jijiga prison, and try and found out where Pound Street is, or was. Apart from the priest, the embassy and the guy at WOFDAJ, have you spoken to anyone else? Have you got anything else to go on?'

Taz shook her head.

'Are you sure?' asked Kirk.

His tone made her pause, look up and meet his stare. She had been about to mention Hugo Ruhl and the montage, but suddenly, she felt deeply troubled. Not breaking eye contact, she said, simply, 'No.'

Behind him, up high, from the corner of her eye, Taz saw one of the circling buzzards seem to stutter in its effortless flight, tumble and plummet, dropping like the curse of a vengeful God onto a hapless, clumsy pigeon. A dusting of feathers, and the vultures leisurely rolled over and followed them down.

❧

Anu and Dave, with a sullen Yusuf Abbas among the McDonald's discards on the back seat, drove round the M25 but stopped at the South Mimms Services well short of the junction with the M4. Once they were settled around a table with tea and crisps, and bottled water for Anu, Dave laid out the ground rules: intelligence only, without caution and therefore of no evidential weight. Fair? Yusuf nodded.

'So what's going on?' Dave began.

Yusuf took a sip of tea from the plastic cup, grimaced and asked if he could have Anu's water. As Anu fetched some more, he smiled for the first time. 'Kids, aren't they?' he said sadly. 'Policewoman? She looks like she should still be in school. Even my niece. Older, but still just a kid, really. What do they know, Mr Bignall?'

'About the life we've lived, bugger all. Whether that's a blessing or a curse, who knows? Been a long time, Yusuf?'

'Has indeed, Mr Bignall. I assumed you'd prefer I didn't recognize you when you pulled out your card. Family?'

'Fine. Yours?'

'Growing up. Causing grief and costing money.'

'And your niece? What gives?'

'I'll be straight with you, Mr Bignall. All I know is that Tasneem is chasing after some story, and somebody broke into my sister-in-law's house, and killed Tasneem's cat, to scare her off. Now you and I both know lots of people who would do something like that. But this isn't the first time someone has broken into Najmabehn's house. It happened once, years ago, back in Uganda, and I made bloody sure they knew never to do that again. So I put out the word. Know what I heard? White noise. Deep, scared silence. There's only one mob that has that kind of muscle these days, isn't there Mr Bignall? And I'm not the one who works with them, am I Mr Bignall? You are. So I'm assuming this is all a performance for the little girl there. Cover up, or the hope of a screw? No concern of mine, Mr Bignall. I'll play my part. Just tell me what it is.'

'That's bullshit,' sneered Dave, 'and you know it. This has got fuck all to do with us, except in so far as it affects your niece. You say you don't want anything bad to happen to her? Well, neither do we, nor do the Indian police. We're all doing our bit, why can't you?'

'India's involved?' said Yusuf, quickly. 'Who? CBI?'

Dave realized he'd made a mistake. He must be losing it.

He would never have let a thieving little toerag like Yusuf Abbas rile him into mouthing off in the old days. He felt pathetically glad Anu hadn't been there to see it. He had been enjoying having one last rookie who thought he knew what he was doing. 'Never you mind. Just take my word for it. Everybody wants her safe.'

'Are you sure? Everybody?'

'Do you know different?'

'All I know is that as soon as you open your mouth about this there's a kind of silent screaming that blocks out everything you've got to say, so no one can hear you. Whatever's going on, it's way out of my league. I don't want any part of it, and I told Tasneem she shouldn't either. I told her to go back to Mumbai, and I'd get her job sorted out for her. That's all. Honest.'

Anu returned with the water. Dave sat in silence as Yusuf sipped at it.

'Mr Abbas knows nothing, apparently.'

'You know where Taz is now, Sir?' Anu asked.

'Ethiopia. She was meant to be back a few days ago, but maybe she was delayed.'

'She changed her flight to stay on longer.' She looked at Dave. 'I've just had a call from...' she glanced at Yusuf Abbas, studiously not listening, 'Imran Khan. Now, she's just changed her ticket again. She's coming back tomorrow.'

'*Al hamdo lailah*,' murmured Yusuf Abbas. 'I wish she was going back to India, though.'

'You think she'd be safer there?'

'Yes, I do.'

They offered to drive him back, but Yusuf Abbas said he'd sooner find himself a taxi. After he left, Dave and Anu sat on, in silence.

'I'd like to meet her at the airport, Guv,' said Anu.

Dave shook his head. 'Bad idea. Too public: too much

drama. Let her get home and then go and see her. In fact, leave it for a day or so. I'll pop in first to have a word. We'll ask Uniforms in Swindon to keep an eye on her, okay?'

'Okay, got it,' smiled Anu, enjoying the fact that the reference to Uniforms no longer meant her. 'I wonder if Superintendent Shastri will come back here too.'

'Sitaram, have you done Firearms?'

'Basic and intermediary. I'm waiting for my advanced course. Why?'

'No reason. Just wondered.'

That night, the heaviest storm for more than a decade exploded over Addis. Sheet lightning ripped the sky and shattered the night as almost continuous thunder roared, banged and rolled off the hillsides, shaking the windows in Taz's room and numbing her senses. The air reeked of ozone and tingled with static. The electricity sub-station was hit, taking out the entire sector, and when she looked out, down to where neat terraced gardens had been, thick, muddy gouts of water swirled, burst through irrigation channels and tumbled down the hillside, dissolving borders and sharp edges and sweeping their contents across the road below and into the bloated gutters and overflowing drains and on, down into winding alleyways which had already become glaucous mudslides.

Such apocalyptic grandeur demanded to be witnessed from the terrace, and wrapping herself in a blanket, Taz felt her way in the strobe-lighting out into the corridor and up the stairs. On the terrace, sheltered below an overhanging roof edge from which the rain cascaded, she found the manager. Hunched, sombre, shrunken. Awed as she was by the sheer scale of raging nature. One by one, other members of the night staff joined them, staring up at the sky in grim silence. Of Kirk, there was no sign.

'Good for the crops,' Taz offered. 'Good for the farmers.'

Not taking his eyes from the sky, the manager quietly corrected her. 'It's the wrong rain, at the wrong time. Another ten minutes of this and 4 million more people will starve this year. Ten more minutes will cost people like us a lot of friends and relatives, and people like you a lot of money.'

10

Taz, in spite of her studied indifference at the sight of him, was secretly delighted to see Mark waiting for her among the phalanx of anxious relatives and bored taxi drivers as she emerged from the customs hall in Terminal 3.

He smiled at her, apologetically, and took the handles of her luggage trolley. He had made out a card with her name on, like the ones various drivers were holding up, tracking each new arrival like sunflowers following light, but clearly, at the last minute, his confidence in its humour failed him.

'Take you home, lady?' he asked, hopefully.

She shrugged. 'If you like,' she said, grudgingly. Then, realizing how much she had just sounded like her own mother, she stopped, turned to him, cupped his surprised face in her hands, and kissed him hard.

'Well!' he gasped, as she withdrew from the kiss. 'Welcome home!'

She smiled up at him. 'It's not my home, anymore. And even if it was, it's certainly not ours. But thanks, all the same. It's surprisingly good to feel welcome, anywhere. Let's not make a big deal out of it, but you are actually the only person in the world I wholeheartedly trust right now. So, until I go away again, let's go back to how things were. OK?'

He nodded, enthusiastic.

In the car, he was only too willing to take full responsibility for the poor terms on which they had parted. Just as he had when they had divorced. It was one of the things she liked and hated about him with equal intensity. Hated, because it made him the dispenser of excuse and the layer of blame: sole arbiter of who was right and who was wrong. Liked though, admired even, because it was one of the many generous things about him; something he intended should spare her any regrets, free her of any responsibility. Something he had always elected to do to discourage the negative introspection she had been too prone to sink into when they'd first met.

Given that, why did he still, as he always had, manage to make her feel so bloody guilty? Like they both knew deep down that really everything, from the fall of man to 9/11 via the Holocaust and the Partition of India, was really all her fault, somehow.

He asked how she had got on; she told him about Addis, and Jijiga, and Kirk, who had left for India the same day with nothing more than a quick kiss and a contact number, and Rama Rao.

With a massive pang of guilt, she remembered she had not even told Rama Rao she was leaving. Not that he would care. Well, actually he would. He'd be relieved. But he deserved the courtesy of a thank you and goodbye. If only because he was a friend of SK's. Shit! She hadn't called him either. She sighed. She knew this was how it would be: reality thrusting itself inconveniently into her life, like an uninvited and imperious relative, as soon as she touched down. And that thought made her think of her mother, to whom she also owed several calls. Oh, well. At least she had Mark. Good old reliable, undemanding Mark.

He was full of questions about Ethiopia: he had looked up a load of guff on the internet so he could engage intelligently with her about it. Trying far too hard, as usual, he was just pissing her off, because his knowledge was so much greater than hers. What did she think about debt relief? She didn't. Nor did she have an insight into or a view on the border dispute with Eritrea or the future of the opposition. She tried to think of something to ask him, but couldn't come up with anything better than the health of his parents.

'How're your Mum and Dad?'

'Fine, fine. Send their love. Hope to see you.'

He asked her what she thought she would do next; she admitted she wasn't sure. She saw a momentary triumph, a proprietorial gleam. She added quickly that if she didn't work out her next steps, she would be going back to Mumbai.

He took the message.

They wouldn't be making love that night. She had thought they would, had intended that they would, but her period arrived, in a breaking wave of released angst, disconcertingly early, 30,000 feet over Eastbourne, twenty-five minutes from landing.

She felt she should tell Mark, so that he didn't build up his hopes, and get too disappointed. She was suddenly uncomfortable about quite how to do so; she recalled that in their seven-year marriage they had never actually spoken about such matters, except in euphemisms. The same applied to a range of other bodily functions. It all seemed too ludicrous that she was still left with that uncertainty; she was determined not to sink back into an adolescent dialogue about being 'off games' or 'not quite up to it'. She was, though, plagued with doubts about quite how to discuss the matter in any other terms. Maybe she was actually more British than she thought.

Their entire relationship, from the initial courtship to post-divorce partitioning of CDs and novels, had been polite, disciplined and constrained. Civilized, Mark called it. That was what he had always been good at; what he made a good living and lots of easy friendships out of—being civilized. Infinite patience, uncomplaining acceptance of responsibility, determined avoidance of conflict and drama. Off-hand, she couldn't recall him ever really losing his temper; maybe becoming a bit exasperated with her, or a flat tyre or a late train. Never really angry, though. Never ever losing it. No, not Mark.

And as for swearing; a 'bloody' or a well-bred 'bugger', was about all.

At times she almost despised him because he was so utterly complete unto himself. Sure, he was lonely, and he wanted her back. But it was a sign of his almost selfish wholeness that since their separation he had not, as far as she could gauge (and she was pretty sure Ma would have been on the phone to let her know if she'd picked up the slightest) made the least effort to get into any other relationships. He was good-looking, in an unselfconscious, comfortably crumpled, English sort of way, and he pulled down a decent enough salary. Plenty of the couples that had been their friends were now divorced, and she was sure that there were several women who would have welcomed his advances—she even knew of two who had made it quite clear they would have been up for it while she and Mark were still married. Cows.

Essentially, Mark was a gentleman. Through and through.

A couple of hours later, he was sitting in her mother's lounge, sipping a ginger beer poured from one of the cans her mother had thoughtfully stocked the lower shelf of the refrigerator with, in the hope that Mark would be a regular guest during Taz's stay.

Taz, fresh from the shower, wore her mother's towelling dressing grown, and rubbed her hair dry with a hand towel.

He stood up when she entered the room.

She shook her head. 'If you're hoping for a screw you're out of luck,' she said, brutally.

'Taz!' he cried, hurt and shocked.

She laughed, and flopped onto the sofa. 'You can pour me a drink. Whisky and soda.' Then, to her own surprise, she added, 'Sorry. Do you fancy something disgustingly unhealthy? Ma has a secret stash of Tesco burgers. She thinks I don't know. Shall we raid her freezer?'

He was sulking, friable and petulant. It was obvious even in the way he held the drink out to her. She knew though that within a few minutes, he would, somehow, be purporting to take responsibility for his disapproval, and apologizing for it.

She took a quick gulp of the whisky. He took a breath, and looked at her gravely.

'And you can have tomato ketchup on yours,' she said, cutting him off.

The words struck her as indescribably funny. She dissolved into near hysteria. He resumed his look of pained forbearance.

Next morning, while Mark, still a trifle prickly, popped out for a 'couple of ticks', Dave Bignall called round to see her. He apologized, automatically, for the mess the SOCOs—the Scene of Crimes Officers—had made. She told him she hadn't noticed any. He asked her what she wanted done with Pudding's remains; she was surprised that she hadn't really given it a thought. She'd assumed that they'd just, well, disposed of him. She frowned.

'We can, you know, have the poor little thing cremated,' Dave said, 'if that's what you want. We thought maybe you'd like to bury him in the garden, or something.'

Taz shook her head, then to her surprise, said 'Yes.'

'We got a vet to look at him; not really a post-mortem, but just to help us with the report. You know, technical terms. That's where the remains are. If it's any comfort, the cat had several tumours. The vet said he'd have needed to have been put down before too long. Sorry.'

Why don't I find that comforting? Taz wondered. She

refilled Dave's mug of tea. 'Where's your colleague, Miss Thingy?'

'Oh, she'll be around. She's your Point of Contact. This is merely an informal call about your cat. Made any progress in this investigation of yours?' he asked.

'Well, I met the priest who was with Armitage Shanks, and met the agency he was working with in Ethiopia. I met someone who knew Armitage Shanks earlier in Africa, visited the prison where he was when he wrote the letter to me. That's about it.'

'Sounds like you've been busy. Sounds like it's for real, too. When we last spoke you weren't sure.'

'Oh, it's for real. I just can't seem to pin down precisely what "it" is. That's why I went to Germany; that's where the guy was who knew Armitage Shanks. That's also why I went to Ethiopia, because that's where whatever happened, happened. That's what I've been doing: Trying to find out who he was, and what happened to him. And why no one has any record of him, or his execution.'

Dave scratched behind his ear. 'It's like one of those puzzles in the newspapers, isn't it? Armitage Shanks? Could it be a code word or is it a conundrum? Doesn't sound like a real name, does it?'

Taz shook her head. 'On the Internet it's a very common alias.'

'An anagram?' He took a slip of paper from his pocket, and a pen. 'Let's see. You can get...' He scribbled in silence for a minute or two, tabulating the letters, jumbling them up and making patterns amidst the confusion. 'Atheism, Messiah, Minaret. Too many letters left over though. SK's Nightmare.'

'That's a good one,' said Taz, impressed. 'Those are my boss's initials.'

'Hmm. Not that good, really. Still got two "A"s left over,' said Dave absently, still absorbed with the puzzle. 'Got it! Mark Against She! Perfect.'

'That's amazing! How do you do that?'

'Dunno. It's a gift. Not much in demand though, except at Christmas and leaving parties.'

'Well I think it's incredible.'

'Thanks. Doesn't help us work out who was so bothered about your curiosity though. Any further thoughts?'

'None.'

'Any more threats since?'

'No. Nothing at all.'

'But somebody wants you to lay off?'

'I guess. What else could it be?'

'Maybe somebody wants her to keep at it,' said Mark, quietly, from the doorway. They both turned; neither had heard him return from the paper shop in the village.

'How do you mean?' prompted Dave.

'Well, it's obvious, isn't it? If anyone knew Esme, Taz, either personally or professionally, they'd know what happened to Pudding would only make her more determined. That's a possibility, isn't it?'

Dave looked doubtful. 'Maybe. What are you going to do next, Miss Dhar?'

'Try and identify who Armitage Shanks was. Follow up a couple of leads...' she said, vaguely.

'Shame you don't have a better description, or know what he looked like.'

She nodded. She had intended to add that she had a photograph, but remembering how she had acquired it, thought it best not mentioned. Mark noticed the omission, and looked at her with one eyebrow raised. She looked away.

'Well, I wish you success,' said Dave, finishing his tea. 'I'll ask around. Don't expect anyone will be able to help, but you never know. I'll tip you the wink if anyone has any bright ideas. Like we did on the location of the priest.'

'That's kind; really kind,' said Taz, gratefully. The detective rose to go. He nodded at the folded copy of *The Guardian* under Mark's arm. 'Much in the paper?'

Mark shook his head. 'Not much. The usual. Another car bomb in Iraq. A Muslim terror cell in Manchester raided and a dozen young men held. Some new outrage by neo-Nazi gangs in Germany. Just the usual.'

∾

A policewoman she hadn't seen before turned up at 9.15 the next morning with what she, echoing Dave Bignall, referred to sombrely as The Poor Little Thing. Taz tried to call it Pudding, but it didn't seem right to dignify the frozen, anonymous package wrapped in thick insulation that the policewoman gravely carried in from the back seat of her car with the name of the object of more of her affection than any other living being in the past two decades. Only her father had she loved more. But like her Pa, Pudding too was gone now. Long gone. This thing simply needed to be disposed of. She wished she'd asked Dave Bignall to tell the vet to do it. Now what was she going to do? She paid for a gardener to call once a week to cut the grass and tidy up the tiny garden for Ma. He was a round, bald man with bad teeth who arrived with his own tools and a severely disabled wife, incapable of speech or independent movement, who would sit, silently staring dead ahead, in the front passenger seat of his tank of a car parked on the driveway, as he did his hour with the lawnmower and edging shears. Ma, Taz knew, had taken to climbing into the driver's seat and treating the poor woman to a monologue on the injustices of life and the cruelty of uncaring children. Just in case the poor bitch didn't have enough suffering in her life. But the man wasn't due for another three days, and in the meantime, there wasn't even a trowel in the place, and she did not want the thing on the draining board beside the sink to begin to thaw.

∾

Anu Sitaram found herself excited at the prospect of seeing Taz again. As she rang the doorbell, she actually felt butterflies in her stomach: anticipation of her first out-of-uniform assignment alone, or an embarrassing legacy of a childhood fan-crush? She had thought carefully about what to wear, which was wonder enough, and rehearsed her greeting and first few questions. She had even gone over them with a grinning Dave Bignall, who told her to stop wasting his time and get on with it.

Taz opened the door. Anu said, 'Hi,' and asked if she was busy. Taz nodded. 'I'm trying to work out how to dig a grave.'

'I've got something to bury in the garden,' she added by way of explanation in response to Anu's bewildered expression.

'Do I need to caution you?' Anu asked.

'No. But you can be an accessory if you like. Come on in.'

A neighbour loaned them a garden fork and a spade, and the two of them set to Pudding's interment. It was a warm morning, and they worked in companionable silence.

'You've been collecting a few air miles, I hear,' said Anu.

'And you've been promoted,' panted Taz.

Anu knelt once they had dug about a cubic foot of earth out of an abandoned patch of lawn and nettles beneath an old pear tree, and began to scrape out the bottom of the hole. 'Not really. It's a transfer out of uniform. Working for Mr Bignall. More travel, more excitement, but same rank and salary. How deep do you want this to be?'

Taz had proposed a shallow pit in one of the flower beds

until Anu had pointed out the risks of a fox, dog or even the gardener disinterring Pudding. She dabbed at the sweat on her forehead and shrugged. 'Think this is enough?' she asked hopefully.

Anu smiled. 'Let's try a few inches more.'

'I'll bet you say that to all the boys. Sorry. Childish habit. If you loosen up the soil, I'll dig it out.'

'It needs to be deep enough to let us get a brick or a large stone in on top to stop anything getting at him. I suppose my transfer must seem pretty small scale after what you've done. Even so, it's like, foreign? Totally different ways of doing things. Different ways of talking. I can't imagine what it must have been like making the move you made.'

'It sounds a lot more dramatic in hindsight than it actually seemed at the time. England to India wasn't such a big step as radio to TV. That was just like you say you're finding your new work. Can you talk about what you're doing?'

'Sure. Keeping an eye on you.'

Taz paused, and rested on her spade. 'Are you?'

'Yes. Look, I'm not going to play games with you. You are clearly under threat and you need to be careful. There are a lot of things that don't make much sense at the moment, and a lot more I'm sure someone at my level doesn't get to know, but personally I'm on your side and officially under instructions to make sure you stay safe while you're in the UK.'

'I don't think I'm in that much danger.'

'Really? What are we doing at the moment?'

Taz thought for a while. She watched this trim, earnest young woman fork through the soil and stones, and noticed the grace and strength with which she reached down and tugged determinedly at a fierce tangle of tree roots, and suddenly felt profoundly safe.

'You might have a long job on your hands. I have no plans to go anywhere.'

Anu looked up, and smiled. 'That's OK by me. Shall I go make a cup of tea?'

∾

'Your boss has quite a way with anagrams, doesn't he?' said Taz as she sipped her tea.

They were standing over the filled-in grave. Anu gently pressed the soil down with her toe. 'Tell me about it. A Harridan Ma At Us. That's his take on my name.' She paused for a moment, then continued in a different tone of voice, 'Taz, can I ask you something?'

Taz sighed. 'There's no such thing as a free cup of tea.'

'Actually, it's your tea. The man you went to meet in Germany? Did the priest tell you about him?'

'No. It was an uncle of mine. He sent me an e-mail with the name and address.'

'Yusuf Asgharbhai Abbas? You see, we had a word with him and he denied doing anything at all to help you. Not because he didn't want to, but because he couldn't find anything out.'

Taz looked doubtful. 'You've interviewed my uncle? Bet that wasn't a cozy chat. You'll no doubt have noticed that the words "police" and "denied doing anything" naturally fit together for him. I hope this hasn't caused him any trouble.'

'Not as much as it has caused me. I got into deep shit for checking out the priest for you.'

'God! Sorry! And I haven't even thanked you properly. I didn't know. Is there anything I can do?'

'No, it's sorted now, thanks to Mr Bignall. But it looked a bit iffy for a moment or two. I mention it only to make the point that I'm not in a position to judge what your uncle may or may not have done to help you, even if I wanted to. Have you still got the message? Are you sure it was from your uncle?'

Taz looked up at the old pear tree above Pudding's grave. Its gnarled bark was flaking in places, like dry, scrofulous skin, but the crabbed branches that had looked dead before she left for Ethiopia now were in bud and held the promise of another season of blossom and bloated fruit.

'I'm not sure of anything,' she admitted, angrily. 'And whenever I think I am getting near to something, someone comes along and convinces me I'm even further away from any understanding that I thought. Just like you're doing now.'

'Taz, I'm sorry but I'm…'

'What?' Taz snarled. 'Just doing your job? And what is that precisely? Hassling my uncle, watching me, confusing me, misleading me? Christ, what I wouldn't give for someone who will talk straight to me about this! It's all a fucking anagram, isn't it? A game, a challenge? Well, I won't be played, lady. And I won't be deterred either. Thanks for the help, but I think you'd better go. No doubt you've got a report to write and file.'

❧

After Anu left, Taz spent a fruitless afternoon trying to get through to Yusuf Kaka, Father Thomas, Rama Rao and S.K. Mehta. None was available. She left messages for all four. She rang her mother at her brother's house in Canada, finally 'fessing up about the break-in and Pudding. Her mother, in clipped, sniffy tones, informed her she had already heard all about it from Yusuf Kaka and was disappointed that she had to learn such things that way. They ended the conversation with a chilly farewell. Taz decided she needed to do something to avoid the spiral of depression she could feel her conversation with her mother plunging her into, and, suddenly sentimental, decided to try and make a meal for Mark.

When he arrived, he was clearly pleased with himself, and his self-satisfied grin slipped dangerously toward a smirk when she told him she was cooking. She could have done without the incredulous laugh; she had enough problems. Most of the meal had come from Marks and Spencer's. She only really intended to make one dish, and that she had followed slavishly from Delia Smith's *Complete Cookery Course*. She had no idea how it should have tasted, but it certainly didn't look like the illustration. She poured him a glass of wine, and refilled her own. When they sat down to the starter, she could see he was aching for her to ask the reason for his ghastly cheerfulness. She felt she owed him that, at least.

'I found out something,' he said, simply.

'About Armitage Shanks?' she asked in disbelief.

'Uh huh. What is this?' he asked, frowning down at a lump of something he poked at with his fork.

'Who cares?' she snapped, exasperated. 'What could you possibly find out that I couldn't?'

'Oh, all sorts of things.'

'What things, for Christ's sake!' her voice rose near to a scream.

'How old he is, perhaps,' Mark replied, smugly.

She leaned forward: 'How could you find that out? I can't even find out who he is, or even if he existed at all.'

'By the application of a bit of lateral thinking, combined with the same amount of common sense plus the awesome power of the Internet. He's less than thirty-seven, or was, when he died.'

'No...' she murmured, frowning, and shaking her head. 'No. I'm sure that's wrong. Anyway, how could you know?'

'Well, my theory does depend on Armitage Shanks being his real name.'

'Which looks increasingly unlikely, but go on. This is obviously the day for party games.'

'Well, if that is his real name, he must be named after the sanitaryware company, right?'

Taz nodded.

'Well,' said Mark, pushing the half-eaten starter from him. The company didn't exist before 1969. I checked out their website. It's all there. There were two separate companies, prior to that. Shanks was one, and Armitage Ware was the other. Totally separate. Until they merged.'

'But... in the letter he talks about a Gene Pitney song that was popular when he was a kid. *24 Hours from Tulsa* was a hit in 1963. I checked that. That would make him much older, wouldn't it? Nearer fifty. Mid-thirties doesn't match with the tone of the letter, either. He's older,' Taz insisted. 'I'm sure.'

'Really?' Mark wondered. 'He talks about being treated like a son or younger brother by the other chap in his cell. How can you be so sure? Can one really deduce age from a letter? Can't an old poet write like a young lover, and a newly qualified solicitor write like a septuagenarian judge?'

'It's not like you to be eloquent, Mark,' she snapped back.

'It's very much like you not to listen,' he muttered, but Taz didn't hear him.

She cleared away the first course in silence, opened another bottle of wine and served the main course. They had just begun to work their way through it when, pushing her mouthful of food into her cheek, she poked a fork triumphantly towards Mark and said, 'He's not less than thirty-seven. I'll bet you anything he's not less than forty. That proves Armitage Shanks must be an alias.'

'Perhaps,' said Mark. 'Of course, there is another possible explanation.'

'No, there isn't.'

'Yes there is. The whole thing is nonsense. A huge, elaborate, expensive hoax. Have you ever thought of that?'

'Of course I've thought of that,' she hissed back. 'Do you

think I'm stupid? Thought of it for four milliseconds and dismissed it. What kind of a hoax would involve priests in Africa, and retired aid workers in Germany, and someone killing Pudding? Whatever it is, it's not a hoax, and only a dickhead would even think it could be. Whatever it is, it's serious.'

Silence.

As so often before, Taz felt Mark had expected and deserved better of her. He had tried, he'd actually been doing what she should have been and all she could do was pick at him, snap and sneer. She raised her glass. 'Mark, thank you for looking it up. It was kind of you and I'm sorry to be so snide, and sorry about this crappy meal too. Stay here tonight. Let's sleep together, cuddled up like an old, married couple.'

He shook his head. 'I don't want to sleep with you when you're drunk, Taz,' he said, quietly.

Drunk? Well, maybe she was. What the hell? 'Whatever. I still owe you one. When I'm not drunk.'

'And when will that be, Taz?' he asked, smooth and easy as a well-stropped razor. She placed the palms of both hands on the table and pressed down. She held her breath for a moment, then looked at him long and hard. 'Get out,' she said softly.

'Taz, I'm sorry...' he began, realizing he'd gone too far.

'Fuck off!' she said, her voice rising. 'Go on, get out.'

He sighed and began to fold his napkin. The gesture seemed so slow, patient and painstaking that something in her snapped. She picked up her wine glass, and threw it in his general direction. It missed; she had meant it to. It exploded against the wall behind him in a spectacular burst of red wine. Even as she watched the horror and surprise flinch into his face, and revelled in the spectacle of the splash across the wall, a bit of her brain was praying the wallpaper was washable and working on how she would clear it up so her mother would never know.

'Taz...'

'Next it's the plate. Then the cutlery. I'd get out now if I were you.'

He left. Taz leaned forward, pushed her place setting and the ruins of the disastrous meal away and rested her head on her folded arms. She had thought she was going to cry, but she didn't. She was annoyed with him; irritated. Very. What was that anagram of Armitage Shanks? Mark Against She? Too fucking true.

The phone rang. She snatched it up. It would be him, of course, crawling like the snake he was. 'Well?' she snapped.

'Miss Dhar? It's Professor Rama Rao.'

'Oh, hi,' she said, flustered and momentarily taken aback. 'Thanks for returning my call. I just wanted to say thank you for all your help and apologize for not saying goodbye before I left.'

'It was no trouble. Literally. I am well aware I was little help and a poor host. I should apologize, but after the last time, neither you nor SK could hardly have expected me to be anything other than unenthusiastic.'

'No problem. Well... er, what last time?'

'That unfortunate young man from Cal who died back in February. Well, good luck, Miss Dhar. Goodbye...'

❧

At around four in the morning, the phone rang again. Taz felt for it, dragged it to her ear and groaned into it.

'Taz!' cried SK, a malicious satisfaction evident in his voice 'Haven't woken you, have I?'

She mumbled something incoherent but obviously offensive back at him and he chuckled. 'I've been calling you and calling you. I have something important to tell you.'

'Sorry. Busy. Just got back.'

'Yes, so I heard from Vijaya Rama Rao. Were you thinking of reporting in on progress any time this century?'

'There is no progress. SK, I'm getting nowhere. I've achieved nothing. Mark found out as much in a couple of hours on the Internet as I managed in Germany and Ethiopia combined.'

'You're not being fair to yourself, Taz. You've been doing fine. You found the priest and you found Ruhl.'

'But I have absolutely no idea what to do next,' she confessed.

'Well, that's what I've been calling about. We think we've got a match on the men in the picture you sent us. They all worked in a refugee camp in Africa, with Hugo Ruhl. How did we get them? Get this: they all died in a boating accident eighteen months ago. Exploding fuel tank.'

'They're all dead?'

'So it would seem. Although only one body was ever recovered. Badly burned. Identifiable only by dental records. Interesting, eh? How sure are you Ruhl identified the writer of the letter as one of those men?'

'I don't know. He seemed to. I was sure at that moment. Absolutely sure. But now, I really don't know.'

'Well, there's only one way to find out. I've e-mailed all we've got on them to you. It's in a zipped file. There's a fair old bit. Images too. You'll need broadband to download it.'

'That's OK. Mark...'

'What?'

'Oh, never mind. Where did they die?'

'Ghana. I've set you up with a local contact. Tasked him with checking out these guys. I think this could be the breakthrough.'

'Can't I just come home?'

'What happened to the big story? No, you can't. Not just yet. Not if you want your job back.'

'You mean it? My job back? You wouldn't just say that?'

'I won't lie to you, Taz. It hasn't been easy, but I think I may just have persuaded the powers that be. You do still want your job back, don't you?'

'You know I do, you manipulative turd. More than anything. OK. Ghana it is.'

'That's my girl.'

She asked how the dyke was doing: SK assured her she was doing fine, and he'd be grateful if she'd refrain from referring to a colleague in that way.

Pompous prat. How'd he like his job given away? That bitch had it coming in spades when she got back.

They talked logistics. Flights and expenses. Then she asked, 'SK, did you send anyone else to Ethiopia?'

'When?'

'You know, that's an odd response. *"Yes, No, Why?"* or *"What the hell are you talking about?"* would all make sense. But "When?" Very strange. Back in February, or in the last couple of weeks, since you ask.'

'No.'

'Then can you check up on a man called Kirk Chopra, from a company called Intuatica in Delhi, dealing in computer information systems. He was in Addis with me.'

'Problem?'

'I don't know. I thought he was just being pleasant company, but he was very interested in what I was doing, and seemed to know more about it than he let on. Said he was staying on, too, when I said I might. Then when I left he promptly pissed off back to Delhi. I've got a number for him.'

'If anyone else is trying to muscle in on this story after all we've done, Taz, we are both in deep trouble,' SK warned, deeply concerned.

'I don't think he was media. But there was something not quite right there.'

'I'll have him checked out. Don't tell anyone, and I do mean anyone, about the Ghana angle. Tell everyone who needs to know you're heading back here. OK?'

'OK. You're the boss.'

'Good. Remember that. Now the other one?'

'Oh yeah. Your friend Rama Rao mentioned some guy from Cal who got killed out there in February. Shit! He's not…'

'The one whose clothes our man was wearing when he wrote to you? Oh, I wouldn't think so, Taz. I'd forget all about it if I were you.'

∽

The phone rang again. Any last chance of sleep that night shattered. A man's voice she didn't recognize said, 'You've been looking for me.'

'Are you… Armitage Shanks?'

'I have been. I don't want to be again.'

'The one who wrote to me?'

'That's right.'

'That's bollocks. You can't be. He's dead.'

'That's right too.'

'How do I know you're for real?'

'I don't know. You could ask me something.'

'OK. Tell me about the Slaughter House.'

'Wise choice. When I was a child, I used to walk to the bus stop, to go to school on Pound Street. There was an abattoir on the way. On Pound Street. They used to slaughter every day. Some days cattle, some days sheep; Wednesdays, I remember, was pigs. In the morning, all you could smell was the excrement from the animals brought in late the night before and held overnight. It was always liquid. A reeking slurry. They whimpered, desperate and despairing, like they knew what was going to happen. Like they knew there was no escape. That's what we used to smell, every morning, on our way to school. In the afternoon, after the slaughtering had been done, they'd hose down the concrete floors, and the bloody water would flood out over the pavement, and into the gutter. The bleach and disinfectant was so strong your eyes would water and it would catch in your throat. My mother would tell me off for walking through it; used to insist I walk on the other side of the road. I never once saw one of those creatures. Never once saw anyone who worked behind the gates and the high walls. But God, could you smell it! It got into your clothes, and in your hair, and in your skin, no matter on what side of Pound Street you walked. Liquid fear, and the trapped wail of foreseen death in the morning. Stale blood and the astringent tranquillity of cleansed death in the evening. That's the Slaughter House on Pound Street.'

'Who were you?'

'You already know that. That's why I had to call. When there was a chance you might not find out, it was better to let you think I really was dead. Now, I have no choice. I am one of the four who died in Ghana.'

'What happened to the others?'

'I don't know. One died there. I don't know what they did to the other two. What happened to Hugo Ruhl?'

'I don't know.'

'I see. I'd hoped he would escape.'

'Where are you?'

'I can't tell you that.'

'But you're somewhere safe?'

'Safe? Who's safe? Where's safe? Safe is a feeling, not location or a state of being. No, I'm not safe. Nor are you. But I am not in any immediate danger, if that's what you mean. Not that I am aware of.'

'What's going to happen to you?'

'Nothing. It's already happened. I represent no threat to them now. So I'm in no danger. But you are.'

'If I can find you, would you meet me?'

'No. I've already been killed twice. That's quite enough, believe me.'

'Don't you think this story needs to be told?'

'No. Absolutely not. It's over, for me. Forever.'

'Well, it isn't over for me.'

'It will be, soon, believe me. Either at your choice, or theirs. Even if you do discover the truth, no one will believe you. They must be sure of that, or they wouldn't let me speak to you.'

'And if you're wrong?'

'Then they'll destroy you. Either in appearance, or in reality. Look, I got you into this, and I'm sorry for that, so let me give you some advice. Please take it. You don't stand a chance. They know you, and if they know you, they own you. Stop now, while you still can.'

'Who are they?'

'The same ones they've always been. They are eternal.'

'Are they watching you now?'

'They are always watching. The price of their power is eternal vigilance.'

'I thought that was freedom.'

'So do they.'

'Why me?'

'Like I said in the letter: you were just a face to focus upon. Sorry, but I really thought they were going to kill me. I really thought they would keep the letter. None of this was meant to happen. None of this would have happened but for that interfering priest. The well-meaning damn more of us to purgatory than all the despots and tyrants combined.'

'I won't give up.'

'Then you are a fool. Killing you isn't the worst thing they can do to you,' he said, and the line went dead.

PART III

PAYING DUES

11

Black Star Weekly

Accra, Sunday 16 September 2005

4 DIE IN LAKE TRAGEDY

Relief Workers Perish in Lake Blast

By a Staff Correspondent

Accra (15 September): For the first time since last week's boat tragedy off Akosombo, official confirmation came today that there was no more to it than an accidental blast. A spokesman for the Inspector-General of Police told the *Black Star Weekly* today that while it is too early to say conclusively what caused the incident, foul play has been ruled out.

It was a sleepy Sunday afternoon on 9 September when four men, apparent picknickers, arrived at Akosombo. Boat, lines and bait were hired. Fried chicken, roast corn and groundnuts were prepared and ready. Bottles of beer were cooling in a net over the side of the boat. They brought with them cards, a clockwork radio and even a laptop and DVDs. Just a Sunday off. But one that was destined to end in disaster.

The four, three Britons and a Canadian, set off in the twelve-year-old launch *Lake Lady* around 2 P.M. An hour and a half later, day-trippers picnicking on the shores of the lake watched in horror as a mighty explosion ripped the fishing-boat apart.

Rescue attempts were launched immediately. Local fishermen raced to the scene, and the *MS Dodi Princess* diverted to join the desperate search for survivors. Among wreckage spread over a large area by the force of the explosion, the body of one of the men, an aid worker, was recovered. Searching continued for the remains of the others for several days. With hope fading, the search was finally abandoned on Thursday.

The owner of the *Lake Lady*, a Felix Sarpong, was arrested but later released without charge. It is understood that future charges of criminal negligence are still under consideration. Kofi Agjei, 47, an Accra-based businessman and close friend of Sarpong, strongly protested the boat-owner's innocence. 'The *Lady* was very dear to Felix,' he said. 'Although he hired her out, she was his boat and he looked after her very well indeed. There can be no question of her not being perfectly maintained. In fact, just a week before this accident, she had been inspected and her licence to be operated as a tourist boat was renewed. If there had been anything wrong with her, how come the inspectors didn't find it?'

The four victims were named as Andrew Carr, 36, of Lymington, Robert Lloyd, 51, of Carlisle, Martin John Peters, 27, of Chorleywood and Dilip Dutta, 41, of Cranbrook, British Columbia. To date, only the remains of Peters have been recovered. His father and sister flew to Ghana last Tuesday to formally identify his remains. A tearful Peters Senior told reporters, 'This has been a horrible few days for my family and me, and my heart goes out to the families and friends of Johnny's colleagues who are also grieving but have the added burden of the absence of any remains to bring home. I know Johnny would have wanted me to say how much he loved this country, and how committed he was to the people he and the others were looking after. In every letter and e-mail, his passion for his work shone through. We were proud of him, and take comfort in our memory of a wonderful young man the world will sorely miss. Finally, I would like to thank everyone for the messages of kindness and sympathy we have received from all over the world.'

The deceased worked for Vancouver-based charity Safe Return, which supports efforts to repatriate refugees and asylum-seekers from the world's most vicious and brutal conflicts. All worked in the Buduburam Camp, home to around 40,000 refugees from Liberia, some of whom fled their country more than fifteen years ago. The camp has recently had bad press: alleged abuses, home of a number of criminal gangs and most recently seen as a recruiting ground for mercenaries for West Africa's many deadly wars. Safe Return's executive director Claire Dickinson, who flew to Ghana immediately on hearing of the deaths, said, 'This is a tragic loss of four dedicated and highly experienced workers, all of whom have served in other conflict zones, including Kosovo, the Middle East and elsewhere in Africa. Their legacy will be our renewed efforts to shelter the innocent and provide a voice, and an eventual homecoming, for the dispossessed, the silent and the scared. As workers, their load will be picked up by other hands. As friends and colleagues, we will all miss their wisdom and their smiles forever.' When asked if guidelines for Safe Return workers would be reviewed as a result of the accident, she declined to comment further.

Joseph Danquah, Ghana's Minister for Tourism Development, said at a conference on 'Eco-Tourism and the Environment' in Kuala Lumpur yesterday, 'This sad matter should not deter people from visiting our beautiful country, where they can be sure of a warm welcome and a wonderful time.'

Jonjo Amin Asante folded away the year-old newspaper cutting, dabbed at the perspiration above his upper lip with a neatly creased handkerchief, and looked around at the excited throng with bleak distaste. They weren't fit to wear trousers, half of them. Slum thugs, beach bums and jungle boys, with no pride, and little enough shame.

He was dressed in a dark suit, shiny, sagging and world-weary as himself. The collar of his white shirt was frayed, and the cheap polyester tie he had bought that morning hung like a piece of stiff plastic over his crumpled shirt front.

It was too hot, and too crowded, to be so formally dressed, but that was Jonjo Amin Asante. Prim as a churchy spinster, prissy, some would—and did—say. Careful about his appearance, and obsessive about his use of English. Most people mistook him for a man of the cloth. Anyone forming that view would now have been instantly dissuaded by the stream of invective he let fly at a loping youth with a pair of reflective glasses and a swagger of attitude who had the temerity to tread on Jonjo Amin Asante's down-at-heel but highly polished shoes.

The youth stood back, raising his hands, as though in surrender, but laughing all the while.

Jonjo called him a crocodile-mouth, and the youth snapped his fingers in his face to signal his indifference. Jonjo looked down at his shoes, he polished the toes of each against the calves of his trousers. The youth's clumsiness set a final, angry spin to Jonjo's plummeting spirits.

He had been standing outside the floodlit Kotaka International airport for over an hour. The night was hot and sticky. A crowd, hundreds-strong and twitchy as a cow's flank under flies, coagulated around the exit from the arrivals hall, on the look-out for relatives, friends, prospective employers or simply an easy touch. The police had twice pushed the heaving, noisy mass back, and Jonjo had treated a female police sergeant to a twenty-second burst of abuse, in a language which he was sure she would not understand.

He had always been an angry man, when he was younger, it had been clever. Cool. Even attractive. Yet as he aged he retained, unlike his contemporaries, the passion and fury that had got him elected on a radical ticket as chairman of the students' union at Achimota—and got him arrested, beaten up and sent down eight months later.

He stabbed a final glare into the crowd; God, how he despised these cheap hustlers and street boys, almost as much as he looked with loathing upon the newspapers several of them read, as they squatted on the still-hot pavement between bursts of excitement as each new batch of arrivals was descended upon.

Jonjo hated what the Ghanaian press had become. That had been why he had become a freelancer; so he could maintain his standards—standards he believed in, even though no one else valued or wanted them. Integrity—he told himself, in an aphorism he repeated like a mantra—may be out of fashion but is never out of style. It was that simple. As with the proper use of English. Half the sentences on most of the front pages, and even in the editorials in the daily newspapers had forsaken as much as a passing attempt at syntax. Despicable. He hated them. They were scum. They couldn't even lie grammatically. And as for the pursuit of the truth? Out of fashion. That's why he'd gone freelance. That was also why no one would employ him any more—that's why he'd ended up having to go cap in hand to the Information Bureau which had found him this assignment.

He checked the handkerchief he had refolded and thrust into his breast pocket; a neat triangle showed, and he fussed with it for a moment, until satisfied. He pressed and pushed at the tight cap of grizzled hair that he kept cut so short these days that even such a cursory attention was unnecessary. He wiped the corners of his mouth with a thumb and forefinger. He sniffed, and swallowed. He even huffed his breath into his cupped hands and tried to catch any odour; he took a sugary pastel from his jacket pocket, and sucked it.

She should appear soon, he told himself. Very soon, now.

He looked around for someone he knew. A few years ago,

there wasn't a high-ranking policeman, army officer, or politician who didn't know, fear and respect the name and the opinions of Jonjo Amin Asante. When he had the 'Voice of the People' column in the *PDG*—*the People's Daily Graphic*. In the days when the *PDG* was a paper to be proud to work for. Before Rawlings closed everything down, and then Rawlings opened everything up again, too quick, too wide, too late. Threw open the floodgates, so any garbage could be printed, and passed off as news.

He knew no one at the airport, these days. They all looked so young he suspected he might know some of their fathers, or maybe even their grandfathers.

He grunted his dismay and anger as he was jostled aside by a family of six, half carrying, half dragging an empty baggage trolley through to meet their returning kin.

He shook his head. Look at them; pushing and fighting and squabbling with another group who were trying to drag the baggage trolley from them. Like dogs in a gutter. Whatever happened to pride and dignity?

He spotted the woman he had come to meet; they had e-mailed a photograph, but he would have guessed anyway. She was a reporter as well, so they said. They said, too, that she was a good one, but when he asked what she'd written, no one could show him anything. Just another big, foreign name on some journey of exploration that he would have to lead by the hand, nursemaiding her as though she were barely potty-trained, while she sent back brave accounts of all the things she saw and did.

What a way for a man like him to have to make a living!

❧

So Ghana now it was to be. And in secret too. Well, what the hell? It was a great deal better than sitting around her mother's new house, which was reeking of spray polish and closet nostalgia, waiting for the story to come to her.

And it got her away from Mark.

He'd come back the next day; she knew he would. Asked her out to a show. Got tickets, and boasted about it like he'd managed to acquire the Ten Commandments five minutes before Moses.

Prat.

She took a malicious delight in calling and telling Mark she was off to India less than an hour before she left for the airport. It felt good, lying to him. Mark Against She. He'd flapped around like a damp fairy, wittering on about changing appointments so that he could drive her, and wondering about what he should tell her mother when she got back. That had made her pause; she had not given a thought to her mother's return seven days hence. She hadn't realized the time had gone so fast.

She put the phone down on Mark while he was still talking, and called Anu. She was round in fifteen minutes. Taz apologized for her angry outburst and told her she was off to Mumbai. Perhaps strangely, she found it harder lying to Anu, but there was a chance, a real chance, of getting her job back and she would have lied wide-eyed to the Archangel Gabriel if it helped her get back on *Good Morning Mumbai*. Clearly troubled, Anu said nothing for a while, then suggested they fill a watering-can and soak in some seeds that she had brought with her to scatter over Pudding's bare little grave. They used a teapot. She asked Taz if an Indian guy had contacted her in Addis, and on hearing he had, felt better, satisfied that Rohit was on the case. She'd alert him to Taz's return to India, as soon as she'd said goodbye.

Together they checked that the house was securely locked up, embraced uncomfortably, and Anu stood and watched, arms crossed, in silence, as Taz departed. She waved, but Taz didn't look back. Instead, she settled into the taxi she had kept waiting for the past half an hour, noting with satisfaction the impressive numbers already clocked-up on the meter.

She told the driver to take her to Heathrow; he asked her if she wanted a fixed price, and she told him to leave it on the meter.

She was on her way back! Life, once more, was chargeable. She still couldn't quite believe it. She was on her way back and she had spoken to Armitage Shanks! He'd actually called her. She was sure it was him. Had to be. She hadn't told SK. She wasn't quite sure why, only that it was the right thing to do.

By the time she was on the plane, she was feeling guilty again about the way she was treating Mark, and SK. Mark wasn't a bad guy, nor was SK. Who had found her Rama Rao, in Ethiopia? Who had identified the men in Hugo Ruhl's photograph? And now, who had sourced this Amin Asante guy for her to work with? God only knew how he did it.

And then she thought of Sidiq in Germany. She chased the thought from her mind. Now was not the time to waste energy on a pointless guilt trip. Maybe sometime she could do something to make it up to him. Letting him down like that...

❧

In the five days since he had received his assignment, Jonjo Amin Asante had been far from idle. From a small amount he had got third-hand from a contact of a friend of S.K. Mehta, he knew it was a story about the Abrunis, the white men that had died on the Volta Lake.

Good, as far as it went.

And enough, too, for him to be getting on with. In his day, Jonjo had been one of the best. He had single-handedly exposed the payments scandal; twice interviewed Rawlings, the last time in an explosive one-on-one which had ended with a clear threat of house arrest. He had been in Liberia with the first wave of ECOMOG—peacekeepers from the Economic Community of West African States—forces, and way back in the expulsions from Nigeria had twice crossed the border illegally, had reported first-hand on some of the atrocities he had witnessed, and as a result still had no less than three extant exclusion orders issued against him. The story could be there, or in Liberia, for the dead aid workers had all been connected with the refugees in Ghana. Or Cote d'Ivoire. Not that it mattered. He had contacts in all three, but so far, no expense account, so he started where he could afford to. With Liberian refugees grubbing out a tragic neo-living begging, or trading trinkets in the dust and exhaust fumes of Nkrumah circle, and out at the block-built refugee camp on the Darko Farm and Buduburam.

It had not been long before he found someone who would talk to him about the white men. He hadn't passed the information back; he had decided to save it for the incoming Taz Dhar.

Taz and Jonjo took an almost instant dislike to one another. A blunter mind than his would have realized that she was not merely jet-lagged, but drunk too, and a more blurred vision than even a semi-drunk Taz's was unlikely to miss the distaste and superiority that tugged down the corners of Jonjo's mouth, and stiffened his back and movements. The airport had exploded in a welter of noise and excitement as Taz and her fellow passengers stepped out from immigration control, and were swallowed up by the hustling, dash-asking melee around them. He had not extended a hand to shake the one she offered when he identified himself, but had merely glanced at her bags, turned and hissed for a coolie, growling a dismissal at the dozen enthusiastic mavericks who descended on Taz's bags like vultures on carrion.

He walked a pace and a half ahead of her to the car, and responded to her overtures of conversation with icy-polite and distant, single-syllable conversation killers.

He was not, he made clear, a holiday guide, or a courier, or a nursemaid. He was a reporter, like her. A professional, he added pointedly. As she was new to Ghana, and as a matter of professional courtesy, he would see her settled in her hotel. Thereafter, they would collaborate on the story, and there was a point or two he would want to discuss about credits at the appropriate time. In the interim, they would work, together when necessary, apart preferably. If she needed a guide, protector, and someone to haggle for her in the curio market, her hotel could recommend one. That was not, never had been, and never would be, his role.

Warm welcome, the Minister for Tourism had been quoted as promising. Hah! She was getting used to being met by miserable bastards in foreign places. One day, she thought, I'm going to arrive in a country and be met by someone who is actually going to smile and say 'Welcome.'

'You're pretty sure of yourself, aren't you?' Taz said, as he handed her a room key in the lobby of the Penta Hotel, and turned to walk away.

He paused, and turned, nodding. 'I am a reporter. One of the best. In Ghana. In Africa. You've seen my portfolio? No? You can. Tomorrow. Wars. Scandals. Executions, corruption. Interviews with Presidents. Insights. Visions. I am pretty sure of myself, because I am the best. You?'

Taz brushed the hair back from her face, and shook her head, smiling, admiring, against her own better judgement, such a granite slab of self-confidence from such a shrunken, tattered character. 'In my own field, I'm pretty good too. Or was. Had a big following. Upped the ratings, crashed and burned the opposition. Does that mean anything to you? Probably not. Now, I'm just a drink problem with good legs. I've got no fat portfolio to show off. Oh, I guess I could create one. Some of my best broadcasts are used on media studies courses. I guess I could lug those around with me if I wanted. But it's not important, you see? I know I've got this one chance. This one story. It's my way back. Of course, a way back wouldn't interest a big reporter like you. Not someone with your track record. You don't need that, do you? You're still at the top of your game. Where are you working now? What paper? What's the dateline on the last thing in this great portfolio of yours?'

The anger didn't so much flare in Jonjo's eyes as it gradually ignited, like a gas flame catching, and being turned up, full. He opened his mouth to speak. Taz, whose years in a studio had taught her a sense of timing of which Jonjo could never even perceive the value, turned, and with a breezy, 'See you at 9.15 tomorrow morning, hot shot', left him stinging in the empty foyer, glowering round at the cheap African masks, puffing and snorting like a wounded bull mastiff.

STATEMENT No 5. RECORDED 12 MARCH 2006
DARKO FARM REFUGEE CAMP, GREATER ACCRA

My name is Purdy Gbalzeh. I am thirty-seven years old. I knew these people who died. One of them came to my house one night with three other men. This one. (Interviewee indicates image of ROBERT LLOYD) They looked like soldiers, but they weren't Liberians. They spoke English to each other.

He told me that I must get my family and get ready to leave. Said there would be a lorry to transport us.

At first, I refused. The war had gone on for a long time, and no harm had come to us. Now it was over. Everyone said so. Why should I leave my home?

He told me that the guerrillas were back and they were about to attack. They were Krahn.

I said I was not concerned with politics. He said it didn't matter. Said my family would be killed.

My home was in the Grand Cape Mount region, in the west of my country. It was a beautiful place. Now, I live here, and I have nothing.

But he saved my life, and my family's. I know that. Others have come since, who have seen what happened then, in the area around my home. Many died. Many more were tortured.

I never saw that man again. He gave us money to get here, and told us who to ask for. I think he pays for this camp, but I don't know that. Only that people say this. Why does God do these things? Why does he take such good people? One day, I would like to see that man again, in heaven. I would like to thank him. He saved my family, and me, too.

Accra was about as far from Addis Ababa as it was possible to get in Africa. On the other side of the continent, down at sea level. But that was merely to site the contrasts physically: Where Addis had been sombre, chill, disciplined and awash with thin soldiers and policemen with AK-47s, and its people reserved, wary and excessively polite, Taz found Accra brash, loud, hot, modern and anarchic. Wide dual carriageways raced traffic from flyovers to fat roundabouts sporting socialist statuary amid a fiesta of exuberant blooms. Tall office blocks reflected sunlight back down onto busy thoroughfares, where pot-bellied policemen on point duty wore British bobby helmets, snowy white, and were armed with nothing more than whistles and mobile phones. Plump, straight-backed women decked out in explosive colours rolled along the street, dignified, calm and easy; like stately galleons with psychedelic sails, wafted by light breezes, indifferent to the honking Toyotas, Fords and VWs with their radios blaring out distorted gospel music, hiplife, high-life and reggae. Battered Tro-Tros, private buses, hawked rides to the Ridge, cantonments, Labadi and Labone, with religious musings and street philosophy offered for free on their front and rear windows: *Respect the Old Man; Are you God?; Rescue the Perishing, Care for the Dying; Give better clap to Jesus, Be Quiet and Shut Up.* Very occasionally, an antiquated, majestic blue mammy wagon would force its bulbous and battered nose into the throng, like a proud old prizefighter coming up to the line one more time. The last of thousands of Bedford trucks, shipped out CKD, Completely Knocked Down, half a century earlier to become the engine of transport, trade and growth in Britain's West African colonies. Once ubiquitous, with their wooden bodies locally crafted, in thick afina wood, mahogany and walnut, today anachronistic as a red Routemaster on the streets of London. Sweat-slick hawkers in stained singlets dipped and dived among the vehicles, offering everything from yesterday's editions of London's papers through Chinese padlocks to fresh fish on loaded trays on their heads, yet the negotiations on price were as often debated in a passionate English accentuated with hints of Brixton, as in clattering, rhythmic Ewe and Fanti.

There was dust and smoke and noise and life and joy: a cosmopolitan Africa this, comprehensible, with a touch of Mumbai and a lot of Saaf London, and comfortable, too, to Taz's Asian fusion eyes.

She was well aware there was another West Africa beyond; obscure places the world never heard of like Upper Volta, Chad, Mauritania and Benin and still others; Sierra Leone, Liberia, Nigeria, which the world knew, but only as the home of obscene slaughter perpetrated by drugged-up and juju-inspired child warriors, or as lands ruled by warlords, palsied despots and brutal military regimes. Names which were bywords for fraud and corruption on such a breathtaking scale they had to invent new words to describe them. Lands of blood diamonds, tainted wealth and sullied beliefs. Why did she know Ghana before her arrival only as the country of origin of a significant part of the workforce that kept London functioning, and as the emerging competition to India in the call centre business? Because it was an unnewsworthy oasis of comparative wealth, vociferous peace and busy tranquillity. A bustling oasis in a region with a grim past of slavery and dark practices and a cruel present of corruption and violence. No wonder Ghanaians would greet one another of a morning with a cry of 'Are we alive?' and be told 'Eh! We are alive, Oh!' and both would laugh and shake hands and snap their fingers at the sheer joy and infinite possibilities, and the minor miracle of another day in Ghana.

Yes, a happy, welcoming people... but with exceptions to every rule.

Jonjo Amin Asante had made it clear that his job description did not stretch to exposing her to the more picturesque aspects of his country, of which he held a less romantic view than hers. So, having been assured Accra was one of the safest capital cities in the world, she wandered the streets after breakfast and absorbed the sights. She stood and watched a funeral procession pass; men in toga-like wraps of shiny purple cloth, so dark it shone almost black, one shoulder bare. She thought about death, and Armitage Shanks, and waited for Jonjo to come around. She wondered, now she was virtually back on the staff, if she should do a piece on Accra. She gave SK a quick ring to ask him. He said no.

On his eventual arrival, she asked Jonjo if he could recommend another hotel; she told him she thought she would probably have a problem sleeping in one so near the Ring Road, and so clearly on the final approach to the airport. He pretended not to hear. She asked him if he wanted tea. He said yes.

She asked him if he had everything he needed to make a start. He glanced at her, his eyes half closed. There was a look of overweening self-confidence about him. He reached into his jacket pocket, and took out six sheets of folded typescript.

'Things I have found out so far.'

Taz's eyes widened. 'You've been busy.'

Jonjo's heavy eyelids dropped once, in a massively smug gesture that she suspected ancient chiefs had used when accepting tributes.

She unfolded the sheets and scanned the neatly-typed notes. They were transcripts of two interviews.

'Did you show them the photograph?' SK'd had the image enhanced, digitized and e-mailed. Jonjo had a wad of copies in his briefcase.

Breath escaped from him like a punctured tyre. She assumed that meant yes.

'What did they...'

'Read,' said Jonjo.

She decided to let that one pass. 'Can you find other people who knew them? Maybe worked with them, or went on the boat trip?'

A hint of irritation flickered across his face. 'That is what you are paying me for. Not to arrange hotel bookings. This afternoon, I am seeing a man who says he went to Liberia with one of them.'

'Do you want me to come?' asked Taz, and then immediately regretted it.

'It would be better not. He will talk to me. If he wants to

talk in Ewe, I can still understand him. If he wants to talk in Fanti, I can talk to him in that, too. With you there? All he will think about will be money. He will say whatever he thinks you want him to say so that he can get more money. You stay here and read what I have got so far.'

The tea arrived. He poured himself a cup, into which he ladled three spoonsful of sugar, and filled the chipped cup to the brim with condensed milk. He did not offer to pour any for her.

Taz suspected that she hated Jonjo Amin Asante. Just as surely as she knew she needed him.

∾

STATEMENT No 3. RECORDED 9 MARCH 2006. NORTH RIDGE HOTEL, ACCRA

My name is Samual Adu. I am twenty-nine years old. My home is in Brong-Ahafu. For three years I have worked with Safe Return in the Buduburam Camp. I knew the Abruni, Mr Lloyd. He said we should call him Bob, but we always called him Mr Lloyd.

He was a good man. A wonderful man. When my baby boy was ill, he arranged for my son to get medicine. It must have cost him a lot of money, because at that time there was a shortage of medicine, and the hospitals were turning people away. He never asked for anything in return. I wish I could have done something for him. I owe him my son's life. What greater debt can there be? What better thing can a man do? What more is there to say?

∾

Gord watched the sun set on the Thames and felt profoundly homesick. Everyone thought him American, though he was actually Canadian—just. From a small town in British Columbia right on the US border, where the hear beat down on his fifty acres of vines and the afternoon sky turned red, purple and grey from forest fires blazing out of control down in Washington State. Ideally suited, the US State Department had said, to play the honest broker. Not an anal retentive Brit. Not a brash and arrogant Yank. Everyone trusted a Canuck.

There was, he thought, something about a sunset. Twilight: half dark. A time for reflection. Something people who live where the sun plops down over the horizon with a heavy indifference for the passing of the light can never truly appreciate. A time to take a last desperate grasp at the day. To steal back meaning and purpose from among the trivia and the meanness before another day has gone forever. Lost, sacrificed, traded. A day that had dawned, just as leisurely, not so many hours earlier, pregnant with infinite possibility, now slipping into the past, surrendered to predictable activity.

He thought of his home and sadly registered the polarizing of another day spent away from it. He wondered what this year's vintage would be like. Better than the last two, please God. Then he could give up this shit and live the life he wanted to, where he wanted to and never, ever travel out of Canada again.

He thought of the vast green Bill Reid sculpture in Vancouver airport he invariably, superstitiously touched every time he travelled abroad: The Jade Canoe. Full of fantastic creatures from Haida mythology: the Bear Mother and the Raven. The Dogfish woman and the Frog, the Eagle, the Mouse Woman and the Wolf, all tumbling, curling and squabbling around the tall, erect figure of the Spirit of Haida Gwaii. And there, easily missable at the Spirit's side, the dour figure of the Ancient Reluctant Conscript.

That was the figure upon which Gord placed his hand. The one for which he felt an abiding affinity; paddling stoically amid the writhing, spiteful anarchy. That was what he identified with. The unwilling, unenthusiastic, un-young.

He strode, hands thrust deep in pockets, to The Morpeth Arms, fought his way through the crowded bar and up the back stairs to the deserted room with the view across the river to Vauxhall. The person he was due to meet rose and advanced toward him, soft drink in hand.

'Good of you to come.'

'Your invitation would be hard to resist at any time, Superintendent Shastri. I hadn't realized you were back in the UK.'

'Officially, I'm not,' smiled Rohit. 'Passing through. Thought we might talk a little as two professionals.'

Rohit Shastri indicated a glass of wine on one of the tables: Gord picked it up, sniffed, turned down the corners of his mouth in disdain, and placed it untouched back on the table.

'I'm listening.'

Rohit had been preparing for this conversation for several weeks. Now the moment was upon him, the magnitude of what he was about to do weighed heavily. He sipped his orange-and-soda to give himself a moment.

'You know,' he began, falteringly, 'I feel so at home here. Britain and India have so much in common. We are the only peoples in the world to share a true appreciation of class and caste. We both distrust simple certainties. We both love ambiguity and delight in secrecy for its own sake. But we Indians, like you Canadians, are custodians of a big country. Britain is tiny. It affects the way people think. We think big. They think small. And we are the future. They are the past.' Rohit leaned forward, and lowered his voice. 'Do you know what I would say if I happened to be speaking to someone from the US State Department?'

'I'm still listening.'

'I'd say the British delude themselves that there is a special relationship between the US and the UK, based on race and language, because that was dead long before the Second World War ended. The US only has one special relationship, and that's with Israel, and it's based on money and influence. But there have to be higher ideals. We are the world's biggest democracy. A secular state...'

'And you think that should make India America's choice for a special relationship in Asia?'

'Much more than that,' Rohit enthused. 'We are smarter, more flexible, much more numerous, far less costly and we are willing to make difficult compromises. Oh, I know, China is bigger, but despotic and unstable. Pakistan is momentarily of greater strategic importance in the War on Terror. But by all the rules America is built on, we are more than their best choice, we are their natural successor.'

'Wow! I don't think I'd say that to them if I were you. You ought to be a politician.'

'Oh,' smiled Rohit. 'I intend to be! But first, I have a duty.'

'Yes' said Gord, sadly. 'We both do. You know Taz Dhar is globetrotting again?'

'So I was informed by our police colleagues.' Rohit stared unblinking at Gord. 'Back to India, they tell me.'

Gord met his stare, and smiled. 'So they say. Is she one of yours?'

Rohit shook his head vigorously. 'A free agent. Far too unstable for us.'

'Someone claiming to be the letter-writer called her four days ago. Know anything about that?'

'Not a thing.'

'Then the purpose of this meeting is...?'

'To ask you to tell your bosses we could do this for them so much better than the British.'

Gord threw back his head and guffawed. 'Are you high?

What do you think "this" is? Some Macdonald's franchise? A sweatshop for Wal-Mart? A call centre that can be shifted from Bradford to Bangalore and no one will notice?'

'That's exactly what I think this is,' said Rohit. 'A back office activity that you need done well but don't want to do yourselves. Ethiopia? Liberia? Is this really where you want this done?'

Gord glanced out of the window. It was full night now. The streetlights were on and the Secret Intelligence Service building across the river, a bastion of sandstone and metal, was lit up like a Disney fortress, its image reflected in the shimmering surface of the river. 'You think "this" is that easy? We are walking a fibre-thin line here. Get "this" wrong and horrible things follow—Nazi death camps are what happens when you authorize innately decent and highly efficient people to abuse their fellowmen. Abu Ghraib is what happens when you give the same opportunity to the God-fearing but inept.'

'That's why we have laws. Work with us,' urged Rohit, his eyes shining like a zealot. 'We can keep the entire thing in-country. No more sub-contracting to places and people you don't want to be dealing with. And remember, the British gave us more than railways and bureaucracy. Around the end of the nineteenth century, they passed an Act to create the Indian Telephone System and a mere six months later, another authorizing phone-tapping. Every one of Britain's colonies had laws empowering the Governor to declare an Emergency and suspend civil rights, and our grandfathers railed against such draconian powers, but you know what? Nowhere did people repeal those laws once they gained Independence. The British bequeathed to us a marvellous raft of laws and powers, more than sufficient to do everything you'll ever want us to without once stepping outside Due Process. Think of it, the world's richest democracy and the world's biggest, working together to make the planet a safer place. Your contract with the organization in Euston has six months left to run, and you are having second thoughts about renewing with them...'

'How would you possibly know that?' asked Gord. 'Even if it were true, which it isn't.'

'Every sixth person on this planet is an Indian. We have the biggest, richest, highest-educated and best-integrated diaspora the world has ever seen. Mention that too when you put our offer forward.'

12

Jonjo Amin Asante found himself warming to the assignment; whilst he had little appetite for eulogizing white martyrs, he rejoiced in the rigours and discipline of the task, as well as in the exercise of old skills he feared, secretly, that he might have lost in the past six years of information bureau document-scanning, text-proofing and occasional copywriting.

His dislike of Taz Dhar grew in proportion to his rekindled enthusiasm. Not only did he dislike her because, as a matter of course, he despised drunkards, he disliked her because he disliked every Indian he had ever met, and there seemed nothing about her to make him revise that world view. He disapproved too of women doing men's jobs. He also knew with a massive certainty he was much better placed to pursue this story than she, and he increasingly felt it to be his story, not hers. That was what shifted obligatory dislike along his spectrum of disapproval and displeasure toward something nearer to hatred: day by day, he marginalized. She asked him to re-interview the people he'd spoken to earlier. Ask them if they knew Hugo Ruhl. He hadn't done so. Partly to annoy her, but mainly because he was pretty sure as soon as he started to let her tell him what to do, she would be in control.

He could, of course, have spoken to them again, and then simply not told her. Or just tell her he had and that none of them had ever heard of Hugo Ruhl, but that was not his style. He would not lie. Ever. To her or to anyone else. But he wouldn't offer her more than, in his view, what she was entitled to. What she was paying for. In the first few days, she had asked him questions about himself; his family. Where he lived. He'd simply refused to answer. Hoping to find some crack in his slate-faced indifference, she asked to see his portfolio. He delivered it to her hotel promptly the next morning.

Taz read through the pieces. There was no denying he had been good. Fearless, viciously confrontational at times, massively compassionate at others. But all, some time ago. But God, could he write! His English was superb, with the ability to put a spit in a phrase that gave it a whole new meaning and perfectly captured the essence of what he had to say.

She warmed to him as she read through the pieces. One, a description of the destruction of a village in Liberia, made her cry. His stock went up even higher when she found, slipped as though by accident into the carefully maintained portfolio, two statements he had not shared with her but had still faithfully transcribed from his antique tape recorder:

STATEMENT No 1. RECORDED 8 MARCH 2006.
POLICE HEADQUARTERS, ACCRA

I know you. You are Joseph Amin Asante. Do you remember me? Ten years ago you said some robber dashed me small to leave him alone. I was demoted for that. Now, I am a big man and you are the small boy, Amin Asante. Clear off. I have nothing to say to you. Don't let me find you hanging around here again.

STATEMENT No 2. RECORDED 9 MARCH 2006.
DAILY GRAPHIC OFFICES, ACCRA

'Eh, it's Jo Amin! I thought you were dead. Put that thing away, old man. Stop playing at still being a reporter. Go home to your village, sit

under a tree and eat guinea fowl with the other old men. What? I don't care what you are working on: go away. You spoil our name simply by hanging around.

When he returned late in the afternoon with the transcripts of two more interviews, she thanked him for letting her see the portfolio, and began to ask him questions. He closed down her interest with the indifferent precision of someone switching off a DVD. He didn't want her as a friend, or even as a colleague. He didn't want her around. He needed her, as an employer, but that role she could serve equally well half a world away.

What he wanted was the Armitage Shanks' story. For himself.

∾

STATEMENT No 6. RECORDED 12 MARCH 2006. BUDUBURAM CAMP

My name is David Birch. I am the co-ordinator of Safe Return's project here in Buduburam. My role is to help and support as many of our clients as possible to return to their homes in Liberia.

We do not like the term 'refugees'. Nor do we use the expression 'asylum-seekers'. These are people who, through violence and intimidation, have had their homes, their livelihoods and their citizenship taken from them. Our aim is to help them to reclaim and repossess what is theirs by right.

I have a team of fourteen working with me. Until the sad death of our friends and colleagues, there were six ex-pats, four Ghanaian nationals and four Liberians. Now, I am the only member of the team who is not an African.

You want to know about our friends and colleagues who died on the lake? Well, where shall I begin? Johnnie Peters, the one whose body was found? Well, he had only been with us about a year. Great fun, heaving with enthusiasm and energy. He could do magic tricks. Organize party games. Just a big kid himself, really. The kids all loved him. So did everybody, really. Before coming here, he had done a few years in the army, even spent some time in Afghanistan, one of those special units. Intelligence-gathering. A very gifted linguist. He could speak Ewe and Twi after just being here a few months. Was fluent in Krahn by the time he died. Just one of those people who had an ear for it, I guess.

He had a girlfriend back in the UK. I met her at the funeral. Lovely girl. Heartbroken, of course.

His work? Well, like the others, he was allocated a dozen families who had expressed a wish to return, and he would make visits to their home areas with them, discuss what they would need to re-establish themselves there; help them find work, get the kids school places and assess the level of risk they might face. That sort of thing.

He worked very closely with Bob Lloyd, and the two of them did well. Had a very high SRR: Successful Resettlement Rate.

Dilip Dutta had been with us here slightly longer. He had worked for Safe Return for some years, but mainly at our global headquarters in Vancouver. This was his first field assignment, and I think between the two of us it had been arranged to get him the necessary experience so he could advance in the organization. Dilip, don't get me wrong, lovely man, was very much an operator: one of those people who really enjoy organizational politics. To tell you the truth, his heart wasn't really in his work here. He found conditions out here tiresome and the pace at which things happened absolutely infuriating. That's the thing about West Africa: you love it or you hate it. You simply can't be indifferent to it. All of us, we love it. But Dilip? Well I'm afraid he hated it. He used to get into the most terrible paddies about things. Little things that he could do nothing about. Power failures, water shortages, people being late for meetings. The rest of us, we accept it. Joke about the fact that meetings will take place according to GMT—Ghana Maybe Time. But not Dilip.

He was due to go home, back to Canada two weeks after the accident. That was one of the reasons for the trip: a farewell treat. Poor old Dilip.

The other two, Andrew Carr and Bob Lloyd were two of our most experienced colleagues. Both had been with *Safe Return* for more than ten years. Andrew had done time, sorry, that sounds like he was a convict or something, doesn't it? Anyway, Andrew had worked for us in the DRC—the Democratic Republic of the Congo, Burundi and Rwanda. Bob Lloyd had been in Sierra Leone and the Lebanon. Both of them had worked together in Kosovo.

Because they were so experienced, they had extra responsibilities. As well as having a dozen families, they were handling for resettling, both represented Safe Return in support of the DDR programme—Disarmament, Demobilization and Reintegration of soldiers as well as repatriation of both people here and internally displaced people.

They have been extremely successful. Both had been nominated for awards. What they achieved together was little short of remarkable. They will be, they will all be, greatly missed.

How do I feel now? How do you think I feel? I lost four friends and four colleagues and had it not been for a minor crisis here, just before they set off, I would have been with them on that boat. How would that make you feel?

∾

Taz liked, felt warm toward and vindicated by the image of Armitage Shanks that was emerging from Jojo Amin Asante's interviews. Of course she was convinced Robert Lloyd was the man who had written to her. Had spoken to her. Bob? Hmmm. Fifty-something. The right age for the reference to the Gene Pitney song. There was a Pound Street in the market town in which he'd been born, and there had been a Slaughter House there. Closed down in the late Sixties. She had checked. It had to be him. Worldly, caring. Just the kind of man to have written such a letter.

The interviews described a brave, committed individual, taking risks for a cause he believed in and for people he cared about. His picture was among those in Hugo Ruhl's montage, and there he was in the group snap of the farewell function. He was the one standing with his hand on Ruhl's shoulder. She could put names to all the faces now. Seated on Ruhl's left, Andrew Carr, and on his right, Johnny Peters. Well, he didn't look like that now, poor sod. She'd seen post mortem photographs and read the autopsy report. Death had been caused by the shock of the explosion. Severe damage to lungs and internal organs. Dead before he entered the water; virtually no water in the lungs. Severe burns to most of the body. Left hand and forearm missing. He was left-handed. Looked like he'd been holding on to or reaching out for whatever had caused the explosion. Best not to think about it.

Robert Lloyd: strange to think she had heard his voice. Not really what you might call good-looking, but decent, amiable. The sort you would trust. She wondered if the others had been renamed Armitage Shanks, and where they now were. If he had somehow survived the explosion, perhaps they had too. Was Dilip Dutta the dead Indian businessman? It would be a bitter irony if Bob Lloyd had ended up wearing his friend's clothes and never knowing to whom they had belonged. Never realizing how close to their late owner he had been. She studied the slightly blurred figure. Unlikely perhaps, they were not of a similar build. Lloyd was taller, broader and heavier than Dutta. But possible still. Something she should follow up? What should she now be doing? She wasn't sure. She settled to the latest interview transcripts.

STATEMENT No 7. RECORDED 13 MARCH 2006. BY TELEPHONE

Claire Dickenson? This is she. Yes it's been a terrible blow to us all. We work in twenty-three different countries at the moment, with a team of over 400, including our headquarters staff. Everyone of our people is important. But Dilip, Bob, Andy and... Martin, were not just colleagues but friends too. Dilip was due to become my second deputy director. Andy and Bob had done wonderful work in the past. All were doing great things in and for Liberia. Now if you'll excuse me...'

Nothing like a manager who knows her staff. Didn't even seem to recall that Peters was called Johnny although his first name was Martin.

STATEMENT No 8. RECORDED 16 MARCH 2006. NOVOTEL, ACCRA

'My name is Antonio D'Silva. I represent the United Nations High Commissioner for Refugees in Ghana. Like everyone else, I was deeply saddened to hear of the untimely deaths of the workers from Safe Return.

I have nothing but respect for the four who died, but you will be aware of the number of concerns expressed about Safe Return. There seems to be a degree of confusion about their objectives and there have been criticisms about their methodology. In particular they seem to have been accommodations reached with a number of highly undesirable groupings both in Liberia and within Buduburam Camp itself.

Don't get me wrong, this is a complex world, and a highly difficult and sensitive area in which to work. But there have to be standards. At times, people claim that Safe Return has crossed the line between what is acceptable and what is not.

Examples? Well, there have been reports, unsubstantiated I admit, but from a number of sources, that funds allocated to support the return of refugees are not being properly accounted for. Safe Return exists to do exactly what its name implies: returning refugees safely to their homes. And its workers have been quite successful at it, but the process seems very expensive and it is difficult to see where all the funding is coming from. So we audited their accounts and found a number of anomalies. When something is going wrong, the usual thing you find is that a single item will be charged for several times. But this is the weird thing: we found exactly the opposite. Amounts we had granted to Safe Return appeared to be being used over and over. That, say, for every $100 we granted, we were getting

$1000 in goods and services. Very strange. Let me stress, these are only allegations at this stage, but they are, shall we say, causes for concern.

STATEMENT No 9. RECORDED 17 MARCH 2006. GHANA JOURNALISTS ASSOCIATION HQ, ACCRA

My name is Confidence Kwame Ampong. Everyone knows me as CK. I am a journalist.

Six months ago, I did a feature on the parlous state of governance in Buduburam Camp. Girls, some as young as eleven years old having to trade sex for extra rations. Gangs of organized criminals—thieves, protection racketeers. Corruption in camp management. All these things.

What does this have to do with the four men who died? They were all involved in it. That's what.

STATEMENT No 10. RECORDED 17 MARCH 2006 JAMESTOWN PRISON, ACCRA.

My name is Okechi Nwodo. I am a Nigerian citizen. I do not know why these people have arrested me. I am innocent of all charges.

They say I have knowledge of drug-smuggling events. This is not true. I knew the men who died. I thought they were my friends. But they were not. They are the ones who are responsible for me being here. This one (interviewee indicates image of ANDREW CARR). He is the drug-smuggler. I am innocent.

Late in 2004, before the Harmatan, he asked me to drive a lorry for him. He gave me money, and papers. He told me everything would be all right. That the goods in the lorry were all cleared by customs and that all the paperwork was complete.

I trusted him. I drove his lorry for him: three journeys, three weeks. Then, he told me to drive to Ghana, and that he would meet me at the Buduburam Camp. He told me he would pay me a lot of money. I trusted him. I was stopped by the police and searched. They found drugs in the lorry. I did not know they were there. I told them about Mr Carr, but they didn't believe me.

I am innocent of the charges. I tell you, this Abruni is the one they want. But when I tell them, they don't listen. They hate me because I am a Nigerian.

OK, she told herself, so Idi Amin, as she had begun to refer to Jonjo in her mind, was dictating the pace right now, and she was slow, and pretty disoriented. Who wouldn't be? But she was picking herself up, and getting things sorted out.

She was looking better, too. With nothing practical to do, she thought about trying an hour or two in a health centre, and was told that the Labadi Beach Hotel might be a good place to try. It had been something, much to her surprise, Jonjo had been only too willing to arrange for her. She had been so taken aback she had agreed to his request to hire a car for his use, with barely a second thought.

SK rang. 'How's this information agency doing? Any problems?'

'No. We're on top of things here. You've seen the transcripts? Idi Amin is good, I have to hand it to him.'

'Idi Amin? Wasn't he some black despot who hated Indians?'

'Got it in one.'

'I take it he isn't with you now?'

'Waiting for me actually. He's going off to another Refugee Camp later on. He's going to drop me somewhere first.'

'And how will you piss away your day?'

She thought about that. Long and hard.

'What?' asked SK, concerned. 'Have I used an inappropriate colloquialism?'

'No, SK. You've said exactly the right thing. Absolutely spot on. That's what I'm doing, isn't it? Pissing away my days. Thanks. Now you must excuse me, I'm going to have a quick word with Idi Amin.'

∾

Jonjo sat in a low chair in the foyer, his arms stretched along the back of the seat, his fingers drumming lightly on the taut material. His lips were pursued in a soundless whistle, and he breathed an old tune he couldn't name, but which came to him in rare moments of peace and tranquillity. He sat with both feet square on the floor: crossed legs crease trousers, his mother used to tell him, and he told his children in turn. Not that they listened. He wore a collarless, sleeveless, tie-and-dye shirt, olive-green trousers, and a wafer-thin pair of sandals. He looked out through the glass doors which held in the chill of the air-conditioning, to the car park, screwing his eyes up against the brightness.

There was a significant contributor to his uncharacteristic joy: the wide, flat and battered white Peugeot he had hired.

He hadn't driven a car for five years; he had been nervous when he'd gone to collect it. Afraid the traffic would be too much for him. Instead, he found the feel of the heavy car, with its lumpy steering and juddering gear stick, easy and familiar, as though he still drove every day.

He allowed far too much time for the journey; he had been outside the Penta at twenty-five to eight, so he had driven down to Danquah Circle, along the Ring Road, and back into Osu, telling himself he was getting the feel of the car and hoping an acquaintance or two would see him.

He tapped his trouser pocket; felt the keys against his thigh. What a surprisingly satisfying sensation. What a sense of power, status and significance a small thing like a car key could impart. He even smiled when he saw Taz; an expression she had not seen before which made her wonder momentarily if he had indigestion. He stood up as she approached, and smoothed his shirt. He held out is hand, formally, to shake hers, as he did every morning.

'Good morning, Miss Dhar! It's the day for the Labadi Beach, the gymnasium. Everything is arranged.'

'Stuff it, Mr Amin Asante.'

Jonjo's eyebrows rose slightly; he thought he may have misheard.

'Are you familiar with the expression "jerking around", Mr Amin Asante?' Taz continued. 'No? Well leaving aside its gender-biased provenance for subsequent analysis, it's a valuable bit of idiom which I commend to you as neatly encapsulating the concept of futile activity, wasted time. As in, "You are jerking me around, Mr Amin Asante".'

Jonjo's eyes half closed, and a long breath, with a groan beneath it, escaped him. 'You don't want to go to the Labadi Beach.'

'Well done, Mr Amin Asante. Nor do I want to go shopping, or to the George Padmore Memorial Library, or the Arts Centre. I want to get back in charge of pursuing my story.'

'Your story?' he began.

'My story.' she confirmed. 'Do you like the car?'

'I have found Hugo Ruhl's wife,' said Jonjo, quickly.

Taz nodded. 'That's better, Mr Amin Asante. When do we go and see her?'

'I thought you might like to see her by yourself. You won't need me to translate. She speaks English. I can carry on with the interviews I have lined up.'

'Better still, Mr Amin Asante. We understand each other. That's good. That's the basis of a working relationship, don't you think?'

Jonjo nodded. 'An equal share of the work, and the rewards.'

'Maybe. Can I see Frau Ruhl today?'

Jonjo shook his head. 'Tomorrow, maybe.'

'Are there arrangements that need to be made?'

Jonjo sniffed, took an envelope from his pocket and held it out to her. She took it with a frown.

'What's this?'

'An airline ticket for tomorrow morning's flight. The woman is in The Gambia.'

The triumph in Jonjo's eyes was mirrored by a sneaking and resentful respect in Taz's as she nodded, and took the ticket.

'How long do you think I'll need to be away?'

'A week, ten days maybe. I've left the return portion of the ticket open, but flights out here are irregular. Maybe two weeks.'

'Meanwhile, you'll carry on here? I don't know, Mr Amin Asante. Maybe I should send you to The Gambia. Maybe you should go and interview the lady.'

Jonjo knew she was bluffing. He knew Ghana: she had met Hugo Ruhl. It would make no sense to do it any other way but how he had suggested. He said nothing.

He's learning about timing, Taz thought.

'Or maybe I should ask the Information Bureau to assign someone else to this job, huh?'

'I am the best,' Jonjo said, simply.

Taz shrugged. 'I don't doubt it. But maybe I want someone who's going to do what I tell them, or maybe I just don't like your face. I guess this job represents pretty big business for your Information Bureau, huh? I expect they'll meet the whims of the client as big as us, don't you? Where will that leave you, Mr Amin Asante? No story, no expense account, no big, white car. The one you hired is that big white one over there, isn't it? I thought it would be. What do you think, Mr Amin Asante? Shall I make that call?'

She glanced down at her mobile phone. 'Or shall we agree to a few new ground rules?' she asked him. 'By the time I get back, I want everything you can get on all four dead friends, Safe Return and Hugo Ruhl. I want the photograph of them all together published in at least two daily papers with a request for anyone who can identify any of the men to contact the Information Bureau, and you can even offer a small reward for new information. By the time I get back I want to know everything there is to know about them, Safe Return and Armitage Shanks too. Are we clear, Mr Amin Asante?'

Any trace of triumph had given way to anger and resentment. For the first time, Taz noticed that the whites of his eyes were pink with age. If she hadn't disliked him so much, she would have felt a twinge of sympathy, but instead she merely prepared herself for what she was sure would be a counter-attack. She wanted to keep him on the story, because she knew he had skills in abundance, and contacts and access to which she could never even aspire. He was the best around here, just as he said: bloody good by anybody's standards. She was even willing to consider giving him part credit for any story that ultimately emerged, but right now, they had to get the power politics sorted out, once and for all.

'Well?' she prompted.

'Well, Miss Dhar,' said Jonjo, slow and measured, 'you are the one in charge. You've got the money. You've got the power. You can dictate the terms, and I have no choice, do I? We'll do it your way. Just as you insist. We'll publish the photograph that you stole, and we'll ask for people to identify the men in it, even though we know one of them is the man you stole the photograph from. No doubt you have thought of that. No doubt you already know how you are going to deal with the charges of theft, infringement of copyright and invasion of privacy. After all, you're in charge. I expect you'll just spend some more of your foreign money, and buy your way out of it. Why should I worry? I'm just some old black man you've hired, aren't I? Someone you can dismiss because you don't like my face. Isn't that right? So I'll go along and get this published then, shall I? You'll forgive me if I just ask the head of the Bureau how he feels about handling stolen goods.

You see, he has principles, just as I do. Old-fashioned ones. Who knows, he may even want to confirm your instructions with the people who are paying us. We wouldn't want them to think we were, what was the expression, jerking them around, now, would we, Miss Dhar? But that won't be a problem, will it? After all, I'm sure all those things you told me after you had had a few drinks weren't really true. You used a nice expression when we first met. Something about people thinking you were nothing more than a drink problem with good legs? After all, you're not like me, are you, Miss Dhar? No one can just get rid of you because they don't like your face, can they? After all, it wouldn't be for any reason like that that you're here, would it? No, no. I'm sure your employers—are they still employing you, by the way? You weren't too sure on your last drinking binge. Anyway, I'm sure they'll be happy to underwrite your illegal activities on their behalf, and even explain to Mr Ruhl how they come to be paying to publish a picture stolen from him. You're the one in charge.'

Taz bit her bottom lip, her face was burning, and she couldn't meet Jonjo's unblinking stare.

'How did you know about the photograph?'

'You talk too much, Miss Dhar. And you want me to think that you're cleverer than you are. So you boast. Although you won't admit it, you want me to respect you. So you try to impress me. The more you drink, the harder you try. How old are you, Miss Dhar? Around forty? When I was little more than half your age, the presidents of three countries had their agents bribe different compositors on the *PDG* to sneak them a sight of my column before it hit the streets. Colonels in their security services had what I wrote copied out in longhand and telephoned into the Castle—an old slave fort, still the headquarters of Government, the President's Office and, in the days of the military rule of the PNDC, a place where people were taken, tortured and never returned from—or radioed out to Monrovia and Lagos. In one week I turned down three bribes, each of which would have kept me comfortable for a decade, and received four death threats. There have been six attempts on my life, and I've spent ten months under house arrest and done a year of hard labour. You hate me because you know I am a better reporter than you will ever be. You want me to respect you. You, whose greatest claim as a reporter is the capacity to read words in big print off an autocue and to mock and insult people who have simply rung up for your advice. You don't even have a right to this story. If there's a story here, it's an African story, and it's going to take more than your money and that letter you received to find it out. It's going to take a real reporter. An African reporter. If you think you have a hope without me, then you just make the telephone call, right now. Otherwise, get packed for the trip to The Gambia, and leave me to find Armitage Shanks in my own way. Take the photograph. Show it to the woman. It may be a comfort to her. Take these interview reports too. They will not. Ground rules agreed?'

STATEMENT 11 RECORDED 18 MARCH 2006. DARKO FARM REFUGEE CAMP, GREATER ACCRA

My name is Penda. I do not want to give my family name. I am thirty-two years old. I came here to escape the war in Liberia. I have been in the camp for eight-and-a-half years.

I knew the White Men. One of them, that one (interviewee indicates image of ANDREW CARR) very well.

He came with the soldiers, when they came to my home. They killed my father, and two of my brothers. They took my youngest brother away. They raped me, in front of my mother. Then they raped my sister. They killed my mother and my sister. They left me for dead. All the time this man watched. Once, he said something to one of the soldiers when he was on top of me. It made the soldier laugh.

He had been to our home before. We had welcomed him, and given him food and shelter because people said he was a good man. He led the soldiers to our home, and he told them lies about my father and my brothers. I hate him. They say someone has killed him. I am glad. I curse his name. I curse all of them.

13

STATEMENT 4 RECORDED 11 MARCH 2006
RINGWAY ESTATE, ACCRA

My name is John Narty. I am thirty-six years old. Until I was retired on medical grounds, I was a police officer. My rank was inspector, and I had nine years' service. I knew these men from Safe Return. On three occasions I was told to follow them. On one occasion I arrested one of them. This one (Interviewee indicates image of ANDREW CARR), but he was released within three hours on the orders of my senior officer.

I charged him with drug offences, but I was ordered to withdraw the charges. He offered me money on two occasions, now I remember. Once, when I had been following him around Accra for several hours, and another time, when I arrested him.

He used to meet with two Nigerians who we suspected were handling the money from drugs deals. We thought these men were all drugs dealers. The people the three of them met with were under surveillance too. This one, who I remember was called Lloyd, the Indian and the younger one (interviewee indicates LLOYD, DUTTA and PETERS). We had built up a strong case, by the time we arrested that one. (Interviewee again indicates CARR.) Then I was told to release him! No one ever told me why. He had big friends, I guess, with wet hands.

Four months after he was released, I was hit by a truck that failed to stop at a road block. I had four ribs broken, and my pelvis was cracked. I was retired on medical grounds. I had kept notes on all the cases I was

involved in, but I had to hand them in when I retired. Now I am a
watchman at The Pride of Africa store.

Taz took a taxi out to Kotaka, and carried her own bag into
the departure lounge. In contrast to the night of her arrival,
the airport was practically deserted; the flight up to Banjul
rarely carried Europeans, and the frenzy she had witnessed on
her arrival gave way to a casual and sleepy sense of timeless
space. She queued up behind a tall woman in purple whose
hair was plaited and meshed into an elaborate saucer-like
structure that tilted at a forty-five-degree angle over her left
ear. A tiny child, sleeping easily, formed a bundle wrapped in
matching cloth tied against the small of her back.

The baby's head lolled and one unfocused eye half opened.
Taz smiled. The eye closed. She felt a tap on her arm. She
turned, to face Jonjo, dressed in his airport suit, the one he had
worn when he had first met her. He thrust a plastic bag of fruit
towards her.

'For your journey,' he said, simply.

She took the fruit and looked down. There was a silence,
and the person in the queue behind her hissed, attracting her
attention, indicating that the queue was moving on. She
turned back, and took two steps nearer the check-in desk.

'I want to…' Jonjo began.

'Those things I said…' Taz said, simultaneously.

They smiled uncomfortably at one another. 'You first,' Taz
offered.

'I have come here to say I am sorry,' said Jonjo gravely. 'I
shouldn't have said the things I did. I was angry. Your words
hurt me. As only truth can.'

'It's I who should apologize. What I said was childish and
vindictive. Everything that you said was true. I deserved it.'

Jonjo shook his head. 'Not from me, you didn't. We are much alike, you and I. Maybe that's why we have a problem being... partners?' he added, suddenly holding out his hand.

Taz nodded, and smiled. 'Partners.'

They shook hands. As he released his grip Taz caught his forefinger between her finger and thumb, and withdrew her hand with a loud snap of the fingers, as she had seen people do in the street. Jonjo laughed, honest and open, for the first time with her.

'Very good! You are learning.'

'I think I am.'

'One more thing,' he added, suddenly serious. 'I told you one lie. When I said things about respect. I do respect you. For fighting to hold on to what is important to you. I didn't. I let them take it all away from me, and said it was alright, and that I was being true to myself, because I maintained my integrity. Because I wasn't prepared to compromise. I made a mistake. I should have fought, like you're fighting. Go and come, Sister Tasneem.'

'Pardon?' she said, thinking she had misheard.

He smiled, and shook his head. 'Pidgin English. It's what the uneducated people say, to a traveller. It means...'

'I can work out what it means. Go and come, Brother Jonjo.'

14

Taz stood in the shade of a large mango tree and watched the children, beyond the rusting fence made out of cut-up and beaten out oil drums, play in the afternoon sun. Their bare feet kicked up powder-fine brown dust. Here and there in the playground, an island of dry grass, burnt to straw and rough stubble, somehow clung on to the talcum topsoil. Beneath the meagre shade of the thin, bare branches of a dead bush, two goats were tethered to an old car tyre. One child pushed a pair of uneven wire wheels on a spindly axle attached to a stick. Three others chanted, danced and skipped on pencil-thin legs in a complex game she could make no sense of. Two more lay on their stomachs, their heads propped in their hands, staring with massive concentration at a minute insect. Taz took off the white sun hat she had brought that morning, and felt a slight breeze cool the sweat on her forehead.

In the compound beyond the dusty playground, a single-storey building constructed of breeze blocks echoed with the raised voice of the woman she'd come to see. The building was roofed with more flattened-out oil drums. Old woven mats and sacking hung over the windows, and the door was half a dozen planks of wood nailed roughly together. A cross had been daubed in white paint on the wall beside the door, and a similarly casual hand had splashed the slogan 'no wetin' in three different places on the perimeter fence. But the stains, and the sour, wheaten reek suggested few heeded the request.

Behind the school, a clutch of palms reared up, their slender bare trunks ludicrously tall, topped by an explosion of green and brown leaves that hissed in the breeze and sounded like the tide on shale. To each top, amid the green coconuts, clear glass bottles were lashed, tapping palm wine.

She heard children's voices chant back, a woman's incantation:

'The plate is on the table.
The knife is on the plate.
The spoon is in the bowl.
The saucer is on the plate.'

Then, a clatter and scrape of moving furniture, and another wave of children exploded into the bright sunlight. They were taller, older than those already at play. But they wore the same dusty, mustard shorts and shirts. A brightly-coloured bird flashed past, squawking from a tree, making Taz start. She looked up, but the sky was so bright it made her eyes water. She blinked, twice, and re-focussed her sun-bleached gaze on the school. The woman she had come to see stood now in the doorway, feeling in the pouch of a smock-like apron for a pair of sunglasses. Taz pushed herself reluctantly away from the shade of the tree and walked past the burnt-out and stripped-down shell of a saloon car to the narrow gap in the rusting fence.

The woman at first failed to see her; it gave Taz time to study her more carefully.

She looked much younger than Hugo Ruhl; mid-thirties, perhaps, to his late fifties. Her hair was somewhere between blonde and ginger, honey-coloured, long, but tied tightly back and half hidden beneath a small blue scarf. She was shorter even than Taz, who barely topped five feet three, stockily built, with plump arms and bare calves pale and solid beneath the apron, blouse and brightly patterned skirt she wore. The children playing took little notice of her. Three, hands joined in a circle, skipped a discordant and foreign ring-a-ring-o'-roses, cannoning into her legs. She bent slightly, and eased them gently aside like a hiker pushing away a bramble in his path.

'Frau Ruhl? Can I speak to you please?'

The woman looked up, her surprise reminiscent of Hugo Ruhl's in Germany when Taz had similarly doorstopped him. She seemed confused, unhappy perhaps, to hear herself called by that name. She took off the sunglasses, frowning, and polished the lenses on her apron.

'Good afternoon,' she began, still frowning quizzically. Her German accent thick, heavy and as out of place in this baked compound as a North Sea mist.

Taz smiled. 'The children have your accent,' Taz said. 'I was listening to them.'

The woman reddened and looked down, and then looked up at Taz, her large blue eyes bright. 'I know. One of the parents has already complained that his son sounds like a German tourist. Are you from the British Council? You are welcome to look around.'

She said no more. She simply stood, looking warily at Taz, waiting.

'No, I'm not, Frau Ruhl... should I call you that?'

'Do not call me that,' she said, glancing quickly around the compound. 'My name is Meissner. Or Leyna. Wait.'

She strode quickly across the compound, and grabbed the threadbare collar of a skinny six-year-old who had been advancing stealthily towards the unsuspecting goats with a sharp stick and a frown of profound, malevolent concentration on his tiny brow. Taz smiled again as the child pantomimed wide-eyed astonishment as he was lifted bodily from behind into the air, his arms and legs flailing like a panicked swimmer. Leyna swung him round, lowered him gently, and murmured a few words to him. The child looked away and Leyna knelt and tugged the tiny bush shirt straight. The child stood stiff, arms outstretched like a crucifix, then collapsed in on himself in writhing giggles as she tickled him and sent him on his way.

She returned to Taz, dabbing at her neck with a handkerchief. 'Not a bad boy, a sweetie really. But there's something profoundly unhealthy about his interest in those goats. I'm sorry. Shall we go inside and talk?'

Inside, the simple school house was hot and dark; two sacking flaps had been folded back to allow in shafts of stark sunlight at the far end of the narrow room, near the blackboard. There were benches, odd chairs, and cheaply made flat tables to work on. In a corner, still encased in polystyrene and wrapped in clear polythene, was a computer.

Leyna followed Taz's glance.

'A misunderstanding. I asked the German Embassy for

materials. What I was hoping for was some coloured chalk, and maybe a few calculators. They sent me that.'

Taz glanced around, up at a battered hurricane lamp suspended from a nail in a crossbeam. She looked at the Leyna, who nodded.

'Exactly.' She smiled, as they sat. 'Now, a wind-up radio, that would have been useful. What can I do for you?'

'Your husband,' Taz began. 'Hugo Ruhl. Do you know where he is?'

'Why?' asked Leyna, rubbing both hands over her face, a gesture of tiredness and resignation which effectively hid her reaction.

'I visited him,' said Taz, reaching inside her bag and withdrawing a sheet of paper. 'In Rastatt, a couple of weeks ago. We arranged to meet again, but he didn't turn up for that meeting, and when I checked out your apartment, he had left. I wondered if you knew where he had gone. I know he was associated in some way with the dead workers from Safe Return. You see, he gave me their photograph with him. I'm investigating their story.'

Leyna Ruhl listened carefully, glanced at the photograph Taz offered her but showed no reaction.

'How did you find him there?' she asked suddenly. 'Not even I knew where he was.'

'Someone told me.'

'Well, if Hugo didn't talk to you again,' she said, 'it would be because he didn't want to. Hugo doesn't do anything he doesn't want to do.'

'How long have you been married?'

'Five years. And I know nothing of an apartment in Rastatt. He must have rented it.'

'You're... separated?'

'Obviously,' snapped Leyna, then she smiled a tiny, tight smile. 'Oh, I see what you mean. Sorry. No, we are not separated.'

Taz looked round, unsure quite what to say.

'I know Hugo was very worried about something, and that was why he left me,' Leyna continued without being prompted. 'But I cannot tell you what it was, or where he went, or anything really. He always kept what he did and our life together very separate. He had his work, I had mine. And you have yours, whoever you are.'

'I'm so sorry!' Taz said, reaching back into her holdall for a card. 'My name is Taz Dhar...'

Leyna Ruhl's eyes widened. 'You're Taz Dhar? I had assumed such a name belonged to a man. You have proof?'

Confused, Taz produced her passport. Leyna studied it, and passed it back. 'I have something for you,' she said, heavily. 'Wait here.'

She returned after a few minutes, holding a single sheet of A4 paper. Taz took the document, a print out of an e-mail, and read:

I am sending this message immediately after your departure from my home. I have agreed to meet you tomorrow, but I will not keep that appointment. If you know anything about this, you know as well as I do I will not be here tomorrow. They will come for me soon. I will try to run, but I have little hope of escape again. You have exposed me, marked me for them. I am targeted. I can sense it, a laser dot on the back of my head. Now, like any prey trapped in his den where it thought it was safe, I must break cover, and that is what they have been waiting for.

Maybe I should have stayed with the others. If I had, maybe they would still be alive, and I, well, what am I?

There is no time for this. I am sending this message to Leyna with a request that if you come to her she gives it to you. I have to tell you, if you are in The Gambia, you are too close. Close to the answer, and close to great danger. I care not at all what happens to you, but I fear the repercussions of what I have done, what you are doing, for my Leyna. She knows nothing of it, she is no threat to them, but they will not care. I do not want anything bad to happen to her. She deserves so much better than the poor provision I have been able to make for her. This now is all I care about.

The least, the last thing I can do for her is to protect her. From them. From you. But it will be at your expense. A devil's deal. But then my friends and I, we are good at brokering the devil's deals.

You must not speak to Leyna again. You must not go near her, or try to find out anything more about her. You must destroy all references to her in any notes or messages, and please remember that means mobile phone records too. You must lay a false trail of research in The Gambia to lead those watching you away from her. That must be your part of the deal. Do this, and I will give you everything you want to know. I have created a website, where you will find all I could have told you, all I know about Armitage Shanks. I have told Leyna she must only give you the address when she receives by e-mail a photograph of you back in England, holding a newspaper on which she can clearly see the date and headline. Do not send it from your own e-mail address. Create a hotmail account for this one message. Once she has verified it as genuine from that paper's online version, you will then be called at a landline number you specify, and given the password you will need to access the site. Once this message is sent, this account will be closed and this laptop will be destroyed. None but the three of us know of this arrangement. Keep it that way, for your sake as well as Leyna's.'

'You've read this,' Taz said, flatly.

'Yes,' Leyna said, her voice heavy and her face twisted with grief and anger. 'And I cannot change Hugo's plan, even if I wanted to. It must be as he says.'

'So you and I speak no more?'

'As he says,' Leyna repeated.

Taz offered her hand, which Leyna glanced down at, and stared back at Taz, silent.

'I am sorry it's like this,' she said, letting her hand fall.

'So am I,' said Leyna, sadly. 'Please go now. I have work to do.'

15

Taz returned to the hotel, deeply troubled. She headed for the bar to still the trembling of her chin and dislodge the weight of tears which pressed like a flat iron across the bridge of her nose. Sure, she was finally near now to understanding what this was all about. But she felt no elation, only a shame, condemned as she was by the pain she had seen in Leyna Meissner's face. She was frightened too at the thought of her responsibility, her unwitting part in Hugo Ruhl's fate, whatever that was.

There seemed little point hanging around in The Gambia; a day should suffice to meet Hugo Ruhl's requirement for a false trail from an investigator as rigorous as her, she thought bitterly.

She was checking out flight details at the reception when she noticed a message in her pigeonhole. She pointed it out and the receptionist handed it down to her.

A man had rung, he didn't want to leave his name, but he'd call back, that evening. Seven P.M.

She wondered if it was SK, or Mark, but thought it unlikely. Neither seemed over-keen to speak to her these days. Maybe it was Jonjo; perhaps he had found out something really important. Perversely, she hoped not, because she did not want to lie to him about the e-mail and the website, but nor could she share the information with him, because she was, belatedly, determined to do right by Hugo Ruhl. To fulfil her part of the deal to the letter. She let the afternoon drag slowly by her, and was back at reception, waiting for the phone to ring, a quarter of an hour before the appointed time. When he called, it was a voice profoundly English, one she didn't recognize. A metallic, neutral voice that could have been a railway station announcer, or a speaking clock, or a BBC newsreader.

'You're looking for Armitage Shanks.' A statement, not a question.

'Who are you?' she asked, feeling her pulse quickening.

'You've got a photograph, haven't you? You showed it to Leyna Meissner today?'

'I've got a photograph, yes. Is Armitage Shanks in it?'

The voice on the phone laughed; the sound made the hairs on Taz's forearms tingle. 'Oh yes.'

'Which one is he?' she asked, annoyed at the sound of desperation in her voice.

'Does it matter?'

'Yes, it matters. It matters a lot. Which one is he?'

'Which one?'

'You heard me. Which one?'

'Armitage Shanks? They all are.'

'All of them?' she shouted, incredulous.

'Yes, all of them.'

'Even... the man in the middle of the photograph?'

'Very good, Miss Dhar! You mean Hugo Ruhl? Yes, even him. But not anymore.'

'You mean he's disappeared somehow?'

'No. I mean he's dead, somehow. That's why he didn't keep his appointment with you.'

Taz's senses reeled. Not only did the voice know about the photograph, but also about the meeting with Hugo Ruhl that never was.

'Who are you?'

'Someone who knows who you are looking for.'

'And knows Hugo Ruhl?'

'Knew Hugh Ruhl.'

'Are you in this photo?'

'Very good, Miss Dhar. I should have been counting. Like twenty questions. How many have you had now? I expect I'm in the photograph. If it's the one I think it is.'

'Can we meet?' Taz asked.

'Oh, I shouldn't think so. You're dangerous to be with. Hugo the Jew met you, and Hugo the Jew's no more.'

'Are you sure? Sure that he's dead?'

'Oh, I'm sure. He was dead before you broke into his apartment.'

'I didn't…'

'No, no. Of course you didn't.'

'I have to talk to you.'

'You are talking to me. You may talk to me again. But only if I think it's safe.'

'Safe from what?'

'Just safe.'

'Can't you tell me anything else? Now?' she pleaded.

'No. Well, maybe, but I don't know why I should. Oh well, here's one for free. Change your hotel. Move to the Bungalow Beach. Goodbye Miss Dhar.'

The line went dead. She could have screamed with frustration. She asked for her bill and packed her bags. Within two hours, she was unpacking in a ground floor flatlet in the Bungalow Beach Hotel.

Having forgotten, in the thrill of a new lead, to leave a forwarding address.

STATEMENT 12 RECORDED 19 MARCH 2006.
FRIENDS CHOP N CHIP, LEBONI, ACCRA
(Note: Interviewee previously known to Interviewer)

My given name is Peno. I do not wish to give my family name, but you know me, Mr Amin Asante. I am thirty-one years old, and unemployed. I knew one of these men who died at the Lake.

The one I knew was called Mr Lloyd. I first met him when I worked at the hotel where he stayed when he first arrived, two years ago. I used to clean his room. At first, he did not trust me, but then, when he found out I couldn't read, he seemed to like me more.

Before, he used to hide away all the paper before I went in. After, he used to just leave them, wherever they were.

He made me promise never to take any away, or even move any. He made me promise never to let anyone else into the room when I was cleaning it.

I always kept my promise.

Maybe a year ago, I lost my job. I didn't do anything wrong, but the manager had someone from his village he wanted to give my job to, so I had to go.

Mr Lloyd said he could use me, in his work. I was happy to work for him.

I made two journeys with him, one into the Western Region by lorry, and the other, by boat, to Monrovia, in Liberia.

This was a very dangerous journey. They said it was all over, but there was still fighting and soldiers were killing people, every day. I was very scared.

Mr Lloyd said we would be quite safe; he said he had friends on both sides who would help us.

I asked him why we had come to such a bad place. He said it was where we had to do a deal.

I remember those were his exact words. Where we had to do a deal.

I don't know what went wrong, but we had lots of trouble, right from the time we tried to get into what used to be Taylor country. A bus full of Mandingo children had been killed a few days earlier, and everywhere was very tense, and very dangerous. Still, Mr Lloyd said it would be alright. No problem.

He seemed to have lots of friends in Liberia; everybody knew him, or seemed to know of the people from Safe Return. People said they had done wonderful things; rescued people from certain death, and stopped the slaughter. People told big stories about Mr Lloyd too, but I didn't believe them all. They said he had come to end the war. To bring real peace back to the country. I don't think that was true, but I know that whenever he spoke, people stopped and listened.

He had lots of money, and often people would come to him, and he would give them money.

Then, one day, about two weeks after we had arrived, we were deep in Taylor country and Mr Lloyd had a meeting with a big man, a chief or a general maybe. Everything went very well. Mr Lloyd was very happy. I saw him hand some papers over, and the big man gave him some money. I don't know what it was about.

Then, next day, we were just sitting by the road side eating. I remember, we were eating fu-fu, and plantain. Mr Lloyd was very happy. Then, soldiers came. They were wild men, with no kind of uniform. Some wore baseball caps, and others miners' helmets. They wore vests and football shirts and they carried big guns. Many of them seemed crazy, like they were drugged.

They arrested everybody; not just Mr Lloyd and me, but everybody. They rounded up all the men in the area and made us get on to lorries. They took us to an old barracks that the army used to have. It had been bombed, and burnt, but there were still some buildings there. They put us in a room, and made us sit on the floor.

I got separated from Mr Lloyd. I never saw him again. They took him away with a lot of others, but I guess he must have been released, or returned to Ghana because I know people say he was killed in Akosombo. On the Lake.

Me? They kept me there for three days, then they beat me and kicked me.

They beat a lot of us, and treated us badly. They took out all the Krahns, and hacked them to death. We could hear their screams. Then there were maybe twenty of us left. Then, as the soldiers went away, they opened fire on us. Many died. Many others were wounded. I was hit twice, once on the hand, and once on the side of my head. I was very lucky I didn't die. But I cannot see anymore. Some people found me, and took me to Monrovia. I still had my papers, so I was handed over to Ghanaian soldiers who brought me home.

I have been very lucky. My youngest brother found me here, and now we beg for money at the crossroads. People are kind, and we make a living.

I have been very lucky.

But if Mr Lloyd was still alive, he would look after me, and I wouldn't have to beg. He looked after his friends. He was a good man.

I have something more to say: a week ago, another man came asking about someone called Armitage Shanks. His voice was not like yours. He was not of us. He smelt of the soap Mr Lloyd used to use. He spoke English, but he spoke it strangely. Not like Mr Lloyd. Someone had told him I knew who a man called Armitage Shanks was, and he asked me questions about this Mr Shanks. Did I know him? Did I know anything about people from Nigeria who sell drugs? I knew then he wants to do harm to Mr Lloyd's name, because bad mouths say evil things about him, and Nigerians and drugs. I have never heard of this man Armitage Shanks. Then he asked me if I knew Mr Lloyd. I sensed this was not good for the memory of Mr Lloyd, so I said I did not know him, either. Even though he offered me a lot of money, I would not dishonour Mr Lloyd's name. Not for any money.

Will you give me money, Mr Amin Asante? I have told you the truth. Only that.

∾

Jonjo Amin Asante was getting scared. Well, perhaps not scared, exactly; he had been in this line of work for too long to be scared. If he'd been prone to fear, on even an averagely brave man's scale of reticence, he would have given in, and knuckled down, and toed the party line years earlier. Not scared, no, but troubled. Not so much by what he had so far found out, as by what he was beginning to suspect.

He was being followed; well that was nothing new. It certainly had novelty value these days, but he had been under police surveillance for so long in the past that the presence of a dark blue Toyota always two cars distant was almost a comfort; a perverse status symbol.

If anything, that exhilarated him; he had thought he would never be a problem big enough to anyone to warrant such interest ever again. Besides, the dangers were a hell of a lot less these days. Little chance now of being dragged down to the cells below the Castle and beaten senseless for six hours. These days, the police were a poor man's friend.

Well, that's what they said in the papers, didn't they?

He remembered an interview eight years earlier with a thirteen-year-old girl in Korle-bu Hospital who had been raped in the back of a police car by three constables, two of whom had children older than her, and he felt the old rage gyrate a turn within him. No, it wasn't them: they didn't trouble him; rather it was where the trail was leading. Back over borders he had no wish now to recross.

He had thought it would take him back into Liberia; he had contacts there still. It would be dangerous, of course. But nothing like it had been: a country torn apart in tribal wars, dressed up in Western fatigues and disguised behind a confusion of abbreviated party names. But now, at peace, of a kind. Now, it was a place no more dangerous for him than for anyone else, and nowhere near as bad as it had once been.

And what about Nigeria? Could that be where the answer was? Where there was still a legally sworn warrant for his arrest, and an informal sentence of death as widely promulgated.

Liberia would be inconvenient. The thought of returning to Nigeria was so awful he preferred simply not to think about it. What could be worse? Well, he had to admit to himself that, if it came to a choice, the thought of giving up the story was infinitely worse.

And these men, what of them? Dead heroes, mythologized. White martyrs fallen in a noble cause. Or so they had seemed at first. But now they were rapidly being revealed as little more than cheap racketeers involved in drugs-trafficking on an almost spectacular scale.

Jonjo mentally withdrew the word cheap. It was as lazy as it was inaccurate. Fit for today's press, but not for a true professional like him.

He wondered how Taz would react to the things he had found out. He felt almost sorry for her. And scared for her too.

This time, scared probably was the right word.

If it was dangerous for him, who knew the ropes, it would be trebly dangerous for a foreign woman wondering around alone, naively asking questions about men who, if his informants were right, were serious players in a bad world.

Jonjo still wasn't at all sure that he much liked Taz, but he was certain he felt a responsibility for her, and wanted no harm to come to her, at least while she was, even at the most tentative level, in his care.

He was glad she was up in The Gambia, among lots of other tourists, safely out of the way. Jonjo shared with most Ghanaians a smug and superior, near patronizing disdain for The Gambia, despite the fact that its economy was far healthier than their own. A ridiculous little country it may be, but The Gambia, despite the odd bloodless coup, was stable, comfortable, secure and solid compared to most of the rest of West Africa.

Taz, he told himself, hoping that he believed it, was a lot better off there than in Ghana, India or even back in England. After all, hadn't somebody cut up her cat to scare her there?

In The Gambia, among crowds of other tourists, she should be safe. She could take tea with Hugo Ruhl's wife and waste her time there while he got on with the dangerous stuff. In respect of which, he was being paid well, in which he was getting well versed and for which, he was already well trained.

He screwed up his nose. There was a peculiar smell coming from the kitchen. He closed his eyes and groaned. His wife was melting candle wax again. Jonjo always told people, with a malicious atheist delight in hollow blasphemy, that his wife had left him eight years earlier for a white man called Jesus Christ.

They had always lived in the same small house her father had rented for them when they first married thirty years earlier, with its bad, bare wiring, and blotchy, powdered damp stains on the walls, and the smell of sewage from the open gutters on two sides. It had never been a dream home. On a street corner in Asylum Down, where traffic lurched around potholes, kids fought, parents screamed and radios blared through permanently open windows at them. Always too crowded and too noisy with no privacy to speak of, until it was too late. By the time their children left home—Rose and Moses into homes and families of their own, David into the army and little, weak Ruth to a child's grave—to be left alone together was the last thing Jonjo and his wife wanted.

They rarely even spoke these days. She spent more and more time involved in the church, and only made a point of cooking for the two of them on Thursdays—a regular, stilted meeting at which any particular problems about their always strained finances could be blamed on one another, and in theory at least, resolved.

And, wonders of wonders, it was Thursday again. My, how quickly they came round! That evening, she would be waiting in culinary ambush, and the dank, stale air of the house would be warmed with the scent of baked plantain.

Today, for the first time in a dozen years, Jonjo looked forward to it. Not that his wife was much of a cook. Never had been. Her efforts always laid heavy on his stomach, which had never fully recovered from a prison diet and dysentery. No, what he looked forward to these days was the once dreaded discussion of money. For the first time in a long time, he was pulling down a regular, decent income, which allowed him to approach these evenings with a new arrogance. Whereas before they would have bickered for half an hour over a thousand Cedis, now, when she demanded money for this or that, he simply said, 'Is that all?' and tossed fat bundles of notes onto the table with an almost sensual indifference.

He went out without telling her where he was going and drove the big Peugeot through the Ringway Estate, simply for the sheer pleasure of driving. He told himself that he thought better behind a steering wheel, and the drive provided the stimulus and structure he needed to sort through the things he had found out. He also told himself sternly not to delude himself: he was doing it because he liked it and there was nothing at all wrong with that, no matter what his wife and her boyfriend Jesus might say about it.

He glanced in the rear view mirror; the blue Toyota was there, right behind him. A sudden lull in the traffic had stripped away the usual intervening vehicle. Jonjo indicated to turn left; the Toyota did the same. At the last minute, Jonjo turned right. So did the Toyota.

He laughed to himself, suddenly surprised that he was laughing aloud; shocked at the unfamiliar sound of his own amusement.

He had got affidavits from people who had known the man who ended up as Armitage Shanks and his friends in Liberia, and in Ghana. Three distinct pictures were emerging, or maybe distinct was the wrong word. Three overlapping but inconsistent images. First, the aid workers, the saviours, supporters and deliverers. A small but significant number of the Liberian refugees who had made it back to their homeland had done so at their instigation, and with their encouragement, protection and funding.

So the man for whom he searched was a good man, one of several; a saint, some had said.

Then there was another perception: let us call him Armitage Shanks, the businessman. The man with a personal computer in a hotel room, who always paid his bill, and went to meetings and had visitors, and kept himself to himself.

Then too there was the shadier side: the colluder in rape and violence, the evil deceiver, the drugs dealer. Or was there? There was suspicion, sure, and allegations, too. But hardly any evidence. Yet.

That hadn't surprised him; not at all. Only when he had spoken to Narty, the retired policeman, did he get near to anything concrete. He wondered, not for the first time, whether there was any chance of getting to see the police file. There would be one, or there would have been one, once. The ability of the police to lose documents however, was legendary. Especially when it was in their interest, either because they had something to hide, or they wanted to up the dash.

He braked suddenly. Inconsistencies. Anomalies. They were not the barriers to the truth as he had thought; they were at its heart.

The driver of the blue Toyota behind, day-dreaming, failed to see the brake lights till almost too late. The unmarked police car screeched to an undignified halt inches from the white Peugeot's battered rear bumper. The driver leapt from the car, stung by the jibes his two colleagues spat at him, a quick-fire comedy act reviewing his driving. He half ran to the white Peugeot, his face working with rage, and snatched open Jonjo's door.

'Where did you learn to drive, old man?' he screamed, high-pitched and indignant. 'Show me your licence!'

Jonjo turned and looked up at him, unperturbed. 'Where did you learn to follow a car, Officer? Show me *your* ID. Eh! Should I petition the Commission on Human Rights for harassment, or just report you for dangerous driving?'

The policeman leapt back from the side of the car as though he had received an electric shock. He kicked the car door shut and called Jonjo a couple of names, but his heart wasn't really in it. Jonjo slipped the Peugeot into first gear and pulled away. The officer strode back to the Toyota, furious still. His guffawing colleagues had thought of three more witticisms to add to his discomfort.

When he got home, Jonjo re-checked the affidavits. It was there, blatant. He told himself the policeman had been right;

he was an old fool. How could he have missed it? There was a massive, glaring inconsistency in the statements he had taken. His only excuse was that he never paid much credence to the dates and times people quoted. People living through crises were notoriously bad at such detail, and in his experience West Africans were the worst of all. And after all, hadn't he heard these tales of brutality and slaughter countless times before?

The attack on the village in the Grand Cape Mount Region: if Robert Lloyd had been there, it couldn't have been more than two years earlier. Ten years earlier, now that would have been different. He remembered those days only too clearly. He'd been there. In Liberia. Not in Grand Cape Mount itself, but in Monrovia, with the ECOMOG contingent.

But two years ago, there was meant to be no war. No massacres, no busloads of children being killed. Yet that was what these witnesses were saying. Not ten years ago, but just two. When Liberia was meant to be well on its way back into the mainstream: headed by the first democratically-elected woman head of state in the history of Africa, a new champion against corruption. From basket case to donor darling. Sure, huge challenges remained: a crippled infrastructure, inefficient and venal officials, but starting to look good for the first time in decades. Facing the future with a modicum of confidence. Or was it? Inconsistencies. Something very strange was going on.

Then there was the statement by this girl Penda. She had been raped and her family killed and Carr had stood by and watched it all, yet she'd been in the camp for over eight years, and Carr wasn't meant to have been around then. So either she's lying, or mistaken, or Safe Return was not telling the truth about what they did, when and where. Jonjo heard his wife return. She banged down a string bag of vegetables on the kitchen table, and sighed. He looked up at her.

'You want to eat out, old woman?' he asked.

Her eyes widened, then narrowed suspiciously. 'Why? You don't like what I cook now, old man?'

'I've never liked what you've cooked. You want to come out with me to celebrate the solving of a mystery, or not?'

'Where?'

'Anywhere you like. Eat what ever you like. As much as you like.'

'Eh! Big man, huh? Big spender, suddenly? What clothes have I got to go out in, except my church clothes?' she asked, sourly.

Jonjo looked at her and shook his head. 'You are a really miserable bitch-woman, you know?' he said, gathering the affidavits together.

'I will pray God forgives you for that.'

'Don't trouble him on my account. Get your Jesus hat. I'll wait in the car.'

Whilst he waited for his wife, Jonjo drummed his fingers on the steering wheel and hummed tunelessly. He should let Taz Dhar know of his suspicion.

Two hours later, after a pinch-faced and silent meal of Red-Red in a street cafe, he made the call. The meal of spicy beans in palm oil lay heavy still on his stomach, like a cold stone. Maybe it wasn't his wife's cooking after all. Maybe it was just her.

Taz Dhar's mobile was switched off. Jonjo tried the hotel, where polite staff checked their records, as he mentally counted the units on his prepay phone that the assignment afforded him ticking away, and then they told him she had left, and they had no idea where she had gone.

He wondered if he should be worried for her, then dismissed the idea. What harm could possibly come to her, up there in The Gambia?

STATEMENT No 12 RECORDED 19 MARCH 2006.
KANESHIE MARKET, ACCRA

'How do you turn this thing on? It's on? Eh, heh! Now, listen. People die. People get killed. People who should mind their own business. People who get involved in other people's concerns. Is that what happened to the men from Safe Return? Who knows? Might that be what could happen to you? That is for you to decide.

My name? Who do I work for? That does not matter. But I know your name, Amin Asante. And I know where you live too. And where your children reside. Think about that. But not for too long.'

16

Taz, in a bungalow not more than 200 yards from the sea, let the pounding of the waves and the hiss and whistle of the sea breeze through dried palm fronds, ease her into a tourist frame of mind. She had been true to her part of the deal. She had destroyed all references to Leyna Meissner in her notes, and made no efforts to contact her or to find out anything more about her. Just how aggressively did Hugo Ruhl's false trail have to be forged?

Most of the other guests at the Bungalow Beach were Swedes, with a leavening of retired Brits. The couple in the bungalow next to her, she learnt within hours of arriving, had built up a very successful organic fruit farm in Kent which their son now ran whilst they took it easy. They were pleasant, and kind to a woman alone. They invited her to eat with them, and tried to see that she was all right in little, generous, unnecessary ways; leaving simple treats on her verandah. Some of the fruit they might have bought that morning, or an English paper.

She still had no idea why the man that had rung her had told her to move here. She refused to call him Armitage

Shanks, although she recognized that, if what he said was true, he had as much right to the name as Robert Lloyd, or whoever the condemned man that had written to her was. She wondered if he was watching her. The receptionist had assured her it had been a local call. Maybe he was. Somehow, she didn't resent it. It was different to the guy who had killed Pudding watching her. Maybe it was because she was abroad, or in a more public place.

It was the fruit farmer in the next bungalow who told her the answer.

It was mid morning and she had been dozing, naked, fan-cooled, on top of the bed. He had knocked on her door, waking her. She wrapped a towel around herself, and slipped back the lock.

He had stood there, on his skinny, varicosed legs, with his leathery stomach, like a deflated bag, over the too-tight elastic waist band of his ridiculously bright swimming trunks, his old, lizard skin reddened. He had beamed at her, eyeless behind dark sunglasses in day-glow orange frames.

'Cyn though you might like this,' he said, holding out a rolled-up magazine.

She took it from him; *Woman and Home*, a month old.

'She got it for the plane. She's read it all. Doesn't want it back. You're welcome to it.'

She thanked him, but he didn't seem keen to leave. She guessed he was bored.

'How is your wife?'

'Cyn?' he said, gratefully. 'Oh, better than nothing. Don't tell her I said that! Well, actually, you can, if you like. I've been saying it for thirty-four years. She's sleeping. Were you?'

Taz nodded, and he apologized for disturbing her. 'It doesn't matter,' she assured him. 'I haven't slept so much in years. I must have paid the bed bank back years of late nights and early mornings. Do you want a drink? A beer, or a coke, or something? I've got some in the fridge.'

He followed her in, and watched appreciatively as she bent to check out the contents of the refrigerator.

'That's what's great about this place,' he observed. 'So relaxing. We've been coming here for years.'

He looked around, and his glance fell on the photograph from Hugo Ruhl's apartment which Taz had propped up on the windowsill against the fine anti-mosquito mesh. 'As have you, I see.'

Taz crouched down, one hand on the door of the refrigerator, not really listening. She frowned. 'I've got lager, or orange juice. Tonic. Some soda, too. Is it too early for something stronger?'

'It is for me. I'll just have orange and soda. You go on, though.' He picked up the photograph. 'Who were they?'

Still crouched, Taz looked over her shoulder. 'I'm sorry?'

'That photograph. When was it taken?'

'I don't know. Two or three years ago, maybe.'

'You didn't take it? I thought these might be people you'd met last time you were here.'

'Here?' Taz snatched the photograph from him, and stared hard at it. 'This was taken here?'

'At the poolside. Can I have my drink now?'

'Show me,' she said, taking his wizened old wrist in her hand, and half dragging him to the door.

'Don't you think you should put something more than a towel on first?' he asked 'not for my sake. I'd be flattered, really...'

'Wait here,' she said, quickly, thrusting the unopened box of orange juice and bottle of Krest soda into his hands. 'Help yourself to a drink, but just don't go away. I'll only be a moment.'

She quickly pulled on pyjama trousers and a tee-shirt, and raked her fingers through her hair. He was still staring at the juice carton and soda bottle, undecided, when she re-emerged.

'We can do that later,' she said, picking up the photograph. 'Show me.'

He had been right. How could she have failed to see it? He led her to precisely the point at which the photographer must have set up the camera, and with the photograph held up in one hand, encouraged her to squat until she was at just the right angle.

She could even identify the table at which they must have sat. It had been night, of course, when the photograph had been taken, but otherwise, everything was the same. How could she have been so blind?

The thought that Robert Lloyd, Armitage Shanks, all the Armitage Shankses, had been in this hotel thrilled her till she wanted to giggle like a child. She took the fruit farmer's arm and almost skipped with glee.

'Come on!' she said, dragging him towards the bar. 'I'm going to buy you the most expensive cocktail we can find. You've earned it.'

☙

On Friday the Harmattan returned to Accra, hot and sour as a hospice death. Dry, and red with dust hauled off the Sahara, it lay itself over the city like a poultice, drawing fetid evils and foul tempers to the surface.

Nobody expected it, not at that time of the year. The Doctor, as it was called, may have arrived early, but as it did every year, it promptly set about sorting the quick from the dead. Like a hard frost in chillier climates, the Harmattan terminated a whole raft of ailments. Some it cured, some it simply ended. The mortality rate in the hospitals at The Ridge and Korle Bu steadily increased as the Harmattan set about its work. Airlines cancelled flights out of Accra and diverted them to Kano and Abijan to avoid the thick pall of dust over the city, where it was oven-hot, searing dry. Jonjo's wife wanted to have an argument; Jonjo couldn't be bothered. He just sat and sweated and tried to remember what it was like to be cool. He thought about hitting his wife. He never had, although the provocation had at times been pretty severe. He knew that with the Harmattan came a general and widespread increase in violence; husbands and wives and parents and children all over the city would be contemplating violence upon one another; it was a fact. Statistically proven. When he had specialized in crime in the mid-Seventies he had read up on it. Research done somewhere or other; the temperature and humidity bands within which more acts of violence take place than at any other.

He had four interviews lined up. Two more Liberian refugees, an old contact on the *PDG*, and a woman who he had been told might be able to help him. He wondered, uncharacteristically, how many he could dip out of. The Liberians could wait. After all, that's what refugees did, wasn't it? Wait on others. And his old friend on the *People's Daily*; he would understand if Jonjo didn't make it. That left just the woman. Jonjo took out his notebook, and checked the address. A place out on the coast road towards Labadi. A good excuse to get out of the city.

She might have been Carr's mistress. That's what his informant hinted.

Without saying goodbye to his wife, he walked out to his car.

Or rather, he walked out to where his car should have been.

He looked up and down the street, confused. At first, he wondered simply if he'd forgotten where he left it. Ludicrous, but it was the kind of thing people think, and do, at moments like that. Then he looked around again, as though, equally ludicrously, the car might suddenly reappear.

It could have been stolen. A simple vehicle theft. Somehow, he didn't think so.

He turned, and walked slowly back towards the house, stepping light, as though the pavement had suddenly turned to eggshell. He didn't get more than halfway to the concrete steps up to the door. He hadn't expected to.

They came at him from both sides. At the first flash of movement he caught in the corner of his eye, he crouched, instinctively.

That was a mistake.

As he went down, a denim-covered knee rose to connect with his chin, snapping his teeth shut and jolting his head back. The things he saw before him changed abruptly, like a camera, suddenly dropped. He was looking up at the grey, blousy sky. He had taken beatings before. He knew he should move to protect his eyes, his head, and his kidneys, but even as he tasted his mouth filling up with blood, he felt he couldn't be bothered. A massive, pained lethargy spread through him, as a booted foot caught him hard in the side, and half rolled him over.

Then the blows and boots rained down so fast he could no longer distinguish between them.

One of them was using a light, vicious cane, its stinging cuts, a screamed treble to the dull bass of kicks and punches.

They were working him over professionally, he recognized, as a wave of bloody vomit retched up through him and he at last curled up, fetal, and wrapped his arms around his head.

His head. Apart from the first knee, they had carefully avoided his head.

So they didn't intend to kill him, he realized, without gratitude.

Yet.

❧

The fruit farmer let himself be persuaded to try a cocktail and Taz ordered a gin and tonic, then changed her mind, and changed it back again. The barman shrugged, and his attention wandered as he waited for her compass needle gaze to stop swinging between the optics.

'Hello?' she snapped. 'Gin and tonic? Today sometime?'

He turned down the corners of his mouth in an eloquent declaration of immunity to sarcasm, and trickled a measure of gin into the glass.

'To you, my friend,' she said raising her glass to the bemused farmer. 'I have to ring my boss to tell him what we've found out, thanks to your sharp eyes.'

She picked up her mobile, but the battery was dead. She had forgotten to put it on charge when she had arrived. 'Fuck! Where can I make a phone call?' she asked the barman, as he placed a dish of groundnuts in front of her.

'From your room, or at reception. They make the call for you, and then you pick it up. Or at the Gamtel office beyond the gate.'

The farmer was still sipping his cocktail when she finished her gin. 'Another?' he asked. She nodded. 'If I were you I'd go to the Gamtel office. The charges here are ludicrous.'

Light-headed with gin and excitement, she ran the limp gauntlet of lack-lustre beach boys slouched in the shade beyond the hotel gates, waving away half-hearted offers to show her the sights, the market, a real African village, or a genuine African wedding, and eased her way through to the Gamtel office. There was a queue for the four hardboard booths, each with an uneven stool beside cheap new Chinese telephones on old painted shelves. She read the instructions of the hand-printed sign, and queued up at the cashiers to book her call and await her turn.

It was only six minutes before she was told to go to booth two, and the phone rang.

'SK? It's Taz.'

He groaned. 'Hi Taz. What did I tell you about a time difference? Try to remember it.'

'Sure SK. Sorry. SK? Are you listening to me? What's wrong with you?'

'What time is it with you, Taz?'

'Oh, about five in the afternoon.'

'Well, it's about eleven at night here, and I just got to bed half an hour ago. You know, the first hour of sleep is the deepest, the most restorative, the most dangerous to disturb in a man of my years. Why don't we just do e-mails?'

'You want me to call back tomorrow?'

'No, I've been trying to call you. You've not been reading your e-mails either, have you? Where the hell are you?'

'I'm in The Gambia. Have been for the past few days.'

'God almighty! And I expect you've kept the hotel on in Ghana?'

'Forget it, SK, the exchange rate is such shit, the room costs less than you tip some peon to water your pot plants when you go on vacation. Anyway, I'll be heading back there, then to the UK.'

'No you won't Taz. Come back here, right now. Your job is yours again, but this whole thing is officially over.'

'What? Why? We're almost there.'

'That's why, Taz. You know you asked me to check out that Kirk fellow you met in Ethiopia? Well, he doesn't exist. But that company he said he worked for does. Premises just near Lodi Gardens. Plenty of staff. Only, they don't seem to have any customers. Now what does that sound like to you?'

'A front?'

'I think so. And I think I can guess who for, too. Because the moment we started looking into them, all hell broke loose, and now not just your future is at stake but mine too. So get back here and everyone wins but your successor, who could benefit from another year or two's experience before she steps into a role like yours, anyway. It's time to pull up stumps. Call it a day. Stop running around the world on expenses, and come on home.'

'But I've got so much, and that guy we hired in Accra is gathering statements from all sorts of people. Doing some really good work.'

'What guy we hired in Accra?' asked SK suspiciously.

'You know, Jojo Amin Asante? The guy from the Information Bureau. Remember?'

'Oh, that guy. Their contract was cancelled the day before yesterday.'

'What? But I need help...'

'Taz, have you been listening to anything I've been saying? All you wanted was your job back. Well, you've got it. But you must be back here by next Monday, or you say goodbye to your job forever. Help? The only help you need now is drying out, detox or therapy.'

'Fuck you, S.K. Mehta.'

'And you spin on it, Taz Dhar.'

'Jesus, SK! If I can't see the gesture, it doesn't mean anything, does it? People don't say spin on it over the phone. It doesn't mean anything over the phone. It just doesn't work over the phone.'

'No, Taz, it doesn't, does it?' agreed SK with a grim satisfaction that left her wondering, as she put the phone down, which of them had actually got the last word.

Next Monday he had said. That gave her five clear days. She went back to the hotel and contacted a travel agent to find out how quickly she could get back to Mumbai, via the UK. After all, it would save the Channel money to utilize the unused portions of her various tickets, wouldn't it? And it would let her get to see the website Hugo Ruhl had so thoughtfully created. Ma was due to return from Canada in three days, and Mark deserved a thank you and the courtesy of a farewell shag. Relationships managed and website accessed, she could then go home to the warm embrace of a city that adored a star and which she loved to distraction in return, with both dignity and story whole and intact, fame fast returning and months ahead in which to exact revenge on the lesbian. It couldn't have worked out neater. Spin on it, indeed!

∾

Two days later, as she was spewed out of baggage reclaim in a wave of tired and ill-tempered travellers, she was surprised to see Anu Sitaram waiting for her. She smiled, another proto-relationship to be sorted, then her face froze as she absorbed the drawn expression and the pained concern in Anu's eyes. There was to be no happy return, that was blindingly obvious. But whatever it was, it couldn't be that bad, could it? If it were, good old Mark would have been there... Mark? Oh, God. No. She realized that she was shaking her head, not wanting this to be real.

Anu half ran toward her, reached out and took her bag. 'We've been looking for you everywhere. Oh, Taz, I'm so sorry. I've got bad news.'

'No,' she moaned. 'Oh, no.'

Anu put her arm around Taz's shoulder, and led her out of the flow of arriving passengers. 'It's Mark, isn't it?' Taz shouted, above the cacophony of greetings, grumbles and announcements.

Anu dropped the bag and turned so they were face to face. She placed her hands lightly on Taz's shoulders. She crouched slightly, so she could look into Taz's face. 'It's not Mark, Taz. It's your mother.'

'My mother?' Taz cried, confused. 'What about my mother?'

'She's dead, Taz. I'm so sorry. We've been trying to contact you in India and in Ghana. Where on earth have you been?'

Taz stepped back, so Anu's hands fell from her. She needed to be self-contained and on her own. 'Thank you, Anu. For coming to tell me. I'm sorry I've caused everyone so much trouble. Do you know where Mark is? Asghar. My brother. I must call him. My uncle too. Yes, I should talk to him. To all of them. I'll need to sort out things. You know, announcements. The burial. Fatiahs...'

Anu looked away, and her mouth twisted as though she had a bad taste in it. 'The funeral was three days ago, Taz. In Toronto. Your uncle and Mark have both gone there. I'm really sorry, Taz. So sorry. Really I am.'

PART IV

KILLING TIME

17

The morning was chill and brittle. The sky was cornflower-blue with just the faintest wisps of high cloud to the east, tinged dawn-pink. There was heavy dew on the grass but there had been little rain for a long time. The garden seemed autumnal, although it wasn't yet through June.

Taz shivered as she hung out the washing.

She had been back in England for three weeks. Living in her mother's house, killing time. Waiting for the forty days to pass, so she could attend the final Jamun Yusuf Kaka would host at the masjid. She told herself, and everybody else, that she was sorting things out. Dealing with things. Well, if that meant overseeing the cutting of the grass, and deadheading her mother's fuchsias, and dusting and polishing, then it was true.

But if it meant taking any decisions about the future, then it was another lie. In any case, there wasn't actually anything for her to deal with.

It had come as no surprise to Taz to discover that her mother had appointed Mark one of her executors. Asghar in Toronto was the other. Taz owned the house, so it was not part of her mother's estate anyway. Everything else, which in reality was not very much, went to Asghar, except for a ring of her father, the one with the opal that he used to let her play with, that she would slip on her finger and which had seemed then so huge and to fit so loosely that she could spin it round and round, like a hoop on a stick. Papa had wanted her to have it, insisted on it, when he was in the hospice, but Ma, uncharacteristically, had been unable to part with it. It had been on her mother's finger when she had died. It was on Taz's finger now, where it fitted, yet strangely. It seemed the ring had shrunk to fit her finger, rather than she having grown to fill it.

Anu had found her a flight to Toronto whilst she freshened up in an airport hotel. While she waited, Taz had rung Mark, and told him she was coming. He met her at the airport, reliable, stable and stolid as ever. Like a probation officer receiving a re-offending youth. Long-suffering, superior and in control. Yusuf Kaka, always undemonstrative, had been unusually distant, even for him. Asghar had made a scene about her not being there, and told her that Ma had wanted his kids to have the house. Mark had intervened, calmed things down, but the chill remained and her departure a few days later went unacknowledged by Asghar and family.

It had been a heart attack, apparently. Her mother hadn't felt a thing, they assured her.

In death, as in life, Taz thought, bitterly.

She hadn't been exerting herself, or anything. She'd just gone shopping, grumbling contentedly about the shortcomings of Canadian stores compared to Swindon. Everyone said she'd never looked better. She'd simply bent down to pick up a bag of something, slipped sideways and died. Like a magnificent yacht, capsizing.

Asghar, Mark, Yusuf Kaka, they'd all tried to contact Taz; tried really hard. There had been emergency messages, but most people thought she was in India, and even SK, who knew she wasn't, couldn't trace her in time.

So they carried on. Had no choice. Burial as soon as the

authorities released the body, and on the third day, the day of her arrival at Heathrow, the Ziarat, Jamun and Fatiah.

From all she'd heard, the functions were precisely what her mother would have wished. Understated, well-organized. Unfussy. Anonymous. Buried where Allah had chosen for her demise, in a new *khubbrastan*, in a foreign land, progressively filling with familiar names. Where her only son and grandchildren could tend her grave and raise her stone.

When she returned to her mother's, no, her house, she had found waiting for her a call on the answering machine expressing S.K. Mehta's deepest sympathy. A week later, unannounced, a cheque arrived. Her severance. In full. She still hadn't banked it. They'd been very generous, in the circumstances.

She hoped Jonjo had got an equally generous pay-off.

Hoped, but couldn't work up the enthusiasm to find out. She thought perhaps she should send him a card or something but knew, even as she was wondering about it, that she wouldn't. It was over. The whole silly, empty, futile game. It all seemed so trivial and irrelevant, in the light of what happened next.

'So it's over?' asked Gord.

'Seems so,' said Tim from Euston. 'Champagne?'

They were sitting in the garden of the Royal Overseas League, just off St James, on the unfashionable edge of London's atrophying club land. A last few octogenarian ex-district commissioners bellowed out from deck chairs in Swahili and Hindi, their words lost on the predominantly Polish staff, whilst upstairs their contemporaries' widows fortified themselves with tea and scones before battling onward with their carrier bags from the shops in Jermyn Street toward the crowded platforms of Victoria and Waterloo. Once the life blood of the League, they were now ghostly reminders of past glories, quaint and picturesque as red-coated Chelsea pensioners, for these days the clientele were mainly visiting members of clubs abroad with reciprocity arrangements, and out-of-town business types who fancied fading grandeur would give status to their London one-on-ones.

A suitably anonymous place for types like Tim and Gord to talk.

Beyond the garden fence and high hedge of firs, crowds of tourists milled. A party of Spanish school children in Green Park shouted and laughed, almost obliterating the thin strains of a selection of hits from Lloyd-Webber musicals that the Guards band was playing for a garden party in Buckingham Palace, just over the other side of the park. In the League garden, still a haven of shady tranquillity, a fountain, a modernist statement in deformed metal and tortured piping, gurgled and dripped, and greedy sparrows snatched a drink before returning to patrol beneath the tables, to beat the thuggish squirrels to falling crumbs.

'Is it appropriate?' wondered Gord.

'I think so, ' said Tim.

'Go on then. You're sure she's out of it?'

'Pretty much so. We've put in progress the necessary steps. She's taken her mummy's death pretty hard. Seems to have lost all interest, but we'll keep her monitored, just in case. If her interest suddenly re-awakens, we'll be the first to know, and you'll be the second. No fall-out across the water?'

'Well, our people are still seriously pissed about the cock-up in Ethiopia, but you've promised not to use them again.'

'Absolutely. It's a shame, because a lot of work went into setting that up, and they were bloody good too. And we're closing down West Africa as well. For a while we'll rely solely on our outlets in Eastern and Central Europe. And some of those are headed by people we are still helping The Hague to investigate crimes against humanity.'

'Yes, it is a shame. We'd sooner have seen the money flow to Africa. Part of our commitment to the poorest nations and emerging democracies.'

The champagne arrived. They sat in silence and smiled appreciatively as the waitress, young and blonde with a heavy accent and braces on her teeth, neatly popped the cork, filled the two flutes, waited for the bubbles to settle, topped them up and placed the bottle in a bucket of ice-water.

They sipped and reflected for a while.

'Sometimes I wonder what makes people like you tick, Tim. How old are you? Mid-thirties? What keeps you doing this?'

'What keeps you?' Tim replied, glancing round the garden.

'That's easy. A Grape. A Cabernet Franc. Which produces a red wine that has a world of herbs, grass cuttings and pencil lead in its aroma, and tastes like everything and nothing all at once. Or it will, when my winery comes good. You?'

Tim shrugged. 'Old friends, new challenges.' He paused, took a sip of champagne and licked his upper lip slowly. 'Riding. I started off in the Blues and Royals. I have a couple of horses. I do a bit of riding school stuff for kids with difficulties. Most Sundays, actually. Take them out hacking, that sort of thing.' Tim reached for the bottle, and topped up their glasses. Gord nodded his appreciation. The band at the Palace broke into *Thunderbirds*.

'Loose ends?'

Tim shrugged. 'Being tied up as we speak. The Indian TV people have agreed to close down her investigation and reinstate her. Sitaram will be shifted off to something interesting and rewarding. Community policing somewhere remote, I think. I'm off to Ghana to oversee the final details of close down there tomorrow.'

'Bignall?'

'Not a problem.'

'And Armitage Shanks is…?'

'Alive and well and looking good for a fair old while to come. Now we're just waiting for you to sign on the dotted line.'

'There may be a delay on that. Look,' said Gord, frowning slightly, 'I have to ask you this: the mother's death. Your lot didn't…'

Tim's mouth fell open. 'Is that meant to be a joke? What the hell do you take us for?'

'Fine, fine,' said Gord quickly, a burden clearly having been lifted from him. 'Forget I ever mentioned it. It was just that when you said about steps having been taken…'

'Oh, I see. No, Mummy's timely demise merely shows we've got a benevolent God on the other side, nothing to do with us at all. I was referring to a discussion we had with Ms Dharwallah's uncle to the effect that some, shall we call it 'candour from Uganda' might prove efficacious. So, why the delay in the contract renewal?'

Gord waived his hand vaguely. 'Conditionalities. Hold-ups on the "No Objection". You know the kind of thing: process problems.'

∾

Jonjo Amin Asante lay for three weeks on an iron bedstead with springs that creaked every time he moved, on a thin mattress, covered with a plastic sheet, in Ward 17 of Korle-Bu Teaching Hospital.

Before that, he had lain for one week on the same bed in the corridor, awaiting another's death or recovery to allow him space in the ward.

His left leg was in plaster, from ankle to thigh. His ribcage was strapped round with tight elastic bandages to help the three ribs to knit together.

He could lie on his back now. For the first ten days, he had had to lie on his stomach, with a single sheet held up on a cage, for the vicious cuts of thin cane had virtually flayed his buttocks and the tops of his thighs.

He had lain, naked, exposed, and greased every four hours, with plenty of time to think.

His wife sat next to him, most days. In silence. Waves of disapproval and disappointment emanating from her like a radio signal.

Now, it was the blood in the urine which kept him in hospital still.

The Information Bureau, full of regrets and apologies, had taken him off the payroll. Given him a payout which met the costs of the first couple of weeks of hospitalization, and even had a whip-round among his half-dozen colleagues which paid for a further day and a half.

The Indians, the head of the bureau explained sadly on his one visit to see Jonjo, had closed down the account, and back-dated its termination to the day of Taz's flight to The Gambia.

For the last eleven days, between Taz's departure and his beating, his efforts had generated no income. Oh, the bureau would meet the costs he had incurred on the investigation, and his hospital bills for the first few days, the head had assured him, even though it would wipe out any profit they might have expected from the deal. But that was it. Too bad, really.

The police came and interviewed him: a decidedly half-hearted interrogation. Old acquaintances looked in, shook their heads and made half-hearted attempts at jokes about the old days, but mostly, he just lay there, thinking, and it was how to pay the hospital for his continuing treatment that occupied most of his thoughts.

He had wanted to discharge himself, but he was simply, physically incapable of doing so. He needed someone to help him out of the place and drive him home and there wasn't anybody.

A few old friends got together, the PDG staff amenities fund forked out a surprisingly generous payment, and his problems were temporarily alleviated.

For at least another week or so. So, he lay on his still tender buttocks, moving as little as possible, staring at the ceiling and thinking about things.

He got into occasional desultory conversations with the staff, all of whom spent most of their time bemoaning the delays in paying their salaries, and with his fellow patients.

The guy on Jonjo's left had gallstones.

The guy on his right, some aging disease which left every limb quaking and shivering, and a permanently surprised expression on his face.

Every thirty-seven seconds, the guy one bed further along, on the other side of the trembling geriatric, let out a low, mournful wail.

Jonjo knew it was every thirty-seven seconds, he had counted them. Over and over.

Then, one morning, Jonjo was moved to a single room at the end of the ward, nearest to the door. A room in which, the day before, a fat old Ashanti businessman, whom Jonjo had more than once crossed swords with over his lucrative past of shady trading and dodgy building, had finally succumbed to the huge pressure his vast girth placed upon his mean heart, and passed away, remarkably quietly, given that his querulous and strident complaints had echoed through the ward for five days previously.

'No extra charge,' the ward orderly had assured Jonjo three times over. 'Guaranteed. No extra charge. Administrative reasons alone.'

So he lay in the comparative luxury of the single room, beside a window which overlooked the vast garbage bins which were as tall as a man and on wheels, into which soiled dressings, food scraps and the general detritus of the large hospital piled.

At five past three on the morning following Jonjo's move to the private room, the night duty nurse sitting beneath the light of a forty-watt bulb at a table in the centre of the main ward, discreetly left for ten minutes, the handful of crisp bank notes in her blouse pocket crumpled and comfortable against her left breast.

A figure eased itself out of the shadows and crossed to Jonjo Amin Asante's room.

Jonjo was asleep. He had always slept well. Now that there was little else to do, he drifted in and out of consciousness, sometimes unsure what had been a thought and what had been a dream.

The figure paused at the doorway and listened to the rhythm of Jonjo's breathing, just on the edge of snoring.

On light canvas soles, he crossed to the locker beside Jonjo's bed.

He found what he was looking for, almost immediately. The head of the Information Bureau had asked for it back; Jonjo had said it got lost in the beating.

The Philips Pocket Memo recording machine on which Jonjo had taped the statements he had gathered.

The tape was still in the machine.

The figure picked up the machine, opened it and was just about to remove the tape within it when Jonjo spoke.

'What will you do if I cry out?' he asked.

The man smiled and sat on the edge of the bed. 'Kill you, I suppose. Are you going to?'

'I don't know. Will you pay for that tape?'

'Sure. Is it yours to sell?'

'No. Take it. Pay me instead for my silence.'

'I was told that couldn't be bought.'

Jonjo looked away and the sigh that escaped him sounded like a soul dying. 'It can now. I have nothing else to sell.'

∾

Yusuf Kaka had appeared on Taz's doorstep unannounced, on the very day Jojo Amin Asante sold his final asset, just past seven in the evening. Taz hadn't heard from him since her departure from Toronto, though she knew he had been due to follow her back to the UK after a week or so. Never one to miss an opportunity to kill two birds, he had used the funeral as an excuse to pursue a number of lost acquaintances and promptly set off across Canada and the States in search of childhood friends.

He seemed uncomfortable, and waited to be asked in. She offered him tea. He asked for water. They sat in silence as he drank it, one hand placed piously on his head, then spoke about their journeys. Yusuf Kaka told her about an uncle of sorts he'd caught up with in Philadelphia, who was doing very well in a catering business, franchised in three different cities.

More silence.

Then, not looking at her, he began. He spoke of the old days in Kampala, and the expulsion from Uganda. The threats and accusations levelled at them by Idi Amin, which made Taz think suddenly, guiltily, of Jonjo. He smiled as he told her how the expulsion turned out to be the best thing for him, as for so many others. How Amin had done them a favour, although it hadn't seemed so at the time, as they stood shivering in bush shirts and saris on the draughty tarmac at Gatwick Airport, penniless, homeless refugees. How bad things soon started to happen to the Africans left there who had so enthusiastically celebrated their departure as a liberation but who almost immediately discovered what tyranny in a crippled economy looked and felt like. Old stories. Family legends, told and heard many times before.

Then he talked of one night, several years before the expulsion. A night when the rains were late and it was so hot and so dry and there had been an attempted robbery at her parents' house. When Pappa had been away working on the road for weeks on end, selling Singer sewing machines in outlying towns and villages, and his younger brother had been supposedly looking after his brother's new home and young bride. But, always the wild boy, Yusuf had been off with a gang of disreputable friends chewing hallucinogenic *miraa* leaves and drinking beer, and had returned to hear Najma screaming in terror. He told, without pride or drama, how he had chased off the three thieves, had caught and half killed one as a lesson to all his type what would happen if they ever messed with a Dharwallah house again. How his blood had been up, and his sister-in-law had been so scared and so lonely, and well, how one thing led to another and…

Taz could not keep the revulsion off her face. Like any another child, she had always found the thought of her parents making love vaguely ludicrous, deeply disturbing and profoundly distasteful. The thought of her strict, prim mother giving way to any sort of illicit passion… Ugh! And with Yusuf Kaka?

'I really don't think I need to hear this,' she said, raising a hand to stop him, the disgust clear in her voice.

'Yes, you do,' her uncle insisted. 'We both knew we had made a terrible mistake. Done a terrible thing. We swore that as long as we lived, we would never discuss what had happened. Never tell anyone.'

'But now Ma is gone you want to make a clean breast of it?' sighed Taz. 'Pretty selfish, don't you think? Muddying my memory of my mother so you can ease your conscience. Does Asghar know? Have you told him too?'

As though she hadn't spoken, he continued. 'Your father found out. He was very hurt, and after, he never treated Najma or me the same again. I think in his heart he never forgave us: never trusted us. How could he? The three of us didn't make a clear agreement, but we each kept that secret. Your Ma and Pappa took it to their graves. But in his life my brother proved himself to be a better man than I will ever be. He came to accept what had happened and deal with the repercussions.'

'What repercussions?'

'You.'

'Me? You mean...'

'Yes, *beti*. You're my daughter.'

18

Taz hated her mother. Hated her for lying, hated her for dying, and hated her for getting herself buried before Taz even knew she was dead. And now, thanks to Yusuf Kaka, the one person she had loved unreservedly and unequivocally, who had loved her with the simple rightness of a good man caring for a devoted daughter, had been taken from her. A father, deeply loved, recast as a pathetic, hollow cuckold, and replaced by a lecherous, sleazy crook. At levels below logic, she knew, with a vast certainty, that her mother had done it all on purpose. She'd had it all her own way and then neatly avoided the final argument. Got the last word, and denied Taz forever the opportunity of either putting things right, or confronting her for them being so utterly wrong.

She couldn't talk about any of this to Mark, of course. She was now part of the tight little cabal of deceit and would, as they all had all her life, pretend that everything was as it appeared to be. That the cracks were purely superficial and the stains as removable as the splatter of the wine she had flung at Mark on their last meal together, before everything changed forever. Anyway, even if she had confided in him, he'd promptly want to take responsibility for sorting everything out, and tell her it was all OK, which he couldn't, and it so wasn't.

But she ought to have known. She smiled sadly at her use of the word 'ought'. Her mother, she had always suspected, was the person for whom, more than anyone else, the word ought had been introduced into the English language. Her mother had savoured its regret, enjoyed its accusation and exploited its quiet outrage to the maximum. 'You ought to have been there, Tasneem.' 'Something ought to be done.' 'You ought to have known that would happen.' 'It didn't ought to be allowed. They ought to tell him.'

Mark too had developed an irritating tendency to use the same word; mostly in 'You ought not worry yourself about that.'

They slept together, at weekends. She and Mark. Back in a safe, middle-aged, reassuring demi-affair, with no risks, and no surprises. But that too seemed false and she couldn't get rid of the thought, illogical though she knew it to be, that Mark believed he was sleeping with the daughter of the man he'd always called Pa, but he wasn't. Not any more. He was sleeping with Yusuf Abbas's virtually incestuous bastard child.

And good old Mark had even found her a job with the local radio station. It paid peanuts, but it didn't really matter. It was work. He was pulling down enough for both of them. 'You ought to get yourself out,' he had assured her. 'They're very pleased to get you; you ought to be flattered.'

Mark was pleased with her; told her so, regularly. She'd

done so well. She ought to be proud of herself. After all, she hadn't had a drink for three weeks, had she?

❧

Anu tried to be a friend to Taz, desperately wanted to be, more so now that her job didn't require her to be, but it just wasn't working. In part it was because of all the differences that lay between them, but mainly it was because Anu, intelligent, competent officer though everyone knew her as, reverted to a clumsy, tongue-tied girl, with limbs too long and elbows that seemed to stick out for miles as soon as she was within a hundred yards of Taz.

Why?

Dave Bignall said that Taz was safe now. Arrangements to keep an eye on her were being stood down. He would be returning Anu to other duties soon, so she should expect to be moving on. Not, he had hinted, back to uniform but out to wider horizons. She had come to the attention of some important people, he told her, and they had been impressed by what they had seen. All in all, it had been a good career move, he had wryly observed, her little bit of unauthorized information-seeking from the Embassy in Ethiopia.

Anu was not particularly bothered that this whole Armitage Shanks thing had petered out to nothing. That was how a hell of a lot of police work went. She just wished she could get Taz Dhar to take her seriously. As what? A confidante? A soulmate? She didn't know. But she wanted to matter to Taz in some way and was painfully aware that even though the Armitage Shanks stuff was no longer exercising her mind, Taz was still deeply preoccupied and her thoughts focussed an infinity away.

On what, she did not know.

❧

The house was too big for her, Taz realized. It had been too big for her mother, really, except that women of her mother's generation had been brought up to clean, and dust and organize houses in a way Taz never had, and to keep spare rooms aired and ready for retuning children, just in case. Far too big and profoundly lonely, with a dearth of happy memories and too many recalled miseries. She thought about selling it, but that would simply rekindle her brother's avarice on behalf of his kids, and she couldn't face another drama about it. She thought of getting another cat, but felt it would be a betrayal of Pudding's memory. So she did nothing. She stayed, delayed, prevaricated, putting off saying yes or no to Radio Brunel, and refusing to decide on anything. Mark came round, and Anu Sitaram hung about too like a moonstruck schoolgirl, but she saw remarkably few other people. What friends she had were in Mumbai, and all had called and sympathized, and cursed the Channel and urged her to return, until they had run out of things to say, and now the Clit restricted their calls to a diary update, on a rota, weekly, simply to maintain contact.

She had planted sweet herbs and lavender on the plot where she and Anu had buried Pudding. She ought to have stopped then, she told herself. Stayed at home, given up this wild goose chase so that she could have been here, and got to Toronto for the funeral, or at least the third day. Done her duty to her adulterous, lying bitch of a mother. Well, it was over now.

So why was it that, since her return, Taz hadn't even properly unpacked? Her travelling bag, with the letter from Armitage Shanks and the photograph and the rest of the montage stolen from Hugo Ruhl's flat, stayed where she had first dumped it on her return from Toronto, in the hallway. As though to open it would be to unlock some Pandora's box her mother's death had permitted, forced, finally allowed to be sealed. As though the ghosts of other dead lurking within were still capable of possessing her.

Or perhaps, the bag sat there by the umbrella stand, just three feet from the door, just where she had huddled when she was warned about her curiosity, as a statement not even she had recognized she had made, about her return. That she were simply waiting for something, or someone, in order to head off again.

∾

The West End Hotel was one of S.K. Mehta's favourite haunts. Gloriously unfashionable, terminally uncool. Totally non-*Aaj Mumbai*.

He waited in the art deco foyer, surrounded by stacks of left baggage, trapped in red netting, and watched the lift attendants in their stained white jackets argue over a tip.

'We still want it,' a voice behind him murmured.

SK didn't turn. He didn't need to. 'Can't be done,' he said.

'Of course it can. We were almost there. She just needs to be… reactivated.'

'It's too dangerous. They're watching her too closely. It's too risky. Look what happened last time anyone got close.'

'That was a mistake. One we won't make again. We'll take care of her.'

'Like you've done so far?'

'Yes.'

'You know what she'd call you? A shitbag tosspot. Something like that. And she'd be right.'

'Rivetting. Look, I really don't have time for this. She has to be reactivated. It's not up for discussion. It's not your decision or mine. It's what has to happen. We have to be able to handle the next few weeks, and like it or not, she's the key to doing it. That's the plan. Make it happen.'

'Don't you ever wonder if this is all worth it?'

'Of course not. It's a matter of duty and the greater good. Get her back in play.'

∾

It was Friday. Taz watched daytime television till 3.30, drove to a supermarket and bought the weekend shopping, then went home to prepare dinner for Mark.

She had drunk so much coffee and tomato juice she felt nauseous. Alcohol substitutes. Shit. She'd decided to sleep for a while, on the old sofa in the front room before starting to cook.

Cook.

That was an exaggeration, if ever there was one. She'd bought yet another series of packaged meals, which required little more than plastic being pierced, a couple of numbers tapped out on the microwave, and a mid-irradiation stir. Still, at least she couldn't ruin that.

She awoke from a powerful and disturbing dream, in which she was being entered, half against her will, by Armitage Shanks. Yet when she looked up, in her dream, to see his face, it was constantly changing, melting and re-forming, like depressingly clever computer graphics.

He was taking her, against her will. Yet he wasn't forcing her. Tricking rather, but with her connivance, or acquiescence. Like some Regency seduction.

He was saying something, but she couldn't make out the words. Some other sound was getting in the way.

A split second before she awoke, she realized it was her own voice, screaming.

The phone. The phone was ringing. Mark. There was a problem. He wouldn't be able to go over that night. Would see her tomorrow. Really sorry.

When she put the phone down she realized that she was actually relieved. She knew that he had been watching her carefully, looking for signs of her returning to drinking. When he kissed her, for the first time, on each arrival, she could tell he was testing her breath.

So, no Mark. Until tomorrow. Good. Ideal opportunity to get pissed. She went to the cupboard in which her mother had kept the ironing board and vacuum cleaner, and took out the emergency bottle of brandy. She sat down and she drank. Drank like she meant it. Urgent, secretive and gleeful. Like a kid dragging furiously at an illicit fag behind the bicycle shed.

She gulped back the first inch or so like it was lemonade, and sighed and leaned back, waiting for the heavy spirit to bring its own, reliable, sanity.

She thought about the little radio station at which she could now work if she wanted. How ludicrously proud they had been to think they might get her. The local paper had written about her; talked about her like she'd been some international mega-star returning to her roots.

They had offered her a chat show, ten to mid-day, each weekday morning, and a two-hour slot on Sunday afternoons. It would keep her out of mischief, Mark said. She ought to be grateful. Ought to be.

Ought to let herself enjoy the adulation.

She poured herself another half-tumbler of brandy.

She'd even been asked to open a local supermarket, and do a prize-giving at a primary school.

Ought to be honoured.

So why did she feel so much like a clapped-out soap opera has-been, reduced to wet Wednesday matinees on the end of a rusting pier in a fading seaside resort?

She held her glass in both hands and pressed it against her forehead. God, she was a maudlin bitch, she told herself. What about Hugo Ruhl? Dead, so the guy who had rung her in The

Gambia had said. Was it true? Had she made any attempt to find out? No. Some reporter. Had she even asked SK? No. Too proud, or too scared or just too fucking indifferent? And Sidiq? Jonjo? Any attempt to contact them? No way. A maudlin, selfish, stuck-up, fucked-up, lonely, shitty bitch!

'Do you care about anybody?' she asked aloud, rubbing her nose with the back of her hand and trying hard to sound like her mother. 'About anything?'

She looked up suddenly, brutally aware of the weight of the ceiling above her. She stretched out on the sofa and stared up at it, frowning. She was deeply troubled by the thought that she had no idea what held it up. She couldn't see any nails, or screws, or anything. She looked around and realized it was getting dark. She reached out to switch on the table lamp beside the sofa and knocked over an ornament she had sent her mother from a trip to Sri Lanka. She swore, but left the shards of pottery where they fell. Why had it shattered? It had fallen on the carpet. Oh, well, screw it, one thing less to have to dispose of. There were half a dozen plants in pots in the room. The thought of their root systems disturbed her, growing, imperceptibly, inexorably. Creeping like veins, or pale, blind worms feeling their way through the soil, sucking moisture out of dirt, taking life.

She thought of Pudding's ripped and rotting body out there, and wondered if roots were forcing themselves into his decomposing remains. Remains. What a grim image that word conjured up. She wondered if Pudding's eyes were still intact, and if his fur still clung to his skin. Did he still have a skin? She thought with a shudder of distaste of the way the soil beneath which he lay had sunk into a shallow dip. Of creeping things feeding.

And the pictures on the walls. Their weight. The strain on the screws and the nails from which they hung. She thought about the heaviness of things pulling apart, and the tortured stresses that pressed things back together, behind the scenes.

The room frightened her. She tried to stand up, but her legs were rubbery and numb. She squinted at the bottle of brandy. She was even more scared by the realization of just how much she had drunk. A sudden ugly wave of sense came like nausea to her brain. Shouldn't there be a mouse coming through the wall? Or a bat? Something hallucinatory. Anything other than this dreadful clarity and ghastly awareness of everything around her? She thought of an old Ray Milland film she had seen years before, the man with the x-ray eyes. She felt like that, just then. Like she could see what was going on, behind things. Through things. Within things. She tried to close her eyes, then open them again, quickly. She wondered if she should try and make herself vomit. Or drink lots of water, maybe. Ought to. Yes, really ought.

She could feel the weight of air on her skin; she really could, she was sure. She sniffed, and then suspected the air streaming into her nostrils was a violation. She wanted to cry at the thought that what she was inhaling was what the geraniums on the windowsill were exhaling. It seemed disgusting, somehow. 'Plant fart. It didn't ought to be allowed,' she said, but it didn't strike her as funny, out loud.

She tried to remember if she'd ever been this drunk before. She wondered if there was something wrong with the brandy. Saliva suddenly filled her mouth, and she knew she was about to throw up. She staggered towards the kitchen and vomited copiously into the sink. She let herself slump to the kitchen floor. Her sweat was cold and clammy on her brow. She was retching again. She vomited where she lay, then heaved, stretched and empty, four more times. Then she passed out. The phone rang. She didn't hear it. It rang every hour, on the hour, throughout the night. She answered it at 5 A.M. Her voice was a strange, ugly croak. Her mouth was bitter with alcohol and stale vomit. There was, she was sure, a livid split down the side of her head, just above her left ear. Brandy, she decided, was off the list.

'Issa middla fuckin' night,' she told the caller. That could have come out better, she ruefully acknowledged.

'Glad to hear you sounding more like your old self,' said SK.

'Waddyou wan'? I don' work for you anymore.'

'I'm calling as a friend. One who's worried about you. You remember that chap in Accra you worked with? Amin Asante? Well, we hear he's been beaten up. Badly beaten up. You need to get out of that house. He couldn't give them what they were after so they think you could be next.'

'Who thinks so?'

'People who know about these things. People I've spoken to. Is there somewhere you can go? Somewhere you'll be safe?'

'Maybe. What do they want?'

'Something about a website Hugo Ruhl set up. Did you check it out? No? Well, no time for that now. Just get the hell out of there. And be careful.'

Still wobbly, she staggered to the hallway, and snatched up her travelling bag. As she opened it, the photo of the gathering at the bungalow beach fell out, together with all the other images from the montage in Ruhl's flat. She knelt down gingerly to pick them up. There was a snap of Jamestown Prison in Accra: She recognized it now. And one of Jijiga in Ethiopia. And the next, the refugee camp outside Accra. There was a picture of a lorry, its smiling driver leaning against the bonnet. And here, Christ, this was a cheerier Rama Rao with an Indian guy in a garden, which could well be in Addis. Fuck! It was all here. Had been here all the time. The photo of the four who died wasn't the key, but quite literally just part of a bigger picture. It was the images all put together that pointed to the answer. Sobering up fast, she switched on her laptop and got the MSN home page. What was it Ruhl had specified? How could she access that website he created?

'I have told Leyna she must only give you the address when she receives

by e-mail a photograph of you back in England, holding a newspaper on which she can clearly see the date and headline. Do not send it from your own e-mail address. Create a Hotmail account for this one message. Once she has verified it as genuine from that paper's online version, you will then be called at a landline number you specify, and given the password you will need to access the site.'

She searched out her digital camera, cursed as she found the batteries were flat. She couldn't find the lead that connected it to the computer either, but then realized Mark had packed it neatly away in the pouch in which the camera was normally kept. Calm down, she told herself. The Tesco superstore in Swindon would be open. It was always open. Batteries and the morning paper: that's what she needed. Next she rang Anu, waking her, only to be told she was a couple of hundred miles away at a family wedding in Manchester and not due to return until Sunday. She apologized for disturbing her. Was there a problem? Did Taz want Anu to come back? Should she call someone to go round there? No, no, Taz assured her. Nothing wrong. Just that she was going away for a day or two. She'd call again on Monday. Great! Now where could she go? Who could she trust? Where would she be safe?

∾

It hadn't taken Anu long to decide where her duty lay. She disappeared into the loo with her mobile in her makeup bag. Though still early, she was meant to be getting dressed. She knew it was a big deal to her mother and aunt, this wedding. Not just for her to be there for the bride and groom, who were suddenly, seriously avowed now, almost irrelevant, but for her to be available and amenable to the parents of half a dozen marriageable, appropriate sons who were unlikely to find the prospect of a policewoman as a daughter-in-law very appealing. And she knew that though everyone laughed at the suggestion and shrugged off the idea as ludicrous, she was among the prospects being offered up, and was herself being gently encouraged to consider potential partners, and she hated it. She didn't want a husband, lover or life-partner. What she wanted, like many of the other sons and daughters dutifully but indifferently presenting themselves, was to be left alone to get on with her life, and her job.

Taz had never called her before, though she'd had Anu's personal cell number for months. Significant? Of course. But indicative of what? No idea. She couldn't really justify dropping her family yet again and racing down south, much as she ached to. No, others less willing would have to sacrifice their weekends.

So she sat on the loo in the en suite of the bedroom she was sharing with a cousin from Slough and made a series of whispered calls.

ॐ

Fourteen-and-a-half minutes after Taz had called Anu, Gord was awoken by an early call.

'I said you'd know as soon as we did if her interest was rekindled,' said Tim from Euston, grimly. 'Well, it is.'

'Oh, no! You know what you are going to do?'

'Uh huh. Want to know what it is?'

'Absolutely not! Just let us know when it's all over. The powers that be are already edgy about your handling of things. If they have any further cause for concern, you can start looking for other career opportunities.'

'Relax. Everything's under control. You just concentrate on getting the contract renewal.'

19

The City Inn Westminster stands, coincidentally, right next door to the square granite headquarters of the Security Service, MI5. Sharp, bland and corporate as it appeared, Taz remembered it not for its location in the UK's heartland for spies and spooks, but from a conference she had attended there a couple of years earlier. Some 'Where Next for Britain's NRIs?' jamboree at which she had been invited to talk. Its recalled amalgam of anonymity and connectivity commended it to her as the ideal place now to go to ground. She arrived mid-morning after an expensive and uncomfortable taxi ride to Heathrow Airport, a train journey in to Paddington on the Heathrow Express and a tube from there to Victoria. All paid in cash. None traceable. She signed in under her late married name of Letcombe, and gave Mark's address as her home. Not terribly imaginative, but the best she could come up with, still viciously hung over and half starved as she was.

In the room on the fifth floor she was directed to, she set up camera and laptop, snapped off a dozen shots of herself sitting on the bed with that morning's *Daily Mirror* (God, she looked like some aging hooker attempting blackmail to fund her crack habit), downloaded and attached the least awful to an e-mail quoting the landline number of the phone in her room. She sent it off to Leyna Meissner in The Gambia from a new account she created, just as Hugo Ruhl had instructed, and waited. She ordered brunch from room service, switched off her mobile, slept, showered and by four in the afternoon started to feel half human once more.

Leyna Meissner's response came at a quarter past five. The website address. Taz hit the Internet and typed it in, remembering even as she did so it was pointless without the password, which hopefully would follow shortly by phone. In the meantime, she wondered if the site name itself held a clue. *www.Indedeusabest.com*. She Googled it: a Latin inscription over the entrance to a 500-year-old dungeon in Turkey used as a torture chamber by the Knights of St John.

Where God does not Exist.

Profound. Deep. Profoundly unhelpful too. She logged off, leaned toward the minibar and, reminding herself of how grim she still felt, slumped back onto the bed. It could wait. So could she.

∾

Dave Bignall was not overjoyed to have to kiss goodbye to a rare Saturday afternoon kicking a ball about with his grandson. Sure, lost and interrupted weekends were all part of a policeman's lot, but up the ranks and near to retirement, you were meant to be, if not free of such intrusions, at least able to delegate their more shitty repercussions to others. Plus, since his son had divorced last year, he saw the six-year-old far less frequently than he would have liked, so the few hours per month access his airhead ex-daughter-in-law allowed them were solid gold. Not to be traded lightly.

He had seen it coming, he told himself. Felt it in his water. Thought something was a bit iffy when their long-lost colleague from the subcontinent, Rohit Shastri, had called up out of the blue for an update two days earlier. Anyway, Dave Bignall trusted Anu Sitaram's instincts, more than those of some blokes he'd served with for decades. She was calm, sharp and logical. So when she said she thought something was going down, he believed her. And if she thought it required him to look into it rather than the local plod, well, that merited serious consideration in his book. She was a good 'un.

Now why couldn't his son have married someone like that?

⌇

When the phone rang, it made Taz jump. Silly really, given that she'd been waiting for it for the past hour. She let it ring twice, three times whilst she calmed herself. This had to be got right.

'Hello?'

'Number One. Letters Papa, Echo, Tango, Echo, Romeo, India, Victor. Number Eight. Repeat it back to me.'

'1-P-E-T-E-R-I-V-8.'

'That's it.'

The line went dead. Taz could see in her mind's eye Leyna Meissner in the Gamtel booth, hanging up. She typed in the password. After what seemed an age, the page changed.

'Armitage Shanks is not the name of a real person, nor is it an alias. It is a process. It is based on the fact that there are Two Worlds, and the potential power of crossing over from one to another.

There are two worlds. Everyone accepts that. The problem is that no one can agree what those two worlds are: the key distinction used to be the Old World, and the New. Then the East and the West. What is it now? The Rich and the Poor? North and South? The Axis of Extremism and the Alliance against Terror?

It is this: the People and the Others.

The People are registered at birth, logged, assessed, measured and monitored throughout their lives. The People have passports, e-mail accounts, mobile phones with global roaming and credit cards that are good the whole world over. For the People, airports are welcoming places, visa restrictions and immigration controls little more than momentary irritants. The People are infinitely mobile, permanently contactable, eternally accessible. Losing touch with one of the People for a day warrants significant action and serious investigation. Billions and billions of dollars are spent selling to the People, loaning money to them, pandering to their whims and keeping them safe. Their lives are important, their happiness matters and their deaths are registered, accountable, significant events.

The People eschew their old-fashioned postal service as snail mail, but their electronic communications better deserve that name, for like a snail they leave a discernable trace wherever they have been and whatever they have done. Every time they make a call, send an e-mail, access a website, open an account, charge a transaction, it is a matter of record. When, where, what for, how much. The key to the People's world is information, its price is privacy and its only remaining despot, time.

But what of the world of the Others? The Others come and go and only their families know. The Others buy with cash, pay by barter, trade in kind. Others communicate by word of mouth, letter, or land line. Tied to the land, the Others represent no problem to anyone, as long as they stay where they are. You see, the Others are unwelcome visitors: they come not as tourists, their wallets and purses stiff with charged-up plastic, but as refugees, indentured workers, asylum-seekers with empty pockets and hungry eyes. The Others are the shabby and the sullen you look away from in Immigration, thankful when they are led out of your queue.

So they will have to sit there for hours? Well, time is different for them. They are not under the same diary pressures the People are. The Others don't even have diaries. Time does not torture them. They can be out of touch for months and no one worries. They may as well not exist. But they do have time. In fact, time is the only thing they have more of than the People.

The Others have no credit ratings, they leave no trails. Their very lives are less an issue to their governments, and they are targeted not at all in commercial advertising. If they are happy, that's nice, but what matters is they should be quiet. Their deaths are not significant as individual events, as the People's are. They only matter on a cumulative basis. In short, among the Others, individuals don't matter. Numbers do.

If one of the Others offends you, you can kill them and no one really cares, no one really notices. But what can you do with one of the People? Kill them? There will be an outcry. And if you happen to be a devout, God-fearing Christian administration, it's not only inefficient, it's also just plain wrong.

Now the genius of Armitage Shanks is in the recognition that it is as effective and morally more defensible to persuade one of the People who represents a threat to become one of the Others, than it is to kill them. No inconvenient post mortems, no prospective civil actions.

It is the logical, the brilliantly obvious extension of Guantanamo Bay and Extraordinary Rendition. It is decent. It is worthy. It is responsible. It is right. It is a fine example of how, when devout men face stark choices, difficult compromises can be made.

Let us take as an illustration of how it worked in the case of the four aid- workers—four of the People—in Ghana. Bob Lloyd, Andrew Carr and Dilip Dulta were committed to achieving the worthy aims of the organization that employed them, Safe Return. Perhaps too committed. They knew securing the safety of the refugees—the Others—in their care would need more than the limited resources they had. So they set about raising extra money through a bit of illicit trading. Fairly innocent at first. Selling goods that they had brought in duty-free. But that didn't raise nearly enough, so they started to deal in more serious contraband. But did it really matter? After all, lots of others were already doing it, but they alone did good work with the money they made. Modern-day Robin Hoods, they called themselves.

But then they had to buy the silence of an increasing number of significant men in the areas where they were resettling returned refugees, and in the camp out of which they worked. So as well as paying these men and providing them with drugs, they started to procure for them the sexual services of some of the Others in the camp. Drug-smugglers and people-traffickers too, now? Maybe. They didn't start it, they didn't profit from it. They merely stepped in and took over what was already going on, ran it more humanely, turned it to their advantage, and continued to do good.

Of course, it was only a matter of time before they were caught out. They would in the normal course of events have simply been arrested, and the due process would have taken its course. But no one wanted Safe Return discredited. And they were privy to something that no one wanted revealed in the inevitable scandal their prosecution would have caused.

That a quiet slaughter was still going on in Liberia.

Now, you may think that massacres in West Africa are hardly sensitive news, or indeed news of any sort. After all, it wasn't Americans, Europeans or Israelis being killed. Not the People. It was Africans. Locals. Others. But it is an indication of how sensitive the People's guardians have become. Because as far as the People knew, Liberia has turned the corner. The warlord Charles Taylor was in custody and facing Crimes Against Humanity charges. Fighters were disarmed. A rogue state returned to the fold, headed now by the first democratically-elected female President in Africa, tight in with Washington and the World Bank. Peace and progress, and both pretty quick. That's what is meant to happen when the People take it upon themselves to become involved in the affairs of the Others. This was a success story. No one wanted the truth about the continuing shambles in Liberia to be revealed before the new President even had a chance to pull things together. So three corrupt aid-workers qualified for Armitage Shanks. They needed to cross over to the world of the Others.

I was the one who did it. I had been the one who had first informed on them, these, once my friends. I agreed to help in their crossover. I thought I was doing them a favour. Saving them from the repercussions of their actions.

It was a shambles from start to finish. They had each been taken at various places: Bob Lloyd in Liberia, Andy Carr and Dilip Dutta outside Accra by an Armitage Shanks operative: the fourth one on that lake that day, Johnny Peters. He took them and I presented them with the alternatives: Armitage Shanks and be remembered as heroes or face disgrace and decades in an African prison. The profilers said they wouldn't take long to make up their minds. Whilst they did so, Johnny set up the charade of the boating trip. In reality only he went. Dilip, Bob and Andy listened to what I said, but they weren't buying it. Not to worry. Sometimes it takes a little longer than expected, the profilers said, eventually they'd see reason. In the meantime, someone needed to put Johnny on hold, because if we were going for trial, or the explosion for real, the plan changed. So someone called him on his mobile.

I was told later the explosive wasn't meant to go off then. They said the call signal must have been on the same frequency as the remote-controlled bomb. Said it was a tragic coincidence. However, it would help persuade the others to be sensible. Because now, there could be no question of them having a choice of disappearance or prison. They were dead people now. That made all the difference. The choice now was whether they would become real dead People, or live Others. Dilip was always the sharpest in the bunch. He got it immediately, and accepted. He is now somewhere in Mauritius, I think. I have no idea what he's called. Andy Carr said yes too. He runs a little beach bar in The Gambia. But Bob Lloyd said no, so they redirected him for further persuasion.

And he warned me too. When I said I had doubts about how much of an accident Johnny's death really was. Told me that wherever I went, I would be no safer than an Armitage Shanks in Africa.

I have no idea how many people qualify for Armitage Shanks. I know they have Outlets, that's what they call them, Outlets in Eastern Europe, Central Asia and the Middle East for processing those who do, as well as the one Andy, Dilip and Bob were processed by in Liberia. I didn't know they had one in Ethiopia too, but if that was where Bob wrote to you from, then I guess there must be.

The process has been going for several years now.

It is authorized by the Americans, but managed for them by the British. Respect for the sanctity of life, well, non-Muslim, People's life, was a precondition to the US Administration and the right-wing Christian backers funding the process. Preservation matters, quality, much less.

When an Outlet is set up in a country, that country qualifies for debt relief and enhanced aid packages. When an Outlet is closed, the aid reduces.

Now, you have been sent the final piece of your story, you should make your choice: the same one they had. Real dead People, or live Other? You won't be able to download or print this. Once you log off, this site will become inaccessible. Just as you will.

You have the final piece.

I told you I would tell you everything. I have.

She scrolled down, but there was no more. She read the whole thing again, making notes. Then there was a polite knock on the door.

20

A flat white expanse, with a single line snaking across it. A faint yellow stain. A ceiling. She turned her head slightly and saw bare walls and a window, curtained over. She tried to move, but couldn't. Her throat felt raw and her mouth full. Breathing was difficult and swallowing even harder.

'Now if I might give you a little advice,' a male voice said, 'and in your position, I'd listen very carefully and take it. I would keep very still and concentrate hard on suppressing your gag reaction. The peculiar tasting cloth in your mouth is your underwear. I wouldn't have thought you were a size twelve. The slight prick you are about to feel on the inside of your left thigh is a cocktail of mind-altering substances including a stimulant, to raise the sensitivity to pain and ensure the subject does not pass out. Ah, I see a picture is beginning to form in your mind. Good. Now, I wonder what's going to happen next? Well, I am afraid I have to tell you I am going to rape you. I also have to tell you I will take no personal pleasure in this, but it's in the *Manual of Special Measures*. So there we are. I will, however, as the *Manual* specifies, ensure it will be both extremely degrading and very painful. Also, I will be, and I am quoting now, 'disproportionately maximizing long-term mental damage'. Isn't that a great phrase? There's an entire 'Annexe' in the *Manual* devoted to helpful hints on precisely how that can be done. Pretty detailed. Well, not actually pretty. Especially the photographs. I've seen prettier things on a butcher's slab. I think the drafting committee got off on it. Anyway, we will get started soon. Oh, and I shall be wearing a condom, but not for your benefit. In a short time I will remove your gag, because the *Manual* says greater psychological damage is achieved when the subject is not distracted by worries about choking on their own vomit and if they can subsequently recall their screams. And who knows, we might actually need your mouth, mightn't we?'

Taz felt herself tottering on the precipice of blind, bellowing panic. She looked around desperately, blinking away stinging tears, searching for what, she had no idea. She lay spread-eagled on a bed, wrists and ankles securely tied. She could feel a pulse she didn't even know she had pounding deep in her belly, like jolts of electricity, and another kicking in her temple. Tim sat beside her, the syringe in his left hand resting lightly on her leg, looking, if anything, rather bored. He checked his watch, and said 'Ok, let's get on with it, shall we? We need you bleeding, gibbering and paranoid by five. That gives us just under two hours. Not much when measured against a whole lifetime, really, is it? An hour and a half let's say, because we'll stop for a short beak halfway through, to mop off the worst of the mess and assess impact.'

He removed the bunched-up panties from her mouth, and Taz hauled in breath, her chest heaving and her throat burning. 'I'll tell you. Anything. Whatever it is, I'll tell you. Please. Just ask. Anything.' The words tumbled out of her. She was sobbing and begging, but she didn't care. Just so long as this could be stopped. He could be stopped.

'Well, therein lies the problem. Or is it a dilemma? I can never remember which is which. You see, there's nothing you know that we don't. This isn't an interrogation, like some old war movie where they say, "Ve haf vays of making you talk." On the contrary, this is about making sure that anything and everything you say from here on is ignored because everyone can see you are, well, bonkers. Once we get to five o' clock, even if you tell them the sky is blue and day follows night, people are going to dismiss every word you say as the ravings of a lunatic.'

In her desperation, Taz caught a tiny glimmer of, if not hope, perhaps purpose. From many hours listening to the ramblings of the people of the night on the graveyard shift of radio phone-in shows, she recognized a talker. Yes, it would be true he would take no pleasure in her suffering, and feel no triumph in her destruction, but not, as he implied, because he was just doing what he was told, but because he was more stimulated by the thought and the verbal description than by the act or its result. But if she was to work him, she needed to maintain the picture of her absolute vulnerability. She let go of the pent-up tears and sobbed wholeheartedly. Bubbles of mucus formed on her mouth and nose. He sighed and wiped her face, surprisingly gently, with the pants.

'So am I to be Armitage Shanks?' she asked in a tiny, gulping voice.

He smiled, and shook his head. 'Great name isn't it? My idea, you know. My first proposal was 'Shit Creek', but our friends across the pond thought that lacked a certain gravitas. Uncle Sam does insist on his brutality being nicely sanitized, even when it's being done for him under licence. Asymmetric Warfare, Extraordinary Rendition. Linguistic Legitimation. No, you won't be Armitage Shanks. Whilst we are realizing economies with every new case, it's still a pretty expensive option. And, as our late friend Bob Lloyd discovered to his cost, it doesn't extend to Muslims.'

'Bob Lloyd isn't dead. I spoke to him.'

'*The Slaughter House on Pound Street?*' he mimicked. '*Liquid fear, and the trapped wail of foreseen death in the morning? Stale blood and the tranquillity of cleansed slaughter in the evening?*' I'd heard all that crap a dozen times from him. God, he was a poor sad twat! You'd think someone who'd done the kind of things he'd, we'd, done would have had a bit more of a full complement down below. It was me you spoke to. An unfortunate misunderstanding, but as soon as that fool Lloyd told his jailers he was a Muslim, they checked their contract and, lo and behold! Muslims don't qualify! So we wouldn't be paying for him, so they topped him. Shame really. Another thirty minutes and we'd have gotten to them and sorted it all out. Imagine, if the daft prat had actually sat down with the priest, he'd still be alive today. There's a message there, though fuck knows what that it is. The only one you spoke to was Andrew Carr in The Gambia, and there is a day of reckoning due him for that.

'Yes, you don't qualify for Armitage Shanks. You are lower down the D process. Like your greasy little friend in Frankfurt.'

Taz would have thought she had no space or spare energy to care about anyone else at that moment, but her heart gave a lurch, and she caught her breath. 'Sidiq?'

That's the chappie. An illegal immigrant leads a precarious existence. That of the Others. Easy victims on the shadowy margins of society. Like you, he neither required nor justified significant expenditure. The D process goes like this: Defuse, Discredit, Demonize, Disappear, Destroy. First we simply contain the threat and defuse its potential for harm. Now, normally with someone like Sidiq, the cheapest option is to purchase his silence. As an illegal, he was already discredited, and pretty much demonized too. But unfortunately your cash and his profound sense of having been used by you forced us to choose the final D.'

'You killed him?'

"Fraid so.'

'But he had a wife and kids!'

'A widow and orphans now. Anyway, you're hardly in a position to be too judgemental. We simply kept the appointment you chose not to, talked him through his feelings, which I have to say were hardly very positive about you, and took the requisite action. Believe me, he felt nothing. What happened to him was a great deal quicker and infinitely less painful than what's about to happen to you. However, he did die cursing your name. Very melodramatic! Could have been straight out of one of those Indian films he so liked. And I must confess to a little bit of subsequent artistry. You see, unlike you, I was genuinely moved by what he said about the attacks on his mosque, the threats he and his kind daily live under. Did I tell you we had a listening device in your mobile? I inserted it after I'd gutted kitty. So anyway, I carved a few swastikas on him, post mortem. SS flashes too. I'm amazed you didn't read about it in the Sunday supplements. As a result, our German partners are at last confronting the cancer of neo-Nazism in their midst. Not our main aim in ending his life, I'll admit, but a very positive by-product none the less.'

'All he wanted was a chance to get to India.'

'Hmm. A chance which you weren't willing to let him have.'

'And Hugo Ruhl?'

'Yes, the good Herr Ruhl is a case which does justify an Armitage Shanks. Currently in an Outlet in Poland. Seems suitable somehow: elegant, him being a Jew. Fortunately our American paymasters have no sense of irony.'

'But what...'

'I think that's enough,' interrupted Tim. He touched the tip of the syringe against the inside of her thigh and she screamed in agony, the pain an order of magnitude greater than the shallow pinprick should have caused. Tim stood, and took a small pouch from his pocket. Opening it carefully, he took out a condom, which he placed unopened on the bed between her feet, and a pair of earplugs, which he proceeded to roll between his fingers and thumbs. 'You hoped to postpone the inevitable by keeping me talking. I needed to give the stimulant time to work, and make sure you knew about Sidiq before we start so you also have your guilt to contemplate. Perceptions. Is it a six or is it a nine? Who's really in control? Well, sometimes, even in this crazy old world, things really are as they seem. You're the one strapped down and shit-scared, and I'm the one with a six-thirty stress counselling session booked to help me deal with just how disturbing the next hour or two is going to be.'

He thrust the earplugs deep into his ears, made two huge, gaping yawns to get them settled, and leaned over so his face was no more than a couple of inches from hers. He let his tongue run slowly up her cheek, and it felt like hot, wet sandpaper on her hyper-sensitized skin. 'Your story cannot be defused,' he whispered in her ear as he climbed onto the bed. 'But you are pretty much discredited. Your grasp on reality, oh, so tenuous. Embrace insanity when it offers you sanctuary, Miss Dhar. It's really your last best hope. Your personal engagement with the war on terror is about to begin.'

&

'You're looking decidedly chipper,' Gord observed as he and Tim took breakfast together at Langham's the next morning.

Tim smiled. 'There's nothing like feeling that you've done your duty, and done it well, to brighten up one's day. It's a glorious morning. In a couple of hours, I'll be leading a string of ponies with happy kids astride them over the downs, and all's right with my world.'

20

Everything. She had lost, had taken from her, every last vestige of her her-ness. Weeks, months ago, she'd had Pudding, a job she'd loved, a mother she provided for, friends who cared for her, and the memory of a father she cherished. A pet, a passion, a role, an identity. Dignity. A life. All taken away. Everything, gone. A large part of her past, and all of her present, taken. They said they would destroy her, and they had. No past now, no present then, and no future either.

Nothing. Nothing to look back on with anything approaching nostalgia. Nothing to look forward to with anything other than vacant resignation. For the doctor who'd examined her had told her that in addition to her breakdown, she was suffering from alcoholic hepatitis, and that another drink could be fatal. Also, and by the way, she was perimenopausal and, as he was sure she appreciated, she was highly unlikely now ever to be able to have children.

All gone. Stolen, taken away, or given up.

How nonchalantly, over the years, had she surrendered these little-valued facets of her: her religion, lightly held, unenthusiastically observed and vaguely traded for the picturesque convenience of a church wedding.

'What does it matter?' She'd snapped back all those years ago at her grumbling mother. 'I'm an atheist.'

'A Muslim atheist,' her mother had insisted, in what had struck her at the time as a breathtakingly stupid observation but which now seemed obvious and sensible.

Pleasant home and amiable marriage, the easy way, easily cast aside like barely worn pantyhose for the dazzle and crash of a new life in Mumbai, where the roads have only fast lanes, and no prisoners are taken. And there had been warnings, too, along the way. The first, whispered suggestions that her drinking might be becoming, not a problem, or even an issue: an issuette perhaps? Denial. That's what they called it, but that was to dignify indifference with effort. There was no denial, merely an easy drift into acceptance. Embracing her need. Adoption of the boozing as a facet of her new persona.

Because none of it really mattered, when it came right down to it, did it? Because nothing is forever. None of this, she repeated as a mantra when the ghosts came, is irreversible. What was that Irish saying? When God made time, he made plenty of it? It was all revocable, recoverable, soluble, and if worse came to the worst (which of course it only did for other people), curable. There was always lots of time and plenty of space to turn and trace a way back. Because it was eternally there. A permanent path, clearly marked, solidly paved. Problems may be acute, but they are never truly chronic.

But then the whispers became statements and statements became shouts: her job, Pudding and the near massacre of those around her, of even the memory of her long dead Pappa. How many warnings did a person need to hear before they bore responsibility for their own demise? How many threats? Two strikes and you're out. How many had she ignored?

Realization: some things can't be cured. There are problems which defy solution. Some pain remains forever.

And when, when would she ever stop crying?

It seemed like she had been crying ever since she'd been found.

Found? Lost.

They discovered her, around four that Sunday morning, staggering, dishevelled, half naked and confused, across Vauxhall Bridge.

The Sikh driver of the hourly night bus that linked London's mainline stations, ferrying late drunks and early migrant workers around the sleeping metropolis, had alerted the police. Not the first potential suicide he'd seen mooching around on a London bridge, and depressingly, probably not the last. But once, three years earlier, he hadn't bothered to make the call and a body had been found, mid-morning. A homeless fifteen-year-old, three months pregnant. Not his responsibility, but on his conscience still. So now, he routinely called them in.

'Been making a night of it, have we?' the policeman had asked as the patrol car pulled up quietly beside her.

She had stared dully back. Eyes unfocussed, lips half shaping words her mind could not fully form. Confused, scared, alone.

At first the officer assessed her drunk and incapable. The usual questions: what's your name? Where do you live? Been drinking? What have you taken? On medication? Anywhere to go? Anyone who can come to get you? Nothing. Just the same dull stare, and one hand, rubbing clumsily, scratching, worrying at her cheek, where she could still feel the hot rasp of his tongue.

'Crystal meth,' concluded the second officer. 'Look at her itching. Textbook stuff. She's out of her head.'

'Listen to me, love,' the first policeman had said, slowly, kindly. 'I think you need a bit of looking after.' He had placed a hand gently, reassuringly on her shoulder, but its weight and clammy pressure on her still screaming skin was unbearable and made her throw herself back, whimpering desperately. 'Steady, steady,' he said, stepping back and holding both hands up in surrender. 'Look at me. Listen to me. OK? I think you are in need of a bit of care. We're going to take you to what's called A Place of Safety, OK? For your own good. Do you understand what I'm saying? Can you get into the car?'

She shook her head and began to sob.

'Garry?' the policeman called over his shoulder to his colleague, still in the car, calling in details. 'We're going to need a paramedic. Step round this side and make sure she doesn't make a break for it.'

At the sight of the second policeman, Taz took another step back and half turned toward the parapet of the bridge.

'Watch her, John,' the second policeman warned. 'She's going to jump.'

His eyes not leaving Taz's, the first policeman put his hand out slowly, waving his partner back. 'She's not going to jump. Look at her. She can't bear to be touched, and she seems terrified of touching anything herself. Look at the way she keeps lifting her feet off the ground. Like the soles are raw. She's no jumper. She's on something. See the way she keeps trying to rub something off her face? Tell them to sample it, just in case. Now, just let her be till someone who knows what they're doing gets here.'

A Place of Safety. The mental health ward at the nearest hospital. Where she could be seen by a general practitioner, an approved social worker and a consultant psychiatrist. A place where difficult decisions could be made about the vulnerable, by competent, compassionate professionals.

Somewhere, someone noted this muddled individual's likeness to the description of Tasneem Dharwallah which Dave Bignall had sent out. Phone calls were made, and by mid-morning, Anu was there.

❧

Taz told her what had happened to her. Painstakingly professional, Anu recorded every word and transcribed it for Taz to sign. The doctor, the social worker and the ward staff had all heard the tale too and had ordered swabs and smears, but found no evidence of semen. Only inconclusive traces of saliva on her cheek. The kindest explanation any could offer, and their initial diagnosis, was the hallucinatory effects of whatever narcotic she'd mixed with heavy alcohol abuse. The social worker who sat in on Anu's meeting with Taz caught Anu's eye, her doubt obvious in her eloquently expressionless stare. It almost broke Anu's heart to see Taz like this. She tried desperately to reason Taz through it. Out of it. A rape? Who was it? How many? Where did it happen? What did he do? When?

And what about the dream Taz had mentioned to the social worker, of being taken by Armitage Shanks? Was that the same occasion? Was it different? What that real too? Was Armitage Shanks the rapist? She claimed to have received phone calls from dead people, too. And they were all called Armitage Shanks? She had to see how hard to make sense of all this was: had any of it really happened?

And what, offered Anu, as gently as she could, about the bottle of brandy in the sitting room of her home, and the vomit in the kitchen?

Then, just when it seemed some glimmer of light might be dawning, they asked Anu to wait outside, because a small group of professionals was ready to assess Taz. To decide if she was she a danger to herself or others. A police surgeon and the psychiatric consultant on call met with the social worker and were ready to talk to her.

Anu headed off for coffee and a place from which she could update Dave Bignall. Whilst she was gone, the two doctors were joined by a fellow clinician in private practice who had arrived half an hour after Anu, explaining that Ms Dharwallah had been consulting him since her mother's death and that Wiltshire police had kindly alerted him to the fact that his patient was in a place of safety. He made clear he would not dream of trying to influence their clinical judgement, nor had he any expectation of taking part in the consideration of the appropriate handling of her case, or indeed interfering in any way. No, no. He merely wanted to be there, as a friendly face, and a helping hand, and so as to be able to offer continuity of care in the future.

As a professional courtesy, his National Health colleagues invited him to be present as an observer. He thanked them, and promised them copies of his case notes, provided his patient agreed to their release.

The patient however reacted very badly to the presence of her psychiatrist. Her eyes widened, and her ghastly, tormented wail of rage could be heard halfway down the corridor. She threw herself at her clearly concerned consultant, who took a step back, to allow the attendants to restrain her, and to hold her down, whilst sedatives were administered. She whimpered, muttered a series of muddled expletives and finally curled up into a ball, facing the wall, a position in which she remained, unresponsive to any and all questions for the remainder of the day.

It was the work of moments for the police surgeon and the consultant psychiatrist to agree the social worker's initial recommendation that she represented a sufficient danger to herself and others to justify being sectioned under the Mental Health Act. Shaking their heads sadly, they signed the required paperwork.

As they left, they passed Anu in the corridor. The visiting professional from the private sector paused in his grave reflections on the sad inevitability of such a profound breakdown, caught her eye, and winked. Anu frowned, turned and watched them depart. She had seen one of them before. The one who had winked at her. The last time she had seen him, he had not been in a hospital, but in a police station. And he had not been a doctor. He had been an ambiguous professional from an anonymous organization in Euston, and everyone had called him Tim.

21

Taz thought she would probably never stop crying. Her eyes burned, her lips were cracked, her face swollen, and her throat, constantly dry.

They kept her sedated. That alone felt good.

It dawned on her how remarkably similar her current situation was to that described in the letter she had received at the very start of all of this. Time passing, without structure. Meals, television, lights on twenty-four hours a day. No privacy, permanent scrutiny. A place of safety indeed. She needed the intervention the priest had offered Bob Lloyd. But he too was in a place of safety. Secure in his sanctuary deep in the countryside, or lost within the labyrinth of the Vatican. Who now could she turn to? To whom could she send her Armitage Shanks letter? How? She thought of Anu, but promptly dismissed her as profoundly compromised. Likely either to report the call to whoever was doing this to her, or to ignore it as the paranoid ravings of a dangerously disturbed individual. Mark, equally unreliable. He'd come to see her every day of course, sat in dismal silence after he'd exhausted the trivia he thought safe to share with her. But he clearly saw her first and foremost as a patient and would undoubtedly, well-meaningly, confide everything she said to the first person in a white coat he came across. Her uncle/father Yusuf Abbas? She hadn't even agreed to see him when he'd visited.

No, she needed someone whom she could trust to either do something, or do absolutely nothing at all. What she could not afford was polite, concerned interest in her welfare and an assumption that some professionals should be informed of her call.

She told the social worker who sat with her for an hour every morning that she was troubled about an aunt in India. Developed a whole saga about an operation and her worry for one of her last remaining relatives in Delhi. The social worker was pleased with her concern for someone other than herself and relieved. Taz was moving on beyond the paranoid fantasy about rape which had so obsessed her to date. This was progress. To be encouraged. She agreed to speak to the consultant psychiatrist and both concluded that a short, supervised call to her cousin, to find out how things stood, would be beneficial, and that, her condition permitting, she could ring India the next day. A call charge card? By all means. Did she know the number? Indeed she did.

She made it to the payphone in the corridor supervised

but unaided. It took her three attempts to punch in the numbers. Her vision was blurred, and her hand/eye coordination was shot all to hell. She felt dizzy with relief when the number rang, and cried when she heard his voice.

'Kirk?' she gulped. 'It's Tasneem.'

A silence. 'Taz? Are you alright? You sound awful. I'd heard you'd been taken ill?'

'It's not your real name, is it?' Taz asked in broken Gujarati, with a glance over her shoulder at her carer.

'*Nehi*. What can I do for you?'

'You can get me out of this… place of safety. Get me back to India.'

'Now why would I do that, Taz?'

'Because I think you are as interested as I am in that thing we discussed in Addis, which in a moment, when I speak in English, I will call Aunty. And I have finally worked out the whole picture. I just need the last piece. And I'm pretty sure I know where I can find it, and what it is. You can have it all, if you just get me out of here.'

Rohit thought for so long that Taz feared he had hung up, or that the call card she had bought had run out, or the line disconnected.

'Give me twenty-four hours,' he said at last. 'Don't speak to anyone else. Sleep and eat. You've got a long journey ahead of you.'

She was sobbing wholeheartedly now. 'I'm delighted to hear that,' she said, in English. 'Give my love to Aunty. Oh, and I need some reading material.'

∾

As agreed, Anu met Rohit in the grounds of the psychiatric hospital the following afternoon. They shook hands, very formal.

'Are you sure you want to do this?' he asked.

'You won't get her out of there without me. How did she sound?'

'Not good. Very disturbed. Deeply distressed.'

Anu noticed the carrier bag he held.

'What's that?'

He glanced down at the bag. 'Something she asked me to bring her. A Bible.'

Anu sighed. 'This doesn't sound good, does it?'

Getting in proved surprisingly easy. As they walked down the corridor, Anu told Rohit about having recognized Tim, walking down the corridor dressed as a doctor. How she'd only learnt a couple of days earlier that it was the sight of him which had prompted the violent reaction from Taz that had led to her being sectioned. What she suspected was going on. How she felt she had let Taz down. How she was glad to have the opportunity to put that right, but just prayed it was not too late.

They found her slumped in an armchair, dressed in a baggy and faded tracksuit, watching re-runs of *Columbo* on daytime TV. A cold cup of coffee, a slick of congealed milk on its surface, and two digestive biscuits lay untouched on a small table at her side.

She looked up at them, like a hunted and hurt animal. 'The Bible?'

Without a word Rohit handed it to her. With her face screwed up in concentration and her tongue protruding, she searched desperately, then thrust the Bible back at him with a despondent moan. 'My eyes. I can't focus. You'll have to do it. Find me *The Gospel According to Peter*. First book, chapter four, verse eight.'

Rohit found the verse and read it aloud. 'Charity shall cover the multitude of sins.'

Taz smiled 'Yes! That's it. God, what a Byzantine mind!'

'We don't understand what you are talking about, Taz,' said Anu, gently.

Taz looked at her, frowning at the funereal tone. 'You wouldn't. You never have. 1Peter IV 8. The password to access the website Hugo Ruhl set up for me. I thought it was nothing more than a random pattern of numbers and letters, but it's the final piece he told me he'd sent. It wasn't just the text he wrote. The password was the answer. The charity. Safe Return. This isn't just about three aid workers gone wrong there. The whole bloody organization has been hijacked. Safe Return is the cover for the entire Armitage Shanks operation.' She looked at the man she had known as Kirk, who nodded, slowly.

'Take me out for a walk, cousin,' Taz said. 'You'll need to support me, I'm pretty shaky. Just around the garden.'

It seemed to take them an age. Taz shuffled along, cautious as a geriatric with brittle bones. They moved slowly and in silence until they were well clear of the building, among rhododendron bushes shedding their bloom like bloated confetti, gaudy and bright on the neatly cut grass.

Anu caught Rohit's eye and mouthed, 'Can she make it?'

'Yes,' snapped Taz. 'She can make it. She can also hear and she's not fucking gaga, no thanks to you. So stop talking about me like I'm not even here. Where do we go now?'

Anu smiled, and her chin trembled as she reached out and threw her arms around Taz who, uncomfortable, patted her lightly on the back.

Anu stepped back, ran her hand through her hair and looked away. 'I'm sorry I didn't believe you.'

'So am I,' said Taz, dryly. 'But you got me out. We'll call it quits.'

'There's a car fifty metres down the road,' said Rohit. 'There's a gap in the fence we can get you through. From there, to India.'

'You happy to go with him?' Anu asked, her voice cracking.

Taz nodded.

'Then go.'

'What about you?' said Rohit, turning to Anu, but with one hand still supporting Taz. 'I can make arrangements for you to come as well. Right now, or in a day or two's time.'

Anu shook her head. 'And then what would I do? India's just another country to me. Go. I'll be okay.'

She watched, shoulders hunched, hugging herself as Rohit led Taz gently away. Then she spun round, aware she was not alone. Dave Bignall walked up and stood beside her, and together they watched Rohit and Taz go.

'Did you sign her out?' he asked, not looking at her.

'No, Guv. No need. We just walked out with her.'

'Many people see you?'

'Several. But only two members of staff.'

'Either of them seen you before?'

'No.'

'Right. Let's get out of here then.'

Anu smiled. 'You are a good man, Guv'nor,' she said.

'No,' he sighed. 'I'm a bloody idiot. Just like you.'

'We can't leave it like this, can we, Guv?' asked Anu as they walked toward the main gate.

'No,' he sighed. 'But there's not much we can do about it either.'

'He raped her. She swears it. I believe it. You suspect it. There must be something we can do.'

'Evidence? Remember that? You saw the Rape Test results. Nothing.'

'No,' she acknowledged. 'But there is the DNA on the swab they took when she was first picked up. The saliva on her cheek. Not hers.'

Dave beamed. 'That's the Met for you, see? Thorough. Quality policing! Gaze in awe, young Sitaram.'

'Not that it's much good,' she reflected, 'without a sample from him. And there's not much chance of us being able to get one anytime soon.'

'Oh, I don't know. Noble cause,' muttered Dave.

'What's that?' asked Anu. 'An anagram?'

'No, a euphemism. It's what I've spent the last thirty years avoiding. Doing right by doing wrong. Helping the case along. Improving on the evidence. Noble cause corruption. We got a DNA trace thanks to some exemplary policing. But we'll only get a match through some iffy work. And you are to have no part in it.'

'No way! I owe her! I owe you. I'm in.'

'No, you're not. You're a good cop, at the start of what could be a great career. And this is going to be dirty business I don't want you to be part of.'

॰ঌ

Early the next morning, Taz Dhar's credit card and chip and pin number were used at Heathrow Airport to purchase a business class ticket from London to Accra on KLM, departing three hours later via Amsterdam. Routine processes for a transaction of that magnitude kicked in, but the card-user answered the preset security questions satisfactorily, and in any case was a regular purchaser of international airline tickets, so the transaction was approved. A subsequent check of Immigration and Nationality Department records in the UK, CCTV images in London's Heathrow and Amsterdam's Schiphol Airports, plus a review of reports from the Ghana Immigration Service's recently installed passport-scanning system all confirmed that Taz Dhar travelled to Accra alone, entered unaided, and promptly, completely disappeared.

Among the other passengers on flight KL1008, a Mr N.C.

Chaudhri, headed for Dubai, attracted sympathetic attention as he pushed a wheelchair in which his seriously-ill wife sat semi-comatose, following investigative surgery on a suspected tumour on her jaw at the Cromwell Hospital in West London. Mr and Mrs Chaudhri and Taz Dhar were spotted together once—the merest glimpse by a harassed KLM staffer who wouldn't swear it was them—as Taz Dhar kindly assisted Mr Chaudhri to manoeuvre his wheelchair-bound and heavily bandaged wife into the disabled toilet in the Platinum Elite lounge.

Taz Dhar, an airport securityman remembered thinking, as he saw her board flight KL 589 at 13.25 bound for Accra, looked even less like her passport photograph than many a mature lady he'd seen, but she was a connecting traveller, her baggage already checked through, her threat profile minimal, and his scrutiny was cursory at best.

Twenty minutes later, Mr and Mrs Chaudhri boarded flight KL 457 for Dubai.

∾

Once again Dave Bignall and Anu Sitaram sat outside Yusuf Abbas's back door and waited, but this time they were in Dave's wife's Renault Megane. He had tried to talk Anu out of being there, but she was adamant, and he admired, respected and finally caved in to her insistence.

And secretly, he was proud to have her at his side.

The moment Yusuf Abbas emerged, turned his back to them and began to lock up, they were out of the car. Dave strode, grim-faced, fast and determined toward him, with Anu half running to keep up a pace behind.

Abbas turned to say something but Dave grabbed him, spun him round and slammed him hard up against the metal door.

'Still trying to impress the little girl, Mr Bignall?' mumbled Abbas, his face pressed up so tight against the door that his words slurred. 'Do us all a favour,' he sneered at Anu. 'Open your legs so he can leave the rest of us alone.'

'You've always been a loathsome shit, Abbas,' snarled Dave, his face inches from him. 'But what you did to your niece. Wow! That was really bad, even for a toerag like you.'

'Yeah?' said Abbas, unrepentant. 'And you know the best part? It was all bollocks. What do you think of that?'

With a groan, he collapsed as Dave hit him hard in the kidneys.

'Steady, Guv,' warned Anu as Dave followed up the punch with a kick.

'I tell you what I think, you turd,' panted Dave, supporting himself against the wall. 'I think it's time you did something for me.'

'You must be crazy,' gasped Abbas, as he rolled out of kicking distance. 'I do something for you and I'll never work again.'

'Don't, and you'll never fucking *walk* again!' shouted Dave, lashing out with his boot and narrowly missing Abbas's head.

'OK! OK!' cried Abbas, wrapping both arms around his head. 'Fuck! Get a grip!'

'I'll get a fucking grip on you!' roared Dave, lunging forward.

Anu stepped in, placing a restraining hand on Dave's heaving chest. She turned, knelt and offered Abbas a handkerchief.

'Someone raped your niece, and we know who it is. You're going to help us get him,' she explained quietly, reasonably. 'You're going to put some Class A drugs in the boot of his car, and you're going to remove one of the brakelights. That's all.'

'And then what?'

'We watch justice take its course.'

'And I suppose you expect me to pay for the drugs?'

'That's it,' said Dave, shaking his head. 'I'm gonna fucking kill him.'

∿

'Good cop, bad cop. Played large and played well,' observed Dave breathlessly as he wiped perspiration from his face. 'If I'd known Noble Cause was this much fun, I'd have gone dirty years ago.'

'Guv?' asked Anu, as they walked back to the car. 'How do you know what he told Taz about him being her dad?'

Dave grinned. 'Tim the Tosser and his shadowy pals at Box aren't the only ones who can seek authority for intrusive surveillance.'

'Doesn't that…This, all of it, make us the same as them?'

'No,' said Dave. 'And if you think it does you have a very great deal left to learn.'

∿

Two days after Taz Dhar's departure from London, Rohit Shastri was driven from the discreet clinic in Old Delhi, just near the Inter-State Bus Terminal, where a patient registered under the name of Mrs J. Chaudhri was receiving care not for a suspected tumour on the jaw but for post-traumatic stress and a range of drug and alcohol-related problems. He headed for Indira Gandhi International airport so he could greet a female colleague with whom, as Mrs Chaudhri, he had left London, and who had then, as Taz Dhar, entered Ghana, and who was now finally returning home on a diplomatic passport issued to her by the Indian High Commission in Ghana, sleep-deprived and jet-lagged, and barely able to remember who she was currently meant to be.

She was accompanied by an African man, old and moving carefully, who knew exactly who he was: Jonjo Amin Asante.

∾

'She's missing?' cried Gord, horrified. 'But she is mad, isn't she?'

'Relax,' said Tim. 'The story is diffused, she's discredited, and she's destroyed. Now, she's disappeared. Full house.'

'Your lot did this?' asked Gord.

'Not exactly,' admitted Tim. 'But there's nothing to worry about. This is what we intended would happen. Don't worry. We have it all in hand.'

22

'One can believe,' the minister boomed, nodding at the wisdom of what he was about to say 'that it was decreed by God that Taz Dhar, troubled and plagued as she was in her final months, and anguished with doubts, should meet death and find her peace, from whence those doubts emanated, in Africa.'

S.K. Mehta glanced once more at his watch, tasted bile and felt a long-forgotten ulcer sting. Hadn't they told the old fool up there, drummed it in to him, over and over, that they must finish on time? This was to be syndicated, for God's sake, and could turn out to be the biggest story of the decade. The last thing they needed was to miss the scheduled news slots. He'd pulled strings, traded in favours, exploited his web of contacts. Hinted, whispered, promised, foreswore, cajoled, begged and now, eight global networks were standing ready for something hot, around midday, Greenwich Mean Time.

Breaking News. That's what they were going for. Not something held over for the next summary, which could so easily fall victim to subsequent events deemed more newsworthy. After all this work, all this planning, to lie for an hour, prey to the whims of fate and the vagaries of a fickle media. It would only take one raided mosque. One severe storm. One crashed plane...

Ash seemed unconcerned, but then little that had to do with anything other than himself concerned Old Ash. The young policewoman, Sitaram, suspended from duty now, sat with them, distant and sad. SK felt for her. To be told you had broken all the rules to get someone so vulnerable out of a place of safety only to send her on her way to her death. Tough call.

There was Taz's uncle, Yusuf Abbas, bruised, but looking as bored and uncomfortable as SK felt. He sat amicably beside a man SK had been told was Sitaram's ex-boss, Bignall. Too old and senior to be suspended too, Bignall had opted for early retirement. More victims. This had all turned out to have quite a price-tag in human suffering. Not for the first time, SK had wondered if it had all been worth it. Too late now, or too soon, to count the cost.

The preacher cleared his throat once more. 'There is a story, in the cultural tradition in which Taz Dhar grew up, which seems particularly relevant. There was once a man who sent his servant to market, and was surprised when the man raced back, and burst in on him, quaking with fear.

"What is it?" the man asked.

"Master, I saw death in the marketplace," the servant replied. "He brushed against me, and stared at me hard. Lend me a horse, so that I may ride to Medina, and escape."

The man lent his servant a horse, and saw him gallop off to Medina. Then he went to the marketplace, and found Death and asked "Why did you scare my servant? Why did you stare at him so?" And Death replied, "Because I was surprised to see him here. I have an appointment with him tonight, in Medina."

'What called, or who sent, Taz Dhar back to Africa that second time? To meet that appointment with death?'

∾

Jonjo sat beside Taz in the Clinic in Old Delhi. He had aged a decade since she had last seen him. They struggled to find words.

Eventually, he spoke. 'I thought if we ever met again it would be you visiting me in a clinic in Accra.'

Taz smiled. 'We've both been in the wars, partner.'

'Partner?' He said the word slowly, like he was tasting it for the last time. Then he shook his head. 'No. I traded my right to that title for thirty pieces of silver. I betrayed you. I betrayed myself.'

'Yeah?' said Tax, brutally. 'Well, I screamed and sobbed and begged and would have given them you and all your family and not thought twice about it if it would have made the pain stop. Forget it. Will you make a statement? Give evidence. On the record?'

'No. I gave my word. My silence.'

'Partner,' sighed Taz, exasperated, 'you may be older, wiser, better and braver than me, but I have to tell you, you don't know fuck from a fruit tree about dealing with shits like these. Keeping your word is not a requirement or a recommendation in this game.'

Jonjo smiled. 'My word. My silence. The words of others? Their voices? Who am I to censor them?'

Taz sat up, her eyes bright. 'You kept the tapes? You star! Don't tell me where. We're not out of this yet. The people who brought us here are better than the ones who attacked us, but none of them can be trusted once they've got what they want.'

'But you have a plan?'

'Oh yes. And it covers us both. How are you for money?'

'I have none,' said Jonjo, simply. 'And I have borrowed.'

'Tell the people who brought you here what you need, and don't skimp on the rounding-up. Tell them what you need to settle up in Ghana and support your family in your absence. How would you like a job?'

'Here?'

'Yes, here. Had any better offers lately? To my shame, someone asked me for a job here, not so long ago, and I abandoned him. Well, not you, partner. We have been in the wars, you and I, and we've been beaten, battered and bruised, but that has not been our fault. But it sure as shit will be if we fail to take the opportunity to emerge on the winning side.'

23

Rohit Shastri sat in the room on the thirty-second floor of the Sheraton Wall Centre in the heart of downtown Vancouver and watched the planes land at Vancouver International. He thought how ludicrously similar the view was to what he had shared with Taz in Addis. Distance, perspective, angle, all the same. Yet oh, how different the intervening vista. Arrow-straight avenues breached at crisp right angles by equally neat streets. They led out down Burrard, to the river and English Bay. Granville Bridge, high and wide, sweeping over the cool and trendy eateries and boutiques on Granville Island. Rich ships at anchor, and beyond, the Royal Vancouver Yacht Club, with its tight bundle of masts like stalks of harvested corn. Green as Addis, sure, the land beyond the water, but brutally populated with tall, indifferent blocks of metal, glass and concrete. Wealth. Power. But not worn brash and arrogant. Polite, uncomfortable, almost embarrassed, but also supremely self-satisfied.

What was it Hugo Ruhl has said? The People and the Others? Here, there were no Others. None here would lie down at the end of day wondering if they or their children would succumb to starvation in the night. Homeless there were: damaged and angry, but the safety net beneath them was wide and deep. Here, hunger was a lifestyle choice.

Rohit sighed at the pointlessness, the obscenity of infinite possibility. Gord had said how happy he was to be home at last. Rohit couldn't wait to return as well to his. This place made him feel deeply uneasy.

'Safe Return was targeted, infiltrated and hijacked in the mid-Nineties. A loosely managed organization with easy access to the world's trouble spots. The perfect vehicle, behind the front of its charitable function, for extricating dissidents under threat of death, or sheltering writers with fatwahs on them. Then, post 9/11, once the US Supreme Court made it impossible for the CIA to be doing it themselves, for moving suspected terrorists around the world to legal black holes where they can be more rigorously interrogated without undue concern for their human rights. Extraordinary Rendition lives on, under the inelegant sobriquet of Armitage Shanks. Thomas Cook tours for the terminally troublesome. One-way tickets to nowhere.'

Gord listened but said nothing. His face gave little away.

'All fine,' continued Rohit, 'until three of the real Safe Return workers, Andrew Carr, Bob Lloyd and Dilip Dutta, started getting involved in drug shipments, and other stuff. You couldn't afford the unwelcome publicity of their arrest and trial. All that inconvenient scrutiny. So they had to be Armitage Shanks-ed too. That was Johnny Peters' job. Now I don't know if his death was an accident as Hugo Ruhl was told, or a deliberate act to eliminate possible risks down the line: we will give you the benefit of the doubt. But the net result was Carr embedded in The Gambia, Dutta lost God knows where and Lloyd, whom Dutta had been grooming for us, in Ethiopia. So we sent one of our people to get him out.'

'Speculation,' said Gord, shaking his head. 'Guesswork. Groundless conspiracy theories.'

'Perhaps,' acknowledged Rohit. 'But what isn't speculation is that Lloyd's untimely conversion to Islam coincided with one of Ethiopia's periodic clear-outs of fundamentalists and infiltrators. Our man got caught up in it too. Executed, we think, one week before Bob Lloyd. He was a good friend and, unfortunately for him, a Muslim too. With his death we lost all hope, but then Lloyd found Taz Dhar's picture in the pocket of my dead friend's jeans and wrote his last letter to her. So we encouraged her to work unknowingly for us. On a long rein. Our main aim had become to get to Hugo Ruhl, because before his disappearance, Dilip Dutta had told us he thought he might be ready to turn too. We sent Taz his address, but we didn't realize you were watching her so closely. You got to him before we did.'

'Superintendent Shastri,' sighed Gord, 'where is this going?'

'Here: we have been watching you for over three years now. We estimate you have Armitage Shanks Centres in six countries and have processed around 400 people through them. Each of those countries has received massive aid packages from the World Bank and others, and to be blunt, we are willing to work for it, but we want it.'

Silence. Both men looked out of the window, at the city, busy yet calm, crowded yet ordered, uncertain yet secure, and saw two entirely different views.

'Evidence? Corroboration? Facts?' said Gord, recalling his wandering thoughts. 'This isn't the way we do business. We don't like negotiating with a gun to our heads.'

Rohit shrugged. 'Nobody does. That's why everybody wants to be the one with the gun. Now, I really don't want to pressure you, but I have to, so let's load the bullets into that gun: one, Taz Dhar, conscious, coherent and very, very angry. That was a terrible thing your people did. Makes grim listening. Two, the Ghanaian, Amin Asante. A well-organized man with a copy of all his interviews carefully preserved. Secure now in our care and recovering well from the beating he took. Three, evidence that our colleague lost in Ethiopia died on your instructions, because he got too close to what was going on. I have more—the driver in Frankfurt, for example—but I have to make a phone call within the next three minutes. What do I tell my people at the funeral? They are performers, and have rehearsed two scripts. First: Step out in front of the cameras, mumble some platitudes and a vague assurance that the search for Taz Dhar will go on. Interesting, but only to Indian viewers, and the story quietly dies. Two: Announce that she isn't really dead, but is safe at an undisclosed location in India, where we are nursing her back from the terrible brutality she has suffered because of her attempts to find out who or what Armitage Shanks was. They will then pause to ensure it's picked up by the networks and then go on to describe all she found out. Scenario one plays out if you agree to transfer the Armitage Shanks process from the British to us. Scenario two plays out if you don't. Full disclosure. In short, if we can't have it, nobody will.'

Gord fumed silently. He chewed his bottom lip and glared at Rohit.

Rohit smiled. 'Now, I realize you would like time to reflect, consider and consult, but I'm afraid I must make my call. Delay isn't an option. They will be coming out of the church any moment now, and if they don't hear from me, the default is full disclosure.'

∾

S.K. Mehta's mobile was switched on, but in silent mode. He was profoundly reassured to feel the double tremor of a message received. Discreetly, he slipped the mobile from his pocket, glanced at the message and smiled. He would ask Ash to say a few words. No one did platitudes better. Not even the preacher who, now it didn't matter, proved as good as his word and brought his peroration to a close within seconds of the agreed time.

He could make a new career in broadcasting, thought SK.

❧

'You have it about right,' conceded Gord, 'but for the numbers. There are currently more than 3,000 Armitage Shanks. Still think you can handle it?'

Rohit's eyes widened. This was way more than any of them had envisaged. 'Of course,' he said, after barely a pause. 'No problem.'

Gord smiled wearily. 'Said with a conviction you don't feel. You'd make a great politician but you'd be a lousy poker player. We will need proof of capacity.'

Rohit shrugged. 'We anticipated nothing less. You have a case in mind?'

Gord nodded. 'What will you call it, this arrangement?'

'We were thinking of Hindware.'

Gord looked pained, and slightly bilious.

'Or American Standard? Not really. We'll come up with something bland and appropriate. Our test case?'

Gord opened his briefcase and removed a file. He pushed it over the table to Rohit. 'He'll be expecting you. But you will need to be quick. I hear others have plans for him too. His name is Tim.'

Rohit smiled broadly. 'Excellent! This one, you can have for free. As a gesture of our goodwill...'

24

'Hello, Taz,' said SK. 'Gosh, it's good to be able to speak to you at last. Ash says hi. How are you?'

'Thirsty. And tired. The time difference?'

SK laughed. It was late afternoon in the UK, and he was waiting with Ash for a taxi to take them to Heathrow.

'Tables firmly turned. But the difference is, I remembered: I just wanted to tell you how well things went.'

'I saw. Jonjo and I watched it on TV. It's a weird thing, watching your own funeral. Thank Ash for the kind words.'

'Well, they say six months, a miraculous discovery in Ghana and you'll rejoin the land of the living.'

'People,' corrected Taz. 'It's the People and the Others.'

'Whatever. You should be proud of yourself. You've done brilliantly. Working out that final reference to the charity. Safe Return offices are being closed down around the world as we speak.'

'But at what cost, SK? And for what benefit? Nothing's changed. So much pain, so many people hurt, and for what? So a bunch of Indian zealots can replace a bunch of British psychos in the shady places?'

SK chuckled. 'You think that I'm one of the zealots?'

'No,' she said, sadly. 'I think you're one of the psychos. Are you sure coming back is such a good idea, SK?'

SK paused. 'I'm not sure I understand you, Taz,' he said slowly.

'Don't you? Rohit's people told you to feed me the address of Hugo Ruhl, because they knew he could expose the details of what was going on. But who told the Armitage Shanks people at Safe Return where he was, so they could get to him and take him out before he talked? It wasn't my uncle, was it? It was you. So I could scare him out of hiding and your boss could take him down. Who identified the photo I took? Oh, that must have made you smile! You knew from the start who they were and what this was all about. And then what you got me to do for Hugo Ruhl, you did for me. You told me to run, and I did, because I trusted you. Right into a trap, and I'll never forget or forgive anyone who had a part in what happened then. Never.'

'You're a crazy drunk, Taz,' said SK, harshly. 'I've only ever done what you asked me to, helped you and tried my best to protect you from harm.'

'It won't wash, SK. Rohit spoke to Rama Rao in Addis. You set up that poor guy when he got too close too. Had him killed. Hugo Ruhl. Sidiq, Jonjo, me. You've got a lot of blood on your hands, SK.'

'Paranoid ravings which no one will believe.'

'Yes,' said Taz. 'That's what your boss told me everyone would say after he'd finished with me. But you both underestimate the inner strength of a severely pissed-off woman. Oh, it's going to take time, but I'm getting over this shit. And you know what's going to help me come to terms with what happened to me? The thought that as soon as I have, I'm coming for you.'

'Proof? Evidence?'

'Oh, yes, thanks for reminding me. I nearly forgot. You see, there was one more picture in that collage of Hugo Ruhl's that I didn't recognize at the time. There was a picture of you.'

'No, there wasn't,' said SK.

'No? Well, there is now. And that's proven sufficient to justify the warrant for your arrest that Rohit got before he set off for Canada. I could just let them take you at the airport on arrival, as they intend, but that would be too easy. I'm giving you a better chance than you gave me. Run, SK. You have a head start. But look over your shoulder. 'Cos, I'll be coming after you.'

Epilogue

Kids' Hero Drugs Bust Shame

Children at the Wood Green Centre were heartbroken to learn that Major Tim Macleod, the highly decorated war hero, was last night charged with possession of a large amount of heroin found by police in the boot of his MG sports car during a routine stop to check a faulty brake light.

Maj. Macleod has links with the discredited charity Safe Return, but is better known for his work with Riding for The Disabled Child.

At a brief appearance in Horseferry Road Magistrates Court this morning, Maj. Macleod was bound over to appear before the Crown Court on 5 October. The Crown prosecution did not initially oppose bail, but in an unusual development, Maj. Macleod advised the court to remand him in custody as, he assured them, if released on bail, he would undoubtedly abscond. He also claimed that outside prison his life was under threat.

'My client strongly protests his innocence,' said Maj. Macleod's solicitor, Munira Sheikh. 'His opposition to drug use and marvellous work among disabled children is well known. We will fight these unfounded charges with the utmost vigour. In the meantime, because his life and liberty are under threat form foreign forces, his personal safety is our priority and for that reason, and that reason alone, he has opted to remain in custody.'

Unofficial sources in the Crown Prosecution Service said that further serious charges of a sexual nature are under consideration.

When questioned, Ms Sheikh refused to confirm or deny reports that Maj. Macleod had refused to provide a DNA sample and one had to be taken by force.

Acknowledgements

It would be wrong of me to close this tale without a thank-you to some people who have made its telling such a pleasure. First, to Val Tullett and Janice Redwood, who worked on the two versions of this story with me. More than a dozen years separates their inputs, but both have made a great contribution in text manipulation, suggestion and transcription. To Rob Packham and Stuart Orr, who read working drafts and shared ideas with unstinting generosity. Rob also clarified police procedure and helped me through the complexities of the UK Police and Criminal Evidence and Mental Health Acts. Whilst, from the location of snuff shops in London to the availability of mini-bars in Frankfurt hotels, Stuart brought to bear an encyclopaedic knowledge coupled with rigorous attention to detail. Any writer should count himself blessed to have even one such resource to call upon. It is a privilege to acknowledge each as a good friend, fine collaborator and easy fellow-traveller.

Once more, and forever, to Uma and Indrajeet Phalke, who, more than two decades ago, welcomed my wife and me into their amazing family and have given us so much that defines our lives.

Finally, my list of acknowledgements would not be complete without mention of the amazing Prita Maitra of Penguin India, who has been a beacon of encouragement, honest critic and kind voice for many years. To her, to all of the above:

Cheers, mates.